IVORY OATH

NOVIKOV BRATVA
BOOK 2

NICOLE FOX

ALSO BY NICOLE FOX

Egorov Bratva
Tangled Innocence
Tangled Decadence

Zakrevsky Bratva
Requiem of Sin
Sonata of Lies
Rhapsody of Pain

Bugrov Bratva
Midnight Purgatory
Midnight Sanctuary

Oryolov Bratva
Cruel Paradise
Cruel Promise

Pushkin Bratva
Cognac Villain
Cognac Vixen

Viktorov Bratva
Whiskey Poison
Whiskey Pain

Orlov Bratva
Champagne Venom
Champagne Wrath

Uvarov Bratva

Sapphire Scars

Sapphire Tears

Vlasov Bratva

Arrogant Monster

Arrogant Mistake

Zhukova Bratva

Tarnished Tyrant

Tarnished Queen

Stepanov Bratva

Satin Sinner

Satin Princess

Makarova Bratva

Shattered Altar

Shattered Cradle

Solovev Bratva

Ravaged Crown

Ravaged Throne

Vorobev Bratva

Velvet Devil

Velvet Angel

Romanoff Bratva

Immaculate Deception

Immaculate Corruption

Kovalyov Bratva

Gilded Cage

Gilded Tears

Jaded Soul

Jaded Devil

Ripped Veil

Ripped Lace

Mazzeo Mafia Duet

Liar's Lullaby (Book 1)

Sinner's Lullaby (Book 2)

Bratva Crime Syndicate

Can be read in any order!

Lies He Told Me

Scars He Gave Me

Sins He Taught Me

Belluci Mafia Trilogy

Corrupted Angel (Book 1)

Corrupted Queen (Book 2)

Corrupted Empire (Book 3)

De Maggio Mafia Duet

Devil in a Suit (Book 1)

Devil at the Altar (Book 2)

Kornilov Bratva Duet

Married to the Don (Book 1)

Til Death Do Us Part (Book 2)

Heirs to the Bratva Empire

Can be read in any order!

Kostya

Maksim

Andrei

Princes of Ravenlake Academy (Bully Romance)

Can be read as standalones!

Cruel Prep

Cruel Academy

Cruel Elite

Tsezar Bratva

Nightfall (Book 1)

Daybreak (Book 2)

Russian Crime Brotherhood

Can be read in any order!

Owned by the Mob Boss

Unprotected with the Mob Boss

Knocked Up by the Mob Boss

Sold to the Mob Boss

Stolen by the Mob Boss

Trapped with the Mob Boss

Volkov Bratva

Broken Vows (Book 1)

Broken Hope (Book 2)

Broken Sins *(standalone)*

Other Standalones

Vin: A Mafia Romance

Box Sets

Bratva Mob Bosses (Russian Crime Brotherhood Books 1-6)

Tsezar Bratva (Tsezar Bratva Duet Books 1-2)

Heirs to the Bratva Empire

The Mafia Dons Collection

The Don's Corruption

MAILING LIST

IVORY OATH

BOOK TWO OF THE NOVIKOV BRATVA DUET

My ex came back from the dead,

and stole me away from my happily ever after.

And somehow, that's not even the worst of my problems.

Because I've also been separated from my son.

My father is trying to kill me.

And my husband thinks I'm pregnant—but the truth is that I lost the baby...

and I don't know how to tell him.

Basically, my whole world's on fire.

So I have a choice to make:

I can take my son and run from this life...

Or I can beg Mikhail to leave it behind with us.

Will we make it if I run?

Will he come with us if I plead?

Or will all our mistakes drag us down the path we swore we'd never take?

IVORY OATH is Book 2 of the Novikov Bratva duet. Mikhail and Viviana's story starts in Book 1, IVORY ASHES.

1

VIVIANA

It was all a dream.

Had to be, right? I'm back in an unfamiliar room with chains around my wrists. Dreaming is the only explanation.

I blink through the heaviness in my eyelids and try to come to quick grips with what is real.

I thought Mikhail saving me from Iakov's prison was real, but… I'm still here. Pacing around a hotel room holding a positive pregnancy test and calculating my next moves *felt* real, but this drab, windowless room makes Motel 8 look like the Ritz-Carlton.

Iakov Novikov must have drugged me again and moved me to another cell in his maze-like underground prison. At least this cell has a bed. Small mercies.

I test the chains, yanking them against the metal footboard a few times. They're heavier than the silver ones I had in the other room. They rattle loudly against the bed frame, the sound like an ice pick cleaving through my aching head.

My brain feels too big for my skull, the way it always does after some heavy-duty crying. Yet another reason why my dream feels so freaking real.

It must have been the drugs. Whatever he gave me made me hallucinate and now, I'm hungover.

I shrug my shoulders around my ears for some semblance of hearing protection and pull on the chains with all I have. They scream like the world is having labor contractions, but they hold fast. Even if they did break free, it's not as if I could Incredible Hulk my way through the locked door to my cell. I'm sure there are half a dozen more locked doors between me and anything resembling freedom.

Panic constricts around my chest like a snake—a snake who *really* needs to read the vibe of the room. Is now a time to be worried about small spaces or should I instead be worried about the psychopath holding me captive who wants to torture and murder me for revenge? I think the answer to that is obvious. And yet I have to take deep breaths to stave off my oldest, most annoying friend: claustrophobia.

When I close my eyes, I'm right back in the dream. I can still see Mikhail standing in the door of my cell. I can feel the way his icy blue eyes scraped over me, assessing me for injuries even as he held himself back. I could tell he wanted me as much as I wanted him. Despite everything, the pull between us was still there.

Or, I dreamt it was there, anyway…

I shake my head and rub my fists into my eyes.

It was just a dream.

Or a nightmare, I suppose. I wouldn't call being exiled from the mansion where your son is living by the man you are

A key slides into the lock of my door and I have just enough time to wedge the pregnancy test between my mattress and the wall before my door bangs open and the impossible becomes impossible to deny.

"Trofim," I rasp.

"Good morning, darling." My ex-fiancé closes the door behind him, twisting his head one way and then the other like a snake trying to decide how to consume an especially large meal. "I thought you might be awake. How did you sleep?"

Oh, God. It was all real.

I'm pregnant.

Mikhail exiled me and kept Dante.

Trofim found me.

A million terrifying realities settle in all at once, but one thought is louder than the rest.

"You're dead," I blurt. "I killed you."

He smiles and it's like an ice-cold finger dragging down my spine. Any time I have had a nightmare about Trofim, it's been of that moment. The way he wheezed when I drove the blade into his chest. The blood coating my hands as I fled.

Trofim walks closer and I slam back against the wall. I curl into myself, getting as far from him as I can manage. But it isn't enough. He pinches my trembling chin and forces my eyes to his. "You think that little poke was enough to kill me? You'll have to try harder than that."

I could barely stab him the first time. I knew Dante's life

depended on it, but I could only manage to stab him once before I had to leave.

When I didn't hear anything about him after that, I assumed…

I jerk my face away. "If you survived, why are you just coming back now?"

I'd argue that there never would have been a *good* time for Trofim to surprise me by magically coming back from the dead, but I'm not sure he could have picked a worse time.

"Because I was waiting for you," he croons. "My baby brother surprised me; I'll give him that. He caught me off-guard and took the Bratva from me. Then my father sided with him overnight without any pushback."

"Because Mikhail was the better choice," I hiss.

In an instant, Trofim is on the bed in front of me, his nose pressed to mine. "If he's so great, where is Mikhail now? He saved you once. Do you think he'll do it again?"

No. No, I don't.

"Mikhail broke tradition and protocol. He stole everything from me and no one did anything to stop him. I wasn't going to come back empty-handed. I needed to have my wife and a strong alliance in my back pocket to reclaim what is rightfully mine. But someone," he chides, leaning back to tap the end of my nose, "disappeared. Until recently, that is. And now that you're back, so am I."

I shake my head. "If you're doing this to get to my father, you're out of luck. I spoke to him and he isn't going to help me. He doesn't want anything to do with me."

Unfortunately, that wasn't a dream, either. My own father would rather get revenge by sitting back and letting me be killed than save his own daughter.

"I'll worry about Agostino. The only thing I need you to worry about is getting yourself wedding ready." He looks me over and his nose wrinkles. "You've really let yourself go."

"I'm sorry that being held captive doesn't agree with me," I growl.

He waves me away. "The blood in your veins is the only thing that matters to me now. Finally, after six fucking years, I'm going to marry a Giordano."

I hold up my left hand, flashing the rainbow-colored disco ball on my ring finger. "Didn't you hear the news? I'm already married."

His dark eyes narrow. They are nothing like looking into the deep blue of Mikhail's eyes. Trofim's are flat and emotionless. It's like looking into a shallow, evil puddle.

"I heard. I also heard you showed up with a five-year-old. I don't need to do the math on that to figure out when you spread your legs for my brother," he hisses. There's murder in his eyes for a second before he backs away with a shrug. "It'll be easy enough to explain away. Mikhail raped you, you escaped, and then he tracked you down and forced you into marriage. Now, I'm back to claim my rightful title and my rightful bride. It'll make a nice comeback story."

"I don't belong to you," I snap. The chains rattling at the end of the bed don't do much to prove my point.

"Oh, but you do," he insists. "Whether you like it or not, you and I are getting married, Viviana. But if you make it difficult for me, your little boy will have to go."

My heart jolts. "He's a child."

"He's a liability," he corrects, stalking closer to me. "He's an embarrassment that you created by fucking my brother like a dirty whore."

"And I'd do it again," I spit.

Trofim's hand cracks across my face before I even see it coming. My cheek burns hot. I can feel the imprint of each of his fingers on my skin.

Six years may have passed, but nothing has changed.

He stands up with a sigh. "I don't know why you make me do this. I want things to work between us, Viviana. It's all I've ever wanted."

"All you've ever wanted is a slave with your last name."

He considers that for a second. "Call it whatever you want, but as long as you're a good girl and do as you're told, your bastard will stay alive."

Dante isn't a bastard. Mikhail and I are married. Our relationship is more legitimate than anything I've ever had with Trofim.

But I keep that to myself as Trofim brushes my hair away from my forehead. "It's a good offer, Viviana. It's more than you'll get from anyone else now that you've let my brother ruin you." He stops in the door, a wicked smile tugging the corners of his mouth. "Think it over."

The door to my cell slams shut.

almost definitely in love with a dream. Add to that having no more than a few thousand dollars in your pocket while one of the most powerful, well-connected men in the city is after you and I'd say we're firmly into "night terror" territory.

I breathe in and out, massaging my temples to manage the pain. Suddenly, a tidal wave of nausea crashes over me.

I barely have time to lean over the edge of the bed before my stomach is turning itself inside out. I heave over the concrete floor over and over again. Nothing comes up, but that doesn't stop my body from trying a few more times, just for shits and giggles.

When my stomach finally settles, I fall back into bed, shivering and weak.

So the pregnancy is probably real.

Test or not, I've suspected it for a few days, anyway. Even while my life has been falling apart, it's been hard to ignore the dizziness, nonstop nausea, and the way my nipples nudging against the inside of my t-shirt brings tears of genuine pain to my eyes. The tears of pain being additional to the tears of fear, sadness, anger, and every other human emotion. I've become an emotional water fountain, just like I was when I was pregnant with Dante.

The newest pregnancy symptom, apparently, is incredibly vivid nightmares.

When I close my eyes, I can relive it moment by moment as if it just happened. I can still smell the musty motel room. I can feel the weight of the pregnancy test against my palm.

When I picture opening the door to my room and finding Trofim on the other side, the same dart of panic sinks deep into my chest.

It's wild to me that my brain even dreamed that up. Trofim is the last person on earth I'd ever expect to see standing outside my door. Mostly because he isn't *on* Earth anymore.

Thanks to me.

It's even more wild to me that, even in my shocked stupor, Dream Me was quick-thinking enough to shove the pregnancy test into my pocket as Trofim backed me into the hotel room.

Then he lunged for me and I… I woke up.

Here.

In a different room from the one Iakov had me in at first. With different chains around my wrists than the ones Iakov had me in at first.

Goosebumps race up and down my arms like my body knows something my brain doesn't yet want to accept.

But… no, it was a dream. Because what happened was impossible. Physically and spiritually *impossible.*

As I reach into my back pocket, I'm already berating myself for being so ridiculous. Even as my hand closes around a small plastic stick wedged deep into the denim, I don't believe it.

It isn't until I pull the pregnancy test free and hold it in front of me that my resolve starts to crack. Because even I can't be in denial about the two bright pink lines in the test window. There's nothing imaginary about those.

It wasn't *a dream.*

It really happened.

Which means…

2

MIKHAIL

"I'd ask where you've been all afternoon, but the smell tells me all I need to know."

I flip my brother off and grab my water bottle from the counter. "I only came back for this."

I would've stayed in the gym until I knew everyone in the house was asleep, but I finished the last of the water bottles in the gym fridge a few hours ago. I've sweat so much that I'll turn to leather if I don't rehydrate.

"You've been in the gym for" —Anatoly checks the clock above the stove. "—six hours today. Feels like enough, wouldn't you say, Raoul?"

Raoul shrugs, ducking his head behind the refrigerator door he has open. "It's a lot."

It is a lot. I can tell because my limbs are shaking and my muscles burn with every step. But the fact I'm still standing means I haven't gone hard enough.

"You're just jealous because you wish you were back in the gym, Nat."

My brother narrows his eyes at me. "I think my surgeon would rather I not undo all of his nice stitch work on my chest."

The fact Anatoly is home from the hospital less than a week after being shot in the chest is amazing to me. It's one of the few good things to come from the last week.

"Well, I wasn't shot in the chest," I point out. "So I'm going to head back and—"

"Maybe not literally," Anatoly interrupts. "But that doesn't mean you're not in recovery, too."

I grimace. "That was some second-tier, discount bin psychoanalyzing, Anatoly."

He ignores me and cruises ahead anyway. "I was shot in the chest, but it's not the physical shit that's messing with me. It's the mental stuff. What I saw. What I lost." He swallows, and I know he's thinking of Stella. We've all been thinking of her. She was part of the family and we loved her. No one as much as Anatoly.

"I'm sorry about Stella, man. You know I am. But she was *your* girlfriend, not mine."

"I'm not talking about Stella," Anatoly interrupts. He hits me with a long, knowing look.

I meet his eyes, refusing to look away. I can't let him think for even a single second that I'm running from the dark tornado of guilt and doubt and regret that has been swirling around my head for days.

"What I'm talking about," Anatoly clarifies, "is that it's okay to be fucked up over what happened. We all lost people we cared about, and another marathon session with your punching bag isn't going to make that better."

You never know if you don't try.

"I did what I had to do for the Bratva and I have no regrets. Now, if you'll excuse me—"

"Dante was a mess all afternoon," Anatoly adds before I can turn away. "He threw a fit for his tutor, refused to eat lunch, and shredded every stuffed animal in his bedroom."

Fuck, what I wouldn't give to be able to ignore him and walk away. But Anatoly knows what he's doing.

It's Dante. I can't walk away from my son.

"Has anyone talked to him?" I sigh.

"We've tried." Anatoly gestures to himself and Raoul. "He doesn't want to talk to us. He wants to talk to—"

"Well, he can't!" I drag my hands through my hair and drop down into one of the stools at the counter. "I told him that she left. I was honest and told him she wasn't coming back. What the fuck does he want from me?"

I know I'm not being reasonable. Dante is five years old. He has spent every day of his life with his mother and now, without warning, she's gone.

"Well, for starters," Anatoly says, clapping his hand on my shoulder, "you could stop getting drunk by yourself and boxing all night and try spending some time with him. I'm sure he'd rather have one parent than zero."

The problem is, without the boxing and the drinking, I'm no good to anyone. I wake up every day with a tension in my body I can't get rid of. It's a buzzing awareness under my skin that something is wrong and I need to fix it. And the only way to get rid of it is to dull the sharp edge with alcohol and then physically burn the rest of the energy away.

I can't sit in the mansion with Dante and do puzzles or go for walks. I can't be around him because seeing his face reminds me of *her*.

My hand tightens around my water bottle until my knuckles turn white. When I look up, Anatoly is looking at it like he's waiting for the bottle to implode.

I force myself to release my grip and stand up. "Bring Dante to the gym. If he wants to talk, we can talk there."

"Sure," Anatoly mumbles as I leave. "That's healthy. I'm not worried about this at all."

I ignore him and shove through the patio doors.

I'm deep in another set when I finally hear the door to the gym open fifteen minutes later.

"Go on," Anatoly encourages. "I'll be out here if you need me."

Dante walks across the padded floor towards me. He looks smaller than I've ever seen him. Like the last few days have physically worn him down.

He stops a few yards away and watches me from the sidelines. I could pause and talk to him, but I don't even know what I'm going to say. Which is exactly why I've been alone in the gym for days on end.

When my knuckles connect with the bag, it's like a circuit finally being completed. The energy in my veins has somewhere to go.

Maybe it can help Dante, too.

I drop my arms and turn towards him. "Hey, Dante. I thought—"

"Where is my mom?" he asks.

It's a blow I'm not expecting. I swallow down the bile in my throat. "She's gone."

"When is she coming back?"

"She isn't."

He frowns. "What did you do to her?"

We've been through all of this before—several times, actually. That doesn't make it any easier to handle now.

"Nothing," I growl. "*I* didn't do anything. It's why I'm here and she isn't. *She* is the one who—"

Who what? How am I supposed to explain any of this shit to Dante in a way that makes any sense?

I saved your mom from my violent big brother, got her pregnant, and now, I have to take care of you on my own because she killed Trofim the way I probably should have six years ago.

"Tangled web" doesn't even begin to cover it.

"Have you boxed before?" I ask instead of finishing my sentence. I reach out to steady the bag in front of me.

Dante frowns, still as suspicious of me as he probably should be. Between me and Viviana, Dante comes by his distrust of authority naturally.

"That's not a box."

I bite back my first smile in days. "No, it's not. I don't know why they call it boxing, actually. But what I do know is that it's fun. Er—it makes me feel better, anyway."

He crosses his arms and I see so much of Viviana in him.

Bringing him here was a mistake. The gym is the only room in the house she's never been to. The only place that doesn't smell like her and isn't dripping with memories of the weeks we spent living together.

But I'll always see her in Dante. No matter how much I wish I didn't.

I blow out a breath and grab the roll of tape from the mat. "Come here. I'll wrap your hands."

Dante's curiosity wins and he inches over to me, a frown on his face.

Ever since I met him, he's been a bright, bubbly kid. He loves everyone and is excited about life. Or, he *was*.

The last few days, he's shifted into something I'm more familiar with. When I look at him, I can see the same rage that swirls inside of me. It's the same storm I've been learning to tame my entire life. Now, it's Dante's turn.

The kid in front of me now isn't as innocent as he was a few weeks ago.

The last thing Viviana made me promise before she left is that I'd let Dante be a little boy for as long as possible. I'm not sure that's a promise I had any business making. Less than a week in, and it's already proving impossible to keep.

"Why are you putting these things on?" he asks, flexing his knuckles through the tape. "I'm not bleeding."

"And we want to keep it that way. Hence the tape." His hands are impossibly small against mine. The tape that just covers my knuckles goes from Dante's fingertips to the middle of his palm. "Maybe one day I'll get you some gloves, but this is all you'll need right now."

"What do I do?"

"Did you see me when you came in?" I ask.

"You were hitting that thing."

I gesture towards the bag. "Do what I was doing. We'll get a baseline for where you're at and then home in on what—"

Before I can even finish, Dante launches himself at the bag.

He's small, but he *flies*. He's a blur of movement as he circles the bag, punching and kicking and wailing. It's a heavy bag made for taking what I can throw at it, but Dante actually gets the thing swinging a bit.

"Slow down. You aren't being timed," I tell him.

But he can't hear me. His breath is coming in uneven huffs and he's gasping as he slams his fists into the punching bag again and again. His chest starts to heave and when he circles around the bag the last time, I see why.

"Dante, that's enough." I grab him by the shoulders and pull him back, but he lunges for the bag again. He's really crying now, big, heavy sobs tearing out of him. "Dante, stop."

"Don't touch me!" He flings the words at me like a punch. "You're a liar!"

I frown. "I never lied to you."

"You promised you'd take care of Mama! You told me you would, but she's gone!" He scrapes the tape off of his hands and tosses the scraps to the floor. "She's gone and today is—" His little mouth pinches together until his lips are white.

"What's today?" I ask him.

He swipes clumsily at his damp cheeks. "I'm six now. It's my birthday."

Oh, fucking hell.

"I had no idea, bud."

As soon as the words are out of my mouth, I know they're the wrong thing to say. Everything I do with Dante is wrong. *Vivian would know what to do.*

"We can still get a cake," I say. "Maybe Stel—*someone* can go to the store."

Dante flinches. He caught my mistake, too. His mom is gone. Stella is gone. The list of people who were there one day and gone the next is growing longer all the time.

"I don't want cake!" he screams. "I want my mom!"

I reach for him, but he twists away and sprints for the door. As soon as the door swings open, Anatoly is there waiting.

Our eyes meet through the open door. There are questions written on my brother's face that I don't have the words to answer.

I'm not sure I ever will.

3

MIKHAIL

I'm still drenched in sweat when I drop down behind my desk and pour myself a drink. It doesn't stop there.

When Anatoly takes Dante upstairs and puts him to bed, I drink.

When Raoul peeks through the door to check on me, I ignore him and drink.

As the rest of the house goes dark one room at a time and silence fills every corner, I drink and drink and drink.

It's hours of sitting in the dark, looking for answers I'm never going to find at the bottom of a bottle that ends way too fucking soon.

When it does, I shatter it against the wall, grab my keys, and stumble my way to the garage.

Last week, I would have done the responsible thing and asked Pyotr to drive. Except now, I know that having Pyotr in the house at all wasn't responsible.

Pyotr was a spy and now, he's dead. Viviana is a murderer and now, she's gone. And I don't have the control I thought I did over any of it.

It started raining at some point in the last few hours. The road is soaked and the tires barely manage to cling onto the asphalt as I tear down the driveway and squeal onto the main road. Thankfully, it's late and no one else is out.

I haven't been to the cemetery where Alyona and Anzhelina are buried since the day of their joint funeral, but I drive the winding road to the gates like I've done it a million times before. In some ways, I have. All roads seem to lead back here.

I park under a tree that is piss-poor protection from the rain and squelch my way across the overgrown grass.

When Anatoly and I were last here, the director was going on about when the headstone would be finished and when I could come see them. The sun was shining and I was standing in front of the fresh dirt of my wife and daughter's graves and all I could think was, *What the fuck does it matter?* An overpriced rock wouldn't change the fact that they were gone. It wasn't going to bring them back.

But as I make my way up the muddy incline, a wide tombstone reflects the little moonlight coming through the storm clouds. The white marble glows like a beacon in the darkness.

Their names are etched in black.

Alyona Novikov.

Anzhelina Novikov.

My father hated that I wanted to marry Alyona. She came from nothing and didn't have anything to offer the family, as far as he was concerned. It's why he gave us the smaller property on the other side of the city. The less she associated with the family, the better. It had been a guesthouse for years, but Alyona and I got married and hid away there. It was the closest thing I'd ever had to the romanticized idea of a home.

Alyona felt separate from the Bratva in that way. Going home was some world removed—a peek into the life I could have had if I'd been born into another family.

But I *wasn't* born into another family.

And Alyona wasn't in a world removed.

Seeing the Novikov name etched forever after her name drives that point home in a way that even her death didn't. *They were mine... and I lost them.*

I sink to my knees in the mud. The grass is long around the base of the stone and I pull it out by the fistful. Big gobs of grass and mud come out of the earth. I use the rain to wash away the leftover mud caked along the base of the marble. I run my fingers along the black letters of each of their names, cleaning away the muck and mold.

Then I drive the heels of my hands into my eyes and scream wordlessly into the storm. The rain swallows the sound of my voice. When I look behind me, I can't even see the shape of the car along the road. If I was still driving, I'd probably have crashed into a building by now.

But I'm not driving. I'm here.

And I have no fucking idea why.

"That's not true," I mumble, continuing the thought out loud. "I know why I'm here. It's because I'm fucking it all up again."

I'm talking to a rock, but it's still hard to drudge up the words. I can feel Alyona's eyes on me. Almost like she's been here, waiting for me to finally show up.

"I should have brought flowers." I tap the empty vase built into the bottom of the headstone. "You probably expected some, after… everything. But I couldn't—" I take a deep breath. "You never asked me to choose between you and the Bratva. You knew that when it came down to it, I couldn't. But I think I did. I did choose. And I made the wrong choice."

The alcohol warmed me from the inside out, but it's fading fast. My soaked clothes hang heavily, dragging me down. The chill is starting to seep in.

"Part of me thinks I deserve to rot here, too. For what I did to you both." My hair is plastered to my forehead. Rivulets of rainwater pour down my face and drip from my nose. "I knew things were dangerous, but I convinced myself that you and Anzhelina were different. *You weren't part of the Bratva. Why would anyone come for you?* I fucking knew better, but I didn't want to admit it. And you died because of it. You're dead because I failed you."

I see Dante's shattered face as he swirled around the punching bag… the rage burning in his little body because of me.

"Now, I'm doing it again."

The buzzing under my skin is back. I drive my fist into the dirt like it's a punching bag. I slam my knuckles into the ground again and again. A rock buried in the earth splits my skin open and blood drips between my fingers and over my wrist, but the feeling inside of me that something is wrong doesn't go away.

"I didn't try to move on. I didn't want to. Didn't deserve to. But Viviana was…" I drag my bloody hand down my face. I'm sure I look insane. Maybe that's okay. I *feel* insane. "For the first time in my life, I didn't have a choice. I wanted her, and I hated myself for it. Which makes everything that has happened even worse. I should have known better. I *did* know better, but I couldn't stay away. Then she lied to me and now my son is in danger.

"When you and Anzhelina were in danger, my choice was between you and the Bratva. If I could go back, I know exactly what I'd choose. It's easy. I would protect the two of you with my life. I would…" I bite the inside of my cheeks until I taste blood. "This is different. I'm choosing between my son and my—his mother. I can't choose them both. I can't save them both."

The rain lets up for the first time in an hour. It's a persistent drizzle now. A few stars even peek out between the clouds. Whatever bubble I was in bursts. The world comes back into focus and I stand up.

My pants are soaked, hanging low on my hips. Blood drips down my finger into the mud.

"I don't know why I came here," I say, talking only to myself now. "I don't know anything anymore."

4

VIVIANA

I can hear the rain. It's making me thirsty.

It feels like such a waste, all of that water pouring into the ground and not a single drop of it making its way to me. The window in my old apartment leaked every time it rained. I stuffed the crack with a towel and replaced it every hour while the rain lasted. Right now, I'd wring that dirty city water straight into my mouth if I could.

The only water I get is with my meals. It's a small cup three times per day. It's enough to keep me alive, but it's nowhere near enough.

Why couldn't there be a leak in the ceiling above my bed? I'd sit here with my mouth open for hours gathering every drop. I'd look like Dante when he ran around trying to eat snowflakes last Christmas.

I dismiss that thought as quickly as it appears. I have to be careful where I let my mind wander. Right now, I can only think about what I can control.

Which isn't much.

I stare up at the painfully dry ceiling and groan with my painfully dry throat.

I can't be buried too deeply underground if I can still hear rain pattering off the roof, right? I choose to see that as a good sign. Mostly because nothing else going on in my life could be interpreted as anything even close to good, and I need a win right now.

The metal bed frame squeaks as I roll over. The mattress is actually not terrible, but I'd give the chains around my ankles and wrists a firm zero stars. My skin is itchy and raw from the constant friction. After two days, I'm at the point of begging to have them taken off, but there's no one to beg. The monosyllabic man who brings me food doesn't seem very sympathetic and Trofim hasn't come to see me in two days. At least, I think it's been two days.

That's a win in some ways, too.

But I also know the only reason he hasn't visited is because he's off cooking up plans on how to torture me for the rest of my life—however long that life may be.

If he was spending his time in this cell with me, I might be able to think this is the worst it will ever get. Unfortunately, I know better.

My hands fall to my stomach. To the baby growing inside.

This would be easier if I wasn't pregnant. It would also be a hell of a lot easier to stop eating and drinking the measly rations Trofim sends and let myself die as a dried-out husk in this room.

But I can't do that without hurting my baby, so I'm still here.

The bolt in the door clicks open and, for a second, I'm shocked that it's already mealtime again. The hours in here stretch like taffy. Each time the door opens and more food is brought in, I'm not sure if it's been hours or days since I've eaten.

But right now, I know it hasn't been very long.

Then the door opens and I see why.

Trofim stops in the doorway, his hands folded behind his back. "Excited to see me?"

I shrink back against the wall. It's easy to think about Trofim as some annoying pest when he isn't right in front of me. Like he's nothing more than some washed-up, has-been loser. It was so easy for Mikhail to overpower him that I can forget how terrifying he is.

Then he looms over me and I can't think about anything else.

"Or are you still waiting for my brother to break through that door and fuck everything up again?" he hisses.

"He saved me." My voice is hoarse. I haven't used it in days. "You're the one who fucked everything up. Mikhail—"

"Isn't coming," he finishes for me. Trofim kicks the door closed and reveals a water bottle from behind his back.

In an instant, my focus changes. Trofim is a threat, but dehydration is a bigger one.

I *need* that water.

Trofim knows this, which is why he takes a long, slow pull on the bottle.

Nothing about Trofim is attractive, but I'm mesmerized by the movement of his throat as he swallows. My body tries to mirror it, but my esophagus is made of sandpaper. My insides grind together dryly.

"Mikhail isn't coming for you, Viviana. He tossed your ass on the curb for me to find." Trofim grips my chin and the only reason I don't flinch away is because it puts me closer to the water bottle in his other hand. "After the way you embarrassed me the night before our wedding, I should kill you. I could… if I wanted."

"You *are* killing me," I rasp. "I'm thirsty."

Trofim ignores me. "But I'm giving you another chance. You get to make the choice you should have made all those years ago and choose the better man. The *stronger* man."

It's hilarious. If every fiber of my being wasn't focused on getting a single gulp of water, I'd laugh in his face.

"Please, Trofim." I rotate my face into his hand, nuzzling his clammy palm with my cheek. "I'm thirsty."

I feel disgusting. Pathetic. Like a street cat begging for scraps.

Trofim runs his fingers through my knotted-up hair and instantly, I want to shave my head. Hell, I want to peel my skin off where he touches me. I'd even go so far as to—

Suddenly, he fists his hand in my hair.

"Ow!" I yelp. My neck strains as he tips my head back.

Trofim gives me a tight smile. "Open your mouth, Viviana."

If I had any extra moisture in my body at all, I'd spit at him. Instead, I slowly let my mouth fall open.

Trofim lifts the water bottle over my mouth, tipping it painfully slowly towards my parted lips. Too thirsty to be ashamed, I fight against his hold on my hair to get closer.

"Be patient," Trofim growls. "I'm going to give you exactly what you want."

The first drop of water splashes into my mouth and I actually moan. It's barely enough to bother swallowing, but I gulp at it desperately.

I'm still waiting for more water when Trofim's mouth crashes over mine.

His tongue dives into my open mouth and I nearly gag from the force of it. I try to jerk away, but he has a firm hold on my hair.

I'm suffocating. He drops his weight onto the chain dangling from my wrists, and I'm pinned down. I can't move, can't breathe.

When Trofim pulls back just an inch, I gasp for air. He tugs on my hair, arching my neck even further. "Don't fight it, Viviana."

He leans forward to kiss me again and I flinch away. I don't have anywhere to go, but he notices.

"The sooner you accept that you and I are going to end up together, the better off you'll be." His eyes are black as he leans down to kiss me again.

I squeeze my eyes closed and let him.

It's a claiming, bruising kiss. When Trofim slides closer, I'm terrified this won't stop at a kiss.

But finally, he pulls back.

He studies my face and I will myself not to cry. I don't want to make him angry. Even worse, I don't want him to like it. As soon as Trofim thinks he can torture me like this, he will.

So I meet his eyes, desperate to give him nothing.

"I can give you what you want, Viviana," he advises, backing towards the door, taking the water bottle with him. "If you'll let me."

He can't give me Dante. Or Mikhail. He can't give me *anything* I want.

I can still hear the rain pounding on the roof as Trofim slips out of the room and closes the door behind him.

When I'm alone, I bury my face in the mattress and sob.

And all I can think is, *What a waste of tears.*

5

MIKHAIL

A trail of water and mud follows me through the mansion. Normally, I'd try to clean up after myself for Stella's sake, but she's dead, so fuck it. The mess stays.

It takes all the energy I have left to lumber up to my office anyway. My clothes are heavy and my muscles ache from too many hours in the gym. I should go to bed, but even as weary as I feel, I can't imagine sleeping.

My office is dark when I push through the door and head to the bar cart. I need a drink more than I need clean clothes or a shower. I need to clear my head for a few blessed hours and—

My senses kick in all at once and I whirl around in the middle of the room. "You must have a death wish," I snarl.

"And *you* must be distracted," my father remarks, stepping out of the shadowy corner. "I could have killed you if I wanted."

I wish you would have.

I'm in front of him in an instant, my soaked sleeve barred across his throat. "You missed your chance. I won't miss mine."

"You want to kill me?" he rasps through his closing windpipe.

"Honor demands it after what you did." I punctuate the point with a hard shove into his throat. "You sent a spy into my house. You kidnapped my wife and child."

"I gave Dante back!" he points out like it matters.

It doesn't.

"You betrayed me and you deserve to die. Plus," I add, leaning all my weight on his chest, "it would be fun for me."

He stretches onto his toes to suck in a desperate breath. Then, unbelievably… he *smiles*. "You're finally ready, Mikhail. I'm so proud."

I'm still drunk and tired enough that the words throw me off balance. I stumble back.

"Really, I knew you were ready when I heard you sent Viviana away," he continues. "I spent years preparing you and I wasn't sure it would ever be enough, but here you are: the leader I knew you could be."

I shake my head, but his words rattle around, refusing to fall into any meaningful order. When he takes a step towards me, I shove him back against the wall. "You raised Trofim to be *pakhan*. He was always going to be your heir. The only reason I'm here is because I took it for myself."

"There are some things in life that even we can't control, Mikhail… like which son is born first." He gives me a knowing look, but I stare blankly back at him. He sighs. "As a father, my duty goes beyond helping my children survive. I need to help you *thrive*. There's a reason animals kill the weak offspring to help the stronger survive. Humans like to think we're more evolved, but you know as well as I do that it's survival of the fittest out there. It's why I cut Anatoly loose when he was young. I needed to focus my energy on you and Trofim."

"Anatoly would have made a better leader than Trofim."

"But he didn't have the lineage," he insists. "His entire reign would have been questioned. He would have been dodging assassination attempts left and right. I didn't want that for him."

I snort. "Don't act like you did him a favor."

"But I did," he argues. "Everyone has their faults. Anatoly's is that he was born to the wrong woman. And Trofim... well, he had more than most. But the one I needed to correct the most is that he let his pride cloud his decision making. The same way your heart clouds yours."

I dig my fingers into his chest as if I'm going to tear into him and come back with his own still-beating heart in my chest. I'm tired, but I might be able to summon the energy for that.

"I spent all of my time shaping both you and your brother for leadership," he explains. "You weren't just *the spare*. You were always a very plausible Plan B. *If* I could make you ready for this world."

"I was always ready," I growl.

He shakes his head. "If that was true, you never would have married Alyona."

The mud from her grave is still under my fingernails. What would my father think if he knew where I was tonight? Would he still think I'm "ready"?

"She wasn't strong enough for our world, Mikhail. You knew that. It's why you kept her away from me. It's why you hid her away in that house, isn't it?"

I don't answer.

I don't need to.

We both know he's right.

Alyona was an exception I allowed myself. The rest of my life would belong to the Bratva, but I carved out a sliver of normalcy with them and pretended I could keep it secret, untarnished, untouched.

"First, it was Alyona. Then, Viviana."

"Viviana was strong enough," I spit. "She was strong enough to kill a future *pakhan*."

He continues on like I haven't said anything. "I could see Viviana was becoming a distraction. It's why I came to you with that evidence. With the tape of Viviana walking out of—"

"I know what was on the fucking tape, Otets."

The footage has replayed over and over again in my head since the moment I watched it. I close my eyes and see Viviana smiling nervously on Trofim's front stoop. He pushed the door open for her and she slipped inside. The next clip showed her walking out through the same door, her hands now covered in blood.

"I needed you to see that she was your last weakness. The Bratva needed you to be able to get rid of her so you could focus on what is important," he implores. "Because Trofim will come back some day and you need to be ready to defend against his attack. You can't do that with his ex-fiancée on your arm and a bastard as your heir. You need to be focused on fortifying your position."

I can physically feel my mind buffering. I blink at my father as his words sink in and register.

"Trofim is—He can't come back." I grab the front of my father's shirt, holding onto him as much as I am holding myself up. "He's dead."

I watch realization dawn on my father's face. His eyes go wide as he understands what he said.

What he revealed.

"Viviana stabbed him," he says, nodding too aggressively. "I showed you the video. You saw it."

"And she killed him. That's what you told me. Trofim is dead."

He regretfully meets my eyes, a weary sigh loosing from his chest. "Not… exactly."

I throw him back against the wall hard enough that he bounces. "You told me he was dead. A coroner told me he was dead! *He is dead.*"

He shakes his head. "He would be… if Viviana had been able to stomach the job. But she couldn't finish it. She stabbed him and ran. Twenty seconds after the tape I gave you cut off, Trofim came stumbling out with his hand over a wound on his stomach. He called a doctor and—"

"You lied to me!" I roar, driving him back into the wall. A frame rattles free of its nail; the glass shatters on the floor. "You manipulated me to get what you wanted."

"I was the only one who told you the truth," he fires back. "Viviana was a distraction and I was the only one who could see it. I had to make the hard call, the same way I did when I ended the war with the Colombians."

"That wasn't a hard call. The cartel murdered my family—an innocent woman, an innocent baby. You had to retaliate."

He nods slowly. "I did. All of our allies were outraged. Almost like someone masterminded the whole thing to drum up sympathy and rally our allies behind the cause."

Suddenly, I'm back in that bullet-riddled house. I can smell gunpowder everywhere. I see the trail of blood leading from the panic room to the bodies of my wife and child.

"You… you let them die," I breathe, still not really believing it. "You left Alyona and Anzhelina vulnerable on purpose."

I expect him to deny it. But my father points to the *pakhan's* signet ring on my finger. "The reason you are wearing that today and Trofim isn't is because I removed the obstacles in your way. I helped you become the ruthless leader you needed to be. You wouldn't be here if you were trying to balance being *pakhan* with being a husband. You can't be both—not the way you wanted to do it. You can only be loyal to one. You have to choose."

I let go of his shirt and step away. Everything I thought I knew is shifting around me. The foundations of my life are collapsing like wet clay.

Every day since Alyona and Anzhelina were murdered, I've blamed myself. I thought I should have done more to protect them. I felt naive for believing the Colombians wouldn't target them.

Now, I know the truth. The Colombians wouldn't have targeted them...

Unless my father put a bullseye on their backs.

And I could have done everything to protect them and it still may not have been enough—not if my father was going to bring the full might of the Bratva down on them. He orchestrated the single worst moment of my entire life... and now, he's telling me it was for my own good.

My father reads my shock as a good thing and moves closer. He dips his chin to meet my eyes. "Mikhail the family man never would have survived this world. You would have died years ago trying to save your wife and child. But the man in front of me? *This* Mikhail?" He gestures to me with both hands like I'm the final prize in a game show. "You kicked your child's mother to the curb because she lied to you. You put the Bratva over everything. And because of that, I know you'll survive."

I knew what I was doing when I sent Viviana away. I made the choice with eyes wide open. I'll do anything to protect Dante.

But protect him from what?

Viviana didn't kill Trofim. Even if she did, Anatoly was right: we should have thrown her a party. Trofim was a monster. I regretted not killing him myself plenty of times over the years since I exiled him.

And sure, the Greeks will start banging their war drums the moment this second engagement with Helen even hints towards falling through, but if I'm the ruthless man my father says I am, then I can take them on.

But if I'm the ruthless, cold-blooded man my father says I am, then I wouldn't want a family in the first place. That man could send Viviana away and never think of her again. That man wouldn't spend hour after hour beating his frustration into a punching bag and crawling through the mud.

Dante thought I was going to protect him and his mom. Viviana thought I could be different if I wanted it badly enough.

As I stand in front of my father now, the question isn't just which man am I—it's which man do I want to be?

"You're right. I will survive." I smooth the rumpled collar of my father's shirt down around his neck. Then I wrap my hand around his throat. "You, however, won't."

His eyes widen as I slam him back against the wall one last time, crushing his windpipe beneath my fingers.

"Maybe I would have exiled you the way I did Trofim, but you've made it clear that was a mistake." He claws at my hand. My thumb is buried in his pulse point. I can feel each desperate pound of his racing heart. There won't be many of them left. "I want to learn from my mistakes, as any good *pakhan* would."

His lips quiver around a word he can't find the oxygen for. Maybe it's my name. Maybe it's a plea.

It doesn't matter.

His knees buckle and he sinks to the floor. I follow him, letting him lie sideways in the shattered glass of the picture frame that fell earlier.

Once his eyes flutter closed, I grab a shard of glass and feel the weight of it in my hands. I take stock of this moment, of exactly what I'm planning to do, what it means, what it will change.

Then I drive the glass into his throat.

6

VIVIANA

I hear the door to my room open, but any connection between my brain and my body has been severed. Or, if not severed, then shriveled up and dehydrated like the rest of me.

I know I should sit up and prepare myself for whatever horror Trofim has lined up for me now, but I can't bring myself to care.

Unless it's a glass of water dancing through the door, I don't want to waste the energy.

"Viviana?" A deep voice sing-songs my name.

I'm hallucinating, I think. *Or maybe I'm going crazy. Can dehydration make you hear voices?* It's the only reason I can think of why I would be hearing my father's voice in my ear.

"Wake up and give your daddy a hug."

My eyes snap open to find my father leaning over me.

I'm still hallucinating, but it's worse than I thought. I'm hearing and *seeing things.*

When my father would be gone for work, he'd come to my room as soon as he got home. It was the only time he ever seemed excited to see me. He'd wake me up and give me a hug. Then present me with whatever trinket he bought for me on his trips.

I used to think it was sweet. Now, I know he just wanted to make sure I hadn't gone anywhere.

"You've looked better." The hallucination that looks remarkably like my father—wrinkles and gray hairs included —assesses me with a wince. I feel like a rotted carcass left to bake in the sun. I can only imagine what I must look like.

I try to talk and break into a coughing fit. Once I can manage words, they come out in a hoarse whisper. "Go away."

"I thought you'd be excited about visitors at this point. Especially a visit from dear old Dad." He lays a warm, rough hand on my elbow.

I jolt up so fast my chains go taut. I cry out as the sores on my wrists reopen. But the pain is gone the second I look at my father again.

"You're really here," I rasp.

"Did you think you were dreaming?" he asks with a smile. "I guess I should be flattered."

My weak heart is sputtering against my chest. I feel like he could blow me down with one breath, but I'm ready to go. To run. *To fight.*

"How did you get in here?" I whisper. "How did you know where Trofim was keeping me?"

Is Trofim still alive? Does Mikhail know where I am? Do you have a gun and can I be the one to shoot Trofim between the eyes?

A million questions swirl around in my head, but they all go quiet as my father's face splits into a cruel grin. "Who do you think loaned Trofim this safehouse to hold you? Who do you think told him where to find you in the first place?"

Dread splashes over me like a bucket of ice water. "You betrayed me?" I gasp.

He leans close, his upper lip curled back. "You betrayed me first, Viviana. Don't act like you didn't have this coming."

He's rotten all the way through.

I'm not sure why I didn't realize it sooner. But it took me until this moment to understand that there is no good in him.

When I turned twelve, the chef at whichever exclusive restaurant my father chose to host our celebration delivered a chocolate sphere to the table. It was bigger than my head and I tried to smile and look grateful, but all I could imagine was breaking my front teeth trying to eat a solid ball of chocolate. Then a waiter arrived with hot fudge. He poured the fudge over the chocolate and the sphere began to melt. It fell away in big pieces and revealed, inside, a decadent, four-layer chocolate cake. The best chocolate cake I've ever had.

I fooled myself into thinking my father was like that chocolate cake. I believed that, inside, he was warm and sweet and tender. He just had a hard outer shell. His role in the mafia and the world required him to be tough. But inside, deep down, he loved me. He had to love me, right?

Now, I know all of that was bullshit. It was nothing but the desperate fantasy of a little girl.

"You aren't even going to try to help me?"

"I helped you once before," he hisses. "I arranged a perfectly fine marriage for you—a better match than you ever could have hoped to find on your own. And you spat on it. You complained and argued. Then, at the first chance, you ran away."

"I ran for my freedom."

"And how are you liking it?" He throws his arms wide and gestures around the room. It's so small that he could stretch out and touch opposite walls if he wanted. "How does freedom feel?"

"The only reason I'm here is because of you. Because you ratted out your own daughter!"

Mikhail kicked me out. Trofim kidnapped me. My father turned his back on me.

I have no one. I'm all alone.

"You're here because we all have to face the consequences of our actions one day. This is what you get for failing to kill Trofim the way you promised." He shrugs like there's nothing else he could have done. "You didn't kill Trofim and you ran from me when I wanted to help you."

"You're mad because I didn't kill Trofim, but now, you're helping him?" I ask incredulously. "It makes no sense."

"It makes sense when you understand that Trofim and I have one big thing in common: we couldn't trust our own family. Trofim's own brother overthrew him and his father put up no resistance."

"Because he was a psychopath and needed to be overthrown!"

"And you," he barks, jabbing a finger in my face, "ran off and left me in the lurch for six years. You made me look like a fucking embarrassment who couldn't control his own daughter."

"Controlling your daughter by forcibly kidnapping her isn't *less* of an embarrassment."

His jaw works back and forth. He's older than I last saw him. His hard edges have softened. "I'd rather you be married to Trofim than dead."

I snort, but it sends me into another round of coughing. My vision starts to go black before I'm able to get it under control. "I'm going to end up dead either way. He's killing me."

And my baby.

Would my father change his mind about anything if I told him I was pregnant? When I was pregnant with Dante, I was able to convince my father that it would work in his favor. I doubt I can manage that again.

He'd probably just tell Trofim about the baby. Then I'd be cut off from any connection to Mikhail at all. At least this way, I can keep a part of him with me.

"He won't kill you if you play along, Viviana. Trofim is going to reclaim his rightful place in the Novikov Bratva and he'll take care of you."

Between the two of us, I'm the emaciated, dried-out husk. And yet, I almost feel bad for my father.

"If you really think Trofim can beat Mikhail, then you have no idea who you're up against."

Disappointment I recognize well settles on his brow. "Just because Mikhail was nice to you doesn't mean he's the better leader. Actually," he adds, "the fact that he was nice to you means he *isn't* the better leader. Because a good leader never would have picked up his older brother's trash."

I want to be offended, but I don't have the energy. I'm being held hostage by a man who is going to die trying to overthrow a man who didn't want me. Who maybe never wanted me to begin with.

What a fucking mess.

"Mikhail isn't nice to me anymore," I mumble.

"That's even more reason for you to grab the lifeline Trofim is throwing you."

"What lifeline?" I retort. "If you're talking about this cell, you should look around. I'm dying in here."

"Because you're resisting," he growls. "But if you cooperate, he'll take care of you. I made him swear he would."

My poor father. He has the audacity to make deals with dangerous men, but none of the common sense to understand when he's being played.

Trofim is never going to take care of me. He might keep me alive. He might wield me like a shiny trophy he won back from his brother. But he'll never take care of me.

"How is he going to take care of me in this cell?"

"He isn't," he says. "Tomorrow, he's unlocking the door."

I sit up. "He's going to let me out?"

"For a special event." He nods slowly. "Tomorrow, you and Trofim get married."

I could scream and fight. There's enough anger inside of me that I'm sure I could channel some of it towards leaping off this bed and wrapping the chain dangling from my wrist around my father's neck.

But he would fight back. As weak as I am, my father would overpower me.

And what would happen to my baby then?

What would happen to Dante?

Mikhail doesn't know Trofim is alive. He doesn't know his brother is coming for him. If Mikhail still sends Dante to that boarding school, Trofim could track him down. He could hurt him. He *will* hurt him if I don't play along.

There's no way out. The only choice I have now is whether I fight for myself or fight for my babies.

The decision is easy: I lie back down on the bed and close my eyes.

I listen to my father leave as silently as he arrived and pray that Mikhail will keep Dante close.

7

MIKHAIL

Blood is still pumping rhythmically out of my father's neck when the door to my office bursts open.

Raoul barges in, ready for anything. Until he almost trips over my father's body, that is. Then he glances down at the blood on his shoe and the paling corpse and looks like he's going to be sick.

"I think he's still alive," I drawl as I turn and do what I came into this room for in the first place—get a drink. "In case you want to try to save him."

Raoul leaps over his twitching legs and stops me mid-pour. "Are you okay?"

I shake him off roughly and top off my glass. "I'm not the one bleeding out on the floor. I'm fine."

"What happened?"

He asks the question like it's simple. Like I can draw a line from dot to dot and end up with some crystal clear picture of this night, this week, this whole cursed life.

What happened is that my father murdered my daughter and first wife and kidnapped my second. And right this very moment, watching his chest convulse, I'm still not sure if he did it because he loved or hated me. Maybe both.

I settle on an easier explanation. "It's complicated."

"No shit," he snaps. "Your father is dead on the floor. That usually comes with some complications."

Raoul has always taken everything in stride. It might be a vestige of the fact that he was technically given to me to be used as a slave. Since this is the twenty-first century and I don't own a powdered wig, I never took Raoul's family up on the offer in full. But still… the dynamic lingers. Raoul jumps when I say jump and he doesn't ask questions.

Until now.

When I called him last week to tell him Anatoly had been shot, he was shaken. Then the dominoes kept falling. Pyotr betrayed us; Stella died; Viviana and Dante were kidnapped. The last week has been a shitshow and now, even the most dependable person I know is in shambles.

I take a long drink and drop down into the leather chair in the corner. The gash in my father's neck is bubbling now, a slow leak compared to the deluge a minute ago.

"My father killed Alyona and Anzhelina."

Raoul blinks at me. He doesn't look surprised—he looks worried. It's well-documented that Ruben Falcao, Raoul's father, ordered the hit that ended with my family slaughtered in their own home. He probably thinks I'm crazy to suggest a different version of events.

"No," he says gently. "*My* father killed them."

"Your father picked the—hell, it wasn't even low-hanging fruit. My father tossed it on the ground. He rolled it to your father's feet." I take another drink, not entirely sure if it's exhaustion or the alcohol making my head spin. "The night they died, my father sent me to the other side of the city and withdrew guards from the property. He might as well have put the key under the mat for the cartel. He *wanted* Alyona and Anzhelina to die."

Saying it out loud makes me want to stand up and kill him again. Maybe I should ask Raoul to revive him after all.

"I always wondered," Raoul mutters.

That wakes me up. The world around me solidifies as I stare up at one of my oldest friends. "What the fuck does that mean? You always wondered what?"

Raoul's face shifts from pity to guilt and back again. He sags like the truth is physically weighing him down. "My father was a brutal man, but he did what needed to be done to protect his family."

Rage rises up in me, fierce and swift. "He protected his family by killing mine! Don't tell me he did the right thing."

"That's just it," Raoul continues. "My father never hurt a child. Not once. I grew up hearing stories about him mounting the heads of his enemies on his wall like trophies. Men whispered about the way he would chop off someone's leg for accidentally stepping on his foot. But in all those stories, he never hurt a woman or a child. Ever."

I frown. "He made an exception for Alyona and Anzhelina, then."

"Maybe." Raoul shrugs, his head sinking deeper between his shoulders. He looks like a turtle trying to hide away. "Or…

maybe he didn't know who was in the house that night. Maybe he had bad information and called that hit having no clue that your wife and daughter were home alone."

Would my father have gone that far to kill my family off? He could have taken them out himself, but I would have traced it back to him. If there hadn't been a common enemy to point to—an imminent threat that needed to be dealt with—I might have realized the hand my father played in their murders even sooner.

"Your father offered you as a sacrifice," I remind him. "He told my father that we could torture you, kill you, enslave you—whatever we wanted to do to make things right. He did that to his own son, but you think he would draw the line at killing one random woman and child he didn't even know?"

Raoul thinks it over, choosing his words carefully. There is no good outcome here. At the end of the day, Alyona and Anzhelina are still dead. Raoul was still used as a bartering chip by his father. My father is going cold in the corner.

Everything is fucked up. But if we can untangle this knot, maybe the future doesn't have to be.

"*Your* father orchestrated the murder of your wife and child and then kidnapped Viviana and Dante," Raoul says gently. "He did that to his own son… Do you think he'd draw the line at feeding bad information to his enemies to get them to do his dirty work?"

Raoul looks at me and I remember the first moment we met.

He stepped out of the car parked in front of the mansion and all I saw in him was myself—the spare son whose only purpose was to sacrifice himself at the altar of his family for no other reason than his father asked him to.

It's another reason why I never considered forcing him to be a slave. We'd both spent more than enough of our lives doing that already.

"No," I finally answer. "I don't think my father ever drew a line. He always did whatever it took to get what he wanted."

A string of curse words from the doorway alert us to Anatoly's arrival. "And who is responsible for this mess?" He gestures to our father like he's a glass of spilled milk before he kneels down in the blood and checks his pulse. "This is bullshit. I miss all the fun! First, Trofim. Now this."

"Your father is dead," Raoul hisses at him under his breath. "Pretend you have some decorum."

Anatoly slowly, shamefully lowers his head and stares down at the floor. He folds his hands in front of him and looks solemn.

Then, after a few seconds, he shakes it off. "I think that was enough mourning, don't you? Now that that's out of the way, *who in the fuck is responsible for this mess?*"

I raise a hand. "He deserved it."

"Obviously. That wasn't in question. But what did he do this time?"

Raoul has always been appalled by our manners. Even though his father shipped him to our house and his likely death, Raoul has never said a bad word about him. Even when I know he's burning up with anger, he's kept a tight leash on his outward response.

But there's no sense in me beating around the bush. Not when the elephant in the room is decaying in the corner.

"He arranged for Alyona and Anzhelina to die and framed Viviana for Trofim's murder."

Again, all eyes are on me.

"He killed Alyona and Anzhelina?" Anatoly asks, finally stunned.

At the same time, Raoul frowns. "Viviana didn't kill Trofim?"

Anatoly turns to Raoul. "Wait, what? Then who killed Trofim? I don't understand anything."

I fill Anatoly in on everything as quickly as I can and watch as my brother practically inflates with rage. He looks twice his normal size, I swear.

"That fucking coward," he hisses. "He murdered his own granddaughter. I don't know why I ever expected better, but this is low even for him."

Anatoly saw more of Anzhelina than I did in the brief few months she was alive. We were in the middle of a war and he was the primary guard stationed at our house. He was there day in and day out until the night my father pulled us both across the city to fight the cartel. The same night he knew Ruben Falcao would launch an attack on my house.

Anatoly clenches his fists at his side. If our father wasn't already dead, Anatoly would be on his way to take him out. "Why?"

"He thought I was distracted. He thought having a family made me weak."

"Of course he did," he spits. "We're talking about the man who ignored me from the second I was born and let Trofim kill my mother. Sentimentality isn't something he ever concerned himself with. Even his beloved firstborn didn't get a funeral after his death. We're all just tools he can use until we snap in half. He never cared about any of us."

Anatoly's teeth grind together with every word. He gave up on our father a long, long time ago. That doesn't mean he's made his peace with him.

Now, he won't get the chance.

"The lack of a funeral might have been on purpose since... Trofim isn't dead."

They both stare at me, wide-eyed. After a few long, silent seconds, Anatoly presses his fingers into his eye sockets. "It's too late for this shit. I should be asleep."

I walk them both through my father's confession about Viviana stabbing Trofim but not finishing the job. About the tape he showed me and what he claimed was on the footage I didn't receive.

"And you believe him?" Raoul asks when I'm finished. "You really think Viviana didn't do it? What if he's lying?"

"Why would he? The only reason I sent Viviana away is because she killed Trofim and I had no clue. It made me realize how much of a distraction she was for me. Which is exactly what Otets wanted. Why would he reveal that Trofim was alive and risk me bringing her back?"

Anatoly holds up a finger, amusement curling the corners of his mouth. "I thought you sent Viviana away because you needed to marry Helen to appease the Greeks."

"That, too," I mutter dismissively.

"Then there's no chance you'd bring Viviana back, so Otets could have lied to you." Anatoly watches me closely as he says it. I know he's paying attention to every flicker of emotion across my face.

There is no chance I'm bringing Viviana back.

There *should* be no chance that Viviana comes back into this house.

And yet…

"Anything is possible," I bite out grudgingly.

"Spoken like a man who's getting married tomorrow," Anatoly snorts. "Or have you forgotten that your wedding to Helen Drakos is happening in less than eighteen hours?"

"I haven't forgotten anything," I lie.

I forget about Helen hourly. I need to keep the Greeks happy to make sure Dante is safe, but I'd be willing to do it in many ways that have nothing at all to do with marrying Helen.

"Because we're going to have a much bigger mess to clean up than our father if you back out of this engagement a second time. The Drakos family is ready to defend Helen's honor if they have to."

There will definitely be some honor to defend once the Greeks find out I'm still married to another woman. Annulment papers were drawn up by my lawyer, but I haven't signed them. I haven't even attempted to track down Viviana and have her sign them, either.

Legally, I can't marry Helen tomorrow.

Morally, I won't.

"Trofim is alive and an imminent threat," Anatoly recounts. "The Greeks are a dark cloud over our heads. We have a lot of enemies and few friends. We can't afford to do anything stupid here, Mik."

I toss back the rest of my drink. I should be trying to clear my head, not make things muddier.

Then again, when I think about it, things have always been clear.

"My father turned me into a ruthless, cold-hearted *pakhan*," I announce, rising to my feet to face my brothers. "I'm finally the man he always wanted me to be."

Anatoly and Raoul share a look before Raoul asks, "What does that mean?"

"It means," I explain, "that I know what I have to do. And nothing is going to change my mind."

8

VIVIANA

Bright white sand sprawls for miles. Turquoise water stretches to the horizon and sparkles in the sunlight.

Dante is down by the shoreline, his swim trunks pulled up to his belly button. He's hurrying around with a red pail and plastic shovel in his hands, trying to finish construction on his sandcastle before the tide comes in.

"It's like a picture." I tip my head back to breathe in the salty air. It almost burns my throat, but I can't really complain. I'm in paradise.

Strong arms wrap around my middle from behind. A stubbled chin rests on my shoulder. I know without looking that it's Mikhail. His hands circle around my stomach.

I glance down and I can't see the toes I know are buried in the sand. My baby bump is in the way. I let myself sink back against Mikhail's chest.

"Because it is," he whispers in my ear.

"Hmm?" I hum, my eyes fluttering closed.

I'm exhausted, but I don't want to leave the beach. I don't even want the sun to set. Each time I open my eyes, the sun looks a little lower in the sky. Dante is working on his castle, but he's getting closer and closer to the water.

I curl my hand around my mouth. "Dante, come back in! You're too close to the water!"

My voice doesn't carry. I realize all at once how thirsty I am. When's the last time I had water?

"I said, 'Because it is,'" Mikhail repeats. "It is a picture."

I have no idea what he's talking about, but the sky is suddenly getting dark overhead. The beautiful day is gone and storm clouds are rolling in. The waves are large swells that rise over my head. The water pulls at Dante's legs, laps over his knees.

"Dante! Come back!" I go to pull Mikhail's hands off of my stomach, but my bump is gone. And it's not hands wrapped around my middle, but chains.

The heat at my back is replaced by an eerie chill. I finally look over my shoulder and see Trofim grinning back at me.

"All of this is a picture," he hisses. "It's not real. It was never real."

I turn frantically towards the water, but Dante is gone. The castle he was working on is underwater and there's no sign of my son anywhere.

"Dante!" I cry, but my voice is gone now.

So is Dante.

So is Mikhail.

"None of it was real," Trofim whispers along my spine. He circles in front of me, grinning like a devil. "Except for me."

He lunges at me and I swing at him.

"For fuck's sake!" a man complains, swatting my hand away from his face. "I thought she was unconscious."

The guard in charge of bringing my meals is standing above me, a growing bruise on his cheek from where I hit him.

"She was," another man insists from the doorway. "I guess she's awake now. Just in time."

"What are you doing here?" I try to sit up, but the man grabs my chain and yanks me towards him.

I wait for the painful tug of metal against my wrists, but it doesn't come.

"Stand up. And if you hit me again, I'll hit you back," he warns.

My chains are loose. The cell door is open.

Half of my brain is still locked in the nightmare, but the other half is scrambling to make sense of what's happening.

"Where are you taking me?"

They don't answer. They silently lead me out of the room and into the hallway.

I'm not sure why Trofim thinks I need two guards on me. I can't even stand up on my own, let alone fight someone twice as big as me.

My legs are shaky. The only times I've stood up in days have been to waddle to the makeshift toilet in the corner. But even that has become less frequent. Can't pee if you have no water in your system.

The hallway is dim, but there are other closed doors every so often. How many other people are huddled behind them, too starved and thirsty to fight back?

Suddenly, the man in front of me turns into a large, open room. There are no windows, so I know we're still underground. A table set up against the wall with a curling iron and blow dryer sitting on top of it. A makeup bag is spilled open on the table.

A woman is standing in the middle of the room, her hands folded in front of her. She can't be older than eighteen and she looks even smaller than I am.

"You can sit here," she offers nervously, gesturing to a metal chair in front of her. Her smile falters the longer she holds it.

I don't move, but the men shove me forward and drop me down in the chair. The cold metal bites through my thin clothes. But nothing is as sharp as the pain that lances through my wrists when the guards re-cuff me to the chair.

"Why?" I ask through a sob.

Why are you doing this? Why are you keeping me chained? Why am I still alive?

No one answers me and the young girl nods to the guards.

"We'll come back for her," one of them grunts. They close the door behind them.

And it's then that all the pieces fall into place.

Because hanging on the back of the door is a wedding dress.

Tomorrow, you and Trofim get married.

My father warned me, but I couldn't process it. As horrifying as every moment of being trapped here has been, my brain couldn't grasp that Trofim would actually force me to marry him.

"This can't be happening." I try to drop my face into my hands, but the chains catch. Blinding pain shoots up my arms and I drop them at my sides.

The girl is wide-eyed. She stares at me for a few seconds before she turns around and grabs the makeup bag from the desk. "I'm supposed to get you ready."

"It's going to take more than that," I mumble.

She chews on her lower lip for a few seconds. Then, quickly, she pulls a water bottle out of the makeup bag.

I feel like the vampire I saw in my first ever scary movie. He'd been starved of blood and lunged anytime a human got close. His purple lips curled away from pointed teeth and his eyes were red and hollow-looking. I was up with nightmares for weeks afterward.

The girl jolts in surprise, but she isn't afraid. She unscrews the cap and hands me the bottle. I wrap both hands around it and drink and drink and drink.

I force myself to stop when it's still half-full. If I keep going, I'll just make myself sick. Then her kindness will be for nothing.

"Thank you." My voice still sounds hoarse, but it doesn't hurt as much to talk.

"If you're dehydrated, then your skin will be dry. I can't do makeup on dry skin." I know she's crafting the explanation she'll give Trofim if he finds out she gave me water.

She took a risk giving me the water. She knows Trofim won't like it, but she did it anyway. Maybe…

"Are there tweezers in there?" I ask quietly. "Or maybe cuticle scissors. You could drop them on the floor without realizing it. I'll use them to pick this lock and then overpower you before—"

Her face creases like she's in pain. "I can't. He'd kill me if you got away."

I know she's right. But it doesn't make me hate her any less.

It doesn't make me hate any of this any less.

"My father told me that at least if I marry Trofim, I won't be dead," I say flatly as she begins wiping away days' worth of built-up grease from my forehead. I meet her eyes to make sure she knows I mean what I'm about to say with every fiber of my being. "But I would rather be dead than marry Trofim."

She snaps her eyes away from mine and doesn't look at me again.

I don't blame her. I don't know why Trofim has her here, but it's not to help me escape. It's not to be my friend.

No one is on my side and no one is coming for me. Not my father. Not Anatoly. Not Mikhail.

The woman dabs blush on my cheeks and swipes mascara on my lashes. She curls my hair and paints my nails. I want to tell her that she might as well be preparing my corpse.

Because this is not a wedding I'm getting ready for.

It's a funeral.

9

MIKHAIL

"Please," the night manager whimpers from where he's cowering behind his desk. "I just hand out the keys. I don't know anything about who the guests are. I don't monitor who they invite or who comes and goes. I don't have any clue what is going on with—"

I cock the gun already pointed at his face. "Shut up. I can't hear what they're saying."

The figures moving around on the screen in front of me are fuzzy around the edges. The security system has to be a decade old, at least. There's no audio, but I lean forward anyway. I want to crawl through the screen and be in that moment.

Like I should have been the first time.

"There is no sound," the manager points out. But the words cut off in another desperate whine when I jab the gun in his direction.

The footage is an eerie mirror image of the video my father showed me. Instead of Viviana standing on Trofim's doorstep, I'm watching my older brother knock on Viviana's hotel room door.

It was easy enough to trace her movements from the mansion to the pharmacy. Then from the pharmacy to the cheapest motel in a five-mile radius. The night manager feigned "guest privacy" for all of three seconds before I pulled out my gun and he logged into the security footage like his life depended on it. Which it did.

"When was this taken?" I growl.

"The timestamp in the corner is wrong," the manager says.

"No fucking kidding. It's not December 31, 1999?" Raoul slaps him in the back of the head. "Tell us something we don't already know."

The manager is innocent of everything except being an idiot. The only way to get clear answers out of him is through threat of violence. So I kneel down in front of him, the muzzle tucked under his second chin.

"How long did the woman stay here?" I ask clearly. "And when did this man knock on her door?"

He closes his eyes and blows out a shuddering breath. "An hour, maybe?"

"An hour? She was only here for an hour?"

He shrugs. "I think. It could have been less."

"So this footage—" I jab my finger at the screen on the desk. "—is from the first night she arrived? Four days ago?"

"I think it was four days. I'm not—She checked in a few nights ago. She was quiet and kept her head down. I didn't pay much attention to her. I was more focused on the room next to her. Men were coming and going from that room all night and the police have been on us about cracking down on prostitution."

"The point," I bark. "Get to the fucking point."

"I was distracted and I didn't see this guy show up," he scrambles to explain. "When she walked out of this room with her key, it was the last time I saw her. The maid went in the next morning and her stuff was still there, but she was gone."

I turn back to the screen, watching as Trofim carries Viviana's limp body through the door and down the cracked sidewalk to his car.

"He knew where she was," Raoul whispers, saying exactly what I'm thinking.

If Trofim was here within the hour, then someone must have told him where Viviana was staying.

Now, I need to know who.

As soon as the thought crosses my mind, my phone rings. I pick up and Anatoly is already mid-sentence. "—there *now*. Get there right fucking now!"

"Get where? What are you—"

"Trofim was spotted thirty minutes ago at a bar the Giordanos own. Agostino was with him. He and Agostino were sitting at the same booth. They're working together." He's talking fast, squeezing as much information as he can into every second. "You need to get there now. If you find them, I guarantee you'll find Viv."

Viviana's father is here in the city and there's no way it's a coincidence.

Viviana's father is working with my brother. He helped Trofim kidnap his own daughter.

Before I can stop myself, I send my fist through the poor night manager's monitor. The screen cracks. The edges flicker with life, but the center is a large, black hole of jagged glass.

"Ah, man," he mutters miserably.

All I can focus on is the rush of blood in my ears.

The only reason Viviana was in this shitty hotel for Trofim to take in the first place is because I kicked her out. I sent her out to fend for herself and she was snatched within an hour.

Now, he's had her for *days*.

"What's happening on your end?" Anatoly asks. "Tell me where to meet you and I'll—"

"Stay with Dante," I order. "Raoul and I will take this."

"I'm always the babysitter," he mumbles.

"There isn't time to get back to the mansion. He's had her for days, Nat. *Days.*"

Anatoly curses under his breath. "I know. You need to get to her."

"And I need to know Dante is safe. You're the only person I trust to take care of him. If anyone comes into the house, shoot first and ask questions later."

"You know I'll protect him with my life. Now, go get Viv."

Raoul is at my elbow the second we hang up.

"You heard everything?"

"Agostino and Trofim are working together," he confirms with a nod. "It makes sense. If Agostino is in the city, there's a good reason. He would have been on Viviana the second she stepped foot off of your property. If Trofim found her within an hour, we know who to blame."

"That means we also know who to kill first," I grit out.

Because I *will* kill Agostino Giordano. Not just for betraying his daughter and handing her to Trofim. No, mostly I want to kill him for thinking he has any claim whatsoever on my wife.

No one touches what's mine.

We fly across the city, but the bar is closed when we get there. Not surprising given it's well after three in the morning. Raoul starts to slow down, but I gesture for him to keep driving. "We're going to pay Agostino a house visit."

It's risky. This kind of operation would usually be in the works for days, if not weeks. But we don't have that kind of time.

We might already be too late.

I'm not going to waste another minute planning or plotting. If Viviana is in her father's penthouse, I'm going to rip the walls down and get her out.

Thankfully, I don't need to explain any of this to Raoul. He already understands.

He slams on the gas and drives headfirst into danger without a single hesitation.

Agostino doesn't own the building his penthouse is in, which is his second mistake. The first mistake, of course, being crossing me to begin with.

The after-hours guards on duty in the underground garage are equipped to hand out parking violations and scare away graffiti artists. The young kid walking around the corner with a nightstick on his belt barely even looks up from whatever video he's watching on his phone when I approach him.

"Take a walk," I snarl.

The twenty-something jolts. Fumbling with his phone and making sure it doesn't end up shattered on the pavement is his main concern until he looks into the barrel of my gun.

His mouth falls open, but I speak before he can. "Take a walk and don't come back within thirty minutes unless you want your brains painted on the walls."

The kid swallows and nods dumbly. It's not hard to tell he isn't a threat. He's not making enough money to lose his life standing up to me. I swipe the keys from his belt before he scurries away silently.

Once inside, I turn every corner expecting guards or security. There's nothing. Just an exhausted doorman next to the elevator. Raoul knocks him out and we use his universal elevator key to make our way to Giordano's penthouse.

"That was easy," Raoul remarks as the floors pass one by one.

He's right, but I hear what he's not saying.

If Viviana is here, there should be more security.

I shove the thought away and focus on the next right step. Right now, that's getting to Agostino.

The elevator doors open with a quiet mechanical whirr, but there's no bell to announce our arrival. No telltale chime. Maybe that's why no one comes rushing out from the hallway to the right to demand to know what we're doing here.

Or maybe no one is home.

The lights are off. Raoul and I make our way through the entryway and across the living room using nothing but the ambient light coming from the floor-to-ceiling windows. The apartment is chic and modern—all sharp edges, shades of gray, and exposed concrete. His penthouse is a midlife crisis if I've ever seen one.

I try to imagine Dante's dinosaur night light plugged into the sockets or Viviana's books stacked on the pristine coffee table. I try to imagine her and Dante living here, part of the Giordano family, but it's all wrong.

Because she doesn't belong here. She never did.

The clock in the sitting room says it's almost five. Raoul and I have spent hours darting all over the city looking for her.

We're wasting time.

"Agostino!" I yell.

My voice echoes off the concrete walls as Raoul lunges for me.

"What in the hell are you thinking?" he hisses, dragging me back. "You're giving us up."

I shake him off. "I'm not wasting anymore time." I tear down the hallway, kicking in doors as I go. "Where is she, Agostino? Tell me where Viviana is!"

The house is eerily silent, but I know he's here. I can feel it.

I approach the door at the end of the hall, gun raised. "Open up or I'm shooting down the door."

"We don't even know if he's in there," Raoul argues quietly. "People will hear you blasting away in here. We can't find Viviana from jail."

Raoul has clearly reached his quota of flying by the seat of our pants. But for the first time in days, I feel perfectly at ease.

"Three!" I yell, cocking the gun. "Two! One—"

The lock turns and the door cracks open. Agostino slides his empty hands through the door first, palms up. "Quite the wake-up call, Mikhail. To what do I owe the pleasure?"

He's wearing a rumpled button-down shirt and dress pants. His eyes are rimmed in shadows. I haven't seen him in a few years, but he looks older. Worn.

He also looks like Viviana.

They have the same angular chin and turned-up nose. The same blood running in their veins.

This man watched Viviana grow up from a baby into the woman she is today, yet he tossed her to the wolves at every opportunity.

Before I can stop myself, I toss my gun to the floor and lunge for Agostino Giordano's throat.

As soon as my fist connects with his face, I regret every punch I wasted in the gym. Hitting Agostino feels *so much better* than any punching bag ever has.

Blood and spit flies. Agostino throws up his arms to shield himself, but he's spent too many years behind a wall of guards. He inherited his position from his father and, when the going got tough, he used his daughter as a bartering chip. Agostino hasn't forgotten how to fight; he just never learned in the first place.

"Please," he begs between blows.

I don't let up. I don't slow down.

I can't.

Not while Viviana is still in danger because of him.

"You're a piece of shit." I kick him in the ribs and feel something inside of him give way. "You sacrificed your own daughter and you deserve to die."

"Mikhail." Raoul speaks low. A warning.

Agostino deserves to die, but not yet. Not until I know where Viviana is.

I fist the front of his shirt and jerk him off the floor. A few buttons snap loose, but he manages to get his feet underneath him. His lip is split and blood pours down his chin.

"Where is she?" I snarl. "I want to know where you're keeping her."

He shakes his head. "I don't—"

He doesn't get to finish the lie. I slam him against the doorframe. His head bounces off the wood so hard that I swear I can see the stars in his eyes.

"You do know where she is. I know you know. Which is why I'm going to pull out a tooth for every second of my time you waste." I look back at Raoul. "Find some pliers."

Raoul is a fan of discretion. He prefers to slip in and out of a hit with as little fuss as possible. It's why I don't send Raoul and Anatoly on runs together when I can help it. They have very different styles of dealing with targets.

Tonight, I'm erring on Anatoly's side. *I want Agostino to suffer.*

Before Raoul can even turn around, Agostino crumbles.

"She's with Trofim! Trofim has her," he blubbers. "He threatened me. I didn't have a choice when he—"

His head snaps to the side when I punch him, the words dissolving into a bloody spray.

"Men like us always have a choice. You should have been willing to die to protect her."

I should have died to protect her. I will if it comes to it.

"I'm going to die now, aren't I? You'll kill me. Even when I tell you she's at my safehouse in Staten Island, you're going to kill me."

I glance over my shoulder and Raoul nods. He knows where the safehouse is.

"You're going to die and it's going to be by my hand, but not tonight." I back away and Agostino falls to a bloody heap on the floor. "Right now, I need to get to Viviana."

Trofim has had her alone for days while I was wasting away in the gym.

I can't waste another second. No matter how much Agostino deserves it.

10

VIVIANA

"When are they coming back?"

If someone had told me two hours ago I'd be anxious for the guards to return to drag me to my wedding with Trofim, I would have called them crazy.

Now, *I'm* the crazy one.

Crazy as in bored. Crazy as in anxious. And crazy uncomfortable in the ill-fitting wedding dress Trofim must have pulled out of some retired stripper's costume closet. It's more mesh than lace and I would not at all be surprised to discover it has tearaway seams.

The girl who helped me get ready, whose name I still do not know, only shrugs at my question.

"You could go find them," I suggest. "See what's taking so long."

I've lost all sense of time, but it has to be late. Or early. She's been fighting sleep for the last hour, her head bobbing every few minutes.

She studies the chains around my wrist to make sure they're still firmly attached to the metal chair. She thinks this is my attempt at an escape. In some ways, I guess it is. I want to escape this room. If I have to suffer through a wedding ceremony with Trofim, I want to get it over with as soon as possible.

There's no sense in delaying the horrible inevitable.

I know there's no chance of me getting out of this house. Not only because Trofim definitely has his beefy, brainless goons stationed at every exit, but also because I am long past having the energy for an escape. I barely have the energy to sit upright in this chair.

I have to admit, the girl did a surprisingly good job with my makeup. When I peeked in the mirror after she finished, I looked halfway alive. Better than the ghoulish vapor of a person I was when I walked in.

But beauty, as they say, is only skin deep. Inside, I feel scraped out, hollow. I have nothing left to give.

Whatever fight was in me is gone now.

I just want to swing from the gallows already.

Locked in the cell, thirsty and shivering, it was somehow easier to stay in the present. I felt like I was on the precipice of something all the time—another meal, another drink of water, another round of Trofim coming to torment me. I couldn't think about anything except when the door would open next.

Now, I know what's happening next and it's an easy slide from thinking about the next hour to think about the next ten years of my life—if I even live to see that many. It's way too easy to think about what's going outside of these four walls.

Like Dante.

Thoughts of my little boy have been strictly off-limits, but now, I can't stop wondering if he misses me.

The better, selfless part of me hopes he doesn't. I want him to be happy, blissfully playing hide-and-seek with Anatoly and telling everyone over dinner what he learned from his tutor. But the desperate, lonely human in me wants to know that he loves me as much as I love him. I want him to be asking Mikhail hourly where I am, even if I'm not sure I want to know what answers Mikhail is offering.

Would he talk bad about me to our son? Would Mikhail try to turn Dante against me?

My eyes burn, but I haven't had enough to drink to waste precious moisture on tears. After I finished the first bottle of water, the girl didn't offer a second. I'm still so thirsty and so weak.

It's impossible to imagine escape when I feel this miserable.

Even if I could somehow get away from Trofim, Mikhail threw me out of the mansion. It's not like he's going to let me pick Dante up every other weekend for ice cream dates and overnights. We aren't going to share custody. Mikhail's new wife wouldn't approve of that.

The image of Mikhail in a tux standing next to the harsh Greek princess I met that night during family dinner... I fold my hands over my stomach, suddenly nauseous.

Mikhail and Dante will move on, if they haven't already. And I'll be here, alone. Even if I end up married to Trofim, I'll be alone in every way that matters. If my baby survives this brutal pregnancy, Trofim will twist them into a monster just like him.

A sob bursts out of my throat.

The girl tries not to look at me, and I don't even have the energy to be embarrassed.

After another five silent minutes crawl by, she finally stands up. "I'll see if anyone is in the hallway."

She disappears. I don't care either way. Alone, with her—it's all the same shit.

Until voices echo from somewhere deep in the house.

She left the door cracked open when she left and someone is talking. Fragments of conversation drift down the hallway to me.

This is the first time I've been left alone with an open door since I got here. A little voice in my head whispers at me to try to break through my chains. To rip the chair out of the floor and run for it.

It's a reflex. An instinct after years of fighting. The difference now is, I have nothing left to fight for.

The voices get louder. *Maybe the poor girl actually found Trofim.* I wouldn't put it past him to kill some teenager because she dared interrupt his breakfast.

Then someone yells and I jolt upright.

It isn't the girl yelling. It's a man's voice.

Deep, guttural shouts reverberate down the hall and through the open doorway.

Then comes the shooting.

My survival instinct, which has been beaten into a shell of its former self after the last couple weeks, comes blaring back to life. I pull on the chains, ignoring the flare of pain through my raw wrists. Understandably, the metal doesn't flinch.

Okay. Plan B.

I lift my skirts and give the chair I'm chained to a formal assessment.

The chains are locked around the legs of the chair, which is bolted to the ground. But the ground in question is just faux-wood vinyl. Maybe if I rock the chair hard enough…

I grip the bottom of the chair and throw my weight forward and back like the world's least-fun swing set. The chair barely moves at first, but after a few rounds of back and forth, I can feel it beginning to wobble. Then the floor begins to creak and splinter.

The yelling is getting closer every second. I don't have any illusions about avoiding whatever danger is tearing through the halls, but I want to be ready for it.

I've sat in this room for two hours praying for a quick end to this suffering—death or numbness, whichever came first. Now, death is here and the truth is impossible to ignore.

I want to survive.

For my baby.

For Dante.

For myself.

There are footsteps in the hallway. Heavy, pounding steps. Someone is running straight for me.

I drum up every ounce of energy I have and hurl myself forward.

Finally, the floor gives way. The chair hangs suspended for what feels like a minute, but can't be more than a second. Then I fall forward directly onto my face.

My jaw slams into the floor and I bite my tongue so hard I taste blood…

But *I'm free.*

I sit up and disentangle the chains from the bottom of the chair, then coil the loose links around my hands. *It's just me and my homemade brass knuckles against the world.*

I face the door and drop into a ready position, ignoring the nausea that twists in my gut and the way my entire body sways with every step.

My tank is almost empty. But after everything I've been through—everything I've survived—there's no way I'm dying here without a fight.

My heart thunders to the same beat as the footsteps. I count down the seconds in my head until the door opens.

I know it's coming, but I'm still not ready when the door flies open so hard it bounces off the wall.

My hands drop to my sides, suddenly too heavy to hold. A sob wrenches out of my chest and I stumble forward, catching myself on the chair I just escaped from. I just can't believe what I'm seeing.

"Mikhail?" I croak.

He stops in the doorway, framed like the most gorgeous

picture I've ever seen. As if my deepest, darkest fantasies are playing out right in front of me.

Mikhail holds out his hand to me. "Come on, Viviana. It's time for us to go."

11

VIVIANA

Blood dots his collar and his knuckles are cracked. Dried mud clings to his pants. Sweat slicks his golden hair back.

Mikhail is disheveled and panting and gorgeous and—

"Here," I blurt, blinking like he might disappear between one shutter of my eyelids and the next. "You're here."

A strangled yell echoes down the hallway behind him followed by a single shot. Then the house goes quiet. Mikhail glances down the hallway once before he extends his hand towards me. "Are you ready?"

Nothing about this is funny, but a laugh chokes out of me. "'Am I ready'? Am I—*What are you doing here, Mikhail?*"

Is he working with Trofim? If this is yet another betrayal, I don't think my heart can take it. On some level, I expected it from my father. But not from Mikhail. I won't survive it.

"I'd think that was obvious," he drawls. "I'm saving you."

It's not obvious to me. Nothing about what is happening right now makes any sense.

"You sent me away," I remind him. "You didn't want anything to do with me."

"And now, I'm here." He says it easily. Like it's normal. Like I should have expected it all along.

I shake my head and the room spins. I stumble to the side, but before I can even think about catching myself, Mikhail is there. His hand is firm on my shoulder. The earthy, citrus scent of him wraps around me and I want to cry.

"You're freezing." He unbuttons his shirt and shrugs out of it. He has a fitted t-shirt on underneath that would make him Public Sex Symbol #1 if he ever walked outside in it. It's been days since I've seen almost any human and now, I'm inches away from the most perfect man I've ever laid eyes on as he drapes his body-warm shirt over my shoulders.

"What are you doing here?" I ask again. The sliver of hallway I can see through the open door is still empty. I don't hear footsteps, but someone must be coming. "Where is Trofim?"

I realize in an instant that Mikhail doesn't know Trofim is alive. No one knows he's alive except for my father. He probably thinks I've lost my mind. *Hell, maybe I have.*

"He's gone." Mikhail's jaw flexes.

I wait for more of an explanation. Is this Mikhail informing me that Trofim is supposed to be dead. Or does he know more than he's letting on?

"*Gone'?* In what way?" I press. "Because there might be some things about Trofim you don't know yet."

"I know he's alive. I know you didn't kill him." Our eyes meet and his are completely unreadable. If I'm forgiven, then he's going to have to spell it out for me.

"Okay, okay." I nod. "So you know he was here, but he left?"

"The coward ran." I can see flickers of what Mikhail would have unleashed had Trofim not run. The raw rage and power Mikhail contains sends a shiver down my spine. "But I'll find him. I'll make him pay for what he did to you, Viviana."

He's going to take care of me.

It's dangerous to let myself rest too hard on that point. It's proven flimsy in the past. I'm starting to think I'm the only person who can take care of me these days.

But the anger on Mikhail's face morphs into something frantic as he drags his hands over my shoulders, down my arms. He takes me in one inch at a time, his icy blue eyes assessing me even as they set me on fire. "What did he do to you? Are you okay?"

"I'm fine," I lie.

Nothing is fine. But nothing matters as much as understanding what's happening in this moment.

"Why are you here?"

Mikhail hesitates for only a second before his hand slips to my cheek. His thumb brushes tenderly along my cheekbone. I don't even mind if he's smearing blood and dirt on my face, because I need this. I sink into the warmth of his hand.

"I'm here because you're here," he breathes. "And you shouldn't be. And I'm going to fix that."

Mikhail doesn't let go of my hand as he leads me out of the room and down the hallway. The guard who delivered my food the last few days is lying in a crumpled heap at the base of the stairs. I step over him without an ounce of sympathy.

Halfway up the stairs, I have to lean against the wall to catch my breath.

"Viviana?" Mikhail's voice is honey to my frayed nerves.

"I'm tired," I admit—a heroic feat in and of itself. I don't like looking weak, but my legs burn and my chest aches. I can't catch my breath. "I don't know if I can make it all the way up the stairs."

Worry etches a line between Mikhail's brows for a second before he scoops me up effortlessly.

I know I shouldn't enjoy being cradled against his body as much as I am. It will only hurt even worse later when he's gone and I'm alone again. But I just had the worst week of my life and I'm only human. So I say to hell with it, lean my cheek against his warm chest, and loop my arms around his neck.

My eyes flutter closed without my permission. I should stay awake and make sure I know where Mikhail is taking me. Every cell in my body trusts him, but I'm not sure if I should. He's still the man who kept my son and sent me out into the dark to fend for myself.

I manage to keep them open long enough to look around the main level of the house.

"This is…" I frown, peeking over Mikhail's shoulder at the vaguely familiar oil portrait hanging above the marble fireplace. "My family owns this house."

I've only been here twice before. Once, the weekend the purchase went through. The rooms were all empty and I got in trouble for sliding down the hallway in my stockings. The second time was after my mom's funeral. I guess my crying was a distraction for my father. He sent me to Staten Island to "get over it."

"He came to see me," I whisper as the picture starts to take shape. "He's working with Trofim."

Mikhail's arm tightens around my waist. "Your father is going to get what's coming to him, too."

I don't even care. I lay my head on his shoulder again and close my eyes. As long as Mikhail is holding me like this, I can forget everything else.

For now.

I drift in and out of sleep. Voices break through my subconscious, but nothing alarming. When I hear Raoul, I know everything is fine. If it wasn't, he'd still be fighting. It's a relief because I can't physically keep my eyes open anymore.

"The house is clear," Raoul reports brusquely. "Men are looking for Trofim. I'll let you know as soon as I know something." His voice softens as he adds, "How is she?"

"Weak. Exhausted." Mikhail spits the words like they make him angry.

"Have you asked her about—"

"That can wait," Mikhail growls. "Right now, I need to make sure she's okay."

Even half-asleep, my heart jolts.

He could mean a thousand different things. He might need me to be okay because the mass grave they're digging for the men they killed tonight is already full. Or he might just want me to be fully cogent before he interrogates me about whatever Raoul was trying to mention before Mikhail cut him off.

Or—and I hold this thought loosely, afraid of what will happen if I cling to it—Mikhail might still care about me.

He settles me into the passenger seat of his car and I rest my forehead against the cool window. "I'm taking you to the hospital." Mikhail's warmth leeches into me as he buckles my seatbelt.

Alarm bells I don't fully understand start going off.

"I'm tired," I respond.

"I know." The car starts and the vibration lulls me into even deeper relaxation. "But I need to make sure you're okay, Viviana."

There it is again. That vague sentence that could mean a million different things.

I'm so focused on what that means that it takes me a long time to consider what's going to happen when the doctor finds out I'm pregnant.

But it's too late to dwell on that. I'm already breathing deeply, giving into the rumble of the car. As I fade, I feel a warm hand spread across my thigh. I want to squeeze the hand, but I can't.

I don't dare to hope that it's there for my sake.

12

VIVIANA

I've never been so happy to see a hospital gown.

The ride to the hospital couldn't have been more than half an hour, but the power nap revived me. I woke up in the hospital parking lot with a head full of questions, half of which revolved around *getting this godforsaken dress off of my body as soon as possible.*

The nurse holds the thin, pale blue bundle of fabric out to me. I snatch it out of her hands with a perfunctory "thank you" and practically escort her out of the door. Then I unzip the wedding dress and happily let it puddle around my feet.

And as the fabric hits the floor, I remember I'm not alone in the room.

Mikhail is sitting on the window ledge, his arms crossed. But his attention is laser-focused on every inch of my exposed skin. There's a lot of it, since I couldn't wear my bra with the strapless wedding dress.

"Sorry," I mutter, turning away from him.

Goosebumps that have nothing to do with the balmy temperature of the room spread down my arms. I pull the hospital gown on and reach around to find the strings to tie it closed.

"I'm going to kill him," Mikhail snarls under his breath.

I don't know what he means until his thumb strokes just above the raw skin around my wrists.

I wince and he drops my arm, but I can feel the warmth of him along my spine. I want to sink against his chest, which is exactly why I force myself to perch on the end of the exam table instead.

"I took your chains off in the car, but it was dark." He forces out a deep breath. "Viviana, I—"

There's a soft knock at the door and then the doctor comes into the room. I'm wary of seeing any strangers right now. I just want to get this exam over with as soon as possible and get this doctor out of my life.

But it's impossible to give Dr. Hamilton the cold shoulder. He is the kindest, warmest man I've ever met. He's like the medical field's version of Bob Ross.

"I don't see a darn thing wrong with you, darling," he says after a thorough ten-minute examination overseen by Mikhail. He pats my knee and reminds me of the father I wish I had. When he looks at my wrist, he clicks his tongue. "Not a darn thing except that wrist. The abrasions are angry now, but I'm going to bandage them up and they'll be much happier."

"Just the cuts?" Mikhail paces back and forth across the narrow room, fingers tugging at his hair. "That's the only problem?"

"It's all I'm seeing." Dr. Hamilton gives sufficient eye contact to Mikhail, putting him at ease. Then he looks back to me. "Beyond that, you're perfect, Viviana."

"I think you missed your calling. You should be a motivational speaker," I tease. "I haven't felt perfect in a long time."

Mikhail crosses his arms and paces away from the hospital bed. I don't want to think about what's going on in his head. A running list of recent examples why I'm not perfect at all, I'm sure.

Dr. Hamilton laughs, but his smile is sympathetic. "I'll remember that if I ever consider retirement. I've never been good at relaxation, but I'm in my twilight years now. Motivational speaking might have better office hours."

"Thank you for coming in. I know it's last-minute."

Especially considering I thought I'd be in chains and married to a psychopath by now.

"My pleasure. Now—" He scribbles something on my chart and tucks it under his arm. "—I'm going to get you set up with an IV. I'd like to see you finish a bag of fluids before you leave."

Mikhail whips around. "You said she was perfect."

"She is. And with some help towards rehydration, she'll stay that way." Dr. Hamilton winks at me. "It was lovely to meet you, Viviana. Once that bag is gone, you're free to go."

The doctor slips away before Mikhail can interrogate him further. A few minutes later, a nurse comes in and inserts my IV.

As she drapes the tubing over the corner of the bed and leaves, I try to name the panic sitting on my chest. It's not claustrophobia, but it leaves me with the same dry mouth, tight lung feeling.

I'm okay. I'm safe.

But Mikhail is pacing back and forth in the corner of the room and I still don't know what he's doing here. Once the bag of fluids next to me is gone, I have no idea what's going to happen to me.

Will I have a home? Will I get to see Dante? Will Trofim hunt me down and put me through this hell again?

I try to keep my breathing shallow and steady, but Mikhail is like a bloodhound, if bloodhounds were trained to know when I'm freaking the fuck out.

"What's wrong?" He looks around the room like he's double checking we're alone. "Why are you upset?"

I shake my head. "It's fine."

"You're lying."

"And you don't know everything," I bite back.

I don't mean to come across as harsh, but days without sleep combined with the existential dread swirling in my head are bound to make a girl grouchy.

"I'm sorry, it's just…" I sigh and pinch the IV tubing between my fingers. "I just spent the last few days chained to a bed. This is different, but it doesn't *feel* different."

He tugs a hand through his hair again. It's immaculately disheveled. "You were supposed to get out of the city. I didn't think—if I knew—"

"You didn't know." Why I feel the need to let Mikhail off the hook, I'll never know. But I do. I don't want him to beat himself up over what his brother did.

He drops down on the end of my bed, his weight tugging my legs towards him. "But did you? Did you know Trofim was alive and looking for you?"

"If I had, you never could have gotten rid of me. I would have tied myself to the gates like the environmentalists who chain themselves to trees."

Mikhail doesn't smile. I don't really expect him to.

None of this is funny.

"Tell me what happened. All of it."

I nod. "Well, you know that my dad wanted me to kill Trofim. If he was dead, then it would clear the way for you to become *pakhan* and it would give Dante a direct line to leadership. All of that would have benefitted my father. But for me..." I breathe through the tightness in my chest. "Everything I did was about my freedom and Dante's safety. That's why I did what I did."

"What exactly did you do? I'm sure you've noticed, but Trofim is alive. You didn't kill him."

"Unfortunately," I grumble. "But that's what I went there that night to do. I got there and everything went exactly like I planned. I knew Trofim would buy that I was there to apologize to him and make things right, and he did. He walked me straight back to his bedroom and kissed me."

Mikhail's hand tightens into a fist. I look away. If I reach out to touch him now, I'll never get through the rest of this story.

"He threw me down on the bed and I knew if I didn't do it right then, I wouldn't get the chance. If he found the knife strapped to my thigh, things would have ended a lot differently. So, as he climbed over me, I drove the blade into his stomach." A shiver moves down my spine. "I still have nightmares about his blood coating my hands. It felt like hot oil and the knife slipped out of my hand. I knew as soon as the blade went in that I couldn't kill him. Taking another person's life, even someone as evil as Trofim, wasn't something I could live with."

"So you knew he wasn't dead?" Mikhail asks, brow furrowed. "When I accused you of killing him, you knew—"

"I knew he wasn't dead when I left," I explain. "Trofim was yelling and stumbling around the room. I got up and ran before he could figure out what was happening. But I had no clue what happened afterward. I figured it just… ended."

Mikhail frowns. "You didn't finish the job. You could have told me that. I accused you and you didn't say anything."

"I wanted to. *I tried*. But I also didn't think it made much of a difference. As far as I knew, Trofim was dead. It had been six years since that night in Moscow and I hadn't heard a word about Trofim. Not one peep. Until you told me he was dead. So I thought… I thought I killed him. I thought that maybe one stab was all it took."

Mikhail is quiet for a long time. It's impossible to tell what he's thinking. If he believes me, if he's still mad at me for lying.

And the longer we sit in the quiet, the more I don't even know what I'm thinking.

Do I care if he believes me? He may or may not be mad, I don't know, but… *am I?*

He dumped me on the curb like an old mattress so he could marry some other woman. He did it to keep Dante safe, sure. I get that. I can understand the impulse—I've spent the last six years of my life doing everything imaginable to protect Dante, including flying around the globe to stab Mikhail's brother in the stomach. Desperate times, desperate measures, and all that.

But there's a big difference between understanding Mikhail's motivations and being just peachy about the way I was treated. Deep down, I have to wonder, *Aren't I worth protecting, too?*

Mikhail tugs another hand through his hair and I can see he isn't wearing a wedding ring—mine or anyone else's.

"Why did you come for me?" I can't bring myself to ask him about Helen directly. I'm pathetic enough, naked except for a hospital gown with smudged wedding makeup on. No need to look like a possessive psycho on top of all that. So I inch as close to the question as I can without tumbling over the edge.

"I already told you: you weren't supposed to be there with Trofim."

"Okay, but why did that matter?" I press. "You sent me away. It's not like I was your responsibility anymore. It wouldn't have made any difference to you whether your brother was torturing me or not. You could have left me."

"No," he retorts. "I couldn't have."

My hands slide across the thin hospital comforter, closer to him. I'm not sure if I want to grab his shoulders and shake answers out of him or throw my arms around his neck and hold him until I fall asleep. I could probably sleep for days—longer, if Mikhail was next to me.

"Is it about jealousy?" I feel stupid even suggesting it. He kicked me out of his life just a few days ago. Where do I get off thinking he's jealous? But it's all that makes sense. "If it was, you should know I did *not* want to be there." I lift my bandaged wrists as proof. "Did you think it would look bad for the Bratva? I guess me marrying you and then turning around and marrying your brother, who everyone thought was dead, could be a bad look."

He snorts, mumbling under his breath. "It's a worse look for the Bratva that I'm here right now."

"Then you should go." It might be easier that way. For both of us. He saved me and now, he can go back to the mansion and Dante... Pain twists deep in my chest, but it'll be worse the longer Mikhail stays.

His jaw flexes. "I can't."

"You can do whatever you want." Finally, I find the courage to close the gap between us, my fingers brushing down his bicep. "So why are you here?"

"Because letting you leave that night was a mistake." Mikhail jerks to his feet, his hands opening and closing at his sides like he isn't sure what to do with them. I'm not sure what I want him to do with them, either.

"We didn't even know Trofim was alive. How could you have known he'd come for me?"

"Fuck Trofim," he grits out. "This isn't about him. It's about —" He spins towards me, his eyes electric blue and wild. "You're all I've been able to think about for days. I've been a fucking wreck. Even before I heard about Trofim, I couldn't sleep. There was this constant ache in my chest like I'd lost something. And when I found out that Trofim was alive and he—" Mikhail can't even finish the sentence. He's about to combust. "I had to come get you. I couldn't leave you there, Viviana."

I wish he'd stop saying my name like that. Like he cares. Like nothing has changed.

Everything has changed.

If he'd said any of this a couple weeks ago, I would have melted into a puddle at his feet. I would have thrown myself at him and begged him to say it all again. To whisper it against my skin as he carried me to his bed.

Now, it feels like he's poking at a still-open wound. It hurts.

"What does your new wife think about all of this?"

He checks the clock on the wall. "As of three hours ago, she became my new ex-fiancée."

Silence. Stunned, gasping silence.

"What?" I breathe at last.

"I skipped our wedding to rescue you." He smirks and the curve of his lip does dangerous things to my insides. "I doubt Helen will handle that insult with grace."

"But… war," I blurt. *Speaking of not having grace.*

"Wars have been fought for many reasons." Mikhail's eyes drift slowly over to me. "And as far as I'm concerned, there's never been a better one."

He's saying all of the right things. I want to lean into the comfort he's offering right now, but I can't. Not if that comfort won't still be there next week, next month. I can't lean on Mikhail now if he's not going to be there for the rest of my life.

Because that's what I want from him, isn't it? Forever?

With one child and another on the way, I need to know he's going to be there.

The words coming out of his mouth should mean that I'm safe. So why do I feel like I'm in more danger than ever?

13

MIKHAIL

Viviana is steady on her feet as she climbs out of the hospital bed. The fluids are gone and Dr. Hamilton cleared her to be released, but I hover close by just in case.

The trash can is overflowing with the wadded-up remains of her would-be wedding dress. Viviana stares down at it, one hand holding her hospital gown closed behind her.

"Are the hospital gowns complimentary?" she contemplates, worrying at her lower lip with her teeth. "Because if not, I'd rather walk out of here butt naked than put that dress on again."

I'm tempted to tell her that stealing the gowns comes with a mandatory life sentence for that very reason. I still haven't recovered from the image of her topless, standing in a puddle of her shredded wedding dress. She's been through a lot and I'm more than capable of controlling myself… but *fuck me*.

I grab my button-down from the end of the bed and toss it to her. It's the same one I draped over her shoulders back at the safehouse. "It's bloodstained, but—"

"I accept." She angles away from me to slide the hospital gown off and pull on my shirt instead. It's not like I haven't seen—*and tasted*—every inch of her before, but I don't begrudge her her privacy. She tugs the shirt cuffs over the bulky bandages on her wrists.

When she turns back to me, she's still doing up the last couple buttons. My shirt drapes around the tops of her thighs. If she was an inch or two shorter, it would almost be long enough to pass as a dress. As it is, she looks like the poster child for a walk of shame.

In a way, that's what this is. My shame walk.

The only reason we're here is because I fucked up. I never should have made her leave the mansion. I never should have let Trofim find her.

None of this should have happened—and I'm going to spend every second proving to Viviana that I won't let it happen again.

She finishes buttoning her shirt but continues playing with the seams. Finally, she crosses her arms nervously over her chest. "I don't really know how to bring this up, but I left all of my stuff at that hotel room. Trofim grabbed me and I didn't… I couldn't grab everything. So all of the money you gave me is gone."

"I'm sure the night manager took the cash. But fuck it. I don't give a shit about a few thousand dollars, Viviana."

"Right. Yeah. But, I do." Her eyes are pale green under the fluorescents. "That money is all I had. I haven't been to work in weeks and I don't even have my wallet to use my credit cards. I can't afford a motel tonight without that money."

"A motel?" I reach towards her, but freeze when she flinches back. I shove my hands in my pockets instead. "You aren't staying in a motel, Viviana. You're coming home."

"To the mansion?"

Where else would home be? I want to ask.

"Yes."

Her eyes shimmer with tears. "Am I going to see Dante?"

"Of course you're going to see Dante. Why wouldn't you?" I say. "I'm not going to save you and then turn around and lock you up again."

It sounds ridiculous to me. I *just* told her that I made a mistake. I confessed that I needed to get her back. What more does she want from me?

But the relief on her face says it all. She still wasn't sure.

"Thank you."

"You don't need to thank me," I grumble. "You're my wife. It's your house, too."

Five minutes after we pull away from the hospital, I look over and Viviana is asleep. One leg is curled underneath her and her cheek is pillowed on her arm.

She must trust me a little bit to fall asleep while I'm driving.

Or she's too exhausted to worry about self-preservation.

After everything she's been through, she has every right to be wary. I just never thought I'd look into her eyes and see fear directed at me. I'm used to it from other people, but never her.

Anatoly and Dante are waiting on the front porch when I pull down the drive. Anatoly has to hold Dante back so I can bring the car to a full stop.

Like some kind of motherly spidey-sense, Viviana's eyes snap open the moment I shift into park. She jolts up, looking around, panicked. Then she sees Dante.

"Oh my God."

She tears out of the car, leaving the passenger door hanging open. The second she drops to her knees, Dante crashes into her arms.

"I think you got bigger," Viviana manages through tears. She strokes his hair and cradles his chin. "It's almost like you aged a whole year while I was gone."

"Because I'm six now," Dante says proudly before pulling her in for another hug.

Viviana kisses his cheek and crushes him to her. "I'm sorry I missed your birthday, buddy."

Eventually, she scoops him up and carries Dante towards the house. Her arms shake and her legs are wobbly, but it's like she's afraid she'll lose him again if she puts him down.

I trail behind them, an outsider to their reunion. I'm just as responsible as Trofim for all of this.

By the time Viviana carries Dante inside, her face is pale. He's in her ear moving seamlessly from talking about the movie he watched last night to the game he played with Anatoly this morning with no signs of slowing down. As much as I know Viviana wants to be with him, I also know she needs to rest.

I pat Dante's hair. "It's time for you to head to school."

He ducks away from me and squeezes Viviana tighter. He lays his head on her shoulder. "I don't want to go today. I want to talk to Mama." He looks up at her, his puppy-dog eyes lethal. "Can I skip school today, Mama?"

She kisses his forehead. "Your dad is right. You should go to school. I need to go lie down for a little while. I'm tired."

"I'll sleep, too!" he chimes. "I'm tired."

Viviana tickles his side and laughs. "Liar. Every time we try to take a nap together, you end up burrowing under the blankets like a mole or kicking me in the back until I get up. You hate nap time."

He smirks guiltily. After a few more clumsy attempts at persuasion, he lets Anatoly lead him to the makeshift schoolroom we've set up in the formal dining room.

As soon as Dante is out of sight, Viviana leans against the wall. "Thanks."

"You looked like you needed a break."

"I missed him so much. Was he okay while I was...?" She doesn't try to finish that sentence.

Exiled? Kidnapped? Imprisoned?

How do I tell her that she can't go into Dante's room until I get a chance to replace his bedside table and half of the clothes in his closet because he shredded through them like a wild animal? I should have been there for him, but I was too lost in my own haze of missing her.

That's what it was, wasn't it? I missed her?

There isn't any good way to tell her any of that. Instead, I say, "He's happy you're back."

Viviana is suspicious, but she's too tired to push it. She's almost too tired to stand up. She makes it up two steps before her knuckles are white on the handrail and she's breathing heavily.

"I can help you."

Viviana waves me away. "That's okay. I just need a second to catch my breath."

But I slide a hand under her knees and one arm around her back. I scoop her up easily and carry her up the stairs.

"Or you can carry me," she mutters, annoyed. That doesn't stop her from leaning into my chest.

She gives me all of her weight and I don't want to put her down at the top of the stairs. I carry her all the way down the hallway.

As we pass her room, Viviana starts to say something, but I shake my head. "You're staying in my room."

She'll be more comfortable there, I tell myself. *This isn't because I need her in my bed.*

Then I walk her through my bedroom door and all I can think about is closing the door, locking it, and never letting either of us out again. *It'll be easy to take care of her in here.*

I let go of her reluctantly, lowering her to the edge of the bed. My hands linger on the warm skin behind her knees and the curve of her waist.

"I would be fine in my room," she mumbles, even as she curls her legs underneath her and slides her feet under my sheets.

She's here. *Home.*

For the first time in days, there's no buzzing under my skin. That circuit inside of me is closed, complete. The ache to follow her onto the bed and spread her across the mattress is deep and unrelenting.

"I don't want you to be *fine*, Viviana." I spin around and grab a pair of shorts and a t-shirt out of my dresser before I can do something stupid. "I want you to be perfect."

"According to Dr. Hamilton, I already am." Her mouth is turned into a small smile, but it's thin. She's watching me closely.

"You can wear these." I hand her the clothes. "If you want to take a bath first, I can help you—"

"I'm fine," she says far too quickly. Viviana clutches my clothes to her chest like she's already naked and trying to shield herself.

"If you get in the tub, I want to be there. I'm not going to let you drown."

"I've taken plenty of baths by myself. I'm not going to drown. I can take care of myself."

"But you don't have to." It all comes out more intensely than I mean it to, so I blow out a breath and try to smooth things over. "I'm here. We're both here now. I can help you."

"I'm here for Dante." She chews on the corner of her mouth. "I just—I can't jump back into the way things were before, Mikhail."

"This isn't like things were before. Before, you were locked in your bedroom. That's why I brought you to my room. There's still a chain on your door and no one has been in to clean it since Stella—I didn't want to put you back in there."

As far as arguments go, this point might go to Viviana. Mentioning the lock I had installed on her bedroom door probably won't work in my favor.

The purple circles under her eyes look even darker in the dim light of my bedroom. She's exhausted and we shouldn't be having this conversation now. I know that. I should wait.

I grind my teeth together. "I want things to be different. We lied and we fucked each other over. But we're done with that now."

"We both *want* to be done with it, but I'm not sure if we know how." She sighs and tightens her arms around herself. "It's been a long couple days. I need some time to sleep. We both need time to think."

I don't need to think about any of this, I roar inside my head. *I know what I want.*

"Take all the time you need," I tell her coldly. "But just know: if you choose to leave, Dante is staying with me."

Before the hurt can settle fully on her face, I turn and leave.

14

MIKHAIL

"Okay, so the reunion didn't go exactly the way you imagined. So what?"

I raise my face out of my hands just long enough to glare at my brother. "My wife won't even touch me. She looked at me like… like I was—"

"Like you were Trofim?" Anatoly offers.

I snarl at him, but only because he's right. "She's treating me like I'm the bad guy here, but without me, she'd be married to my brother right now. Actually, without me, she would have been married to Trofim six fucking years ago."

"True," Anatoly agrees. "Then again, you're also the only reason she was almost forced to marry him this second time. If you hadn't kicked her out of the mansion, Trofim wouldn't have kidnapped her."

"I still saved her."

He wrinkles his nose. "Yeah, but it's kind of like asking for an award for putting out a fire you started."

"I didn't start shit," I growl. "If she hadn't lied to me about stabbing Trofim, then I wouldn't have kicked her out."

It's so much more complicated than that, but I'm not in the mood for nuance. I want Viviana and she wants time. Nothing else penetrates.

Anatoly flops back on the sofa, but I can't stop pacing. I'm surprised there aren't tracks worn into the carpet by this point.

"I rescued her," I repeat. "I risked my life to break into her father's house and interrogate him. Then I broke into the safehouse where Trofim was keeping her without any fucking clue what was happening inside."

"Raoul mentioned it was well-guarded."

"Because it was! I took out three guards on my own. Raoul and his team cleared out ten more, at least. They're still getting rid of the bodies. We could have died, but she needs time to think." I snort derisively. "Think about what? Everyone in her life has fucking tossed her under the bus, but I'm here trying to take care of her."

"After tossing her under the bus yourself." The look I fix him with must look as lethal as it feels, because he holds up his hands in surrender. "I'm just playing devil's advocate over here, brother."

"How about you play the role of pretending like you're on my side?"

"I'm always on your side, but my job is to argue with you when I think you're making a mistake."

"What mistake? I haven't done anything wrong."

Anatoly leans forward, elbows on his knees. "Tell me right now why you saved Viviana today."

"Because Trofim is a monster."

He circles a finger in the air to tell me to keep going.

"And she's the mother of my son," I add with a shrug. "Because I felt responsible for her."

"Why?"

"She's my wife."

"You were supposed to marry another woman six hours ago," he argues. "That's not a very compelling reason. Try again."

"You're the worst therapist I've ever had."

"You've never had a therapist. And I don't need to be a therapist to see what's going on here."

"I know you don't, because I already told you: Viviana is my wife and I couldn't let her marry Trofim and be tortured for the rest of her life."

"Why?" he asks again. Anatoly has the nerve to look frustrated with me, as if I don't want to lunge across this room and wring his neck. He sounds like Viviana in the hospital room.

I'm not used to people questioning my decisions. I don't even question them. My gut instinct is always, always right.

"Why?" he asks a third time, eyebrows raised.

"Because it would have been wrong."

He clicks his tongue in disappointment. "Why did you skip your wedding to Helen and risk your own life to save Viviana?

Why did you care that she was imprisoned by Trofim? Why are you pacing around this room now, preoccupied about what *she* wants, when we are going to have the entire Drakos family beating down our door by dinner? Why?"

"Because I love her!" I yell. "Is that what you want to fucking hear?"

A smirk the likes of which I've never seen before spreads across my brother's face. He leans back on the couch, hands folded behind his head. "Actually, it is. That is exactly what I wanted to hear, Mikhail. Thank you."

Regret settles in immediately. Fuck only knows what Anatoly is going to do with this information in his back pocket. Nothing good, I'm sure.

I finally drop down into my chair, feeling more drained than I have in years. I can't remember the last time I slept through the night. I actually can't remember the last time I slept. Period.

"None of it matters anyway. It doesn't change anything. Viviana doesn't care."

Anatoly whistles. "Things really have gone topsy-turvy if even Mikhail Novikov has lost his mojo."

I roll my eyes. "I haven't lost anything."

"Okay, then buck up and show her exactly how much you care."

"I already showed her. I showed her by rescuing her," I point out. "As much as I'd love to make a slideshow of all the men I killed today to rescue her, Raoul is currently burning their bodies."

"Charming," Anatoly snorts. "I was thinking more along the lines of a nice apology. Maybe a heartfelt confession. You can toss in some flowers and chocolates if you want to get really stereotypical."

My face twists in disgust before I can stop myself. "I've done more than enough to show her how I feel."

Anatoly's eyes widen. "You blamed her for something she didn't do without letting her explain, locked her in her bedroom, and then exiled her from your house and kept her son. Which part of that screams 'big, romantic gesture'?"

"He's my son, too," I mutter.

"The point is," Anatoly continues, ignoring me, "you two have been through a lot. You can't just tell her that everything is better now. You have to *show* her."

In the last six years, I've acquired companies, turned enemies into allies, and built a gunrunning empire. I overthrew my own father and brother to claim what was mine.

But one thing I've never had to do… is grovel.

"Well?" Anatoly is annoyingly smug. "What's the plan?"

For the first time in my life, I don't have an immediate answer.

"The plan is to focus on something I know how to do." I push back to my feet and continue pacing. "Like to talk to the Greeks."

Find a distraction. Yes. That's the plan.

"War it is," Anatoly sing-songs. I shake my head and he groans. "I hate diplomacy."

If killing everyone who annoyed me was a solution, I'd have filled a cemetery by now. Anatoly would be dead ten times over, too.

As if on cue, my phone rings. For the fifth time in two hours, it's Christos Drakos.

"Speaking of the devil." I hold out my phone so Anatoly can see who it is.

"The father of the bride." He winces. "Put it on speaker."

I lay my phone flat on my desk and answer. "Hello, Christos."

"*Hello, Christos,*" he mimics. "That's the first thing you say to me after disappearing on your wedding day? We waited for you for two hours. *Helen* waited. She didn't want to take off the dress because she was sure you'd show up."

Helen never was the sharpest knife in the drawer. I told her to her face on several occasions that I had no interest in being married to her beyond what her father could offer me. She seemed to think I'd change my mind. Up until the very end, apparently.

"Something came up."

Anatoly seesaws his hand back and forth. He doesn't care for my explanation. Diplomacy isn't my specialty, either.

"Don't toy with me, Mikhail. I know exactly what came up."

I look at Anatoly and he shrugs. Raoul and I were discreet. Unless Agostino ran his mouth—the same way he did when he called ahead to warn Trofim I was on my way—no one should know what happened today.

"This is about that bitch, isn't it?" Christos spits.

A low growl rumbles through my chest before I can stop myself. Anatoly lays a hand on my shoulder in silent warning, but my hackles are up. It takes every ounce of restraint for me to blow out a deep breath and speak evenly.

"She's my wife."

"My *daughter* is supposed to be your wife! We had a deal, Mikhail. *Two* deals. I gave you a second chance and you embarrassed me. You embarrassed my daughter."

In my opinion, making your daughter a term and condition of a business arrangement is embarrassing enough. If Helen had any other prospects, she would have moved on by now. My guess is the marriage market is looking bleak for her.

"I could have married her and spent our entire relationship cheating on her with the woman I actually love." It's shocking how easily the words come. How simple it is to speak the truth—to everyone except Viviana. "I think doing things this way saved Helen a lot of embarrassment."

Christos is silent for a second before he cackles. "You should have taken your time and come up with a better excuse than *love*."

"I don't need to make any excuses to you. It's only as a courtesy that I'm explaining myself at all."

"We had a deal!"

"And we'll make a new one," I say with a calm I don't feel.

As sideways as this has all gone, I wouldn't mind ending this whole ordeal with a new pact. Preferably one that includes the ability to move my products at every Drakos-owned port.

"The time for a new agreement is over, Mikhail. We sat across that negotiating table and you told me what you wanted: access to my ports. I told you what I wanted: a husband for my daughter. That's my deal. It's the only deal you're going to get from me."

"I can't accept it. I'm married to someone else."

"Then she'll die," he says flatly.

I snatch my phone off the table like I might be able to lunge through the phone and grab the Greek don by the throat. "Think carefully about what comes out of your mouth next, Christos. Don't say anything you'll regret."

"The only thing I regret is thinking I could trust a man who could publicly disrespect his own family to get to the top. You don't know the meaning of the word 'honor.' And now, you're going to lose your Bratva and your pitiful excuse for a family."

"Don't do this, Christos. I'll kill you. I'll slaughter you all if you come for my wife and child."

I wonder if I sound as tired as I feel. A week ago, I was ready to do whatever it took to avoid a war with the Greeks—to keep my plan on the rails. All of it mattered so much… until the second I heard Viviana was in danger.

Now, I know what matters, and it isn't Christos. It isn't Helen.

I need to make things right with Viviana, no matter what it takes.

Christos laughs. "I look forward to seeing you try."

Once the line goes dead, Anatoly sighs and leans back on the sofa. "Wow. L's all around today, huh?"

"We're at war. You do realize that, don't you?"

"It's not like we didn't see this coming."

He's not wrong. I didn't really expect Christos to accept my apology and sketch out the parameters for a new deal over the phone, no matter how nice that would be.

Still, it's annoying. I'd like for at least one thing in my life to be going the way I hoped.

"What's the plan?" Anatoly asks for the second time.

"The plan is for you to give me a better idea than flowers and chocolates. This may be my first apology, but I'm anything but stereotypical."

Anatoly grins and claps me on the back. "Fuck yeah, brother. Let's get you your woman."

15

VIVIANA

I'm still half-asleep, but my heart is racing.

Someone is in here with me.

The room is dark and I'm too terrified to move, but I know someone is in this room. *Mikhail's room,* I remind myself. *In Mikhail's house. I'm safe here.*

I repeat the words to myself, but I don't even know if that's true. I'm not sure I'm safe anywhere anymore.

I stare up at the ceiling, afraid to breathe in case the person realizes I'm awake and lunges for me. Maybe if I pretend I'm asleep, they'll leave.

A floorboard near the bed creaks just as a figure appears over the mound of blankets around my head, looking down at me.

"Holy shit!" I gasp, both in utter terror and deep, palpable relief. "You scared me."

"I wasn't trying to," Mikhail replies simply.

"Try harder *not* to," I bite back. My wasted fear morphs into aimless anger. My heart is thundering against my rib cage so hard it's almost painful. I press a hand there and force myself to take deep breaths. "Here's a tip: don't sneak into my room in the middle of the night."

"This is my room," he points out calmly, hands shoved into the pockets of his dark gray sweats.

Does he ever not *look good?* I wonder idly. I'm grateful that I woke up a few hours ago and took a shower. I wanted to take a bath just to spite Mikhail, but he made a good point—it would've been embarrassing to survive a kidnapping and imprisonment just to drown in a tub because I couldn't stay awake.

"Another reason I should have slept in my own room. You just rescued me from a psychotic kidnapper, so having anyone lurking around my bed in the dark is definitely a bad idea."

"I didn't come here to lurk." He holds out a hand to me. "Come with me."

I'm still annoyed, but I slide my hand into his on pure instinct. It's the way you try to catch a baseball that's flying towards your face. When something dangerous comes your way, you react.

Lord knows there is certainly something dangerous about the shimmer I feel under my skin when Mikhail touches me.

"It's late. Where are we going?"

He grabs a flannel shirt from the closet and holds it out for me, stopping only to let his eyes slide down my body. Well, *I don't need to worry about getting chilly if he keeps looking at me like that.*

"You're wearing my shirt," he observes.

I can't get a read on him. He saves my life and then tells me that I can never leave his house with my son. He gives me a shirt to wear, but when I put it on, he looks at me like I killed someone and am wearing their skin around as a suit.

"They're the clothes you gave me earlier." I tug on the hem of the shirt as if I might be able to make it magically fall to my knees instead of barely grazing mid-thigh. "I took a shower and changed. I hope that's okay."

He drapes the flannel over my shoulders. "I wouldn't have given it to you if I didn't want you to wear it."

Mikhail takes my hand and leads me into the dark hallway. I expect him to head towards the stairs, but he moves to the end of the hall and opens a door I've never noticed before. It's paneled with the same wainscoting as the lower half of the wall and is painted the same warm white as the upper half.

"A secret door?" I sound casual, but there's a twinge of panic low in my gut.

He told me he wasn't going to lock me up, but what if he's changed his mind? Am I willingly walking into a *Jane Eyre* scenario? I cannot be locked in some attic somewhere while Mikhail marries and lives with another woman one floor below me.

"Relax." I didn't notice Mikhail turning towards me, but his chest is a solid wall in front of me. He pulls me close, his lips next to my ear. "You're safe here, Viviana."

Of course he noticed my fear. Nothing gets past Mikhail.

When my breathing evens out, he squeezes my hand and opens the door.

We step out onto a deep balcony. It's shielded by the house on three sides, which might be why I never noticed it before. Not even when Dante and I would play in the backyard. It's tucked away, hidden from view and the wind. But the view looks down over the lawn and the tree-lined property beyond the fence.

"A balcony?" A soft night breeze blows through my hair and I still don't believe it. "You have a secret balcony?"

"It's not a secret. It's just… private." He closes the door to the hallway behind us. "I don't tell most people about it."

"But you're telling me?"

"You're not most people."

I frown. There aren't many ways to interpret what he's saying, but I still won't let myself believe any of this is happening.

Instead, I twist away from him and look around the balcony. It's not elaborate the way the rest of the house is. There are no Adirondack chairs or large umbrellas to lounge under. It's empty, except for a thick duvet spread out in the middle of the patio with a telescope set up on the corner.

"You do a lot of stargazing out here?"

"Never," he laughs.

I gesture to the telescope. "Then how do you explain this?"

"Good question." He drags a hand through his hair and for the first time since he peeked over the blankets at me, I realize… *Mikhail is nervous.*

I'm not sure what to make of that, so I stare at him, waiting.

"You and I didn't get to know each other the way most people do. We never had a first date." He stops, considering that point. "I've never had a first date with anyone, actually."

"Are you trying to humble brag about how women throw themselves at you without the promise of a free dinner and drinks? If so, I'd like to go back to bed."

I pretend to walk away, but Mikhail grabs my elbow. He draws slow circles over the inside of my arm with his thumb. Awareness thrums through me.

In his defense, it's not hard to understand why women throw themselves at him.

"What I'm trying to do is tell you that there has never been a woman who made me want to try. Until you."

I'm just as frozen as I was in bed. I'm just as terrified, too. I don't want to make any sudden moves in case this moment shatters.

"I told you before that I was a wreck after you left. And I told you that I had to come save you from Trofim because you didn't belong there. But it wasn't because I felt guilty about sending you away or because I was jealous that you were going to marry some other man." He blows out a breath. "The reason I was a wreck and had to come save you is because I'm in love with you."

Mikhail is staring straight into my eyes, saying words I never thought I'd hear, and I can't move. Can't speak. Tears slip down my cheeks, and I can't even wipe them away.

So Mikhail does it for me.

He cradles my face, using his thumbs to dab my tears away. "I was wrong when I made you leave, Viviana. Even if you had killed Trofim, I still would have been wrong. Because I should have killed Trofim six years ago when I saw the way he was throwing you around that hotel room. I should have killed him for having you and being stupid enough not to realize how fucking lucky he was."

I choke out a sob, barely managing to wrangle the emotions raging through my chest. "But the Greeks…"

His mouth quirks into the most gorgeous smile I've ever seen. "I already told you: being able to have you is the best reason I can think of to go to war. I'll kill them all to keep you and Dante."

The tears won't stop. I bury my face in Mikhail's shoulder, sobbing while he holds me.

"This was supposed to make you happy," he whispers in my ear.

That, of course, only makes me cry harder.

He's patient with me, holding me close until I can pull myself together and look in his eyes without dissolving into more tears. "So what's the telescope for?"

"I tell you I love you and you're still focused on the telescope?" He shakes his head. "Reminder for next time: show her the star you bought and named after her and *then* confess how you feel."

I pull back, still clutching his shoulders. "You bought me a *star*?"

He directs me down to the blanket and checks the telescope. Then he points for me to look.

The section of sky I can see through the viewfinder is dark, white pinpricks splattered like paint.

"Actually, I bought three stars. Do you see the small cluster on the left? There are three of them. One for each of us." His hand settles on my thigh. "You, me, and Dante."

My heart swells. A million thoughts run through my head about what this means and where we go from here. Then I see another star just underneath the cluster of three.

When I tell him the news about the baby, will he buy that one, too? So all of us can be up there together. Forever. What if there's more in our future? What if we buy the whole galaxy and fill it with little Novikovs?

"Do you like it?"

"It's perfect," I choke out.

"Anatoly mentioned flowers and chocolates," he says dismissively, "but this felt better."

I finally look up at him, my cheeks flushed. "You talked to Anatoly about me?"

"Shocking, I know." He chuckles. "He was unbearable through the entire process. That should be proof enough that I'll do anything it takes to show you how I feel. I probably didn't need to do the rest of this."

I squeeze his hand and press my cheek to his shoulder. He's solid and warm—a safe place to land. "I'm glad you did the rest of it. It's nice."

"Nice enough for you to forgive me?"

It's funny that I asked Mikhail for time to think. Now, we're sitting here on a blanket under the stars and I can't imagine what there is to think about. The truth is embedded in my bones, as much a part of me as my own heart.

"Of course I forgive you, Mikhail." I turn into him, my hand curling above his heart. "I love you, too."

His eyes widen. He's stunned for just a second. Then he grips my waist and pulls me into his lap. "Show me."

16

VIVIANA

"I didn't think I'd ever have this again." I arch my back, letting Mikhail stretch the collar of his shirt to nip at my collarbone. "I can't believe it."

During the worst of it—being trapped in that cell with nothing to look forward to except visits from Trofim—I would let myself imagine *seeing* Mikhail. I couldn't think about Dante without falling to pieces. But for a few seconds, I could imagine a future where I was able to take in the square line of Mikhail's jaw and see his furrowed brow. I just pictured his face and felt something like hope spark in my chest.

Now, I'm straddling his hips with his stubbled face in my hands. He kisses me like I'm water and he's dying of thirst. I'm more than familiar with that level of desperation.

"Believe it." He palms my breasts and then leans down, circling his mouth over my peaked nipples. He sucks on them through the thin cotton material until I'm rocking against him. "You're going to have this again and again… and again."

He grabs the hem of my shirt and I lift my arms to help him peel it off of me. In the back of my mind, there's a delusion that he'll be able to see my baby bump. But that thought, along with every other thought in my head, disappears as he presses my breasts together and lavishes each of them. He pivots back and forth to flick his tongue over my nipples and scrape his teeth over my sensitive skin.

"Mikhail," I moan.

A growl rumbles through his chest, deep enough that I feel it vibrate through me. Then he tips me backwards. In one move, he's on top of me. Trailing his tongue down my body. Circling my belly button.

When he rises onto his knees and looks down at me, there isn't a drop of nervousness in my body. There's no space for it amidst the bright, searing happiness. Mikhail's eyes are dark and wild. He's looking at me like I'm something precious he's found and wants to keep for himself. I know that he loves me exactly as I am.

Mikhail hooks his fingers in my panties and peels them down my legs.

"Perfect," he breathes, spreading my thighs and pressing a kiss behind my knee.

He teases his mouth closer and closer to where I want him until I'm whimpering with need.

"I haven't even touched you and your legs are already shaking." Mikhail smirks. Before I can accuse him of being a smug tease, he dips his face between my legs and slides his tongue over my slit.

"Oh my God." I throw my arms over my head, fisting my hands in the blanket as he laps at me.

He curls his hands around my ass and lifts me off the blanket, angling me against his mouth until I don't need to open my eyes to see stars.

I stroke my fingers through his hair, surrendering to his tongue and his touch. He delves into me, thrusting again and again until I'm squirming in his hands. My thighs clamp around his ears, holding him exactly where I want him until I fall apart.

The orgasm roars through me and tears burn in my eyes. It's not until I'm on the other side of it with Mikhail gently bringing me back to earth with soft kisses to my clit that I realize why I'm crying.

"I forgot that I could feel like this," I pant. "No pain. No fear. Just… you."

Mikhail crawls over my body, his lips slick with my release. "I'm making it my solemn duty to make sure you never forget again."

I lazily swipe my thumb over the crease between his brows. "I don't think there's any reason to be solemn about it. I certainly won't be."

He claims my mouth, kissing me in long, heady strokes. I curl my leg around his hip and draw him closer. Being with him like this feels like fucking. I could do it for hours.

But his erection is hard and hot against me, straining against the front of his pants. I reach between us and slide my hand under his waistband.

"Fuck," he groans, dropping his forehead to mine. Beads of sweat dot his chest. Heat pours off of him like a furnace as I give him a rough stroke.

"Did you forget what this felt like?" I whisper.

Mikhail grips my chin, forcing my face to his. "I'll have to die before I forget what you feel like around my cock, Viviana. Maybe not even then."

I shove his pants down. He kicks them away and then he's there between my legs. He teases his tip against my opening, parting me slowly.

"Please," I beg, clawing at his lower back.

He draws his hips away, toying with me. "What do you want, Viviana?"

"I want you." I thought the pawing and panting was obvious, but apparently, I have to spell it out for him.

He drags his nose along my cheek, turning every touch into some new erotic experience. "But how? There are so many options."

I lift my hips, but Mikhail pulls away again. I groan. "I only see one."

Suddenly, he pins one of my arms over my head, careful to avoid my bandaged wrist. His breath is hot on my neck as he presses his lips to my racing pulse. "I could drive into you deep. I could split you open until you scream my name."

"Yes," I breathe.

Nerves flutter low in my stomach and between my legs. I think I'll combust if I don't feel him inside of me.

He chuckles low against my jawline like he's making a point to trace every inch of my body with his lips. "Or," he offers, skating his fingers tenderly down my arm, "I could slide into you inch by inch. I could fill you one gentle fraction of a thrust at a time until you're desperate for more. Until you beg me to fuck you. Until you think you'll die without my cock."

I dig my nails into his back, drawing a wince from him. "You're already killing me, Mikhail."

He reaches between us to grip his erection, dragging himself up and down my slit. "You're so wet," he groans, circling my clit with the head of his cock.

"I don't care how you fuck me, Mikhail. Take me any way you want." His eyes darken with desire and I nod. "Yes. Like that. Whatever just crossed your mind, you can take me like that."

He shakes his head. "You don't know what you're signing up for, Viviana."

"Yes, I do." I curl my palm around his stubbled cheek. "I'm signing up for you and all that comes with it. Just please, *please* fuck me, Mikhail."

Mikhail's mouth crushes over mine at the same time he slams himself deep inside of me. I cry out, but he swallows it, claiming my mouth with his tongue and my throbbing pussy with every single inch of his hard cock.

He scrapes a hand up my thigh, curling around my ass to lift me closer. He tilts me against him and thrusts.

"Thank you." I arch back and he kisses the slope of my throat, the hollows beneath my collarbones. He's in my head, between my legs, palming my breasts. I've never been so consumed by any person in my life the way I'm consumed by Mikhail Novikov. I clench around him, drawing him even deeper. "I feel you everywhere."

He slams into me, our bodies slapping together. "I love the way you take me. The way you pulse around me when you're close."

He's so big that the smallest flutter is all it takes to feel him against my walls. I wrap my leg over his hip and roll against him, grinding as I milk him from the inside.

He whimpers and that alone might be the single most vulnerable thing he's ever done. More than his apology or his confession. Mikhail drops his forehead to my chest and groans, telling me in his own way exactly how much he wants this.

And it's enough to completely unravel me.

"I'm coming!" I cry out into the night. I fist my hands in his hair and ride him. When my body gives up, Mikhail grabs my hips with bruising force and drives into me.

"I feel you," he snarls, pumping into me again and again. "You're so tight."

A few more pumps and his hips stutter. He spills into me, finding release deep inside my core. Then he collapses, his head pillowed on my chest.

I hold him, grateful for the weight of his strong body. For the way I can still feel him twitching inside of me.

I've never been this close to another person before. *How can I still want more?*

When he finally raises himself up on his hands, I drag a finger through the hair on his chest and try to fight away my nerves. I didn't plan to tell him this. Then again, I didn't plan on any of this. If it was up to me, Dante and I would still be in our tiny apartment. I'd be working for a boss with Funyun breath and coming home to Dante after dark every night.

Maybe it's past time I throw away my plans.

"You're gonna have to buy another star soon," I tell him, my voice shaky.

"I will if we keep at it like this." He chuckles and smooths a hand over my stomach. His fingers dip dangerously low, somehow stoking desire in my limp, sated body. "I came so fucking hard and I already want you again, Viviana. I want to see you pregnant with my child. I want everyone to know that you're mine."

I'm his. He's mine.

Thank God.

I'm so relieved I can barely keep the words in. The confession pours out of me. "We can do this as many times as you want and nothing will change… because I'm already carrying your baby. I'm pregnant, Mikhail."

The smile is frozen on his face for a few seconds… before it begins to slip.

Mikhail pushes back so he's kneeling between my spread thighs, outright frowning down at me.

So much for post-orgasmic bliss. It feels like he just dumped ice water over me. "Mikhail?" I start to ask. "You're scaring—"

"Why the fuck didn't you tell me?"

17

MIKHAIL

Viviana looks almost silver in the moonlight. There's a sheen of sweat across her skin and she's breathing heavily. Her lips are swollen from my mouth. I can see the marks my hands left, bruises darkening where I gripped her hips and pumped into her.

I was inside her without a single clue that she was pregnant with my baby.

"You should have told me," I snarl.

She grabs the flannel shirt I gave her and pulls it over her body like a blanket. "I *am* telling you. That's what I'm doing right now."

"You should have told me immediately." *Before I sent you away. Before I let you get kidnapped.*

She gestures around wildly. "What do you want from me, Mikhail? You know where I've been."

She's been with Trofim for days. Chained. Dehydrated. Terrified.

None of that can be good for the baby.

"Exactly. I know where you've been. There aren't a lot of pregnancy tests in captivity. I doubt my brother ran out for a test and some folic fucking acid."

Her indignation dims slightly and I know I'm right.

"You knew before you left the mansion that night," I accuse. "You knew you were pregnant when you got in my car and drove away from me."

"I didn't *know* anything," she argues. "I felt nauseous, but I wasn't sure."

"You should have told me," I repeat yet again.

"Told you what?" she fires back. "I would have sounded desperate! Like I was just trying to convince you to let me stay. You wouldn't have believed me."

She's right. We both know it. And still…

"Also, considering I'd been held at gunpoint, drugged and kidnapped by your father, and then rescued by you, only to find out you wanted nothing to do with me…" She lets that hang in the air, the accusation landing like a punch to the sternum. "It wasn't out of the realm of possibility that I was just stressed."

"Okay, fine. So you didn't *know* you were pregnant. But when did you *suspect*, Viviana? When did you take a test?"

She chews on her lower lip. Her cheeks flush and, for the first time, she doesn't have a ready answer.

"When did you take a test?" I growl again. "You were only out on your own for a couple hours before Trofim found you, right? And I know you left here and went straight to a pharmacy."

"Why are you asking if you already know the answer?" she snaps. "What do you want me to say?"

I grab my pants and yank them on. "I want you to admit that you lied to me."

"I didn't tell you because I didn't think it would make a difference."

"It would have been the difference between you being kidnapped from a rat-infested motel room by Trofim or you being safe and sound here with me."

Viviana stands up and slides her arms into the flannel shirt. I get another view at every inch of her bare skin. The swell of her breasts, the soft curve of her waist and the flare of her hips.

She's going to look incredible carrying my baby. I want to throw her down and fuck her again at just the thought of it.

She wraps the shirt around her, holding it closed. "If I'd told you that night, you would have let me stay here… but it wouldn't have been because you wanted me here. You would have let me stay here until I gave birth and then you would have kept the baby and sent me away. And I didn't want to be some breeding cow to you, Mikhail. That's not what I wanted."

"You could have died!" I roar. "Both of you could have died. Do you fucking understand that, Viviana?"

I could have lost you both.

Her face softens. She reaches for me, but I step away. "I took you to the hospital. You could have told the doctor. You didn't even ask Dr. Hamilton to check on the baby."

"I didn't—" She blows out a sharp breath. "I didn't know what was going to happen to me. I didn't want to say anything until I knew what the plan was."

Until she knew I wasn't going to dump her on the curb like garbage again. Until she knew she could trust me.

I hate myself for putting that thought in my head.

I hate Trofim for endangering Viviana and our future family.

I hate that this is good news and all I can think about is the million different ways that it can all go wrong.

"Mikhail," she breathes, "I'm sorry. Can we start over? I'm happy about this. I want this with you. Don't you want it, too?"

Before I can answer, my phone rings.

I probably shouldn't answer it, but it's late. Too late for anyone to be calling me unless it's an emergency.

I answer without looking to see who it is.

"Hello?"

"Mikhail." Raoul's voice is hoarse. He's yelling over what sounds like a white noise machine in the background. He coughs, a nasty, hacking sound.

"What's happening?"

Viviana steps forward, her hand on my arm. We're in the middle of a fight, but she can tell something is wrong.

I ignore the way that makes me feel and press the phone more firmly to my ear.

"Cerberus Industries," Raoul says. "It's on fire."

18

MIKHAIL

The building is a hollowed-out husk by the time I get there. Flames erupt from what's left of the third-floor windows and crawl upward, taking the floors above out one by one. It's not hard to tell where the fire started.

But why?

"I tried to put it out when I first got here." Raoul coughs into his elbow again. There's soot on his neck and ash in his hair.

I was standing on a balcony yelling at Viviana about how she could have gotten herself and our baby killed—meanwhile, my second was running into actual burning buildings.

Can everyone keep themselves alive for one fucking night without my help?

"You're not a firefighter, Raoul. That's not your job."

He frowns, taking that personally. "My job is to make sure things run smoothly. A fire brigade marching into our office and discovering all of our secrets isn't the kind of smooth sailing we strive for. I thought I could handle it on my own."

"You should have called me," I growl. "We could handle it together."

"It was late," he mutters.

Raoul throwing himself on the, in this case, literal flames is a problem I'll have to handle another day. Right now, my latest investment is a bonfire and I need to know why.

"How did you even know it was on fire?"

He swipes sweat off of his forehead, spreading a layer of gray ashes across his skin. "The security cameras I installed caught movement. I saw them starting the fire."

I don't want to ask—mostly because I already know the answer. But I have to. "Who?"

"The Greeks. Christos Drakos's second and a few of their foot soldiers."

"Fuck," I grumble. "I should have known when I got off the phone with him earlier. He's pissed and—"

"The Giordanos were there, too," he adds.

I snap my attention to him. "Christos *and* Agostino?"

"They're working together," he confirms. "At least, as far as I can tell. That or they separately had the great idea to burn down your new business on the same night."

It's so fucking late. Late enough that there aren't even that many bystanders watching the blaze. Raoul and I have the sidewalk mostly to ourselves as another fire truck roars around the corner. Firefighters encircle the building. The spray from the hoses looks like molten gold against the flames.

I haven't slept for days and while I was busy confessing my love to Viviana, balls deep inside of her, my enemies were launching attacks.

I have to fight the deep-seated instinct to think I made a mistake. I walk back my knee-jerk reaction to convince myself that Viviana is a distraction I can't afford.

Not only can I afford her kind of distraction, I need it. I know what it's like when she's not in my life. There was an ache in my bones every second she was gone. It muddled everything in my life. If I go back to that, I won't survive it.

Plus, none of this is Viviana's fault.

It's *mine.*

"I should have killed Agostino when we found him in his penthouse."

I expect Raoul to agree, but he just shrugs. "If you had, Trofim may have had time to marry Viviana and then immediately gone on the run."

"Or I could have killed Agostino and still made it in time to save Viviana," I counter.

"Then Christos could have heard about Agostino's death and realized even sooner that you were going after Viviana and weren't going to marry Helen. He would have had even more time to launch this attack." Raoul lets loose another round of hacking coughs before he turns to me. "There's no time for regrets, Mikhail. You did what you thought was best in the moment and I supported you every step of the way. If you fucked up, then so did I. We're in this together."

Together. There's been a lot of that tonight. Anatoly helping me win Viviana back. Telling Viviana how I feel. Now, this moment with Raoul.

There's only so much sentimentality my black heart can handle. But I push the limits one last time.

"Funny hearing that from you after you ran into a burning building that you knew could be filled with our enemies, *alone*." I glare at the man who is my brother in every conceivable way that matters. "If we're in this together, I need you to not be a fucking martyr. Next time, call me *before* you run directly into the flames."

Raoul smirks. "I'll try to remember that."

We watch the fire for a few minutes. If it wasn't the start of yet another war, it would almost be beautiful.

"We have a big shipment of weapons coming in soon," Raoul mentions regretfully, like he doesn't want to shatter this moment, either. "As much as I'd love to stand here and watch the building burn, we need to figure out how we're going to offload the money from that sale without raising eyebrows. Cerberus was our only plan and now, it's gone."

A few weeks ago, I would have been scrambling. I spent six years crafting this gunrunning plot and putting all the pieces together: securing the weapons shipments, gaining the port access, buying a shell company to launder the money.

Now, it's all gone to hell.

But I'm still here. I have Viviana and Dante. I have my brothers.

None of my plans have worked out the way I thought they would, but they've all worked out the way they should.

"Then we'll make a new plan, Raoul." I clap him on the back, banging another round of coughs out of him. "We'll figure it out."

19

VIVIANA

I wake up to reminders of Mikhail everywhere.

There's a soft ache between my legs where he stretched me. My nipples are sensitive from his lips and his teeth. The possessive way he clung to me left bruises that are still blooming on my hips and my thighs.

I feel him everywhere except in the bed next to me, which is where I want him most.

After the phone call, he left in a hurry last night. He didn't have time to explain what was going on, but I could tell by the worry in his eyes that it was serious.

"We'll talk about this tomorrow," he said before he left me in front of the door to his bedroom.

He still wants me to sleep in his bedroom, I thought. *That has to be a good sign.*

Before the poorly thought out pregnancy announcement I made, the entire night was one good sign after another. I mean, Mikhail named a star after me. I've spent my life looking up at the stars and trying to make sense of the universe. Now, tucked amongst the celestial landscape are three little dots. My family, together, forever.

My insides melt just thinking about him choosing those stars for us.

They melt even more when I remember how it felt to have his voice in my ear. The dirty things he whispered against my skin have absolutely ruined me for anyone else.

I want to see you pregnant with my child. I want everyone to know that you're mine.

After everything he said last night, I'm not worried that Mikhail is going to change his mind about me. I'm not tiptoeing around the mansion the way I was yesterday, worried that the slightest wrong move would get me tossed out on my ass.

But I hate that things are unresolved between us. I want to smooth this misunderstanding out and then, if I'm lucky, Mikhail will smooth me out, too.

I stretch my arms over my head and climb out of bed.

I could go down the hall and get my own clothes, but Mikhail's closet is too tempting. I pull on a pair of his athletic shorts. I have to tighten the string and roll the waistband an absurd amount of times. Plus, it looks ridiculous with his flannel shirt. But I don't care. I'm wrapped in the woodsy citrus scent of him as I pad downstairs.

I barely manage a single step into the kitchen before a small body slams against my legs.

"Mama!" Dante squeezes my knees together and jumps up and down. "You're here."

I scoop him up, feeling much steadier than I did the last time I held him. It's miraculous what a lot of rest and a love confession can do for your stability. "I'm going to be here every day, buddy. I'm not going anywhere."

I plop him back in front of his bowl of cereal.

"That's what Anatoly said. I wanted to come see you this morning, but he said you needed to sleep." Dante rolls his eyes. "He said you had a long, hard night, but you've been sleeping for, like, a million years."

I make a mental note to punch Anatoly in the arm later. Hard.

"Where is Uncle Nat, anyway?" I ask through gritted teeth.

There's a small bowl of cereal and half a banana on the island for Dante, but I don't see signs of anyone else's food. Before… *everything*, I'd come downstairs and find Stella in the kitchen with Dante. She always had French toast and freshly-squeezed juice for him.

The image of her crumpled on the cold garage floor, a gaping wound in her chest, flashes behind my eyes. My heart clenches hard, but I fight back the tears. Today is a happy day. My first day back in the mansion with Dante. I don't want to do anything to ruin it.

Dante climbs back into his barstool and shrugs. "He said he had somewhere to be. He told me to eat my breakfast and wait for school to start."

Weird.

The reason I've been able to let my guard down since Dante and I moved into the mansion is because everyone here is as protective of him as I am. I was hesitant to admit it right away, but it's so obvious that Raoul and Anatoly are just as concerned about Dante's safety as Mikhail and me.

If they left him here alone, there must have been a good reason. Maybe the same reason Mikhail rushed off last night and hasn't come back yet.

"Just the two of us, then," I say with forced cheer. My morning sickness has eased a lot the last couple days, but I still gravitate towards plain buttered toast just to be on the safe side. I push two slices down into the toaster and lean against the counter. "Are you still being tutored by Mrs. Steinman?"

He nods his head and talks around a big bite of banana. "Do you know how to subitize?"

"Scuba dive?" I ask, confused.

He swallows his bite. "No. *Subitize.* Here, look." He plucks a few pieces of cereal out of his bowl and lays them on the counter. "How many are there?"

I point to each one slowly, counting. "One, two, three, four—"

"Wrong! You're not supposed to count them."

"But you asked me how many there were."

"Mrs. Steinman says that subitizing is when you know how many pieces of cereal there are without having to count them. But it doesn't have to be cereal. It can be anything."

I'm ninety-eight percent positive Dante is making all of this up or Mrs. Steinman is teaching him nonsense, but then I pull out my phone and Google it.

"Wow. It's a real thing," I exclaim.

Dante beams proudly. "I told you. I'm learning so much."

He really is. Mikhail and I haven't had time to talk about Dante going to boarding school again. We haven't had time to talk about much of anything except the pregnancy. Considering the nosedive that conversation took, I'm not exactly eager to talk about anything else. But we have to.

When Mikhail first wanted to send Dante away, it was out of a sense of desperation. He wanted to keep him safe. But a lot has changed since then.

Hopefully, he's had a change of heart. I mean, no one could look at his mop of golden brown hair and bright blue eyes and wish that he was halfway around the world in boarding school, right? I'm sure Mikhail will agree.

Once we talk through the pregnancy, I'll bring up boarding school.

"Dante?" Mrs. Steinman pops her head into the kitchen. If his tutor is surprised to see me standing there, she doesn't show it. She just smiles and then turns her attention to Dante. "Are you ready to start the day?"

Yesterday, Dante wanted to skip his lesson to spend time with me, but today, he hops out of his chair and bounds over to Mrs. Steinman. He takes her hand and they walk to the schoolroom together.

Just me for breakfast, then.

I butter my toast, make a cup of coffee, and retreat upstairs. If I have to eat alone, I might as well do it from the comfort of a king-sized bed.

Mikhail's bedroom door is cracked open. I twist around and push it open with my back, balancing my plate in one hand

and trying not to splash myself with steaming coffee. I scoot backward into the room and kick the door closed, triumphant.

Then I turn around and drop everything in my hands on the floor.

The coffee soaks into the carpet and the bottom of my socks, burning the soles of my feet. But I barely feel it. Because all of my attention is locked on the end of the bed...

Where my father sits, staring back at me.

Agostino clicks his tongue and sighs bitterly. "Look at the mess you've made, Viviana."

20

VIVIANA

"What are you doing here?" I ask with trembling lips.

A lot of other, more menacing, questions ricochet around my head. Like, *How did you get in?* and *What are you going to do to me?* and *Am I losing my mind?*, but I stick with the most obvious.

The coffee under my feet is already going cold. The nausea I haven't felt all morning twists my stomach.

"I came to see my daughter." My father rises gracefully to his feet and turns towards me. A bruise I didn't notice before covers the entire right side of his face. His eye is swollen slightly and his lip is cut.

"Did Mikhail do that?" I can't help but smile.

"Oh, this?" He gingerly touches his face and winces. "Yes. Mikhail won that battle. I'm not quite the fighter I used to be. But I have my ways of fighting back. Don't you worry—the next one went to me."

"I wasn't worried," I drawl.

I have no idea what he's talking about and I don't care. My eyes flick to the window over his shoulder. It's twenty feet down to the ground below, at least. Unless I want to snap my legs backwards at the knees, that's not an escape option.

If I dive into the hallway, I could probably make it to the door to the private balcony Mikhail and I were on last night. But it's secluded and would also end with me and my accordion knees lying in excruciating pain on the ground below.

I could just scream, but the house is empty as far as I could tell from the kitchen. I have no idea who is close enough to hear me, aside from Dante and Mrs. Steinman. And the last thing this situation needs is my six-year-old busting through the door to find his grandfather trying to murder his mother. No, I don't want to rope them into this.

"Stop looking for an escape route," my father says irritably. "I'm not going to hurt you."

I snort. "Funny, coming from the man who helped my ex-fiancé kidnap me. You haven't exactly spared any fatherly concern for me recently. Or ever, now that I think about it."

"Because you've never been anything but defiant. What kind of message do you think it sends to the world that I can't control my own daughter?"

"Probably that I'm a grown woman who makes my own choices."

His upper lip curls. "Choices like marrying your fiancé's brother? A man who is already engaged to the daughter of one of our allies? It's reckless."

"All of those marriages were arranged against the will of the people involved. Are you really surprised they failed? Besides, your alliances have nothing to do with me."

He bristles upright. "Except it is my alliances that have kept you alive this long! Trofim would have killed you if I hadn't convinced him to marry you a second time."

"That was you?" I growl. "You really think you did me a favor? You saw me in that cell. You saw what he was doing to me. Do you expect me to thank you for that?"

"However you may feel about it, you are still my daughter, Viviana. You are the daughter of the don of the Giordano Mafia. You belong to me."

Wrong. The only man I have ever and will ever belong to is Mikhail Novikov.

I lean forward, each word hissing out of me slowly so he can grasp exactly how serious I am. "I would rather die than spend another day under your thumb. I would rather die right this second than spend a single moment of my life married to Trofim."

He shakes his head. "That's exactly how you'll end up if you don't reconsider."

"Is that a threat?"

"It's a fact," he spits. "If you can't give up this sad attempt at domestic life with Mikhail, you and your lover and your bastard son are all going to end up dead. You have no idea how many people you've pissed off. If you don't fix things now, it'll be too late."

Fear pricks at my heart. At one point in my life, my father's speech would have terrified me into submission. I would have dipped my chin and apologized. I would have begged for forgiveness and mercy—for me, for Dante, for Mikhail, for all of us.

Now, I know it's all a trick.

There is no peace on the other side of my submission. There's no safety with my father for me or Dante. It's just a different kind of fear.

And I'd rather be scared and free than safe in a cage.

"You have no say over how I choose to live my life," I tell him evenly. "I don't even consider you part of my life anymore. You don't belong here and, unless you get the fuck out right now, I'll scream for Mikhail. I highly doubt he'll offer you the chance at escape."

I don't think Mikhail is even in the mansion right now. But my father doesn't need to know that.

"When this blows up in your face, Viviana…" He smiles, but his eyes are narrowed to slits. "… remember I tried to warn you."

He brushes past me and walks into the hallway, leaving the way I presume he came without another word.

21

MIKHAIL

Viviana is quiet in the passenger seat. She's been quiet since the second she told me Agostino was in my house and I told her at once to pack a bag.

Probably because I didn't *tell her* so much as I violently roared at her to pack her things while I demanded Anatoly and Raoul check the cameras and secure the mansion.

Agostino was in my house.

He was with my wife.

And I had no fucking idea.

My hands tighten on the steering wheel again. I've been white-knuckling it most of this trip. No matter how hard I try, I can't unsee the last time someone broke into my home. It didn't end well for my family.

The thought that I could lose Viviana and Dante in the same way is maddening.

"How much farther?" Viviana asks softly.

I force myself to loosen my grip. "Half an hour."

The road is narrow and surrounded by trees on either side and has been for the last twenty minutes. I didn't buy a safehouse in the woods for it to be easy to find.

"Do you think this is necessary?"

"He was *inside* the house," I grit out. "He was in our bedroom, Viviana."

You could have died, I want to add. But I don't want to scare her. Not when I can tell she's already terrified enough. She was still shaking when she told me her father had come to see her.

Her hand is steady now as she reaches out to touch my elbow. Her fingers are gentle. They settle some violent, stormy part of me. I feel like I can breathe a little easier.

"I know. Believe me, I was there." She holds me a little tighter and I get the sense I'm not the only one who needs the comfort. "It was terrifying. I just mean… You have guards at the mansion. Can't they just increase security and make sure this doesn't happen again?"

"We are going to increase security and this will never happen again. That's what they're doing right now. But until I know it's safe, you and Dante aren't staying there."

Part of me wonders if we shouldn't stay out in the woods permanently. It was Agostino breaking into my house this time, but Christos isn't going to be satisfied with burning down Cerberus. I left his daughter at the altar. I ruined his hopes for her future. He won't stop until he's ruined mine, which means Viviana and Dante are likely targets.

It's why I need to keep them safe and strike out at him first.

Viviana is staring straight ahead, her full lower lip pinched between her teeth. I can see the anxiety etched in her face.

I release the wheel and turn my hand over, twining my fingers through hers. "I'm not going to let anything happen to you, Viviana."

She blinks and the cloud of fear dissipates. "I know. I trust you."

I reach over, laying both of our hands over her stomach. "The stress isn't good for the baby."

"Are we talking about that now?" she asks softly. "I didn't want to bring it up again with so much going on."

I've thought a lot about how I reacted. I never even told her how happy I was. How happy I *am.*

"I was scared. For you and the baby. I just—" I blow out a breath. "I hate that I put you and our child in danger when I sent you away."

"You didn't know." She frowns. "Which I guess is kind of why you were mad, so maybe I shouldn't bring that up again."

I chuckle. "I'm just glad you're safe now. And I'm going to do everything I can to keep it that way. So you need to relax and try to take it easy. For the baby's sake and Dante's."

She turns around, peeking back at Dante snoozing in the backseat. "I don't want him to know what's going on. I don't want to scare him."

"Agreed." I nod. "As far as he knows, this is another adventure we're going on."

"Perfect. But maybe, after this, we try to have fewer

adventures." She grimaces. "I wouldn't mind testing out a normal, quiet life for a change of pace."

I squeeze her hand. "I'll do my best."

Dante's eyes pop open as soon as I shift the car to park in front of the cabin. He undoes his booster seat and jumps out.

"This is our new house?" He gawks at the A-line roof and sprawling screened-in porch.

Viviana wraps her arms around his shoulders from behind. "Temporarily. It's an adventure."

She peeks back at me, a knowing smile on her face. And for the first time since she told me her father broke into our house, I can take a deep breath.

No one is going to get to them out here.

Dante inspects every room inside, loudly declaring "dibs" on the room with bunk beds. I snap my fingers in sarcastic disappointment. "As much as your mom and I would have loved sleeping on top of each other in the bunk beds, we'll let you have them, bud."

Dante is digging through the bags of food looking for a snack when Viviana sidles up next to me, her lips pressed against my ear. "No bunk beds, but I vote we still sleep on top of each other."

My cock perks up at that idea. But there's still so much to unpack. And after his nap in the car, Dante probably won't be asleep for hours.

I readjust my pants and keep settling in. There will be plenty of time to perfect our sleeping arrangements tonight once Dante is asleep.

"Do bears live here?" Dante turns away from the large picture window. "The three bears from the Goldilocks book lived in woods just like this."

"Some bears live out here, but they won't bother us inside the cabin."

Dante's eyes widen. "What about when we're outside?"

There's fear there. If I don't handle this correctly, he'll wake up terrified and end up in our bed. And I cannot have that. I have plans for his mother.

I stay calm as I explain. "Black bears aren't very aggressive. They hardly ever attack people. As long as we are alert and keep our distance, they won't bother us."

"What if we don't keep our distance?"

"If we run into one in the woods, we just stay calm and back away slowly. And if that doesn't work—" I flex my arm and wag my brows at him. "—I can take any bear."

Dante laughs. "No, you can't. Bears are ginormous."

"Are you saying I'm not ginormous?" I sweep an arm out to scoop Dante up by the waist. Then I lift him over my head and roar like an animal. "What do you have to say now?"

He can't say anything. He's too busy giggling until he's red in the face and panting.

As much as I wish the circumstances were different, I'm excited to have some time to solely spend with Dante. We haven't had good quality time since Costa Rica. Plus, sending Viviana away took our relationship back a few steps. It's nice that we can all be together again.

When I finally plop him down on his feet, he's grinning from ear to ear. I get the feeling I'm going to make up ground fast out here.

"If all else fails, there's this." Viviana pulls a can of bear spray out of a bag and tosses it to me. "Any time you are out in the woods with Dante, I want you to have that with you."

"You don't trust that I can fight a bear?" I tease. "Do I need to toss you around to prove it, too?"

She presses her lips together, biting back a grin. "Prove it to me later tonight, Mikhail."

Again, I strain against the front of my pants.

It's going to be a long afternoon.

22

VIVIANA

"All my stuffies can sleep on the bottom bunk and I'll take the top."

Dante steps back, hand on his chin as he assesses this configuration. It's the fifth one he's tried. His stuffed animals are apparently a lot pickier about where they sleep than he is.

He immediately shakes his head. "No, no, no."

I can hear Mikhail moving around the kitchen. I have no idea what he's cooking, but it smells incredible. By this point in my pregnancy with Dante, I gagged at even the blandest of spices. I couldn't even put black pepper on my food. But whatever cumin and chicken concoction Mikhail is cooking up has my mouth watering.

"What if your stuffed animals share a bed with you?" I suggest, tossing all of the stuffed animals onto the top bunk. "I'd recommend the top bunk. It's the most fun."

I grab Dante and toss him up onto the bed. He giggles and

dives under the covers. "This house is the funnest. I want to live here forever."

For good reason.

When Mikhail told me back at the mansion that we were going to his cabin, I imagined more of an Abe Lincoln setup. A log cabin with drafty windows and a damp fireplace we had to constantly chop wood to feed.

I'm not sure what about Mikhail's multi-million dollar mansion made me think we'd be roughing it out in the woods, but I knew the second we pulled up that I was dead freaking wrong.

The two-storey A-frame is the stuff *HGTV* wet dreams are made of. The entire backside of the house is a wall of windows looking out on a huge pond nestled amongst snow-capped pine trees. It's perfect.

The romantic picture is made even more perfect when we walk downstairs and find Mikhail dishing out plates piled high with grilled chicken and green beans.

If someone had told me a few months ago that I'd walk in on Mikhail cooking me and Dante a gourmet meal in a loosely-buttoned flannel and a dish towel tossed over his shoulder, I would have said, "You're insane." Now, I wouldn't say anything. Mostly because I'm too busy internally screaming and fanning myself like a Victorian maiden on the verge of fainting.

"Are you two ready to eat?" he asks with a smile.

I'm ready for a lot *of things.*

We sit down and even Dante is excited about dinner—a small

miracle, with his six-year-old taste buds. In between bites, he can't stop talking.

"Dad is going to let me hunt with him tomorrow. In the woods," he adds, as if there's anywhere else to hunt. "We're going to leave early in the morning and pack a lunch. He said we might have to spend most of the day out there because you have to be patient to catch animals. I'm super patient. I can wait for a long time." He stops talking for all of three seconds. Then he looks back and forth between us, eyebrows wagging. "See?"

I bite back a laugh. "Wow. So patient. I'm sure tomorrow is going to go super well for both of you."

Mikhail gives me a knowing smile and shrugs. "It'll be a good time."

He's patient with Dante. And gentle. Two things I never would have pegged him as when we met.

"You just make sure you listen to your dad tomorrow, Dante. Hunting can be dangerous if you don't pay close attention."

Dante lifts his chin. "He's going to teach me. I'll learn. I'm a fast learner."

Mikhail squeezes my knee under the table, soothing away the worries I haven't even consciously thought of yet.

I meant what I said. I trust Mikhail—with my life and Dante's.

After dinner, the woods beyond the window are dark. All I can see in the glass is the three of us reflected back. Mikhail at the sink with Dante on a chair next to him, me hovering in the background like I'll scare it all away, this whole blissful domestic fantasy, if I get too close.

Mikhail washes while Dante rinses. I join in with a towel, drying our plates and filing them away in the cabinet.

It's so… normal. Peaceful.

It's a peek at the life we could have had—if we were different people in a different time.

"Can you read me a bedtime book?" Dante asks.

I'm about to agree before I realize he's tugging on Mikhail's sleeve, not mine.

Mikhail looks over his head to check with me and I nod. The time of me being jealous over their relationship is long over. All I ever wanted for Dante is a father figure. Now, he has one. How could I ever begrudge him that?

"Sure, kiddo." Mikhail ushers him off the stool. "Brush your teeth and change into pajamas. I'll meet you in your room."

Dante groans. "I don't want to go alone. I want you to come with me."

"I have to stay here and finish the dishes. Hey," Mikhail says with a sly smile, "do you wanna race? See if you can brush your teeth before I finish—"

Mikhail can't even finish the sentence before Dante streaks down the hallway. He yanks his shirt over his head and tosses it on the floor behind him on his way to the bathroom.

I take Dante's place at the sink. "It took me years to learn that trick—turning everything into a race."

"I'm a fast learner," Mikhail teases.

He's joking, but he's right. A few weeks ago, Mikhail told me he didn't want a family. He made it clear that he had no desire to be a husband and father in the traditional sense. And yet, here he is.

He's learned how to become an irreplaceable part of our lives in only a matter of weeks.

"Dante loves you. It's so obvious."

Mikhail smiles. "That's good. Because I love him, too."

Our eyes meet. His are a sapphire blue in the glow from the fireplace in the corner. I don't have to wonder if he's thinking about our night on the balcony, the confessions we made to one another. I'm thinking of the exact same things.

"I love his mom, too," Mikhail whispers. He turns the water off and steps closer to me. His arm snakes around my waist, yanking me against his body. I feel a hard bulge against my stomach.

Heat radiates through me. I feel Mikhail's touch everywhere. I swallow down a knot of desire, trying and failing to find the words to respond.

But maybe this isn't the time for words.

I stretch onto my toes, dragging my body against him and drawing a groan from his chest. I press my lips against his—just as footsteps clomp down the hallway.

"I win!" Dante cheers, out of breath. His pajama shirt is on backwards and his hair is sticking up in every direction. "I beat you!"

Mikhail drops his forehead against mine and sighs. Then he turns to Dante with a big smile. "You sure did, bud. You got me good. Now, hurry and pick out books to read before I get there."

Dante runs down the hallway to his room and I move to turn back to the dishes. But Mikhail grabs my waist and plants me on the countertop. He spreads my thighs and steps between them like he was made to fit there. Like we should always be like this.

I can't breathe.

"Remember how you feel right now." His hands drag slowly up my legs. His fingertips brand my skin.

I sigh and part my legs wider. "There's not a chance in hell that I could forget."

Mikhail snatches my lower lip between his teeth, tugging on it for one perfect moment before he turns and walks away. Leaving me to slide to the floor on shaky legs and sit there all by myself, remembering how to breathe again.

23

VIVIANA

When Mikhail finishes putting Dante to bed and walks into the kitchen thirty minutes later, I promptly throw myself at him.

Never one to be caught off-guard, Mikhail scoops me out of the air like he expected it all along and presses me against the fridge. There's a refrigerator magnet digging into my spine, but I barely feel it. I'm too busy hooking my legs around his waist and crushing my mouth to his.

"You obey directions well," Mikhail observes against my mouth between kisses. "It feels like I never left."

I arch away from him and grab the hem of my shirt. I yank it over my head in one fluid movement and toss it. It lands in the sink, but I don't care. It could be shredding in the garbage disposal and I wouldn't let go of Mikhail to save it.

"An hour ago, I would have told you the kitchen was the least erotic room in the house. But that was before I spent the last thirty minutes cleaning it."

Mikhail kisses down my chest. He flicks the front clasp of my bra open and groans when my breasts spill free. "Does the smell of bleach get you going?"

I roll my hips against his erection, giving us both the friction we want. "No, but imagining you fucking me on every single one of the flat surfaces in here did the trick."

He slides me to the floor so he can unbutton my pants. He slips his hand inside the waistband and cups my already-damp panties. "Fuck, Viviana. I had plans tonight. I was going to take my time with you."

He caresses his fingers against my slit. I fist the front of his shirt in my hands, clinging onto him before my legs give out.

"You had plans? Tell me about them."

Instead of answering, Mikhail picks me up and carries me through the French doors to the screened-in porch. The night is cold, but there's a fire going in the wood-burning stove. Twinkle lights zigzag across the ceiling and there's a pile of fleece blankets spread out on the hardwood floor.

"You did this for me?" I ask in surprise.

He bites my earlobe. "After the day you had, I thought you could use the release."

For a brief second, I remember my father standing in our bedroom. The fear. The anger.

But I don't want to think about any of that tonight. Not when Mikhail is in front of me offering to help me forget.

I gladly and wholeheartedly accept.

I press my hands to his chest. His heart thunders against my palm as I slowly drop to my knees in front of him.

"Viviana…" His voice breaks on my name and I love knowing I have that kind of power. I love knowing that Mikhail Novikov is the strongest man I know, but I can make his heart race and his voice shake like no one else in this world can.

I unzip his pants and free his erection. He shudders when I lean forward and press a kiss to the very tip of him.

Then I take his velvet length into my mouth.

Mikhail tangles his fingers in my hair, holding loosely to the back of my head as I swallow him down again and again. I pause frequently to lick the underside of his cock from base to tip. I swirl my tongue around him, loving the pleading noises that come from the back of his throat as I let him touch the back of mine.

"God, that mouth," he growls, thrusting gently against my face. "It's so perfect."

I could finish him like this and be perfectly content. Making Mikhail whimper is a surefire way to get me out of my own head.

But as I pick up the pace to push him closer and closer to that edge, Mikhail slides his hips away from me. He grips my chin and brushes his thumb over my lower lip. "Another time, I'm going to fuck this perfect mouth until I come all over you. But not tonight."

His promise is still shivering down my spine when he presses me back into the cushion of fleece blankets and settles between my thighs. He flattens his hand on my stomach and slides it down until he's just above where I want him. My pussy quivers in anticipation.

"I should be gentle with you," he rumbles, regret staining his voice.

"Why?" He's barely touched me and I'm already breathless.

He shifts his hand higher to curl it around my stomach. The lost ground is devastating. My hips arch towards him as I grab his wrist and push him back down. He resists going all the way, but it's not for lack of trying on my part.

"The baby is safe in there," I argue. "Unless you plan to kill me with your cock tonight, there's nothing you could do that would hurt the baby."

Death by Mikhail's cock doesn't sound like the worst way to go, actually.

His jaw flexes. "I'm big, Viviana. And you haven't been seen by a doctor yet. I don't want to—"

"Someone is confident," I interrupt in a teasing lilt.

But Mikhail is right: he *is* big. Which is why I'm desperate to get every inch of him inside of me right now. So desperate I'm willing to stoop to reverse psychology.

"I've taken you plenty of times before, Mikhail. It's always been fine." I place special emphasis on that final word. *Fine.* The idea alone is laughable. Mikhail Novikov is a million different things, none of which are *fine.*

He's glorious. Intoxicating. All-consuming.

With the way his icy blue eyes are freezing me to the bone right now, he knows it.

Suddenly, both my arms are pinned to the blankets above my head and Mikhail is hovering over me. He refuses to touch me except for where his hands are around my wrists and the tip of his dick is whispering against my opening.

My heart is beating a wild rhythm in my chest, but I try to keep my voice steady as I ask, "Are you going to fuck me or are you going to leave me unsatisf—"

I don't even get the question out before Mikhail slams into me.

Our bodies are barely touching, but I'm full of him. I arch against where he has me pinned—with his cock and his hands—and cry out.

"How's that, Viviana?" he whispers over me. "Is that *fine*?"

I whimper. "S-so… good."

When I open my eyes, Mikhail is smirking. "Are you ready for the rest?"

I frown and glance down to where we're joined. Correction: where we're *half*-joined. Mikhail isn't even halfway inside of me and I had no idea.

I roll my eyes, both from annoyance and the excruciating way he flexes his hips into me, teasing every bit of pleasure out of where we touch. "You're going to be so smug about this, aren't you? You're never going to let me live this down."

"Wipe the word 'fine' from your vocabulary and I'll forgive you." He crushes his lips to mine at the same moment he slides home in me.

I should be used to the way Mikhail fills me by now, but it still catches me by surprise. He swallows down my scream, his lips sealed over mine. When he finally breaks away to drag his mouth over my jaw, I press my head back into the floor. "Fuck."

"That's better." He nips at my collarbone and traces his tongue between my breasts. "Nothing about the way you feel around me is 'fine,' Viviana. It's fucking *perfect*."

He drags slowly in and out of me, making sure I experience every glorious inch of him. The friction is unbearable. It's only made worse by the way I'm pinned to the floor.

"I want to touch you," I beg.

Mikhail smirks and lets go of one of my wrists. But before I can even move my arm, he gathers both my wrists in one of his hands.

"How about I touch you instead?"

Then he slides a hand between us and presses his thumb to my swollen clit. Whatever argument I was going to make dissolves into a broken moan.

He works my clit as his cock stretches me again and again. I lift my legs, splaying my hips wide to take him deeper.

"Viviana…" he growls, sinking into me.

The glow of self-satisfaction is short-lived when he enters me at a new angle. His head glances over my g-spot, and I'm completely and utterly gone.

My body goes taut, my entire spine lifted off the floor as I arch against him. The pleasure is searing and I cry out, screaming Mikhail's name as he fucks me to the beat of my own pulsing pussy.

When I finally sink back into the blankets, sated and limp, Mikhail lets go of my wrists. He kisses my chin and the thundering pulse in my neck. His soft lips suckle around each of my nipples before trailing down my stomach. He slides out of me and I hate the loss of him.

Gently, Mikhail wraps a large hand around my hip and rolls me onto my stomach.

A weak flutter deep in my core draws a whimper out of me. "I can't take any more."

"You seemed to think death by fucking was impossible," Mikhail remarks as he digs his hands into my ass.

"You know I was lying." I would've said anything to get him inside of me.

I spread my legs and I can feel the cool air against my dripping center. Mikhail must be able to see it, because he swipes his thumb there, soothing away the ache.

"I know," he murmurs. He grabs my hips and props me up on my knees, his hands seated in the curve of my waist. "I was lying, too."

My cheek is pillowed on the blanket as I twist back to look at him. "About what?"

His eyes lock on mine, dark and wild. "About ever being gentle with you."

Mikhail doesn't enter me halfway this time—he drives every inch of himself inside of my still-throbbing center.

My back bows and he presses a palm flat to my lower back. He bends me further, angling me so he can slide into me exactly how he wants.

"This is how I'm going to fuck you when you're swollen with my baby." His hands tighten around my waist and he pulls me harder against him. "This pussy is always going to belong to me."

I spent most of my life straining against the chains my father put on me. I wanted nothing more than to belong to myself —to be free.

But belonging to Mikhail Novikov is the best kind of freedom I can imagine.

"I'm close," I gasp, stretching my arms in front of me and sinking back against him. "I'm going to come again."

His hand slips around my hip and he circles two fingers over my clit as he pumps into me.

"Come with me, Viviana," he commands. "Now."

As if my body was just waiting for him to give the order, as soon as the word is out of his mouth, I grip his cock.

He lets out a string of curse words, his thrusts growing more and more purposeful until he stutters and warmth floods through me. I can feel him twitching inside of me and it prolongs my own orgasm, his pleasure somehow carrying mine.

I collapse on the blankets and Mikhail spoons his warm body around mine. The air smells like citrus and sex. My thighs are sticky with the evidence of what we've done.

But I'm as safe and content as I've ever been. I lean into the steady rhythm of his chest and fall asleep.

24

VIVIANA

The heat is biting, but it's a delicious kind of pain. I sink lower into the tub until the water laps against my chin.

We've been at the cabin for days and this is the first time I've been able to relax in the tub.

To be clear, I've been in the tub plenty of times. The moment I saw the claw-footed beauty nestled in the corner of the bathroom, a huge skylight in the sloped ceiling above and a ring of candles around the rim, I knew me and this tub were going to get very close and personal.

The trouble is that the tub and I haven't had any alone time. Every time I start running water, Mikhail appears in the doorway with eager eyes and grabby hands.

Last night, Mikhail fucked me over the end of the bed until I couldn't stand. Then he dropped to the floor and ordered me to sit on his face. I fell off of him, every muscle in my body quivering, and begged him to run me a bath so I could recover.

But halfway into my soak, he slipped into the tub with me. He was all innocent eyes and raised, *Who, me?* hands, but within ten minutes, he was finger-fucking me under the water while I lathered his cock in honey vanilla body oil.

When I remember the way he pumped his dick into my fist and his fingers into my pussy until we both fell apart, panting and limp below the bubbles, I can't even be mad at him for interrupting my tub time.

I never knew a person could be sore from too many orgasms, but here I am. Sore and sated in all the best ways.

None of that means I'm not enjoying *this* alone time, though.

Dante loved going hunting with Mikhail the other day—even though "hunting" for him consisted of wearing a camo sweatshirt and standing behind Mikhail as they stalked through the woods—and he's been begging to go again every morning when he wakes up.

The thought of my little baby boy anywhere near a gun sends a dagger of panic into my chest. Then I remember he's with Mikhail and the worry eases.

I trust Mikhail.

If I didn't trust him, there's no way in hell I'd be casually sipping sparkling cider and shriveling my skin beyond recognition in this soapy water right now. Especially because being pregnant usually makes my anxiety unmanageable.

At least, that's how it was when I was pregnant with Dante. I was on edge all the time. It could have had something to do with being on the run and having no idea how I'd pay for my next meal, let alone afford diapers when the time came. But I'm pretty sure at least a portion of the extra anxiety was my raging pregnancy hormones.

Maybe the fact I'm not anxious now means I'm having a girl this time.

I slide my hand under the water and stroke my still-flat stomach. "Are you a little girl, hm? Is that why I haven't been as sick?"

I'm hesitant to say my morning sickness is over since it's still so early—and lest some goddess of fertility somewhere notices my lack of suffering and hits me with the kind of all-day, nonstop nausea I had with Dante—but the vomiting peaked and waned in a matter of a week. I haven't been nauseous at all recently. The only nipple tenderness I've had has had a very direct link to Mikhail and all the naughty things he does to me when it gets late and we're alone.

He's been so gentle with Dante. I don't know exactly what happened between them while I was away, but I noticed a little tension between them when I first got back. Dante kept checking to make sure I wasn't going to disappear again and he narrowed his eyes whenever Mikhail walked into a room.

That's all but gone now. Dante once again worships the ground Mikhail walks on and Mikhail seems to genuinely enjoy spending time with Dante. It's the only reason I can think of for why they spend from breakfast to lunch every day tromping through the woods with nothing to show for it.

Last night, Mikhail told me he would have caught something by now, but Dante is a heavy walker for being so light and is scaring everything in a three-mile radius away.

I clicked my tongue and patted his shoulder condescendingly. "Sure. I bet it's Dante's fault. Whatever makes you feel better."

"If all you care about is making me feel better…" Mikhail pushed me to my knees in the middle of the kitchen and fucked my mouth just like he swore he would the first night.

I bite back a smile and wonder if it will always be like this.

When the rest of the world settles down, will things with our little family always feel this easy? Or will having a little girl change things?

Mikhail has repeated to me over and over again the last few days that he is "all the way in" with me—and not just when he's literally all the way in *me*. He's showing me in every way he knows how that he isn't going to send me away again. Our family is a priority for him.

But he had another family before. Another daughter.

What if our baby girl reminds him of Anzhelina? What if the reminders of the way his firstborn died make it hard for him to love *our* daughter?

I wouldn't even blame him. How could I? If something happened to Mikhail or Dante, I'm not sure how I'd pick up and carry on. I can't imagine a world without them in it. I'd die a thousand times over to save either of them. The fact that Mikhail has suffered the way he has and is still as caring with me and Dante as he is is a miracle. Or a testament to the strong man he is.

Being strong doesn't make him impenetrable, though.

"Mama!"

The shrill voice echoing through the house is enough to send my heart lurching against my chest. I sit bolt upright in the tub, sudsy water sloshing over the sides as every thought in my head disappears, replaced by images of smoking guns and bloody limbs.

But before I can fully start to freak out, Dante yells again. "Mama! You gotta come look at this!"

I blow out a harsh breath and sink into the tub.

He's okay. He's fine.

"Just a second," I call back.

"Hurry," he repeats. "It's so awesome!"

It better be awesome, considering I almost had a heart attack.

I do my best to work past the adrenaline Dante just unknowingly dumped into my system and step out of the tub. I dry off quickly and wrap up in a fluffy bathrobe before I head downstairs.

I'm only halfway down the stairs when Dante appears at the bottom, bouncing from one muddy boot to the other. A massive grin is spread across his face. I can't find it in me to be annoyed with him for scaring me half to death or for tracking mud across the wood floor I swept and mopped less than an hour ago.

"What's going on, bud?"

"I shot a deer!"

"You shot a deer?" I frown. "Like, Mikhail shot a deer? Or—?"

"It was me!" He grabs my hand as soon as I touch the first floor and drags me to the door. "I pulled the trigger. I shot it. It was me."

I make myself take a deep, deep, *very* deep breath. I wouldn't have let Dante go into the woods with him if I didn't trust that he would be safe. If he pulled the trigger, Mikhail must have thought he was ready.

I trust Mikhail. I trust Mikhail.

I repeat this to myself all the way through the house and out the front door. Then I see an ATV appear between two trees, a dead deer tied to the back of it.

The animal is at least three times the size of Dante and, suddenly, I can't believe I ever let my baby boy walk into those woods alone.

But I swallow all of that down when Dante jumps and cheers as Mikhail pulls to a stop, both of them wearing the exact same grin.

"Did he tell you the good news?" Mikhail hops out of the driver's seat. His pants stretch over his muscular thighs and there is something deep-seated and instinctual going on with the way my stomach flutters as he undoes knots and hauls the deer across the gravel towards the detached garage. I'm horrified, but I also can't stop thinking about how easily he is handling this massive animal and what it means for how easily he can handle me.

"That he killed the deer, you mean?" I ask.

Mikhail smiles wider and holds out his hand to Dante for a high-five. Dante jumps and their blood- and dirt-crusted hands slap together.

"Yeah, he told me." I consider holding my hand out for a high-five, too, but I'm not really in that kind of mood. I'd rather wrap my arms around Dante and hold him there, safe and sound, for the rest of time.

Maybe my pregnancy anxiety isn't as absent as I thought it was.

"How did this happen?" The question sounds like an accusation, so I try to reverse and try again. "Why did Dante have the gun?"

Somehow worse. Oops.

Mikhail drops the deer on the cement floor and Dante circles it, examining his catch from every angle. While he's busy admiring the dead animal, Mikhail eases over to me.

He takes in my wet hair and robe and his eyes darken retroactively. "Were you in the bath?"

"I was trying to relax." A feat that would have been impossible if I'd known my six-year-old was handling a weapon in the middle of nowhere. "You let Dante hold the gun?"

"He was ready."

"How do you know that?"

"Because I wouldn't put him in danger," Mikhail says confidently. He strokes a calloused knuckle over my cheek. He smells like sweat and fresh air. "And because he needs to learn how to protect himself."

"From *deer*?!"

"From everything."

I hate that soft resignation in his voice. Like we have no choice.

"That's what *we're* for," I argue. "*We* are supposed to keep him safe. He doesn't need to know how to use a gun."

Dante is behind Mikhail, toeing his boot at the deer. He's not strong enough to shake the animal, let alone roll it over.

Mikhail lowers his voice. "No, but he needs to trust himself. He needs to have confidence that he can take care of himself. It's the same thing I'm trying to teach him in the boxing ring."

My eyes snap to his. "Boxing? Since when does he box?"

"Since a couple weeks ago." Mikhail shrugs. "He had some frustration to burn. It'll be good for him to know how to use his body."

He *does* know how to use his body, I want to argue. Dante just learned how to skip a couple months ago. When he thinks really hard, he can roll his tongue into a burrito.

Those are good, useful skills. They're all his body needs to know, as far as I'm concerned.

But it isn't just up to me. Not anymore. Mikhail and I have to make these kinds of decisions together.

Before I can even pretend to reach a compromise, Mikhail curls his hand around my cheek. "I'll tell him this is more than enough meat and we don't need to go hunting anymore."

I nuzzle my face into his hand. "Thank you."

"But he isn't like other kids, Viviana. Dante is going to have to grow up sooner than you want him to."

I nod, but only because I don't know what else to say.

I was sitting in the tub this morning so worried about how Mikhail would handle raising a daughter that I forgot to be worried about how the two of us would handle raising any child together.

As Mikhail teaches Dante how to gut and clean the animal, to show respect for its sacrifice, it's hard not to think about how different we are. Mikhail wants to hand down the things he was taught as a child; all I want to do is run from my past.

I have no idea how we'll navigate any of it. All I do know is, right now, Dante is happy.

That'll have to be enough.

25

MIKHAIL

"I like hunting with you," Dante says, a speared marshmallow held over the fire we built. "It's fun."

"I like hunting with you, too, kid."

I promised Viviana no more guns, but there's still plenty I can teach Dante in the woods. Like how to build a fire. And, just as important, how to make a s'more.

Plus, being outside makes it all seem so much more... manageable.

The last few days in the cabin have been amazing. It's like taking a deep breath after a lifetime of hyperventilating. Never slowing down. Never relaxing.

It also feels like a dream. Like a peek into the peaceful, domestic life I could have had if I was someone else. The longer it goes on, the more I just want it to end—because the more of it I experience, the worse it will hurt to let it go.

I know better than most what letting go feels like.

Viviana and Dante are not Alyona and Anzhelina. I know that. That doesn't stop my brain from drawing the parallels.

My wife and daughter needed me and I wasn't there for them. Why do I deserve a second chance at happiness now?

The question doesn't have an answer, but I still ask it to myself countless times every day. When I wake up with Viviana's silky hair spread across my chest. When Dante fills the bathtub with more bubble solution than water and turns it into "bubble mountain." Every time something even resembling contentment dares to settle in my chest, the question rears its ugly head.

Why do you deserve this when Alyona and Anzhelina are dead?

The only time I can get a single second of guiltless peace is when Viviana is coming in my arms or I'm outside in the fresh air. Since I can't fuck Viviana every minute of every day, no matter how much my body wants to, sitting around a fire in the late afternoon roasting marshmallows is a fine backup plan.

Dante points at the end of my stick. "Your marshmallow is on fire."

"Shit." The black, bubbling mass isn't even recognizable as a marshmallow. I flick it into the fire and spear a new one.

"That's a bad word. Uncle Anatoly told me not to say it when Mama is around."

"What about when your Mama isn't around?" I ask.

He can't quite bite back his smile as he whispers, "Shit."

Classic Anatoly.

I should tell Dante to watch his mouth. It's what Viviana would say. But if a boy can't cuss in the middle of the woods with his dad, when can he?

"That stays out here," I tell him. "When we're hunting together, you can cuss. But that's the only time."

He nods and scrunches up his forehead, his gaze cast to the fire. I just know he's searching his brain for every other curse word he knows. God only knows what else Anatoly has whispered to him.

Once he's covered in melted marshmallow and chocolate, Dante and I load up and head back to the house. Today amounted to little more than a hike and some birdwatching, but that's fine. Time in the woods with my boy is enough.

We're close enough to the cabin that I can smell the smoke from the fireplace when Dante reaches out and grabs my hand.

Instinctively, I flinch back. But Dante doesn't even seem to notice. He keeps a firm hold as if linking hands with me is as natural as walking on two feet.

I glance down and he's smiling to himself, staring off at the forest around us.

Anzhelina was murdered when she was still so little. The closest we ever got to this moment was when she wrapped her little hand around my finger in the hospital. She was blotchy and covered in slime, but I placed my finger against her palm and she held it tight.

If she was still alive, would I be holding each of their hands right now? Would they be dancing around my feet, fighting with each other and racing through the trees?

The image plays in my mind for a second before reality settles in.

If Anzhelina was here, Dante wouldn't be.

If Anzhelina was here, I'd still be married to Alyona. I never would have slept with Viviana. I probably wouldn't have tried to take over the Bratva from Trofim at all.

If Anzhelina and Alyona were still here, my life would be entirely different and Dante's never would have started. Viviana wouldn't be inside waiting for us right now.

This reality I'm living is as fragile as the tiny, clammy hand settled against my palm. I know exactly how quickly it can all be snatched away.

I squeeze Dante's hand just a little tighter.

26

VIVIANA

"What's wrong?"

Mikhail doesn't startle when I break the silence we've been stewing in all evening. More and more these days, I think it's impossible to surprise him. He just blinks and turns to me. "Nothing."

I tap the side of his now-cold mug of hot chocolate. "You never even took a sip of this and you haven't said a word in half an hour."

He places his mug on the coffee table. "I'm just enjoying the fire."

I'm tempted to let my weird feeling go. It's been a good day. Dante came home all jazzed up from his "boy time" in the woods. He was sugared up and muddy. I gave him a bath and read him one and a half books before he was softly snoring and drooling on his dinosaur pajamas. Now, Mikhail and I are curled up in front of a fire with mugs of hot cocoa.

It's the kind of stuff Hallmark movies are made of. It's perfect.

Except it's hard to relax when tension is radiating off of Mikhail like nuclear fallout.

I slide closer to him, my knees curled against his strong thigh. "I like staring into a fire as much as the next person, but you're not staring into it." I reach over and trace the deep line etched between his brows. "It looks like you're trying to become one with it. I'm a little worried you're going Johnny Flame on me and this whole cabin is about to be reduced to ashes."

Mikhail doesn't move. "It's just work stuff. I'm fine."

If his goal was to end my line of questioning, he'll have to try a lot harder than that.

"What work stuff?" I press, trying to hide the tinge of panic in my voice. "Are we still safe here?"

Finally, he drags his eyes from the crackling hearth to meet mine. "I'll keep you safe, Viviana. I can handle your father."

"So this is about my father?"

He shakes his head.

I want to scream. No—I want to drill into his brain and pour his thoughts out into a sifting pan so I can sort through the mess. It seems to be the only way to get to the root of what he's thinking.

"You seemed fine earlier. Did you get a call while I was putting Dante to bed? Was it Raoul or Anatoly? What's happening back at the mansion?"

Mikhail brushes his thumb across my lips. "It's nothing for you to worry about. Everything is fine."

I nip at his finger with my teeth and then snatch his hand away from my mouth.

"Except for you," I point out. "You're not fine. There's something going on in that handsome head of yours, and I want to know what it is."

He smirks. "Handsome, huh?"

"Don't act like you don't know it." I roll my eyes. "Now, is this about our safety? Or Dante? What happened in the woods today?"

"Nothing happened. He's a good kid, Viviana. You've done a good job with him."

He's distracting me with compliments, but I'm just vain enough to let him. "Thanks."

"Once he gets a proper education, he'll be on the right track."

Suddenly, I'm the tense one. Five seconds ago, I was starting to sweat under my fleece blanket. Now, I'm cold as ice.

"He loves Mrs. Steinman," I add woodenly.

"She's fine for now," Mikhail agrees, refusing to meet my eyes. "But there are good schools he could attend. Good programs where he'll learn to be independent and—"

"Never mind," I blurt.

Mikhail looks at me, that pesky line pinched between his brows again. "Hm?"

"I've changed my mind. I don't want to talk about this." My

heart is racing like I just ran a marathon and all I want to do is stop. All of this. *Now.*

Bringing up the boarding school conversation has been at the top of my to-do list for the past week, but I've been pushing it for more important tasks. Tasks like... doing literally anything else in the world aside from having that conversation.

"Why not?"

"It's like throwing a turd in a swimming pool."

A startled laugh bursts out of him, and *yes,* I want to scream, *let's go down this path instead. The one that ends with Mikhail smiling at me.*

"I just mean, we're having a good time here, aren't we?"

Mikhail nods. "We are."

"So let's not ruin it with shitty conversations and fighting."

He tucks a lock of hair behind my ear. "You think it will end in a fight?"

"A big one," I confirm. "Atomic. There will be casualties."

"I'd never hurt you, Viviana."

I trail my hand up his thigh. "Cute for you to think *you'd* be the one doing the hurting."

He snorts, but I'll do anything to keep this little family of mine together. I won't let him send Dante away.

I shove the dark thought away and focus on the way his body feels under my hand. "Things will get ugly, so I think we should skip the fight and go straight to making up."

Mikhail watches my hand slide higher and higher up his leg. As I trail my fingers over the seam of his pants, he spreads his thighs slightly.

"I'll take that as your agreement?"

Mikhail grabs my waist and lifts me onto his lap. "Stop talking or we'll be in a very different kind of hand-to-hand combat."

I arch a brow. "Then you better keep my hands busy."

He grips my neck, his fingers pressing into my spine while his thumb settles over my pulse. When his lips press against mine, I'm sure he can feel my heart rate pick up. It's why his lips are tilted into a smug smile.

That smile is why I pull away so I'm kneeling on the floor between his legs.

Finally, a flicker of surprise.

"That was a good idea," I tell him, dragging his zipper down slowly, "but I had something else in mind."

He's already rock hard and I have to fight through a fresh wave of nerves when I pull him free of his boxers.

I lean forward and his cock twitches in anticipation. When I press a kiss to the base of him, his thighs flex.

I drag my tongue along his underside, pressing wet kisses everywhere except the swollen head of him. That's on purpose. After a few passes, Mikhail knows it.

"Viviana…" he warns, fisting a hand in the hair at the base of my neck.

His corded neck is taut. There are red splotches high on his chiseled cheeks. He looks like he's seconds away from popping an aneurysm.

"Huh?" I mumble, too busy flicking my tongue along his length to enunciate. I stop short of where he's shiny from precum and meet his eyes.

They are black and searing.

"Don't give me that innocent, doe-eyed look," he growls. "You know what you're doing. You also want it as much as I do."

He's not wrong. Teasing him has left my panties a mess.

"Now," he orders, wrapping my hair around his fist in a makeshift ponytail, "open that pretty mouth and let me fuck it."

I want him too much to even attempt to argue. I press up onto my knees and take him between my lips.

Everything in Mikhail relaxes as soon as he's in my mouth. He groans, his hold on my hair loosening and his head tipping back against the couch.

He's fucked me out of my own head more than enough times. It's only right I do the same for him.

I wrap my hand around his base, pumping in time with my mouth. When I glance up, Mikhail is watching me again. He brushes his thumb over my cheek, eyes glazed over as he watches me work. When he starts lifting his hips in time with my movements, I remove my hand and take as much of him as I can into my mouth.

My eyes water when he touches the back of my throat, but the awe written on his face is all the motivation I need to stay there.

"Fuck, Viviana." He palms the front of my neck. "You look so good swallowing my cock."

I pull back for a breath, but before I can take him again, Mikhail lifts me up and settles me on his lap.

"Hey," I complain, wiggling against the erection pressed firmly against my ass. "I wasn't done."

Mikhail captures my mouth, silencing my argument with his tongue. Then he lifts me over him and slides deep inside of me, silencing any further arguments.

I moan, arching back as he stretches me. The second he's seated inside of me, he hooks my useless legs over his shoulders and stands up.

I yelp and cling to his neck, but Mikhail doesn't falter. He holds me like I weigh nothing and bounces me against him.

A string of incoherent curse words rush out of me. Somehow, I went from being in control to not being able to move a single muscle… And I've never been happier.

All I can do is cling to Mikhail's thick shoulders as he grips my hips and slams me against him again and again. The sound of slapping skin and my cries echoes around the room.

"Take off your shirt," he orders, still pistoning in and out of me.

I'm nervous to let go of him, but Mikhail has a tight hold on me. I lean back, at a perfect ninety-degree angle from his body, and ease his XL t-shirt over my head.

A strangled sound works out of his chest and he pulls my body against his. My legs slip from his shoulders, but I cinch them around his waist before they fall to the floor. He stumbles forward and sandwiches me between his chest and the wall, never slowing his thrusts.

"You're so fucking perfect." He dips his head to suck my breast into his mouth and I slide my fingers into his hair.

My body is in a frenzy, clawing at him and drawing him closer, but I've never felt more at peace.

"I love you," I gasp. I've already said the words before, but I still tense as they leave my lips. Every muscle in my body tightens and Mikhail growls against my neck.

"Again," he demands, his teeth scraping over my skin.

"I love you," I repeat, clenching around him again.

I say the words and tighten around his cock until he's glistening with sweat and shaking in my arms.

I'm on the edge, but I want Mikhail to fall first. I press my lips to his ear. "This pussy is yours. Fill it up."

His hips stutter and he roars as he pumps into me.

I feel him twitch deep inside of me and, suddenly, the clenching is beyond my control. My orgasm milks Mikhail's until we're both spent. Until we have no choice but to sink to the floor in a pile of sweaty limbs.

"Well, did we make up?" he asks a few minutes later, pressing a lazy kiss to my peaked nipple.

I throw my arm over my eyes and nod. "With interest. I think we can skip the makeup sex portion of the next five fights, at least."

"You think we'll fight five more times?"

"Maybe by tomorrow," I laugh. The sound cuts off sharply when he slides his tongue down the center of my stomach. "What are you doing?"

"You know I like to be prepared." He grips my thighs and presses them apart roughly. His warm breath tickles over my sensitive skin. "We should bank a few more, at least. Get ahead."

He lowers his mouth to me and we make up for hours.

27

MIKHAIL

I stare at the message notification for the tenth time, waiting for the will to respond.

Anatoly messaged yesterday and said the new security protocols were in place at the mansion. As of eighteen hours ago, my mansion became the safest place in the state for Viviana and Dante to be.

As of twelve hours ago, Raoul warned me that the Greeks are about to make a move.

Still, even with the real world threatening to bang down the door, I can't quite bring myself to leave this cabin.

"Why are you awake?" Viviana mutters sleepily. Her eyes are still closed, but she presses her naked body into my side and flops her arm over my chest. Her body is warm and soft.

"It's morning."

She shakes her head. "It's morning for people who didn't have hours and hours of sex last night. For us, it's still the middle of the night."

I kept her up long past midnight, wringing orgasms out of her until she swore she'd die. Even then, I didn't want to stop. Stopping meant that our last night in this cabin would be over.

We were sitting on the couch in front of a fire with mugs of hot chocolate like we were in a goddamn Christmas puzzle. The night was perfect—and I could feel it slipping through my fingers.

I was deep in my head and I almost fucked it all up. I was quiet and sullen. As is her way, Viviana pulled me out of it.

It was a nice way to say goodbye.

I kiss her arm and slip out from under the blankets. She whines behind me, stretching herself across both sides of the bed. "Stay here."

"Someone has to load the supplies."

Finally, her eyes open. She sits up and leans against the headboard. The comforter falls to her waist, revealing the swell of her bare breasts and the curve of her waist.

Fuck the supplies. Maybe I should stay in bed.

She rubs at her sleepy eyes. "Supplies for what? Do we have plans?"

I turn away from the temptation and tug on my thermals. "I told Dante I'd take him ice fishing if the ice was thick enough. It's been below freezing for the last week. The lake should be ready."

I slide into snow pants and turn back as Viviana stretches her arms over her head and rolls her neck side to side.

I bite the inside of my cheek to stop myself from lunging across the bed at her. If we only have a few more hours in this cabin, I want to spend them inside of her. But we have our son to think about.

"Okay," she hums.

"Okay, what?"

"Okay, I'll come."

I blink, clearing my lusty head. "You're going to come with us? Fishing?"

"Ice fishing," she clarifies. "Yeah. Might as well. I want to be with the two of you."

"It's going to be cold."

She rolls her eyes. "You know, I actually guessed that. The 'ice' in the name kinda gave it away."

"You hate the cold." She spent all of last night with her ice-cold toes wedged under my calf.

She stands up and pouts, the blankets falling away behind her. "I can handle it. I'm made of tougher stuff than you think."

After everything she's been through, everything I did to and on and inside of her, she isn't wrong. The fact she's still standing is a miracle.

"A mafia princess roughing it in the woods." I shake my head and pull her naked body flush to mine. "That wasn't on my bingo card."

"What about being outfished by a mafia princess? Was *that* on your bingo card?"

"Is that a challenge?" I tease, pinching her waist.

She yelps and whacks my hand away. "It's a guarantee, Mr. *Pakhan*. Prepare to be dazzled." Then she sashays into the bathroom, leaving me achingly hard but smiling like a damn fool.

"I caught one!" Dante cries out, no doubt sending whatever tiny fish might have come our way in the last half-hour darting back to deeper waters.

Viviana tosses me a look over one of the three ham sandwiches she packed. They were meant to be for lunch, but she's been so bored that she's eaten everything she brought for herself only an hour into our excursion.

"Are you sure?" she sighs. "You've said that a few times and every time—"

"I'm sure!" He tugs on his little pole, jerking like he's fighting with a shark under the water.

Last time, he was standing on his own hook. I'm actually curious to see what he "caught" this go around.

I push up from my folding chair and cross the ice. "Let's see, bud. What do we have—"

Dante pulls back and loses his hold on the reel. It starts to spin.

"Holy shit, he actually caught something." I stop the reel and start reversing course, bringing the line in.

"Holy shit, I caught something!" Dante yells over his shoulder.

Viviana chokes on a laugh. "Dante! Watch your mouth!"

"Dad said I could!" he proudly announces.

I'm too busy reeling in the fish to think about how much trouble that little line is going to get me in later. "You must have caught a whale," I tease.

Dante's eyes snap to me, wide. "Really?!"

"No, not really. No whales in this lake. But this must be a big one. It's putting up quite a fight."

I let Dante take control as much as he can, so the back-and-forth goes on longer than it needs to. Finally, the little fish flops up onto the ice and Dante throws his hands over his head, victorious. Well, he tries to throw his hands over his head. The layers of bulk Viviana insisted he wear make it hard for him to move, let alone celebrate. But he gives it his all.

"I catched a fish!" He runs in a circle around the hole we cut, skipping and twirling. "I catched a fish!"

Viviana is grinning, but she waves him back. "Careful of the hole, bud. Don't fall in."

"He wouldn't even fit with all the layers."

She rolls her eyes at me. "Still. Be careful. Dying of hypothermia definitely isn't on the bingo card."

I gave Dante a long lecture before we even stepped foot onto the ice about staying away from the mouth of the river. The flowing water there makes the ice thin. But it's around a bend in the trees and Dante is still too scared of bears to venture far from us.

"Are we going to eat it?" Dante sidles closer to me, watching his fish flop on the ice. "I can clean it by myself. I watched you do the deer."

"Cleaning a deer is a lot different than cleaning a fish."

"I can do it," he insists. He grips my sleeve, tugging hard. "Please, Dad. Pleeeeeeeeeeeeee—"

"Fine." I laugh and hold up the line. "But turn around and take a picture. Your mom is going to want to remember this."

Just as I suspected, as soon as we turn around, Viviana is kneeling on the ice, her phone out and ready. "Say cheese!"

Once the Kodak moment is captured, Dante is all business. He leads me to the camp we've set up along the bank and unrolls my collection of knives.

"I can't watch this," Viviana declares before Dante even touches a knife. I'm not sure if it's because of her morning sickness or the fact her baby boy is holding a knife. Probably both.

Then we get to work.

My entire life, I've struggled to watch people do a bad job at something that I know I can do perfectly. I've never been able to stand by and let someone struggle. But teaching Dante how to control his blade is so rewarding that it's worth all the hunks of fish meat lost to his clumsy movements.

"Like this?" he asks, slowly moving the knife down the fish's backbone.

"Perfect, bud. You're doing great."

He grins and keeps going and I do my best to savor this moment. To remember the angry kid who crashed into my gym a couple weeks ago and taught my heavyweight bag a lesson. In that moment, I was positive I'd ruined him.

But just like his mom, Dante is made of tougher stuff than that. He's resilient.

I think he'll turn out just fine.

Once the fish is prepped and there are no dangerous weapons involved, Dante's interest wanes. "I want to skate!" He tries to twirl in a circle, but the bottoms of his snow boots grip the ice and he ends up kind of staggering around.

"We're about to eat." Viviana gestures to the picnic lunch she packed. "You can find the napkins or pour the soup into—"

"I'm going to skate." He glides clumsily along the surface of the ice. His breath puffs in front of his face in little clouds.

"Be careful!" Viviana calls after him.

Dante waves his puffy arm over his head at her in his version of confirmation.

"He'll be fine. Don't worry."

"Of course *you* would say that." She wipes her hands on her coat and stands up, eyes narrowed. "When did you tell our six-year-old that he could curse?"

Here we go.

I wrap an arm around her waist, pulling her close before she can get mad and shove me away. "I told him it was okay if we were hunting."

"And fishing, apparently?"

I shrug. "He extrapolated. It was a moment of excitement. It was all in good fun."

"Tell that to Mrs. Steinman when he drops an F-bomb after acing his spelling test," she snaps.

"Better an F-bomb than an F." She tries to look annoyed with me, but she can't quite manage it. Her mouth twists at the corners and I bend down and press a kiss there.

"He's a good kid. A few curse words won't kill him."

She wraps her arms around my waist, tightening until it's almost painful. "No, but the moment he flings one of those curse words at me because I tell him to eat his vegetables or make his bed, *I'll* kill *you*."

I pretend to think it over. "Seems fair."

She rolls her eyes and tries to turn away, but I hold onto her. How can I not? This is it. This afternoon is the last one we'll have out here. The last peaceful day we'll have in a long while, if Viv's father and Christos Drakos have anything to say about it.

Viviana softens against me. "What's wrong?"

I should tell her—warn her that we need to leave. But I don't want to shatter the moment. As it turns out, I don't need to.

The sound of cracking ice and Dante screaming shatters it for me.

28

MIKHAIL

Viviana and I break apart, both turning and running towards… nothing.

The lake is empty. Dante is nowhere in sight.

"Dante!" Fog clouds in front of my face, blocking my view.

How long has it been since I last saw him? Thirty seconds? A minute? How far could he have gone?

"Dante!" Viviana cries just as I see his boots.

He must have kicked them off to slide better on the ice. They're laying a few yards from the bend in the trees that marks the mouth of the river. Which is why I break into a dead sprint.

My feet slip out from under me again and again, but I keep moving. The world flies past as each second stretches and morphs. It's been five seconds since he screamed. Ten, at the most. That's not a long time… unless he's underwater. Unless the layers he's bundled in are waterlogged and he's slipping deeper and deeper into the dark.

I lower my head and run faster.

"Dante!" Viviana is calling his name again and again behind me. I can hear her falling back. I want to turn around and tell her to stay put, but I know it won't do any good. That's our son out there. There's no way she'll wait patiently on the bank.

I jump over his snow boots and follow the edge of the water around the bend.

For a single second, my chest eases.

Dante is standing on the ice. He's above water. *He's alive.*

He turns towards me and his eyes are two black circles in his pale face. He's terrified.

"Dad…" he whimpers.

He takes one step closer to me and the ice shatters.

The cracking sound is like gunshots. But instead of ducking, I lunge forward.

I only make it two more steps before the ice starts to thin. I drop to my stomach, spreading out my weight as far as I can to keep the cracks from spreading further.

"Kick!" I yell, army crawling towards him. "Kick your feet, Dante! Fight!"

He's splashing, but I can't see if he's above water from this vantage point.

I might be too late. He could disappear under the water.

I shove the grim thoughts aside and focus on getting to him.

I hear the moment Viviana rounds the bend behind me because she screams. "Stay back!" I yell over my shoulder. I don't have time to stop to make sure Viviana is following orders; I just have to hope she's smart enough to know I can't save them both.

I might not even be able to save him.

I'm making achingly slow progress towards the cracked ice, but if I want to get Dante out of here alive, this is the only way. It would take longer to crash through a different spot in the ice and have to fight my way towards him like that. I need to get to the hole he fell into.

As I get closer to the fracture point, the ice is thin and gray. It splinters under me, painfully cold water creeping over the surface and cutting straight through my coat and thermal layers. I hiss, but I don't stop. Dante's bright blue coat is a blotch of color below the surface of the water. His face is submerged and he isn't moving.

"Dante!"

He doesn't budge—and everything I've ever been taught goes out the fucking window.

I should stop at the edge and strip down. The fewer layers I have on, the more likely it is I'll be able to get us both out.

But there isn't time.

I throw myself the last few feet into the water.

The cold filets me. It freezes the breath in my lungs and everything in me wants to *get out*. But I splash closer. Dante bobs in the water like a dinghy, still and lifeless. A small sense of relief floods through me when I get my numb arms around him and drag him above the surface. The relief is gone as soon as I realize how rigid he is.

His lips are blue and he isn't breathing.

"This way!" Viviana is standing on the bank, waving me towards her. "Come this way. It's faster."

I'm so cold that I can't even think about whether she's right. I feel my body shutting down with every passing second. If I don't get out now, we never will. So I move towards Viviana.

She's like an angel in her white coat set against the dark trees. I follow the dot of light as black creeps into the edges of my vision. I do my best to keep Dante on my shoulder and out of the water. Not that it matters. He's twenty pounds heavier, at least, just from the frozen lake water his clothes soaked up.

The water gets shallower as I approach the edge. I have to break through the ice with my shins to make it to the shore. I'm sure I'm cut to hell, but I don't think about any of it. As soon as I'm clear of the shore, I lay Dante on the ground, rip open his coat, and press my hands into his chest.

Viviana collapses next to him. She tilts his head back and blows into his mouth.

Neither of us know what the fuck we're doing, but there's nothing else we can do. We have to try.

Viviana blows another breath. As soon as she's done, I start pumping on his chest again. It feels like it's been hours of breathing and compressions, but it can't have been more than thirty seconds. Then, between one pump and the next, Dante coughs.

Water pours out of his mouth and I quickly roll him onto his side to help him get it all out.

"Oh my God!" Viviana presses his soaked hair back from his forehead. Her hands are shaking.

Dante coughs again and then starts to cry.

It's the most beautiful fucking sound I've ever heard.

"We have to get him inside." My teeth are chattering so hard I'm not sure Viviana understands what I'm saying. But she grabs Dante's arm and helps me lift him.

He isn't heavy, but it feels like my arms are frozen solid. I can barely bend my elbows.

Viviana leads the way through the trees, cutting through overgrown bushes and disregarding the path entirely. We don't have time for it.

After what feels like hours, the cabin comes into view. "We're almost there, kid," I whisper through my chattering teeth. "Hold on."

Dante has stopped crying, but only because he's shaking as hard as I am.

As soon as we get inside, I head for the bathroom off of the main bedroom. It's the only tub large enough for both of us.

Viviana drops to her knees and turns the hot water on.

"Undress him," I tell her, gesturing to Dante. Then I turn the knobs back to lukewarm, at most. As bad as the cold water felt, dipping our half-frozen bodies into hot water would be just as painful. We need to warm up slowly.

Viviana tears away layer after layer from Dante while I peel my snow pants and thermals down. I strip down to my boxers and step into the half-full tub. The water is barely above cold, but I hiss as I lower one foot and then the other. I slide beneath the surface reluctantly and hold my arms open for Dante.

"Hand him to me. Now."

There are still tears streaming down Viviana's face, but she's focused. Her mouth is set in a determined line as she lifts our pale, shivering son off the floor and hands him to me.

As soon as he touches the water, he recoils, but I force him in little by little.

"I know it hurts," I soothe. My teeth are still chattering, but it's less intense. "This will help."

Dante is too weak to fight, so I curl him against my chest and hold his body under the water.

As the pain starts to ebb, I make the water pouring into the tub a little warmer and then a little warmer still. After a few minutes, we've both stopped shivering. A few minutes after that, Dante is asleep in my arms, too exhausted to keep his eyes open.

It's only then that Viviana falls apart.

She claws at my neck and shoulders—every part of me she can reach above the water. "You saved him, Mikhail. You saved him."

I lean my cheek against the crown of her head. "Of course I did. I'll always save him."

But I was almost too late.

I can feel Dante breathing steadily in and out, but I'll never forget the way it felt when he was still and damn near dead in my arms. I'll work my entire life to make sure I never get that close to losing him again. *Either* of them.

"When you went in, I didn't know if—" She sobs, burying her face in my neck. Her breath is hot on my cool skin. "I thought I was going to lose you both. I thought we were all going to die out there."

"You weren't in the water," I remind her gently.

She pulls back, her green eyes clear and bright as she takes me in. "I was going in after you. After both of you. There's no point in me being alive if you two aren't here."

I wanted to keep Viviana at arm's length.

When we got married, it was out of some twisted obligation to take care of her and our offspring. I didn't care about her.

Not the way I do now.

"Viviana," I breathe.

She looks me over like she's searching for something she can fix. "Yeah? What is it?"

I hold Dante tighter against my chest and curl my cold hand around Viviana's neck. She flinches, but then leans into my palm, giving me her weight.

I want all of it.

All of this.

"Will you marry me?"

29

VIVIANA

"Did you hit your head?" I ask. I run my fingers through his damp hair to check for myself. A few chips of ice cling to the ends, but there's no blood. No cartoonishly-large goose eggs that I can see. He looks perfect. So I gently remind him, "Mikhail, we're already married."

"That didn't count. It wasn't real."

"It's not real?" I pull back. "It wasn't…"

There was a priest. Rings. Vows.

Sure, the ceremony was thrown together at the last minute and I wanted the "'til death do us part" chapter of things to happen much sooner than later, but it seemed real enough.

"Breathe." Mikhail grabs my arm, his thumb working a soothing circle along the inside of my wrist. "The piece of paper is real, but the feelings weren't. Not back then. Not the way they are now."

Oh.

He's watching me so closely I feel like he's inside my head. Like my thoughts are playing out on a Jumbotron for him to enjoy. Funnily enough, that doesn't scare me the way it used to. There's nothing in there I don't want him to see.

No doubts. No secrets.

He knows all of me… and he still wants to get married? *Again*?

I don't realize I've said that part out loud until Mikhail answers. "I don't want anyone to question who you are to me." He thumbs the column of my throat possessively. "Especially not you."

Mikhail's hand shifts to my cheek to dab away the tears that finally forced their way through my shock. He gives me a tentative smile. "Are these because you're happy?"

After the emotional Tilt-A-Whirl of the last few hours, I'm barely functioning. Self-awareness definitely isn't on the table.

"I d-don't know," I stammer. He frowns and I rush to correct myself. "I mean, yes! Yes. Of course I'm happy. I just don't know—I didn't see this—I don't have a dress."

He raises his eyebrows. "Is that your only argument against? Because, to be honest, I prefer you without one."

A wild laugh bursts out of me. "Are you telling me you like the way I look naked in the middle of our marriage proposal?"

"Only if it means you're going to accept." His calloused fingers slide down my hand to circle the gaudy ring I chose for myself a couple months earlier. He strokes the length of my finger and my God, I didn't know knuckles had so many nerve endings. "Though I'm definitely not above forcing the woman I love down the aisle again."

That's me. I'm that woman.

I'm not sure I'll ever get used to that.

I turn my hand in his, stroking my fingers over his rough palm. "Another forced wedding? You never learn, do you?"

"There's nothing to learn. I'm just finally admitting what I knew all along: I want you to be mine forever, Viviana."

Tears flood my vision at the tenderness in his voice. All I see is the blurry shape of him reaching for me and pulling me against his neck. I reach beneath the warm water and grab Dante's little hand. He's still sleeping, but he squeezes back. Like, even in his dreams, he knows it's me.

That's the way it's been with Mikhail. The moment I saw him, I felt it. Felt this.

We've been fumbling through the dark for years, always moving towards each other even when we had no idea why. Now, we're finally here, and I'm never letting him go again.

Anatoly and Raoul are at the cabin within the hour with a doctor in tow. Where they found a doctor willing to commute on short notice to the middle of nowhere for a cabin call is none of my business, I decide.

"I didn't have to put a gun to his head, if that's what you were going to ask," Anatoly whispers in my ear when they arrive. He pulls me into a tight hug that lifts my feet off the floor.

"I wasn't going to ask anything." Was I thinking it? Obviously. I'm not stupid.

"Tell that to your judgmental face." He kisses the top of my head. "It's good to see you."

Being in this little bubble with Dante and Mikhail has been a little slice of magic, but it's not a lie when I tell Anatoly I'm happy to see him, too.

I step back to let Raoul through the door, but he surprises me by wrapping his arms around me and squeezing tight.

"Anatoly didn't put a gun to his head," he repeats, his voice low. "I did."

It makes sense, then, why the doctor gives Raoul a very wide berth as he tromps through the door.

He's a middle-aged man with a thick mustache and even thicker glasses. He offers a tight smile. "I'm Dr. Price. Where's the patient?"

Dante has been bundled in the bottom bunk in his room since we took him out of the tub. He seems fine, just exhausted. I'd never be able to completely relax until a professional looked him over, though.

"You did everything right," Dr. Price tells us after a thorough examination.

I squeeze Mikhail's hand. "It was all Mikhail. He pulled Dante out of the water and did compressions."

"She gave him mouth-to-mouth," Mikhail adds.

"But I turned the water on hot when we got inside." I shake my head, still disappointed in myself that I didn't know better. "You're the one who turned it to the right temperature. If you hadn't been there, I would have burned him."

"Are we having a compliment battle?" Anatoly is leaning against the doorframe, his arms crossed. "Someone tell me how pretty I am."

Mikhail rolls his eyes and presses his lips behind my ear. "It was a team effort. You did great, Viviana."

Dante leans around Dr. Price. "I think you're pretty, Uncle Nat."

Anatoly winks at him. "That's because you have impeccable taste, little man."

Dr. Price looks Dante over three times in total, assuring us each time that he is perfectly fine. His lungs sound clear and his body temperature is normal.

"He's young and resilient," he announces, wrapping his stethoscope around his neck. "I'm sure he'll bounce back."

"I'm sure he will. Especially since you're going to stay and monitor him tonight." Mikhail arches one brow in a silent challenge.

Given the fact the good doctor had a gun to his head no more than two hours ago, he isn't in much of an arguing mood.

"It never hurts to be thorough," he mutters, dropping his medical bag at the foot of the bed with a sigh.

It turns out abduction is hot when it's done in the name of protecting my child. Who would've guessed?

Dante drifts to sleep a few minutes later and Mikhail and I meet up with Anatoly and Raoul in the kitchen.

"I want one of you to sleep in the room with Dante," Mikhail orders. "I don't care which of you it is, but I don't want the doctor alone with him all night."

"I can do it," I offer.

Mikhail starts to answer, but Anatoly cuts in. "On your wedding night, Viv? Absolutely not."

"My wedding—Who told you?" I look from Mikhail to Anatoly. "It just happened an hour ago."

Anatoly bats his eyes at his brother. "Lover Boy over there just couldn't wait to share the news. He called and told me to bring a doctor and a priest."

"So you did hear me. I wasn't sure, since you didn't fucking listen. One out of two isn't a great showing." Mikhail wraps an arm around me. His hand is splayed across my hip and I lean back into him.

"We don't need a priest," I whisper. "It can be just the two of us. You and me."

He swoops his thumb along my hip bone, sending tremors through me. He saved our son's life and proposed to me in the same day. With the way I'm feeling, it might be best if a man of the cloth isn't around to judge.

Anatoly claps his hands together. "Well, you'll be happy to know—"

"They really won't." Raoul drags a hand over his jaw and gives me a sympathetic grimace. "I swear, I tried to avoid this."

"You'll be *happy* to *know*," Anatoly repeats, a little louder to be heard over Raoul's shit-talking, "that after the last time you made me run around the city looking for a justice of the peace who made house calls, I decided to take matters into my own hands."

"What the hell does that mean?" Mikhail asks as Anatoly digs in his pocket for his phone.

He clicks on the screen and turns it towards us.

I squint, reading the bolded words on the webpage as virtual confetti falls down from the search bar. *Oh, dang, you're ordained.* I look at Anatoly over the phone. "That can't possibly be legit."

"I promise you that *Vow or Never* is a very legit business. I paid thirty dollars and my official certificate is coming in the mail within the next sixty days."

"No," Mikhail says, aghast.

"Unfortunately, yes. I would have it already, but my name was misspelled on the first one. Somewhere out there, Anthony Novikov is an ordained minister and has no idea."

"I meant, 'No, there's no way in hell you're officiating my wedding.'"

Raoul claps a hand on Anatoly's shoulder. "I told you he'd hate it."

Anatoly shakes him off. "You expect too much, Mikky. Kidnapping a medical professional and a man of God in the same afternoon is too far. Luckily for you, I'm the next best thing."

"If you're the next best thing to a man of God, then God help us all." Mikhail pinches the bridge of his nose like there's a headache threatening to end his life.

Anatoly pockets his phone and presses his palms together. "You know I'm Team Mikiana. Or Vivail. Whichever you prefer. The point is, I'm on your side and I would never disrespect the sacred ceremony that will be your *second* shotgun wedding."

I tip my chin back until I can see the hard line of Mikhail's jaw and the amusement he can't quite hide dancing in his eyes. "I don't mind, if you don't. I just want to be married to you."

His hand flattens over my stomach and he pulls me tight against him. I feel his hard length against my back. "As long as we end the day joined forever, I don't care."

There's a double entendre there somewhere but I'm too busy staring up at him, breathless, to find it.

"Sooo…" Anatoly whistles awkwardly. "Am I suiting up, then?"

Mikhail releases me to grab the front of his older brother's shirt. "Don't fuck this up, Nat."

Anatoly just grins.

30

VIVIANA

We get married for the second time at the base of the stairs.

While I was busy making myself look like I hadn't spent the day ice-fishing, saving my son's life, and then crying both horrified and happy tears, Raoul and Anatoly placed candles on every step and draped a set of extra bedsheets from the ceiling like a canopy.

It's more than I expected. More than I need, for sure.

I would have happily made these vows to Mikhail in our bed, wrapped in each other and a sea of blankets, without any witnesses at all. The only thing that matters is the man waiting for me. And the little boy cuddled in the chair just behind him.

"You look pretty, Mama," Dante whispers as I approach.

My heart swells and I kneel down in front of him to press a kiss to the end of his nose. "Thanks, bud."

Anatoly showed up with a backseat full of dresses. Mikhail

heard me stammering about having nothing to wear to a wedding and covered his bases. Smart man.

I was worried none of them would fit now that I'm getting close to ten weeks pregnant, but they all fit perfectly. I settled on a white off-the-shoulder number with lace sleeves and a long skirt, and against all odds, I actually feel like a bride.

What really drives home that feeling is turning to face my husband. The man I love so much I'm going to marry him twice.

Mikhail is wearing dark chinos and a cashmere sweater that highlights his broad shoulders and tapered waist. There isn't a tux in the world that could make him look better than he does right now.

Plus, a sweater is easier to peel off, so the pros definitely outweigh the cons.

He holds out a hand to me, the edge of his full mouth tilted upward. "You ready?"

"Always," I breathe, moving to stand next to him.

The last time we stood like this, I wanted to hate Mikhail with every fiber of my being. Part of me really did hate him.

I hated him for tracking me down and upending my life.

I hated him for forcing me into what he promised would be a loveless marriage with him.

Most of all, I hated him for making me want him so badly when I thought he didn't want anything at all to do with me.

Now, I know the truth—and I couldn't pretend to hate him even if I tried.

We make our vows in a happy daze, which must mean Anatoly didn't try to sneak anything ridiculous into the ceremony. Even if he did, I might not have noticed.

"By the power vested in me by *VowOrNever.com*," Anatoly intones with all the seriousness he can muster, "I now pronounce you husband and wife. Mikhail, you may kiss your bride."

Mikhail snaps me against him and grips my jaw with firm fingers.

"Is the kiss legally binding?" I whisper, biting back a smile. It's the same question he asked after our first wedding. When we left without a kiss and slept in separate rooms. When I was still trying to convince myself I didn't want him.

Now, I'm putty in his hands. Even while I'm teasing him, my head tips back and my lips part.

"No, it's not," he says, leaning over me. His breath is hot on my skin. I shiver. "But we're doing it because I really fucking want to."

The kiss is gentle, but desire is threaded through every second. His fingers flex on my jaw. His hand tightens around my waist. As he parts my lips and sucks the tip of my tongue, I feel the restraint required not to take it further.

Restraint I sure as hell don't have.

I cling to him, moaning softly into his mouth like we're alone. Which we definitely are not. Anatoly clears his throat once. Twice.

"Alrighty then," he finally announces. "I now present Mr. and Mrs. Novikov."

Mikhail slides his hands to my waist and pulls me gently away from him. "Later," he promises, squeezing my hip. "Later."

We all eat a slice of some frozen cheesecake they found in a bodega on their way out of the city. It's white chocolate raspberry and not half-bad. Then Anatoly announces it's time for them to go.

"Go where? You're staying here," I tell him.

"No," he says, "we're not."

"Anatoly and Raoul are going to take Dante and the doctor back to the mansion for the night," Mikhail informs me. "They're going to stay there while we—"

"Consummate your marriage loudly and energetically," Anatoly finishes.

I slap his arm. "That's not funny."

"It was one hundred percent not a joke. I have no desire to listen to you all through the wall all night. Plus, Dr. Price has been through enough." He hitches a thumb over his shoulder to where the doctor is sitting in the corner, watching us all with a mixture of disbelief and wariness.

Clearly, he's not sure what to make of this hostage-situation-turned-wedding. Listening to his captors go at it all night might be the poor man's breaking point. And as much as I want to correct Anatoly and tell him Mikhail and I can control ourselves, I don't have a lot of evidence to back that up. What I *do* have is a flutter deep in my core whenever Mikhail's body brushes against mine.

My face flames and I turn to Mikhail. "You think this is a good idea?"

"I do." He runs a hand over his chin. "I probably should have taken you both back to the mansion yesterday. Now that the new security system is up, it's the safest place for both of you. I just wasn't ready to leave."

"Neither was I." The last thing I want is for him to think Dante's accident this morning was his fault. I would have agreed to live out here if he'd suggested it.

Mikhail fists the fabric at my waist and I don't think there's anywhere in the world I wouldn't follow him.

"Now, neither of you have to leave," Anatoly says suddenly. "But I do. Because the sexual tension in this room is unbearable."

Mikhail takes a swing at Anatoly and he laughs. I dodge both of them to kneel down in front of Dante. He's only been awake for a couple hours, but his eyes are already starting to droop closed.

"Your dad and Uncle Nat were talking and they think you should go back to the mansion tonight, but—"

"You're staying here." He rubs at one of his eyes sleepily. "I know. Uncle Nat told me."

"Is that okay?" I ask. "Because if it isn't, I'll come with you. We can all go back to the mansion tonight. It would be nice to be back in my own room."

Although, when I blink, I see my father sitting on the end of my bed, waiting for me.

I shove the thought away and focus on Dante's face. "You don't have to go alone if you aren't ready. I'll come with you."

"Uncle Nat said we were going to have a boys' night. It can't be a boys' night if you're there," he points out.

"Then it doesn't have to be a boys' night. It can be a family night instead."

He wrinkles his nose at that idea. "I want to go with Uncle Nat and Uncle Raoul. It will be fun."

He feels safe with them.

He's happy.

He has a family.

These are all good things. Knowing that doesn't stop me from planting wet kisses all over his face. "I'll miss you. I love you. I'll miss you. I love you."

"Ew!" he squeals, giggling and trying to fight me off. "Gross, Mama!"

"Tell me you love me and I'll quit," I threaten between a kiss to each of his cheeks.

"I love you!" he gasps. "I love you."

I hold his precious face in my hands and rub our noses together. "I really do love you, bud."

He rolls his eyes, but smiles.

Anatoly and Raoul make quick work of loading all of Dante's things into the Jeep. Dr. Price follows after them, glancing once towards the trees like maybe he'll make a run for it before thinking better of it and getting into the car.

Then they're gone.

And we're alone.

Anatoly wasn't wrong about the sexual tension. The air sizzles with it. It's frigid outside, but I barely feel the cold.

I fold my hands in front of me. "Well, what now?"

Before I can even turn to look at Mikhail, he scoops me off my feet, cradles me against his chest, and carries me across the threshold of the cabin.

31

VIVIANA

The candles have burnt down to useless nubs, trails of smoke curling into the air when Mikhail carries me through the cabin and straight up the stairs.

"Where are we going?"

"Our bed," he growls, kicking open the bedroom door only to kick it shut behind him a second later.

He lowers me to my feet at the end of our bed and stands back. His eyes trace the line of my dress, lingering where the neckline dips low over my chest, where my hair curls against my shoulder.

I log the look on his face as one to remember. Something to pull out when I'm not feeling my best. If a man like him can look at me like this, things can't be too bad.

"I've dreamt about this moment." He reaches out to stroke my collarbone, leaving goosebumps in his wake.

"Having sex with me?" I laugh nervously. "You've done that before."

His careful assessment is setting me on edge. I'm used to falling into heady lust with Mikhail and tearing each other's clothes off. But this slow admiration is still new.

I feel like my skin doesn't fit right over my bones.

His hand whispers over my shoulder, slow, thoughtful. He fingers my lace sleeve before gripping my elbow, like he somehow knows I'm seconds away from diving under the blankets to hide from how *seen* I feel.

"Having sex with *my wife*," he clarifies.

"I've been your wife for months."

He ignores me, wrapping his arms around my back until he finds the zipper along my spine. He draws it down carefully, the vibration tickling across my skin. "Do you have any idea how much I wanted you the day we got married?"

The oxygen in the room is gone. I should tell him I can't breathe, but I'm too busy enjoying the slow suffocation. His body is feverish against mine.

"I remember you saying something about having some frustration to burn off."

He laughs. "More than you can imagine. I was lying to myself and to you. I told everyone it was just a business deal, but I couldn't fucking *think* when you were close to me, Viviana."

I thought the way Mikhail touches me would be the death of me, but his heartfelt confessions are ruining me ten times faster. I'm frozen, trapped between attacking him with every ounce of the desire burning through me and standing perfectly still so that he keeps saying such lovely things.

His hands slide under the delicate fabric of my dress. They float around my ribcage and then tighten, enveloping me until I'm crushed against him. He works his fingertips down my back, kneading and stroking his way under the skirt of the dress, and dragging our hips together so I can feel how hard he is against my stomach.

We're still clothed. He's giving me a hug. That's all this is—an intense, erotically-charged hug, but a hug nonetheless. It shouldn't feel this good. It wouldn't if he was anyone else.

But Mikhail isn't anyone else.

He's mine.

"*I* can't think now," I admit breathlessly. "You feel so good."

His hands scrape lower, caressing the backs of my thighs like he's trying to memorize my topography. Like there might be a test later. If there is, I volunteer to proctor that exam.

"It all got so much worse when you were gone." His breath is hot on my neck.

All I can think about is how much I want his lips there instead. How much I want him to take a bite of me. But I'm also hanging on every word. We haven't talked about what happened after he sent me away. Not really.

"I couldn't sleep." He kisses my thundering pulse. "I couldn't eat. I spent every day beating a punching bag, trying to forget the way you feel, the way you smell…" The flat of his tongue follows the curve of my jawline. I curl my fingers through his hair as his stubble scrapes my cheek. "The way you taste. I was going crazy."

I shouldn't like the idea of Mikhail suffering over me, but send me straight to hell because I really, *really* do.

"I'm going crazy right now, Mikhail." I press away from his chest and drag my dress down so it's pooled around my waist. My nipples pebble from the cool air and his hot gaze. "I need you."

He drops his forehead to mine, stroking his hands over my waist and higher to curl around my breasts. He flicks his thumb over the point, making me shiver.

"And *I* can't fuck you again until you understand what this means to me. What *you* mean to me."

Is it possible to orgasm from words? From soft touches?

"I know what this means. I do."

He shakes his head. "You don't. Because we were in the hospital and you thought I might send you away. You didn't tell me you were pregnant because you couldn't trust me."

"I'm sorry. I should have—"

He silences me with a kiss that has me stretching onto my toes for more. I circle my arms around his neck and I think we've said enough. When he kisses me like this, what else is there to say?

His lips press against the corner of my mouth, my cheek. "I should have told you right then what I knew the first moment I saw you. I should have told you last week, last month, and every single day of the six years we lost."

My chest shudders and I have to grip his shoulders to steady myself. "Told me what?"

"That I want you, Viviana. All of you, in every way I can have you. In my bed, in my head, in my cold, busted-up heart." He cups my face with hands that are strong enough to tear apart the world, but right now are the only thing holding mine together. "I almost lost you. Today, we almost lost Dante.

And I—fuck, I can't spend another second worrying that you don't know exactly how much you've fucking destroyed me."

He's breathing hard like we've already had sex. Like tearing that confession out of his chest took everything he had.

I don't have the right words to respond to him. I'm so desperate for him I can barely stand. So I press my hand over his thundering heart and stretch onto my toes, dragging every inch of our bodies together. "Mikhail Novikov, I love you."

All at once, the tension in him eases. His arms soften around me and his lips find mine. The kiss is soft for a handful of seconds before he tips my head back and parts my jaw. Before his tongue is swirling over mine, licking over the roof of my mouth like flames.

I moan and he trails more fire down my neck and my chest. He drops lower, taking the rest of the dress with him until I'm shivering in front of him in nothing but a pair of white satin panties. He licks the soft material, sending sparks up my spine. Then he shoves them aside and presses his warm mouth to me.

"Mikhail!" I fist my hands in his hair and struggle to stand. He bands a strong arm behind my thighs, holding me against him while his tongue dips into me again and again.

I gasp for breath like I'm coming up from underwater, but the pressure in my chest ratchets up with every press of his mouth.

Then he slides two fingers into me, and I'm gone.

The moment they curl inside of me, stroking nerve endings that are already sizzling, I bow back and scream.

Mikhail's free hand shoots up my spine to keep me from falling backward. His fingers spread wide across my back, holding me steady while he absolutely undoes me.

As the pleasure ebbs away, he flicks his tongue over my clit. I'm oversensitive and I pull on his hair, bringing him up to my mouth.

He's smiling like he knows exactly what he's doing. His mouth is shiny with me and I drag my tongue over his lower lip. He growls, chasing my lips, kissing me back onto the bed. It's heat and desire and need, but when he sits back on his calves and looks down at me, the moment turns soft.

"I'm almost naked and you're still in your clothes," I complain.

He grabs the bottom of his sweater and pulls it over his head in one quick movement.

No human has ever been this beautiful. It's impossible. How am I expected to do anything else when he looks like *that*?

I lunge forward and unbutton his pants. I shove them down his muscular thighs as he kicks them away, laughing and falling against me.

The laughter quiets as we find each other, touching and stroking until we're breathless—and he still hasn't even been inside of me yet.

"I've had sex, but I've never had this. I've never had…" He swallows hard. His thumb presses into my hip bone, shaping me until I'm open for him. "It's never been like this with anyone."

Something like guilt flashes in his eyes.

If we lived in an ideal world, Mikhail and I would have found each other years ago. There wouldn't be anyone else before; no one after. He never would have been married. I wouldn't have watched my first fiancé be killed in front of me.

We are both painfully aware we don't live in that world. This one is complicated and messy. It's been brutal and dark and bloody and awful more often than not.

But it's none of those things right now.

I stroke his cheek, holding his face in my hand. "You deserve to feel happy, Mikhail. You don't have to feel guilty for the life you had before me."

He kisses the palm of my hand and my wrist. He works his way down my arm until he's over me, his heat between my legs. "Sometimes, I feel like there wasn't anything before you."

I want to tell him that's okay, but he presses his hips forward and the gentle slide of him inside of me steals my ability to speak. When our bodies are flush and he's panting against my skin, I decide there's nothing I could say that isn't being said a thousand times better by the perfect way we fit together.

Mikhail lifts himself onto his elbows, his nose pressed to mine. He looks into my eyes as he slowly pumps into me. It's like we both need the reminder that we're here, together.

Despite everything, we found each other.

I lift my hips, meeting his thrust, and he bares his teeth. "I've never been so turned on in my fucking life."

A wild laugh bursts out of me. "Me, neither."

"Just the way it feels sliding into you makes me want to come."

I scrape my nails over his hips, drawing him closer, deeper. "Do it. Please."

He grits his teeth and pumps into me with obvious restraint. Each tender pull of him in and out is sending me into the stratosphere and all I want to do is come down. I claw my hands up his neck and into the sweaty hair curling at the base of his head. "We have all night, Mikhail. We can do this all night. Forever."

The tight grip he's kept on his self-control thus far snaps. His fingers sink into my hips and he lifts me off the bed as he drags me against him harder and harder.

He hits a new angle inside of me and I can't hold back. He's wringing the orgasm out of me and there's nothing I can do to stop it.

I cry out, "I'm coming," and my body clamps down and he stutters, driving deep inside of me before I feel him twitch. Warmth floods inside of me, swirling to my fingers and my toes. Making me dizzy, trembly, *gone*.

"Fuck, Viviana." He collapses next to me, his arm slung over my heaving chest. He kisses my shoulder. "Have I told you I love you?"

I grin. "I think you just did."

"You think? You *think*?!" He clicks his tongue and rolls over me, lifting me off the mattress and into his arms.

I squeal, clinging to him so he doesn't drop me. "What are you doing?"

He bites my collarbone, a wicked gleam in his eyes. "Taking you downstairs to tell you again. And again. And again."

Hours later, limp and breathless on the floor in front of the fireplace, I curl against Mikhail's chest and fall asleep.

I've never felt more loved.

32

MIKHAIL

I'm kissing Viviana before I'm even conscious. The soft skin of her shoulder. The slope of her neck.

It might have something to do with the fact that I fell asleep kissing her. Since the second my brothers cleared out of here with Dante, every second spent not touching her feels like a waste of time.

She sighs and stretches against me. The only thought in my head as I grip her hip is, *She's mine.*

"We have to leave today," she rasps.

I finally open my eyes and her lower lip is pouted out. I can't resist pinching it between my teeth. "Hush. We're not talking about that yet."

"About what?"

I press my lips to the hollow of her throat. "About anything outside of this room. Anything that doesn't involve the many different ways I could have you screaming my name."

She laughs, her long lashes fluttering against pink cheeks. "There's a lot to pack up. We never put the candles away after the ceremony yesterday. I think the cheesecake is still on the counter, so it's probably rotten. There's a lot to do and—"

"And we can worry about that later." I cup her breast, enjoying the weight of her in my hand. "After I make you come."

I slide my hand down her stomach and she stiffens. She snaps her legs together and grabs my arm.

I frown. "What is it?"

Her cheeks darken, turning red. "I'm just—dirty."

"Fuck yes, you are."

"No," she laughs. "Not like that. Like, I am sweaty and the inside of my thighs are a sticky mess. I need a shower."

"I don't give a shit about any of that. For better or worse, remember?"

I swat her hand away, but she coils into a ball like a naked armadillo. "For better or worse is for when we're old and gray and have fallen and can't get up. It can't start on the morning after our wedding!"

I grimace. "Fine. Suit yourself."

She eases back down slightly, peeking at me over the blanket. "Really?"

"Really."

She blows out a breath. "Okay. Good. Let me shower and then—"

I throw back the blanket and scoop her up. She yelps, but it's already too late. I'm up and heading down the hall.

"What are you doing?" she shrieks, covering herself like I haven't seen and tasted every inch of her.

I walk into the bathroom and turn the shower on. She lunges for the door, but I slam it shut, backing her against the wood until she has to tilt her head back to meet my eyes.

"I'm giving you exactly what you want, Viviana." She swallows and I tip my head towards the steaming shower. "Now, get in the shower before I change my mind."

Her chest is rising and falling fast. I can tell she's debating staying put and taking whatever punishment I decide to dish out. I can guarantee she'll enjoy it. But after a second, she marches past me and steps into the shower.

I make it as far as squirting body wash into the palm of my hand when Viviana presses her palms against the tile and wiggles her ass in my direction.

"There's no sense cleaning up if we're just going to make another mess," she suggests, her green eyes wide and innocent.

Dirty, indeed.

I fuck her into the shower wall.

I drive into her hard and fast—the exact opposite of last night. When she screams my name, I grab her hair and arch her back, letting her wail it to the sky.

When her legs are too shaky to stand, I pick her up, wrap her around my waist, and press into her quivering body slowly. I draw out every last second of being in this cabin with her until I can't hold back.

I spill into her, giving her everything I have.

Then I grab the body wash from the shower floor and clean her up like I promised.

The moment I park the car in front of the mansion, I see Raoul.

Actually, I see a lot of my men.

There are new guards posted at the gates and men milling around the driveway. The cameras posted along the fence are as big as ravens. If anyone comes through the gates who isn't supposed to, it won't be because they didn't know they were on camera.

"Different vibe here," Viviana remarks softly from the passenger seat. She's sunk down in the seat, looking as reluctant as I feel to climb out and face reality.

"It's safer."

She reaches over the console and squeezes my wrist. "I know. And thank you. Knowing Dante is safe here is the only reason I could enjoy last night."

I arch both brows. "I don't think that was the *only* reason you enjoyed last night."

She rolls her eyes. "Of course not. Your excellent lovemaking was the number one reason, Mikhail. All hail your glorious penis, amen."

I grip her chin and bring her lips to mine. "I'll be busier the next few days, so repeat that to yourself every so often. I'd hate for you to forget."

"If I forget, will you remind me?" she asks, voice all innocence. But I see the mischief burning in her eyes.

"On second thought, go ahead and forget. Often and repeatedly."

She kisses me. "You got it, boss."

The newlywed haze follows me out of the car and halfway to the front door. Then Raoul steps off the porch, his mouth set in a firm line, and it dissipates.

"I need to talk to you."

I hand my luggage to the new driver Anatoly hired while I was away. The kid trips over his own feet reaching for my bag and then trips himself with the wheels twice on his way inside.

"Is it about that?" I mutter, tipping my head at the poor kid.

Raoul shakes his head. "A clumsy new hire is the least of our problems."

Viviana brushes her hand along my back. "I'm going to go see Dante. Are you coming?"

I want to.

Fuck, I want to.

But reality has finally come knocking and I have no choice but to answer the door.

"I need to talk to Raoul. We'll be in my office."

She kisses my cheek and smiles at Raoul before she leaves. As soon as she's through the door, I sigh. "Let's talk business."

The long and short of it is that the world did not stop turning while I was away. "The Greeks and Italians won't stop until they win this war," Raoul explains. His hand is tight around the drink I poured, but he hasn't taken a sip. "They've been poking holes along the edges of our territory for days."

"No one told me."

"You were busy," he says. "You needed the break."

"It wasn't a fucking 'break,'" I snap. "Agostino Giordano broke into my house. He was in my bedroom while Viviana was home alone."

He dips his head, eyes on the floor. "Security is my job. That never should have happened."

I know Raoul feels guilty. He told me over and over again before we left for the cabin. I tip back my drink and place the empty glass on my desk. "You were putting out another fire. We all were. I get it."

"But if anything had happened to her—"

"It didn't," I interrupt him. "Now, our security gaps are covered and she and Dante are safe here. So let's stop talking about the past and figure out what the future looks like, yeah?"

He reluctantly nods.

"If Christos and Agostino are working together, we can't afford to sit back and wait for them to find another way through our defenses."

"Especially if they're going to keep burning down our businesses," he mutters. "What do you have in mind?"

I snatch Raoul's untouched drink out of his hand and toss it back. "If they want to go after our biggest assets, I think it's only fair that we go after theirs."

33

VIVIANA

I'm doing this because I'm bored.

That's what I tell myself, anyway, as I pull an off-brand pregnancy test out of the box and shred through the plastic wrapping.

This is what days without adult social interaction will do to a person. I'm so starved for entertainment that I'm manufacturing drama in my head. Actually, to be specific, Google manufactured it for me. I dove head-first down one too many internet rabbit holes and things got bleak fast.

As soon as I take this stupid test, I'm going to write a strongly worded email to whichever sadistic algorithm curated my search results. No matter what pregnancy-related topic I searched for, the results pointed me straight to fetal abnormalities or sudden death. And not even sudden death for the baby—for all of us! A couple nights ago, I was seconds away from texting Mikhail that we might all have brain tumors. I talked myself down eventually, but it took a while.

"This is the kind of stuff that happens when you're left alone for too long," I mutter to myself as I sit down on the toilet.

Stuff like talking to yourself.

And taking pregnancy tests even though you're ten weeks pregnant and there isn't a chance in the world the test will be negative.

I mean, sure, I haven't had the most pregnancy symptoms. But every pregnancy is different. I know because that's the cliché line every listicle writer on the internet likes to add after articles like "10 Ways You're Ruining Your Child Before They're Even Born" and "7 Silent Symptoms of Miscarriage."

With Dante, I had nausea morning, noon, and night. There was no relief. I was slung over the toilet constantly. When I couldn't be slung over a toilet, I had an actual barf bucket I stashed under my desk for emergencies.

This pregnancy has been... different.

But that's fine. I'm only peeing on this stick because there's nothing better to do.

Mikhail has been busy since the moment we parked in front of the mansion. Raoul was waiting for him, grim-faced as usual. They walked into Mikhail's office and I'm not completely positive they walked out again.

I think I saw Mikhail slipping into the hallway early this morning, but the sun wasn't up yet and it was still dark, so I can't be sure.

Two nights ago, I might have felt him drop into bed beside me, but I'd been asleep for hours already and was barely conscious. By the time I woke up the next morning, the bed was empty.

He has work to do and I get that. The peaceful bubble we lived inside at the cabin was never going to be forever. It had to burst at some point.

It isn't just Mikhail; Anatoly has been busy, too. I used to be able to count on him to pop in and annoy me at least a few times every day, but lately, he seems to dart out of every room I walk into. I'd accuse him of avoiding me if I could pin him down long enough.

Even Dante has Mrs. Steinman to talk to for a few hours every morning.

I have nothing and no one.

The afternoons stretch on and on. That's the only reason I can't stop stressing about the pregnancy. If I had something else to occupy my mind—human interaction, work, a half-decent TV show to watch—I wouldn't be hunched over my bathroom sink, staring down at a pregnancy test I don't need to take.

I already know what the result is going to be.

When the timer goes off, I flip the test over. There's a smile on my face. I'm actually amused with how ridiculous I'm being.

Then I see the test window and freeze.

Nothing.

The square, plastic window is utterly, incomprehensibly blank.

I snatch the test off the counter and shake it like that might change the answer. I don't have any idea how pregnancy tests work, but some sort of chemical reaction should be happening in there, shouldn't it? Maybe the pee got stuck inside the stick and didn't make it to the test. I angle it one way and the other, but nothing changes.

"I peed on it," I mutter. "Right?"

Maybe I didn't actually pee on it.

It's stupid, but it's the only thing that makes any damn sense.

But of course I peed on it. I remember because it happened less than three minutes ago! Because while I was peeing on it, I thought to myself, *You're being ridiculous. Of course you're pregnant. You don't need to be doing this.*

My heart is pounding loudly enough that it's all I can hear as I dump the rest of the tests on the counter.

Every pregnancy is different.

I only had morning sickness for a few days this time. That's fine. Normal, even.

Though all of the nausea did happen while I was being held captive. On the sliding scale of normal or not, being kidnapped and chained to a bed is definitely less normal.

The nausea could have been stress or dehydration, I guess... But that still wouldn't explain the positive pregnancy test I got in the motel. The same test I wedged between the mattress and the wall in the cell Trofim had me locked in.

I don't feel quite as ridiculous as I pee on the last two tests and plop them on the counter next to the first.

A lack of symptoms is why I went down the first internet rabbit hole. **Can a healthy pregnancy have no symptoms**, I typed.

Turns out, for ninety percent of women, the answer is no.

Thirty seconds pass and nothing. I can see the test working, but there's no little pink line.

Why isn't there a little pink line?

I stand at the sink, frozen, for the entire three minutes. As the timer winds down, I cling to the pitiful hope that the last fifteen seconds will change something. That the tests will magically show that I'm pregnant with Mikhail's child and everything is fine and I've been worried for days over nothing.

But deep down, I know the truth.

I think I've known for a while.

That doesn't stop a sob from tearing out of my chest. I shove my hand over my mouth to stifle the sound and slide to the floor.

I stay there for a long time, crying until I'm all emptied out.

No one comes to check on me.

No one's even around to notice I'm gone.

"Where's Daddy?" Dante grumbles, kicking the toe of his shoes into the tile with every step. He's been walking in a circle around the dining room table for twenty minutes.

On lap one, he stepped on only the grout lines. Lap two, he jumped from tile to tile and screamed if he even got close to the grout. Now, he's shuffling his feet, shoulders slumped.

He looks how I feel.

"He's working." I've answered this question a lot this afternoon. He's only asking because I haven't been great company.

"Then can *you* play with me?"

"I already told you, I can't. I'm busy."

"You're just sitting there," he mumbles. "That's not busy."

If he had any idea how much energy it took to drag myself off the bathroom floor and sit up in this chair, he wouldn't be saying that.

But I never even told Dante I was pregnant. Mikhail brought it up a few times at the cabin, but I didn't want to overwhelm him. I was waiting for the right time to share the good news.

Now, I'm waiting for the right time to tell Mikhail that it was all some cosmic joke.

For the first time in days, I don't care that it's dinnertime and Mikhail isn't home yet. It's easier if he stays away. I'm terrified that the moment he walks through the door and I see his smiling face, I'll fall to pieces.

It shouldn't be this hard. I was barely pregnant. I don't even know if it was a boy or a girl. I technically don't know if it was anything at all.

For all I know, I was never pregnant. The first test could have been a false positive and the few symptoms I did have were all in my head.

I might be heartbroken over something that never existed.

But when I close my eyes, I can still feel Mikhail's warm hand pressed to my stomach underneath the covers. He was excited. He wanted this.

I wanted this, too.

Whether the baby was real or not, the future we were painting was achingly real. And now it's shattered.

"Mama." Dante shakes my arm and I blink. He's standing in front of me and I have no idea how long he's been there.

"Sorry, bud. What?"

"I'm hungry," he repeats. "My stomach keeps growling at me."

Great work, Viviana. Get so lost in your head that you let the child you do *have go hungry.*

"That's a problem we can solve. Let's go find something to warm up."

Anatoly and Raoul chose a replacement for Pyotr while we were at the cabin, but they haven't hired anyone to replace Stella. I don't think Anatoly is ready for someone else to fill her shoes. I get it; I'm not ready, either.

In the meantime, a chef has been delivering meal-prepped dishes every morning that we can warm up. Tonight's offering is chicken piccata and roasted asparagus.

Dante wrinkles his nose as soon as I peel back the lid. "What are those?" He pokes at a caper and then flicks the sauce off the end of his finger. "It's disgusting."

"It's not disgusting. You like chicken and pasta."

"I want the chicken Daddy made," he says. "At the cabin."

The image of Mikhail standing at the counter, a knife in one hand and a dish towel tossed over his shoulder, flashes through my mind.

I want that, too.

"Daddy is busy. He can't cook tonight. But I can warm this up for you."

Dante crosses his arms. "I want to eat my fish. I never got to eat the fish I catched."

"The fish you—" I pinch the bridge of my nose. "Bud, we left the fish on the lake."

He groans. "You left it? It got wasted?"

"You fell through the ice and we had to make sure you were okay."

He frowns like he has no idea what I'm talking about. "Daddy said I could eat it. He promised."

"That was before he knew you were going to drown, Dante! That was before we had to restart your heart!"

Dante flinches and regret floods me immediately. After days of wishing there were more people around, I suddenly wish I was alone. I'm not in a great place.

I set the dinner dish on the counter and kneel down in front of him. "I know you were excited to eat your fish."

His lower lip pouts out, but he tries to suck it back in. "It was the first fish I ever catched."

"It probably would have been the tastiest fish in the world. But you were our first priority, bud. We had to leave the fish behind to make sure you were safe. I'm sorry."

His eyes are glassy, but he nods. "I'll eat the chicken potato."

I manage a smile. "Chicken potato coming right up."

Ten minutes later, Dante is at the table munching away and

I'm heading towards the dining room with my plate when the front door opens.

For a few minutes, I almost forgot. Taking care of Dante distracted me. But as soon as Mikhail appears in the hallway, it all rushes back.

I'm not pregnant.

I have to tell him.

It's the first time I've seen him since we got out of the car three days ago and there's a hollow ache in my stomach. It takes everything I have to keep hold of my plate.

"Hi." I'm not sure how I force the single syllable out of my tight throat, but I do.

Mikhail looks surprised, like he didn't expect anyone to be home. He's half-turned towards the stairs, but he stops and looks back over his shoulder. "Hey."

Don't tell him.

You can't tell him right now.

"Are you hungry?" I hold my plate towards him. "I can heat something else up for myself if you want to—"

"I'm not hungry." His jaw flexes and somewhere deep in my head, I wonder if somehow he already knows. It's the only reason I can come up with why he's looking through me like I'm not even here.

"You should eat something. You haven't taken anything from the fridge in a few days. Working as much as you have been, you need to refuel and—"

"I know how to take care of myself," he snaps.

I slam my mouth shut.

His brows pinch together. I think he might feel bad, but before I can get a good read on him, a chair scrapes away from the table and Dante hurls himself down the hall.

"Daddy!"

For the first time since he walked through the door, Mikhail smiles. It's tight and dimmed, but he ruffles Dante's hair. "How's it going, kid?"

"Can you read to me tonight?" Dante asks, ignoring the question. "I want you to put me to bed."

Mikhail glances at his watch. That's all he has to do for me to know he's going right back to work. He didn't plan on us being right here. He was going to slip inside, do what he needed to do, and leave again.

"I'll put you to bed, buddy," I offer, trying to let Mikhail off the hook. "It's my favorite part of the day."

I wink at him, but Dante frowns and tugs on Mikhail's pant leg. "Pleeeease. You let me sleep with four stuffies and Mama only lets me have three."

Mikhail looks at me. The longer he stays, the more likely it is that I blurt out the news. I sigh. "You can have as many as you want tonight, okay? Just let me do it and—"

"I want Daddy!" he snaps.

Don't we fucking all?!

I take a deep breath, ready to tell Dante that we don't always get what we want. Life is hard. The sooner you learn that, the sooner it can beat you down.

Thankfully, Mikhail interrupts me. "I have time to put you to bed. I'll shower while you eat and we'll meet in your room."

Dante does an actual happy dance back to the table to finish dinner. I can't even blame him; I'd do a happy dance if I could get away from me, too.

By the time I turn back to the stairs, Mikhail is gone.

34

MIKHAIL

Raoul and Anatoly are waiting for me in my office. Raoul is a dark shadow in the corner. His face is drawn and his hands are folded together tightly between his legs. His direct opposite in every way, Anatoly, has tossed himself over my couch, legs loosely crossed and his arms thrown wide.

"I almost thought you forgot about us. I was about to bang down your bedroom door and make Viviana share."

Anatoly thinks I was with her and I don't correct him. It's better than the truth.

The first time I've seen her in days and I snapped at her like an asshole. She wanted to make me dinner and take care of me, but all I wanted to do was wash the blood off my clothes before she could see it.

I wanted to wash this entire fucking night off, if I could.

I drag a hand through my damp hair. "I'm here now. Do we want to talk about what the fuck happened tonight?"

Anatoly's face falls. He's good at putting on a front, but tonight sucked as much for him as it did for the rest of us. There's a limit to how much death and bloodshed he can handle.

None of us want to talk about it, but we can't afford not to.

"They saw us coming," Raoul grumbles finally.

"They didn't just see us coming; they prepared for it," Anatoly counters. "We've had eyes on that warehouse for months. I could have told you every single motherfucker inside by name on any night of the week. But tonight, there were three times as many people as I've ever seen."

"I should have pulled back. We weren't ready."

If tonight's failure was anyone else's fault, I'd be the first to point the finger. As *pakhan*, it's my job to make sure we're as strong as we can be. If someone is fucking up, they need to hear it and they need to fix it.

Tonight, the fuck-up is me.

"Bullshit." Anatoly jumps to his feet and paces. Anxiety ripples off of his tall frame. "We all went in there willingly. You didn't force anyone through that door."

"I didn't have to. You all trust me to make the right choice. Tonight, men who trusted me died. That's my fault."

Christos's men were ready the second we got through the door. It was a barrage of gunfire and blood. I can still smell it.

But my concentration was in tatters. Men were falling at my feet, and all I could see was Viviana and Dante. Usually, a fight hones my senses. Tonight, my head went somewhere else.

To a cabin in the middle of nowhere. Viviana's soft breathing in my ear.

"You're such a fucking martyr," Anatoly snarls, snapping me back. "It was my bad intel."

"And mine," Raoul adds somberly. "I had no idea that many men were inside. Christos moved them in secretly. I have men looking for tunnels right now, but—"

Anatoly snorts. "Tunnels under a fucking warehouse? They use that place to store stolen laptops they sell online and rent it out to shoot shitty pornos. You really think they're organized enough to tunnel underground like moles?"

"They were organized enough to get the jump on us," Raoul fires back. He's not used to being outmaneuvered and he isn't taking it well. "I'm going to look into every possibility until I know how they knew we were coming and what we can change."

"We need to divide Christos and Agostino." I take a long drink. The two of them could go back and forth like this for hours, but I already know what needs to be done. "I should have killed Viviana's father as soon as I knew he'd handed her to Trofim. I didn't and now, he's teamed up with the Greeks against us. That's my fault, too."

Anatoly rolls his eyes, but doesn't try to defend me this time. As much as he wants to, he can't.

"We're stronger than each of them separately. Together, they're a bit more of a problem."

"If you're suggesting we take one of them out, that was the entire point of tonight." Anatoly drops down on the edge of the couch, his elbows resting on his bouncing knees. "Even when shit hit the fan, I was looking for Christos. I didn't bring my hunting knife to *not* rip his insides out."

"Taking out Christos tonight would have been a bonus, but it wasn't the mission. We were there to take out one of his strongholds and weaken him financially. Now," I say carefully, "I'm suggesting we set our sights on one of the figureheads. Christos or Agostino, take your pick."

Anatoly's eyebrow arches and he grins. My brother is a golden retriever ninety percent of the time, but at the first mention of bloodshed, he turns into a shark. "Why choose? I say we go for both."

Raoul shakes his head. "We can't split up. If we go in with half the men and get surrounded the way we did tonight, even fewer of us will make it out."

Liev wasn't even twenty-five. He was one of the first soldiers cut down once we got inside. If he didn't die from the initial wound, he probably wishes he did. I don't assume Christos was in a merciful mood when it came to dealing with captives.

Right now, my *vors* are delivering the news to Liev's fiancée along with a payout. More than enough to get her back on her feet.

It could have just as easily been Viviana getting the bad news tonight. Widowed, days after our wedding. Dante left once again without a father.

I blink hard to clear my head. "Christos's niece is getting married tomorrow. I say we crash the wedding."

Even Anatoly looks tense. "She's marrying the D.A.'s son. You think he'll risk showing his face at a high-profile function like that?"

"He arranged the entire marriage. He's going to want to make sure it goes off without a hitch." Men like Christos—men like my father—don't know when to let go. They'll cling to whatever scrap of control they can get until the very end. "Christos would rather die than admit that he's scared of me. He'll be there just to prove that he isn't."

Raoul stands up. "I'll check out the location."

Anatoly frowns up at him, clearly surprised to be the only one pushing back. After a few seconds, he sighs. "I guess that leaves me to round up the soldiers and weaponry."

Before I can say anything else, my phone rings. I recognize the number immediately and pick up. "This is Mikhail."

"Nice meeting," Anatoly whispers, standing up. "Goodbye to you, too."

I roll my eyes and he only laughs.

The way he can flip his work brain off and on like a switch is as annoying as it is impressive. I'd probably be better off if I had the same switch. The only way I can seem to relax is when I load my family up and get off the grid.

The other end of the phone crackles and then a familiar voice cuts through. "Mikhail. Good to hear from you again. This is Dr. Rossi."

"Thanks for getting back to me. I know it's late."

"I gave up normal hours the second I started medical school," he says with a laugh. "Babies don't keep a nine-to-five schedule."

He made the same joke when I met him almost ten years ago. Alyona was so nauseous I had to pull the car over five times on the drive to his office so she could be sick. We walked in thirty minutes late and found him eating lunch. He waved us in anyway.

"You left a message with the nurses station and they told you I wasn't accepting new patients," he recounts, clearly reading the notes in my file. "Well, what Marcy didn't know is that you are not a new patient."

"No," I breathe. "I'm not."

There's a beat of silence before Dr. Rossi speaks again. "I was so sorry to hear about Alyona and Anzhelina. You can't imagine how sorry."

A house fire. That's what the papers ran with. It's what my father paid the papers to run with, to be more accurate. I burned the house to the ground because I couldn't stand looking at it, and my father made it work in our favor.

Dr. Rossi would be even more sorry if he knew the truth.

"Thank you, Doctor."

The heaviness hangs there for a second before Dr. Rossi chimes back in, voice chipper. "But most people don't call me unless they have exciting news to share. I'm assuming you have a new little one on the way?"

"My wife is pregnant."

Saying it out loud still gives me a rush. That Viviana is my wife. That we have a family. I wasn't sure I'd ever want this again, but now, I'm biting back a smile. After the clusterfuck of a day I've had, that's almost a miracle in and of itself.

"Congratulations, Mikhail! I'm thrilled for you. So let's see what we can do." He hums and I can hear him drumming his fingers on his desk. "It's short notice, but I can see your wife tomorrow afternoon. Would that work for you?"

I should have taken Viviana in sooner. The second she told me she was pregnant. But, as always, life had other plans. I snag the appointment and thank Dr. Rossi for squeezing us in.

I wasn't able to be there for her or Dante the way I should have been, but I'm going to make up for that now. There's a lot I can't control, but I can do absolutely everything I can to make sure this baby is healthy.

"Yes," I say quietly. "That's perfect."

35

MIKHAIL

As soon as Viviana stretches an arm over her head and strokes her fingers through her golden blonde hair, I regret every morning I've ever slipped out before sunrise.

This is a little slice of the cabin I can keep. Even with a war raging just outside the gates, I can wake up next to my wife every morning.

Her lips purse and she rolls onto her side, facing me. Her eyes are still closed, but I see them shifting beneath her lids.

I lay my hand softly over her cheek.

Suddenly, her eyes snap open. She jerks away so hard she almost falls off the bed. She would have, except I loop an arm around her waist and haul her against me.

Her heart is thundering. "You scared me," she breathes when she comes back to her senses. Every muscle in her body is tense. Her eyes are wide, pupils dilated. She's in fight-or-flight mode in her own bed.

"I didn't know sleeping next to my wife would be so shocking."

"Only recently." As soon as she says it, her mouth curves into a frown. "I'm sorry. I know you've been busy."

I flatten my hand on her lower back. Her tank top is twisted around her ribs and I can feel her sleep-warm skin against my bare chest. It's been too long since we've been this close and my cock is standing up and taking notice.

"I have been busy, but I shouldn't take it out on you."

She peeks up at me beneath long lashes. "You're talking about last night?"

"I had a bad day." I press a kiss to her neck, where the early morning light is painting her gold. I can see her pulse fluttering. "Instead of letting you make it better, I decided to be on my own. I can tell you right now that it was the wrong choice. This is where I should have been."

Her hand wraps lightly around the back of my neck, but she's still rigid. Her body is as stiff as a board underneath me. Even when I kiss the hollow of her throat again, she seems to pull back.

I lift up on my elbows, eyebrow arched. "You're mad."

"No. I'm not. I'm really not. I'm—" Her teeth sink into her lower lip, pulling at it. "I'm just tired."

I nip at her collarbone. "Let me wake you up. Make it up to you."

Her shirt slides higher and I band my hands around her ribcage. I trace my thumbs underneath the soft swell of her breasts, working over the point of her nipples. Viviana shivers, but her jaw is still set.

"You're going to make me work for it, huh?" I almost have to force her stiff legs apart with my knee before I can settle between them.

"It's not that."

I work my fingers up her legs, trying to stroke some warmth into her. Goosebumps trail my touch. When my hands slide under the short hem of her shorts, the front of her panties is soaked.

"I know it's not a question of whether you want it." I smirk, but she won't even look at me. Her eyes are fixed on the ceiling.

Somewhere in the back of my mind, alarm bells are ringing. But I don't pay them any attention. I can't. Not when she's bare and wet beneath me like this.

"Let's play a game," I whisper, kissing my way up her thigh. "Let's see how long you can stay mad at me while you're screaming my name."

On instinct almost, her legs shift open. I manage to flick my thumbs under the thin material of her panties before she snaps them closed.

"I need to shower."

"What a coincidence," I growl, looping my arms beneath her back and lifting her against my chest. "Me, too."

She laughs, but it's strangled, hesitant. "I think I'm just… out of it this morning. I'll shower and then—"

I circle my mouth around her breast, wetting the thin material of her shirt until it clings to her pebbled skin. She moans, arching into me even as she presses on my shoulders.

"I'll shower and then we can t-talk," she rasps, already breathless.

"It'll be hard to talk with my tongue buried inside of you," I murmur, lavishing her other breast with the same attention. "Even harder when you're screaming for mercy and begging me for more."

She whimpers. "Mikhail… you're making this hard."

"Hard… like this?" I lower her against my jutting erection, sliding along her perfect ass until she buries her fingers in my back. Finally, she's warm and languid in my arms. "I'm going to fuck you just like this if you don't stop me, Viviana."

She nuzzles her face into my neck, breathing heavily. She doesn't say anything, but she doesn't need to. The way her body sinks against me says more than enough.

"Good girl." I shift her panties to the side. "It's better we do this before your shower, anyway. I don't want the doctor to see the mess I'm going to make of you."

All at once, she's rigid again. She jerks back, falling on her ass on the mattress and staring up at me with wide eyes. "What doctor?"

She's so close to the bulge in the front of my sweats that I can't look at her without imagining her mouth wrapped around me. Maybe that's why I initially miss how pale she is. The dark circles under her eyes. The fear burning just under the surface.

I fist her hair and tip her head back. "I made you an appointment with the best OB-GYN in the state."

I'm seeing the world through a sex-crazed haze. It's the only explanation for how Viviana is able to dart away from me and make it to the bathroom before my now-empty hand even falls to my side.

She streaks across the room, and there isn't enough blood going to my brain for me to do anything other than follow her stupidly.

Viviana is leaning over the sink. Her knuckles are white on the edge of the countertop and she's taking deep, slow breaths.

"Is the morning sickness back?" I grab the trashcan under the sink and place it next to her.

"No."

"But you're sick," I guess. That's the only thing that makes sense. The only reason she'd throw herself out of bed rather than let me touch her.

"No." Her voice wavers. Dimples appear in her chin as her lower lip wobbles.

She's about to cry and I'm standing here with a fucking erection. I ignore the throbbing below my waist and grab Viviana's chin. I gently tilt her face so she's looking at me. "Talk to me."

"I'm not pregnant," she blurts.

The words bounce off my brain and skitter away. They're there and then gone again, impossible to grasp. I don't even try. I'm still holding Viviana's face in my hands, staring down at her blankly.

She turns towards me, reaching for me for the first time since she woke up. Her cold fingers loop around my wrists. "I'm so sorry, Mikhail. I should have told you—"

"Told me what?" I ask.

I misunderstood.

She misspoke.

That's all. Something here is wrong and I'm going to figure out what it is.

Her face falls. As she pulls away—dropping my wrists, turning her face away from my grip—some of the initial rush of words come rolling back.

"You're not pregnant." It's not a question or a statement; it's some in-between thing I can't name just yet.

Everything in my life is up in the air at the moment. The only thing that makes any fucking sense to me is this woman and our son and the family we're building.

And now…?

"I should have told you sooner, but I didn't know how." Tears roll down her cheeks, but I don't even know if they're real.

Viviana lied to me. Again.

She kept something from me. *Again.*

And I didn't notice.

Again.

"You tell me by *fucking telling me*," I snarl.

She flinches and I back away from her. For the first time in my life, I'm worried I'll hurt her.

Hours and hours of conversations play back in my head. I search through every word, trying to understand how we ended up here.

"Mikhail, I—"

"Is that what the cabin was about?" I snap.

It makes sense now. Of course there was some dark underbelly. No moment in my life can exist without one. Dante almost drowning wasn't enough, apparently. There had to be more. There had to be *worse.*

She blinks at me, softly shaking her head. "The cabin was— No! I don't even know what that means. The cabin was just… *us.* It was perfect."

"It was the perfect cover for you to get pregnant if you weren't already." I hate the words the moment they're out of my mouth, but I can't reel them back now. It's too late. "Is that what happened? You lied to me about being pregnant. When it worked, you decided to make it real. You needed a baby to keep me close."

She clutches at her chest like I hit her. In a way, I did. "Mikhail!" she gasps. "No! I didn't. I wouldn't." She looks horrified at the suggestion, but it wouldn't be the first time her acting had me fooled.

"You did. And now, you're realizing it didn't work and you have to come clean," I continue numbly. My throat burns like I'm spewing acid. It might as well be, based on the way Viviana stumbles back.

"You really think I'd do that to you?" she asks with a quiet kind of horror.

I don't know what to think. About anything.

"I'll cancel the appointment."

"Mikhail…" She reaches for me, but I'm already out of the bathroom. I'm already pushing through the door of our bedroom.

Our family was the one thing I thought I got right.

Now, I don't even have that.

36

MIKHAIL

Anatoly and Raoul are loading the car when I step into the garage wearing a suit. "You're a little overdressed for a meeting with your realtor." Anatoly eyes me warily, already suspecting what I'm going to say.

The plan was for me to be seen at coffee with my realtor. I'd be spotted signing documents for the new location of Cerberus Industries while Anatoly and Raoul discretely attended the wedding of Christos's niece. If the wedding turned violent, I'd be across town. Plausible deniability and all that.

After this morning's debacle, though, I have too much energy to sit down for coffee. I want to get my hands dirty.

"I signed the contract digitally and my afternoon freed up." I throw my bag into the trunk. "I'm going to the wedding."

I don't need to see my brothers to know they're looking at each other, silently trying to decide what to do. Who should speak up first.

I whip around, arms crossed. "Say whatever the fuck it is you're going to say so we can go. It would be rude of us to walk in late."

Raoul lifts his chin and keeps his mouth stubbornly closed, leaving Anatoly as the unwilling sacrifice. He rolls his eyes and slams the trunk closed.

"Okay. Well, first, this wasn't the plan, Mikhail."

"Plans change."

"Not at the last minute. Not when you're the one who made the plan to begin with," he points out.

"The plan was to secure a new location for Cerberus Industries so we have somewhere to funnel the shit ton of money we're going to make when the shipment of weapons arrives." I shrug. "I've done that. It's being taken care of as we speak. I'm not changing the plan; I've just finished my part of it. Now, I'm helping you with yours."

Anatoly almost manages to smother a snort at the suggestion that he and Raoul could use my help. "You're recognizable. If anyone sees you, they'll know immediately that we're the ones who—"

"That we're the kind of people who don't make idle threats. They'll know not to fuck with us."

Anatoly growls. "Something is wrong and I don't want to go into a fight with you if your head isn't in the right place."

For a single second, my head is in a bedroom upstairs. *Is Viviana still in the bathroom? Is she looking for me? Do I want her to find me?*

But I shake it off and meet his eyes. "All of me is right here. I started this mess by refusing to marry Helen, so I'm going to take care of it. All that matters is taking out Christos and Agostino. All that matters is the Bratva."

Anatoly arches a brow. He wants to argue, but he has enough sense to know it won't do him any good. Whether I go to that wedding with the two of them or by myself, I'm going.

And he knows it.

Anatoly pulls the keys out of his pocket. "Do I still get to drive, at least?"

"Be my guest. So long as you can drive and walk me through the plan again." I slip into the passenger seat and pull the door closed. "I want to make sure you know what the fuck you're doing."

Anatoly curses under his breath. "And yet everyone calls *me* the bastard."

I let him complain. The only thing that might turn this day around is watching Christos Drakos choke on his own blood. No amount of griping from Anatoly is going to stop me from making that happen.

The reception is in shambles.

At least, it *sounds* like it's in shambles. I don't know much about weddings, but that much screaming can't be celebratory.

"Hurry up," Anatoly hisses, poking his head through the swinging door into the kitchen. "We have to go."

The three of us watched the ceremony from the rooftop across the street, but Christos never showed. He wasn't in the wave of arriving guests or in the processional after the ceremony. His niece and her new husband, the son that will tie the Drakos family to an influential District Attorney, left through a tunnel of bubbles.

But Uncle Christos was nowhere to be seen.

Anatoly and Raoul were ready to scrap the plan and go home. "We'll regroup," Anatoly said. "Figure out where to hit Agostino and try that."

The thought of going home to sit and wait and sit some more made my skin crawl. Slowing down means stopping long enough to assess the steaming garbage heap that my life has become.

I'd rather turn someone else's life into a steaming garbage heap.

Which is why I now find myself behind a stainless steel shelf of pots and pans with my hand around Damon Drakos's throat. The mother of the bride is leaning against an industrial-sized refrigerator, softly weeping as she gawks down at her husband thrashing in my grasp.

"I'll be done as soon as Damon tells me where his brother is," I growl back at Anatoly.

Damon coughs, spraying blood down his chin. "I don't know where he is. I don't—"

I drive my knee into his stomach—into the bullet wound I put there sixty seconds ago. About the same time the screaming on the other side of the door started.

"You know something. Otherwise, you'd wonder why your dear brother isn't here today. Why would Christos arrange this marriage and not come to bless it? Huh?"

"We haven't seen him!" his wife sobs. "It's been weeks. We don't have anything to do with him or his business!"

"Except pimping your daughter out to his allies." I fix her with a hard glare. "Don't waste my time with lies."

Her thin lips seal closed. *Good. Someone needs to survive to pass along my message.*

"You have nothing to say?" I ask Damon, giving him one final chance.

He meets my eyes, summoning the last of his dignity as he silently awaits his death.

I nod and turn back to his wife. "When you do see him, tell Christos that this ends now. Tell him that he leaves my family alone or he'll end up like his brother."

Before the woman can even wonder what I mean, I press my gun to Damon's neck and pull the trigger.

When I push the front door of the mansion open, Viviana is in the entryway.

She opens her mouth, ready to launch into an explanation or an apology or whatever the fuck it is she might want to say to me. Then she sees Raoul and Anatoly shuffling in behind me and her mouth slams shut.

There's blood crusted under my fingernails. Probably dotting the collar of my shirt, too. But I don't care. Let her see it. I'm tired of pretending I'm above this.

She may want to keep secrets, but I don't. Not anymore.

The time we spent at the cabin was a fantasy. It might as well have been a dream. *This* is who I'll always be at the end of the day: the man coming home late with blood on his hands.

But if Viviana sees it, she doesn't say anything. She steps closer, her voice soft. "Can we talk?"

"We'll talk when I'm ready." I turn towards the stairs, but she slides in front of me.

Up close, I can tell she's been crying. There are tear tracks down her cheeks. Her eyes are bloodshot. "Mikhail. Please."

I can feel Anatoly watching me. Even Raoul is tuned into the drama, no matter how much he'll deny it later. If they had any doubts about why I changed the plan and went homicidal on Christos's brother, they don't anymore.

Trouble in fucking paradise.

"If you knew where I'd just been, you'd know I'm in no mood to talk," I grit out. "For your sake, we'll do this later."

Viviana looks up at me and I expect fear. I expect her to cower the way Damon's wife did when she watched me kill her husband. Part of me even *wants* it.

But Viviana just nods and stands to the side.

I navigate around her and walk into my office. Not even a minute later, Anatoly opens the door. "I'd knock, but I'd hate for you to think I was your wife," he says, pushing the door closed behind him. "I've seen how you treat her."

I pour myself a drink and sit down in my chair. "Well, I'd offer you a drink, but I'd hate for you to think I want you to stay."

He chuckles humorlessly. "Killing Damon didn't have the lasting relief you were hoping for, eh? Turns out wanton murder might not be the solution to troubles at home?"

"Get out, Anatoly."

"I thought your days of taking out your frustrations on a punching bag were over. I guess I was wrong," he says. "You just found a living, breathing punching bag instead."

The fact that I'm not sure if he's talking about Damon, Christos, or Viviana is damning in a way that pisses me off.

"Leave. I'm not in the mood."

"I know you're not." He drops down onto the sofa, making himself right at home. "I don't care."

We sit in silence for a few minutes. If he's waiting for me to be the first to break and start this confessional, he'll be waiting forever. I have nothing to say.

Finally, he sighs. "What happened back there?"

"Christos was tipped off, obviously. He bailed on the wedding because he was scared of facing me. And the asshole didn't even have the decency to warn his brother that I was coming."

"I'm not talking about the wedding. I know what happened there." Anatoly's jaw flexes. His hands rub together and I get the sense he has some frustrations to work through himself. "You charged into a building full of public figures and Drakos soldiers so you could kill Christos's brother for the low, low price of, let's see… *zero new information.* If Raoul and I hadn't followed you inside, the guards in the lobby would have killed you."

"Good thing I knew you were going to follow me inside."

That's a lie. I told them to wait outside and I didn't see the guards waiting around the pillar. They would have cornered me from behind and I wouldn't be here right now.

Anatoly shakes his head, and I know he doesn't buy my bullshit. "I want to know what's going on in your own house. With you and Viviana."

I shoot him a warning look, but Anatoly doesn't know when to quit. He gets that from our father. He stares back at me, anticipating answers I don't have.

"It's called a relationship. Marriage. You should try it."

His face darkens. He *did* try it. For the first time in his life, Anatoly was a one-woman kind of man.

Then he found that one woman dead in our garage.

I'm being an asshole bringing it up, but I told him to leave. Twice. He has only himself to blame...

Right?

"I've seen you and Viviana together long enough to know what your relationship looks like. Usually, I can't be in the same room with you without getting nauseous. But it was icy back there. She looked upset."

"Probably because she is." I shrug. "So am I. It happens."

He groans. "Care to elaborate? It's hard to be your confidant when you don't tell me anything."

"You aren't my confidant."

"You're right. I'm your brother. It's an even deeper bond."

I snort. "Ask Trofim how he feels about that. The next time I see him, I plan to kill him. What kind of bond is that?"

"Don't lump me in with Trofim," he snaps. "Don't sit here and lash out at me because you fucked things up."

My molars grind together. "I didn't fuck anything up."

"You're pissed with Viviana about something, so you threw yourself into a fight with the Greeks and killed someone we had no plans to kill. Now, you're walling yourself off in your room. I'd say you fucked several things up, man."

"You don't know what the fuck you're talking about, Anatoly." I point to the door. "Leave me alone."

"Once again, no. I left you alone before. Maybe you don't remember because you were drinking yourself into the ground, but we've done this whole shebang already." He circles a finger at me and the glass I'm crushing in my fist. "You drank and worked out until you couldn't stand. I understand what you were going through, so I let you grieve. But we don't have time for this now."

"I've managed this Bratva long enough on my own. I can manage myself."

"You're being reckless," he spits, "and I deserve to understand why."

"You don't deserve a fucking thing from me!" I roar. The anger hits me sideways, rising up from the place it's been hiding all day. Simmering. Waiting. I fling my glass against the wall and jab a finger at my brother. "My personal life isn't your fucking business. If you aren't here to talk about work, then get the hell out of my office."

Anatoly sits tall, shock flickering across his face as he takes in my shaking finger and the alcohol dripping down the wall.

He runs his tongue over his teeth and I wait for some quippy remark. Some perfect Anatoly-ism that will cut through the tension—through the dark cloud that has been this shitty day.

Instead, for the first and probably the last time in his life, he does exactly what I ask.

He simply leaves.

37

VIVIANA

"Why can't Daddy be here, too?" Dante whines. It's been his constant refrain since we left the house an hour ago.

I thought he was having a good time at the park, so the reminder that we're here without Mikhail takes me by surprise. I have to turn away quickly so I don't turn into a sobbing mess in front of all the other parents at the park.

"Your dad is busy today," Anatoly chimes in easily. "Hey, go climb the rock wall over there and I'll take a picture of you and send it to him."

"Okay!" Dante chirps back.

As soon as Dante is out of earshot, Anatoly drops down onto the bench next to me. "He's busy being a grouchy asshole."

When I told Mikhail that Dante was asking to go to the park, he turned away from me like I didn't even speak. Like I wasn't there. Five minutes later, Anatoly strolled in with his keys and offered. Apparently, I'm the only one Mikhail is icing out.

I sniffle and swipe at my cheeks. "At least he's talking to you."

"You say that like it's a good thing. I think the silent treatment would be better."

"Don't be so sure," I mumble under my breath. "Where did he even sleep last night? Because it wasn't in bed with me."

I know because I was awake tossing and turning all night.

The days we spent at the cabin were a bright spot in a long stretch of darkness. Now, Mikhail thinks all of it was some manipulation. I look back on our time there and see how great we can be together. What does he see? How badly is he twisting those memories in his own head and will I be able to twist them back?

Anatoly turns to me. "What even happened with you two? You guys were the picture of wedded fucking bliss a few days ago. I've never seen Mikhail like that before. He was... happy."

A few days ago. It feels like a lifetime.

"I probably shouldn't say..."

If Mikhail wanted Anatoly to know what is going on, then he would have told him. But there's no one else for me to talk to. I've been sitting with this secret—with this shame—for days and I can't carry it anymore.

"Come on, Viv." Anatoly rubs a hand on my back. "What's going on?"

It's all the encouragement I need. The truth rushes out of me. "I'm not pregnant," I blurt.

Anatoly frowns. "Are you supposed to be?"

"He didn't tell you that, either?" I can tell from the blank look on Anatoly's face that Mikhail didn't. Anatoly has no clue. "Well, great… Now, he can be mad at me about that, too."

"Wait." Anatoly shakes his head. "Are you—You were—What?"

"I *thought* I was pregnant," I explain in a stop-and-start stutter. "I took a test before Trofim kidnapped me. It was positive, but I guess i-it was a false positive or something. I don't know."

"And now, Mikhail is mad at you?" Anatoly's brows pinch together. "He's mad at you for a false pregnancy test?"

I sigh, sinking down on the bench. "It's complicated."

Anatoly opens his mouth to say something, but Dante's voice rings out across the park. "Look at me, Uncle Nat!" He's standing on the ledge on top of the small rock wall, his fists raised over his head in triumph. "Take a picture."

Anatoly stands up and snaps a few shots, giving Dante an air high five. When he's done, he sits down next to me, sliding a little closer and lowering his voice. "You're going to have to make sense of this for me, Viv. Because even my hard-headed brother isn't unreasonable enough to be pissed at you and, by extension, me, over something like *this*. This isn't your fault. It was a shitty test."

"It's not just the test; it's the timing of all of it. The fact that I didn't tell him right away." I drop my face in my hands. "I knew for a couple days. I suspected for even longer. But things were going so well that I didn't want to ruin it."

He lays a hand on my shoulder. "You didn't ruin anything."

I choke on a laugh and gesture around wildly. "Look around, Nat. It's ruined. Mikhail won't even speak to me."

"For now. He isn't speaking to you *for now*. But give him time. He always comes around."

I want to believe him, but I know better than to hope for the best. "Every time things start going well for me, they have a habit of falling apart. Maybe Mikhail and I have run our course." The words lodge in my throat. I can barely force them out without sobbing. "We could make it work out in the middle of nowhere, but when we're back in the real world, there's too much baggage."

"Baggage." Anatoly groans. "That's what it is, you know? Between our useless father and Trofim and then Pyotr… Mikhail has a hard time knowing who to trust."

Anatoly isn't saying I'm like any of those men, but that's what it feels like. That's what I'm afraid of: Mikhail sitting in his office, imagining me as some conniving liar who used him.

I'd give anything to rewind time a few days. I'd tell him the first time I noticed I didn't have pregnancy symptoms. I'd bring up the fact that I only took one test and never had it confirmed. All of the little doubts that were swirling around in my head, I'd say them out loud. I'd confess everything to Mikhail.

But there's no going back now.

"I didn't even mean to keep it a secret from him. I was waiting for the right time. But it turns out, there isn't a right time to dump terrible news in someone's lap."

"Unless that someone is your husband," Anatoly says softly. "Mikhail wants to take care of you, Viviana. He doesn't need you to hide things from him. Whatever is going on with you, he can handle it."

The question was never whether Mikhail could handle the news.

It was whether *I* could handle it.

We stay at the park for another hour, letting Dante burn through the endless energy he seems to have. He climbs the rock wall so many times that he can literally do it with his eyes closed by the time we leave. On our way back to the car, he hangs limply over Anatoly's shoulder, pretending to snore.

That doesn't stop him from announcing, thirty seconds later, "I want to go swimming!"

Anatoly smiles through a groan. "Aren't you tired?"

"I want to go swimming," Dante repeats like that's answer enough.

Anatoly and I take turns tossing sedentary options at him—puzzles, movies, video games—but Dante is a boy who knows what he wants.

"Fine. I'll swim with you," Anatoly relents as we walk into the house through the garage. "But I'm lying on a float the entire time and you're definitely *not* going to tip me over into the water."

Dante giggles, his eyes sparking with the kind of mischief that used to make me wonder if urgent care centers offered frequent flyer miles. "Okay."

I ruffle his hair. "Go get changed into your swimsuit and then we can—"

"Daddy!" Dante is a floppy-haired streak down the hall before he launches himself into Mikhail's arms.

I didn't even see Mikhail standing there. Probably because I wasn't looking. I can only get my hopes up so many times before I accept that Mikhail isn't going to show his face until he's good and ready.

But here he is.

He obviously heard us come in, and he didn't dissolve into the shadows like Batman. I try to take it as a good sign, but it's not like he greeted us at the door, either.

"Hey, kid." He bends down to hug him without looking at me or Anatoly.

Anatoly pads into the kitchen with an ease I couldn't fake if I wanted to. "Dante is dragging me to the swimming pool. You wanna come?"

"Please!" Dante pleads, yanking on Mikhail's pant leg. "Please swim with me!"

Mikhail sighs. "I have a lot to do, but I could—"

Dante shrieks with excitement before Mikhail even finishes the sentence and whips those baby blues around to me. "You, too, Mama?"

"Oh." I glance at Mikhail and his jaw is set. His eyes are drilling into the top of Dante's head like he might be able to plant his own thoughts there. *You don't want your Mama to come with us.*

It doesn't work. Dante slips right back into shameless begging. "Please, Mama! Pleeeease!"

Dante will be so happy we're all together that he probably won't even notice his dad and I aren't talking. I can fight through the tension on Dante's behalf if Mikhail can. We're both adults, after all.

I manage a smile. "Sure, bud. I'd love to."

No sooner than the words are out of my mouth, Mikhail takes a step back and glances at his watch. "Actually, it's later than I thought it was. I have something to take care of. Sorry, Dante."

Dante's face falls, but the words rush out of me first. "You've got to be fucking kidding me," I growl.

Dante gasps. It's the first time he's ever heard me curse. I'd be worried about that if I wasn't infinitely more worried about grabbing the vase next to me and hurling it at Mikhail's head.

Sensing the dark turn things are about to take, Anatoly swoops in and ushers Dante towards the stairs. "Come on, *amigo*. Last one to the pool is a rotten banana."

"It's a rotten *egg*," Dante laughs.

Anatoly scoops Dante up and balances him over his shoulder, fleeing the kitchen like it's on fire.

It might as well be.

My skin is hot and prickly with days' worth of frustration simmering under the surface. The intensity notches even higher when Mikhail finally deigns to look at me.

"You're really going to disappoint him because you're mad at me?" I snarl viciously. "Whatever is going on with us, I didn't think you'd let it affect your relationship with—"

Before I can even finish, Mikhail turns… *and walks away.*

I gawk at his broad shoulders and long legs as he takes the stairs casually, pretending I don't even exist.

I'm stunned, but I'm not hurt.

No, I'm too angry to be sad.

I stand motionless for one second, five, ten. Then the sound of his office door snicking closed snaps me out of it.

Anatoly told me to give Mikhail time. *He'll come around*, he said.

I charge up the stairs, my hands in tight fists at my sides. If he doesn't want to come around, that's fine. I'll *bring* him around.

For the first time in his entire life, Mikhail Novikov doesn't get a choice.

38

VIVIANA

Thankfully, Mikhail's office door is unlocked. If it wasn't, I probably would have slammed face first into it, which would have lessened the overall effect. As it is, the door flies open hard enough it bounces off the wall and I'm steaming in the doorway.

Mikhail doesn't even look up.

He's sitting behind his desk, his hand wrapped around a crystal glass like it's the only thing keeping him on the ground. His knuckles are white.

"We need to talk."

"I'm busy," he grits out.

I slam his office door closed behind me. "Then we better talk fast."

Mikhail lifts his head slowly, moving with practiced ease that sends a shiver down my spine. His eyes meet and hold mine.

This is a good idea, I tell myself. I truly believe that. Even as the anger inside of me shifts into something flushed and uncertain. Even as I fidget from one foot to the other, trying to decide how to stand my ground while he's pummeling me with his icy blue eyes. Mikhail is my husband and we have to talk this out. I press my shoulders back and meet his glare with one of my own. "You can ignore me if you want, but—"

"Apparently, I can't." He gestures to where I'm standing in the doorway.

I huff and continue. "But you can't ignore Dante."

"I was going to spend time with him, but *you* couldn't walk away. You can't tell him no."

"So you'd rather disappoint him than be in the same room with me?"

He leans forward, hissing his words with a shocking amount of venom. "I'd rather disappoint him than let you use yet another child to get my attention."

Baggage, I remind myself. If Anatoly was here, he'd remind me of that, too.

So many people in Mikhail's life have lied to him and manipulated him. He's trained to assume the worst in people. Even though his words land like a sharp jab to my sternum, I stifle the pain and try to rise above it.

Then, I very promptly tunnel directly underneath it.

"And I'd rather get a false positive on a pregnancy test than have another kid that you'll ignore whenever it suits you."

When they go low, you go lower. My life motto, apparently.

Heat crawls up his neck, which is the most reaction I've gotten out of him in days. It's intoxicating, even if it means he's pissed at me. At least this time, he's mad about something I've actually done.

"I don't even know why you're upset," I continue. "You didn't want this baby in the first place. It's not like you'd have time, anyway. You don't want to spend time with the kid you already have."

Between one blink and the next, the desk between us dematerializes. That's the only explanation I have for how Mikhail goes from sitting behind it to standing directly in front of me.

The energy pouring off of him is enough to press me back against the door and lodge whatever I was going to say next in my throat.

His eyes are black and his nostrils are flared. "You don't know a single fucking thing about what I want, Viviana."

It's hard to feel powerful when I'm cowering against the door, but I do my best. I have to. Mikhail is used to pushing people around and getting his way.

Now, it's my turn.

"I know you don't want to be sitting in this office alone. I know you could pick me up and throw me out this door if you actually didn't want me here, but you haven't."

He snaps his hand to my neck, banding his long fingers loosely around the column of my throat. "Keep talking and I will."

The frustration flowing through me congregates in the places where his body touches mine: my throat, the brush of his knee against my thigh, his hot breath on my temple. I swallow and I know he feels it against his palm. Mikhail Novikov is aware of his effect on people; on me most of all.

"Maybe I don't know what you want," I admit. "But you don't know how much I wanted that baby."

I'm not going to cry. I look over his head, focusing on the ceiling to send the tears flowing in reverse. This is my chance to tell him everything I wanted to say when I broke the news. I'm not going to sob through it.

"When Trofim was holding me captive, knowing I was carrying your baby was… It was the only reason I had to stay alive. I laid on that stupid bare mattress for hours, stroking my stomach, desperate to find a reason to take my next breath. It wasn't about getting you back, Mikhail, or having a bargaining chip. You didn't give me any reason to think I'd ever see you again."

I'm snarling my way through this confession. I'm taking the fragile pieces of my heart and flinging them at him like darts, hoping at least a few of them leave a mark.

"I didn't tell you when I started having doubts about the pregnancy because I *wanted it*, Mikhail. I wanted this baby, this life… you, me, and Dante. I wanted a fourth little star in our cluster."

Tears well in my eyes. I try to look away, but Mikhail's hand is like iron around my throat. It's not tight enough to choke, but it's enough to keep me exactly where he wants me.

If he wants me here at all.

"That false test is the only thing that got me through captivity. It's the reason I found the strength to survive and I will never, ever regret that." With nowhere else to look, I meet his dark eyes at last. "You didn't want the baby in the first place, so cheer up. You're free."

"I already told you, Viviana: you don't know a thing about what I want."

The fingers from his free hand dig into my thigh as he snaps my leg up and around his hip. He presses closer, his hard body melding against the soft curves of mine. I can feel what he wants prodding against my hip bone.

I slowly stretch onto my toes, sliding our bodies together. "Then t—"

His eyes flash as he tightens his fingers around my throat. I can't speak. Can't move.

"You think I didn't want this baby?" His lips brush over mine. I can barely breathe, and I lean towards him like he's oxygen. "I could show you. I'll prove to you how much I wanted this baby."

"How?" I rasp.

We still have our clothes on and the friction is enough to have me panting. Black dots speckle the edges of my vision, but this would be a fine way to go.

Mikhail drops his lips to my ear and snarls, "I'll fuck another one into you right now."

He says it like a threat. Like I should be terrified.

In a way, I am.

I'm terrified he won't follow through.

39

VIVIANA

The air is still and heavy for three, maybe four seconds. Mikhail is rigid against me, frozen except for the scrape of his dark eyes over my face.

Then he snaps into dizzying motion.

My feet are off the floor and he crushes me against his chest. The air whooshes out of my lungs as he spins me towards the center of the room.

But as it turns out, I don't need air.

I don't need gravity or oxygen or any of those useless fundamentals of life. The only thing that matters is the way he throws me down on his desk and settles his weight between my legs.

With one swipe of his arm, the desk is cleared. A cup hits the wall, pens skittering across the wood floor. Papers are still fluttering to the ground like confetti when he grabs the hem of my shirt and yanks it over my head.

There's no time to think about what we're doing. As soon as I toss the shirt to the side, his mouth lands hot and needy on my chest. He shoves my bra aside and takes my nipple between his lips, rolling it with his tongue.

I cry out, sliding my hands into the silky weight of his hair. I'm feverish, out of my mind. I came in here to yell at him and now, I'm arching my breast deeper into his mouth and grinding myself against his thigh.

I fist the front of his shirt. "God, I missed you."

His mouth is too busy tasting every inch of my skin to stop for conversation. His lips have important work to do. They blaze down my ribs. I wouldn't have called the belly button an erogenous zone, but Mikhail is making a strong case for inclusion.

"When I found out you gave birth to my son, all I could think about was seeing you pregnant," he growls against my flat stomach, curling his hands there. "I hate that I didn't get to see what you looked like carrying my baby."

I'll paint him a lovely picture once I regain the ability to string words and sentences together.

I was enormous. My ankles were swollen and I couldn't even fit into my narrow, piss-poor excuse for a closet. I had to pile all of my clothes behind the couch for the last two months of my pregnancy. I felt like a whale.

But the reverent way Mikhail talks about it makes me think he would have made me feel beautiful.

I also hate that he wasn't there.

He slides his hands from my waist to my jeans, tearing at the button and dragging them down my thighs along with my panties. He reaches out and strokes his thumb over me. I don't have a choice but to open my legs wider. To give him more.

And he takes it.

He toys with me up and down and up, spreading my wetness around before he slides one finger into me. I sigh in momentary relief before raw need yawns open inside of me. It's a sinkhole, taking everything with it. I want Mikhail to feed it until we both collapse in on ourselves.

"Mikhail, I—"

I want more, I want to say. But then he turns his wrist and strokes his thick finger along my insides.

All at once, it's too much.

We just started and I'm already spasming, gripping the edge of his desk. *He's going to kill me in under thirty seconds with the tip of one finger.*

But I want his weight against my chest. I want to feel how solid he is.

I grab the collar of his shirt and pull him up to me. "Fill me now."

I reach for his pants, but he's already there. Already unbuttoning. Already holding the hard length of himself in his palm.

"I came in my fist so many fucking times, Viviana… imagining it was you." He slides a second finger inside of me, stretching me. "I was waiting for the day I could fill you up again. With me. With our baby."

He gives his cock a rough stroke with one hand as he pumps two fingers into me. It's good, but it's not what I want. I want it to be him inside of me. I want it to be my skin, my warmth, my body wrapped around him.

"Mikhail," I whimper.

He doesn't seem to hear me. Or, if he does, he doesn't care. He slides his hand up and down his shaft, timing it with the speed of his fingers in and out of me. He's working both of us with his hands while he's one thrust away from being buried inside of me.

I don't understand it.

For years, I'd lie in bed with a toy between my legs, thinking about Mikhail in that bridal suite. The way he fit inside of me. The way he teased me.

Like this.

Now, he's *right here* and I still can't have him.

"I thought about you," I confess. "Every time I touched myself. Every time I came. It was always you."

A deep rumble moves through his chest. He drops his forehead to mine and lets out a ragged breath. "Fuck. You're so wet for me, Viviana."

So take me, I want to scream.

"I want you, Mikhail."

He circles his thumb over his head and strokes again. He's stretched so tight it looks painful.

Lord knows *I'm* in pain.

"I know you do. I can feel how much you want it." He finds a spot inside of me and circles his finger. I buck off the desk and he holds me down.

I'm clenching, pulsating around his fingers, and I can't stop. "I don't want—I want—Please."

"Tell me what you want, Viviana."

There's an urgency in his voice, but I can't make sense of it. I can't think about anything except the pressure building at my core. The way Mikhail's abs are flexing, pumping his hips into his own hand instead of into me.

"I want you," I whine. "Don't you want me?"

I sound pathetic even to my own ears, but the sinkhole in my chest has apparently swallowed my self-respect. I need answers more than I need dignity.

He grabs my hand and wraps it around the velvet length of him. He's warm and solid. He groans as he drags against my palm.

"Feel how much I want you. How hard I am, just *thinking* about putting my baby inside of you."

I groan. I've never been this turned on and this frustrated at the same time. I slide my hips to the edge of the desk, taking his fingers deeper, willing them to fill me the way I know he can.

"You're killing me," I whimper. "I want you. You want me. What are we doing?"

"When I came inside of you six years ago, it was because you felt so good. Because *this* felt so good that you didn't want me to pull out. It wasn't because we wanted a baby. This time…" His voice trails off as he thrusts into my hand, losing his train of thought to a groan. "When you get pregnant this time, I want both of us to want it."

"I want it, Mikhail. I want it."

I've wanted it for so long. Months. Years, probably, if I feel like being dangerously honest with myself. There was always something about Mikhail Novikov that drew me in. Even before I was willing to admit it.

"You want *me*," he counters. "You want my cock inside of you right now. I can feel how much you do. But when this is over, I don't want there to be another doubt in that beautiful fucking head of yours about what this is and what we're doing here."

He's worried that this is the lust talking.

I accused him of not wanting our baby and now, he's making sure we both go into this with eyes wide open.

His concern for me would be sweet—if it wasn't so absolutely ridiculous.

"I know what it's like to carry your baby, Mikhail. I've done it before and it was the single greatest thing I've ever done in my entire life." I take his face in my hands and look him in the eyes. "If I didn't want this, I wouldn't have charged up here and walked through that door. Now, put another baby inside of me right now. Please. I'm begging you."

His eyes flare just before his mouth crashes over mine, bowing me back. Our tongues slide together, tasting and teasing. I moan as he slips his fingers out of me. Then he pulls back and brings them to his lips, tasting me.

He licks them clean. If I wasn't horny out of my mind, I'd memorize the pull of his lips over his fingers. The way he savors me.

As it is, I have tunnel vision. I want to skip everything in the middle and get to the blinding light at the end. My body clenches hollowly, aching for him.

But Mikhail doesn't drive into me.

He grabs my hips and slides me off the table.

"What are you—"

He spins me around and presses on my shoulder until my ass is in the air and my bare breasts are smashed against the top of his desk.

Then he cracks his hand against my ass.

My skin ripples from the force of it. The sound echoes in the quiet room and I'm frozen. From the pain blistering on my backside… and the jolt of pleasure that is still vibrating directly between my legs.

"You spanked me," I breathe, too stunned to move.

Mikhail cups my ass in his large hand, smoothing calloused fingers over the red hot skin. "That's for ever doubting me."

Before I can tease that he's tempting me with a good time, Mikhail grips my hips and finally slides into me.

There are no soft, building thrusts. He presses and presses like he's as desperate for this as I am. Like we're making up for lost time.

I cry out when I'm sure I've taken all I can. But Mikhail soothes a hand down my spine and thrusts deeper as he coos, "Just like that." His legs are flush against the backs of my thighs. "Do you feel how perfectly we fit?"

I nod weakly. It's all I can manage. This is all I've wanted since he sat me on the desk, but now, it's more than I can handle. My brain is short-circuiting.

Mikhail wraps my hair around his fist and tugs, arching my back, pushing himself just that little bit deeper. "I asked you a question, Viviana."

I open my mouth and a desperate, pleading sound slips out. I have to search the lusty, muddied waters of my brain to find a single syllable. "Yes."

Of course I feel it. How could I not? Sex with Mikhail has never been just sex. It isn't enough for him to claim my body. He needs my mind, my soul. All of me.

Well, he can have it.

Each thrust has me stretching onto my toes, nearly lifting off the floor. I'm pinned between the table and his body, completely at Mikhail's mercy.

"This is how deep I'm going to be when I come," he says, sinking into me to illustrate the point. "This is how I'm going to put my baby inside you."

He's toeing a fine line between torture and pleasure. I'm panting and pleading. "Yes. Please."

Suddenly, his hand is around my throat and I'm lifted up, up until our bodies are flush together. My shoulder blades press into his sweat-damp chest and my head is on his shoulder. I'm pinned, unable to move, unable to do anything but take him at a new, devastating angle that has my eyes rolling back in my head. I reach for any bit of his skin I grab, settling on digging my nails into his muscled thighs.

With him right behind me like this, I can feel the ways he's falling apart, too. His heart pounds against my back. His breath is wild on my neck. He kisses my throat and my shoulder and I've never felt more out of control and more protected than in this moment.

Mikhail's voice is a dark whisper in my ear. "Come with me, Viviana. Let's make a baby together."

The words push me over the edge.

My body clenches, tightens. I hold him inside of me, gasping in time with his small thrusts until his hips slam against me and hold. His hand tightens around my throat and we're perfectly still, save for the pulse of him between my legs.

Finally, he lets me go and we collapse forward, a panting, sweating mess on top of the desk. He's still inside of me when he kisses the base of my neck. "I want every part of you, Viviana—inside and out. Never doubt that."

40

VIVIANA

As soon as I wake up, I reach for Mikhail.

It's only been a few days of this—fumbling for each other in the early morning and sliding together—but it's already an instinct. "The human desire to multiply," Mikhail joked one morning, running his finger along my opening as his *"desire to multiply"* leaked out of me and stained our sheets.

He's not even wrong. We're having sex—really, *really* great sex—but it's sex with a purpose. We are making a family and Mikhail never lets me forget it.

You're going to look so good carrying my baby.

Everyone is going to see you and know that you belong to me.

All of Mikhail's intensity is focused on getting me pregnant, and I love it.

"Food," Mikhail decides, sliding out of me from behind and rolling out of bed. He grabs my robe from the bathroom door and holds it open for me.

I press my legs together. "I need to clean up. I need to—"

"Leave it." His eyes darken, tracing over every naked inch of me. "Hold me inside of you. Maybe it will help."

"I don't see how it's going to make any difference. We're fucking more than we're not the last few days. I don't think we need any more 'help.'"

He yanks me to my feet and slides the robe over my arms. "It will help me get through breakfast without throwing you down on the table and filling you again."

I flush from head to toe. "Oh. Well then."

"That's what I thought." He pinches my lower lip between his teeth. "Let's eat."

Even sitting across the table from each other is sexually charged. I can't watch Mikhail butter his toast or take a bite of eggs without thinking about all the dirty things he's done with those fingers and that mouth.

Is this what people call the honeymoon period? Or am I always going to feel like this?

I'm not sure, but I enjoy the tingle down my spine and the warmth in my chest.

I pull my eyes away from him and focus on sustenance. After last night and this morning, I need the calories.

"I figured Dante would be awake by now."

"He's on a field trip with Anatoly and Mrs. Steinman." Mikhail eyes me over his coffee. "Anatoly told you about it last night. At dinner."

I frown. "I don't remember—" Then it hits me and my face flames.

Mikhail smirks, far too pleased with himself. "Was your mind somewhere else?"

Yeah—*in the gutter.*

I remember pretending to listen to Anatoly, nodding and smiling along with whatever he said. Under the table, Mikhail was dragging his hand up and down my thigh, inching higher and higher. It's what I deserved for wearing a dress to dinner. That's what Mikhail told me once we were alone, anyway.

When he finally slid his finger over the lace between my legs, I almost skyrocketed out of the chair.

I jab the tines of my fork at him. "You're becoming a distraction. We're not going to be able to pull this kind of stuff once we're back at the office."

I would have been more upset about Cerberus burning down if anyone had been hurt—which, thankfully, they weren't—and if it hadn't meant a prolonged vacation for me—which, thankfully, it had. Something about being kidnapped—*twice* —left me in need of a work sabbatical. But now that things are creeping towards something like normalcy, I'm excited to get back to it and settle into a new office.

"When did you say the offices would be ready?"

Mikhail is suddenly very focused on his nearly-empty plate. "Tomorrow."

"I need to tell Anatoly."

"He already knows."

"Right. Of course he does," I mutter, my brain whirring with a thousand new thoughts. "Is he going to be here at the house with Dante after his tutoring? Someone will need to be here with him since I won't be home until the late afternoons now. I hear my boss is a real hardass."

I smirk up at him, but Mikhail isn't smiling. "No one needs to be here with Dante." I'm about to argue before he adds, "Because you'll be here."

Mikhail drops the bomb and gets up from the table. As if this conversation is over. As if I'm just going to let him walk away.

"I'll be here tomorrow?" I ask cautiously. "Or…"

"Every day. Most days," he amends. "Since you won't be working."

Somewhere in the back of my head, a record scratches. "And why won't I be working?"

He meets my eyes with a sigh. "Think about it, Viviana."

"No." I jab a finger at him, shaking my head. "*No.* Don't say it like that. Don't say it like I'm being ridiculous and I should understand this. When we got married, I told you I was going to keep working."

"When we got married *the first time*."

"I didn't realize I needed to re-up my terms and conditions before the second ceremony," I snap.

"There are no terms and conditions this time. That's why this is different. Our marriage isn't a business deal anymore; it's a relationship."

Some girlish part of me is giddy hearing him say that, but I squash it down. This isn't time for fawning, lovesick Viviana. It's time to be serious.

"Great point, Mikhail. This *is* a relationship. Which means we each have needs and desires that need to be fulfilled and we should respect those."

Mikhail edges around the island, stalking towards me. "Believe me, Viviana, I have the utmost respect for your needs and desires."

I take a step back. "I'm not speaking in euphemisms here. I'm being serious."

"So am I." He keeps moving forward, backing me around the island. But each of his steps are worth two of mine and he catches up quickly, cornering me against the countertop. His arms bracket either side of me. "I can't meet your needs and desires if you get yourself killed in the breakroom."

He smells like citrus and maple syrup. I want to take a bite of him. "You're being dramatic."

"There's no such thing when we're at war. They burned the last building down. I'll never be able to trust that you're safe there."

"So I'm supposed to sit around the mansion all day and wait for you to come home?" I ask incredulously. "You expect me to be happy with a social circle that includes you, yourself, and your penis?"

"You've been thrilled with that social circle the last few days." The deep rumble of his voice vibrates between my legs. I'm painfully aware that he's still dripping down the insides of my thighs.

"Don't change the subject."

"I'm not." His mouth whispers over my neck. I close my eyes and take a deep steadying breath that doesn't do a damn thing to steady me. There's no such thing when he's this close to me. "The fact that we've been fucking like it's our full-time job is very much the subject. You're going to be pregnant with my baby soon, Viviana. The target on your back will only get bigger."

"So hire more security. I'll take Raoul with me everywhere I go."

Mikhail pulls back to look at me, annoyingly at ease. "He's not a bodyguard and he'd hate you for even suggesting it."

"Then find a bodyguard. I don't care who it is. You can't make me quit."

"Okay." He nods, thinking it over. "Then you're fired."

I shove against his chest, but he catches my wrists in his hands and curls them harmlessly against his chest. "You can't do that!" I argue, even though I know he can. "I'll sue you for wrongful termination."

He kisses my knuckles and my wrists. He slides the large sleeves of my robe higher, tasting my skin.

I try to pull away, but he pins my hands to the edge of the countertop and looms over me. The front of the robe gaps open and he notes it for several heated seconds before his eyes meet mine again. "You told me this is what you wanted, Viviana. You told me you wanted my baby."

"I do, but—"

"Do you want to be a personal assistant more than you want to be pregnant?"

I sigh. "It doesn't have to be black and white like that."

He catches my mouth, kissing me until I'm liquid. He presses his forehead to mine, breathing hard. "Right now, the entire world is black and white. There are good guys and bad guys. There's safety and danger. I'm not willing to risk you or Dante or the baby-to-come," he says, brushing his hand over my stomach, "in some gray area. Until I know it's safe, you're fired."

What he's saying makes sense, which is somehow worse.

"So what am I supposed to do until then?"

He takes me by the waist and lifts me onto the counter. His eyebrow is arched, his pupils expanding with every breath. "I have a few ideas."

I don't want this conversation to be over, but what more is there to say?

Mikhail loves me. He wants to keep me safe. How can I be upset with him about that?

I slowly untie my robe, letting it gape open. "I thought the goal was to make it through breakfast without having sex again."

"And we did. Breakfast is over." Mikhail shoves my robe off my shoulders, leaving me completely naked on the counter. He drags a finger slowly between my breasts. "That's an accomplishment worth celebrating."

He slides me to the edge of the counter and pushes into me. This morning, the sex was slow and gentle. Now, he spreads each of my knees against the counter and slams into me. It's fast and rough.

I tug on the roots of his hair, meeting each thrust halfway

until we're slapping together. Until my screams echo off the tile and Mikhail is grunting against my neck.

I clamp down around him a second before he dives deep and stays there, twitching into me.

"Soon, you're going to be carrying my baby." He bites my neck, soothing the hurt with his tongue. "You'll be pregnant and nothing else will matter."

I still don't know what I'm going to do every day. I don't know when I'm going to be able to leave the house—when we'll be safe. But when Mikhail is holding me like this, none of those questions seem nearly as important.

If this is all I ever have—Dante and Mikhail and the baby-to-come…

It's enough.

41

VIVIANA

Mikhail, Dante, the baby we're trying for... that's enough for me.

They are *more* than enough for me.

I laid in bed all night, feeling the truth of that deep in my bones. But I couldn't ignore another, just as persistent truth: knowing they are enough doesn't mean I can't want more.

Mikhail is in the kitchen with a mug of coffee when I walk in, armed with nothing but a middle-of-the-night plan and unearned optimism. He looks up and then looks harder. It's like a double take, but from the moment he sets his eyes on me, they never waver.

He slams his mug on the table and I have to fight not to flinch.

If I had to guess, I'd say he's probably pissed because I'm wearing my go-to work outfit—a navy blue pencil skirt with a pale blue button-down. The top few buttons are open, revealing the barest hint of business-appropriate cleavage.

The heels are three inches high—tall enough that I meet most men in the office at eye-level, but short enough that I can be on my feet all day without wanting to throw myself out of a conference room window.

"Viviana." Mikhail grits out my name. I'm not sure if he's mad at me or seconds away from fucking me on the countertop the way he did a few days ago. He always had a thing for this skirt.

"Good morning," I chirp, turning away from him to pour myself some coffee.

He curses softly under his breath.

A second later, he's behind me. We aren't touching, but I can feel him. It's a pull like magnets getting too close.

"How did you sleep?" I ask innocently.

"Peacefully," he snarls. "Because my wife respects my decisions and doesn't pull ridiculous stunts to get my attention."

I hum in agreement, nodding along even though I want to elbow him in the ribs. "That's great, Mikhail. I slept well, too."

"Viviana." He repeats my name again, lower this time. "Don't do this."

I turn to face him. My hands are shaking so badly I have to leave my coffee on the counter. I don't want to spill it on my shirt. "I'm not doing anything, Mikhail."

He pointedly looks me up and down. "Then what's this?"

"It's not a stunt to get your attention, that's for sure."

"Well, you've got my attention anyway. What the fuck is this about?"

I sigh. "I want to go back to work."

"No."

"You can't just dismiss me like that. I'm your wife. We are in this together."

"You *are* my wife," he agrees. "And I'm not going to let my wife die in this war because she wanted to get paid by the hour to make copies and schedule meetings."

"Don't dismiss what I do! Don't act like it means nothing."

"But it *does* mean nothing." He cradles my cheek in his hand, stepping closer so I have to tip my head back to take in all of him. "Everything means nothing compared to you. You are the only thing that matters to me, Viviana. Keeping you safe is more important than anything else."

My heart cracks open at the tenderness in his voice, but I steel myself. I knew there was a real risk I would cave to his warm hands and soft lips and deep voice. God knows I've caved more than enough times already.

That's why I practiced this. I press my shoulders back and repeat the line I prepared. "If you won't let me work at Cerberus, then I'll apply for a job somewhere else."

His hand drops to his side. His eyes narrow. "Not without my permission."

"You're my husband, not my prison warden. I don't need your permission." I reach for his hand, stroking my thumb over his thick wrist. "You can't force me to stay home, Mikhail."

He looks down at where I'm touching him. For a second, I think he might be ready to compromise.

Then he raises my arm over my head, bends low, and tosses me over his shoulder like I'm a fresh kill, like the deer from the woods. He might as well bind my hands and legs and drag me across the floor toward the clean-up shed.

"Put me down!" I pound my fists on his back all the way up the stairs and down the hall, but it's about as worthwhile as punching a concrete wall. Feels about the same, too. My hand is throbbing, but he doesn't even have the decency to pretend I'm hurting him. "Mikhail, put me—"

He drops me unceremoniously on the bed. *My old bed*, I realize as I fall face first into a comforter that doesn't smell anything like Mikhail.

I felt powerful when I put this outfit on this morning, but now, it's twisted around my waist and rumpled. I feel like a newborn giraffe taking its first steps as I scramble to the edge of the bed.

"What in the hell was that for?"

"I can't trust you to do the smart thing, so I'm doing it for you."

I gape. "You're locking me in here?"

"You aren't giving me another choice."

"You have a million choices. You live a blessed life where every choice is yours—even other people's!"

He rolls his eyes and I take the opportunity to lunge for the door.

Mikhail catches me around the waist easily and slings me back on the bed.

"You have guards all over this house," I remind him. "You don't need to lock me up in one room to keep me here."

"I know you better than anyone, Viviana." He curls a finger under my chin. I swat him away and the asshole just smirks. "Which is why you and I both know I absolutely need to lock you in this room if there's any chance you'll behave today."

I fight with him all the way to the door, but he pins my arms to my sides, kisses my forehead, and then pushes me away from the door just before he slams it closed.

For the first hour, I alternate between banging on the door and lying on the bed, my head dangling off the end. As if a different perspective on the room might reveal some escape hatch I missed earlier. A secret tunnel or one of those spinning bookshelves from the movies.

But it's the same old room. A balcony that's too far from the ground to jump off and a locked door that, even if I could get through it, would leave me facing down a small army of guards who would rather make a lifelong enemy out of me than go against Mikhail's orders.

Eventually, I flip through a few books and try to lose myself in mindless television, but the minutes crawl by.

There's one brief burst of excitement when the door cracks open mid-afternoon and Anatoly's face appears. He's there only long enough to hurl a protein bar and a bottle of water at me before snapping it shut again.

"Ow!" I shout at him, rubbing the sore spot on my thigh where the water bottle pelted me. I swear I hear him laughing as he walks away.

It's as I'm pulling the hem of my skirt up to inspect my thigh that an idea hits me.

I kick the protein bar under the bed and run into my picked-over closet. Most of my clothes have migrated into Mikhail's room, including all of my favorite pajamas and most comfortable leggings. But what this closet is absolutely lousy with is lingerie. Between Mikhail working nonstop the first few days we were back and our fight, I haven't had much use for it.

Until now.

I undress, swap out my nude bra and undies for something red and lacy, and then re-dress. But this time, I hike my skirt a little higher on my hips, rolling the band under so the hemline falls to my mid-thigh. I also unbutton my shirt until my business-appropriate cleavage is something closer to "ripe for an HR complaint." So much of my chest is visible that just walking through the front doors in this shirt might be considered sexual harassment.

If that isn't, then texting photos of myself in this outfit to the CEO's personal phone *definitely* qualifies.

But locking me in this room against my will is abduction, so I think said CEO has it coming.

I balance my phone on a pile of books at the end of the bed and embark on the boudoir session of Mikhail's dreams. If he thinks he can drop me in this room and forget about me from nine to five, he has another thing coming.

I start off slow—a few stereotypical sexy assistant shots where I'm biting the end of a pencil and crawling towards the phone with my shirt draped open. Then I start thinking about how Mikhail will respond when he sees these photos. What he'll do…

To himself.

To me.

I send the first batch of photos and don't wait to see what he says before the skirt is in a rumpled pile next to the bed and my shirt is unbuttoned. I let the sleeves slip down my shoulders as I run my hands over myself, imagining they belong to Mikhail. I snap photos from every imaginable angle, sending them as fast as I can take them.

By the time the sun is sinking low outside my window, I'm wound tight. I texted Mikhail more than enough photos that suggested I took care of myself all day, but I never actually finished. Coming from my own hand while my traitorous brain pictured Mikhail would feel like a hollow victory.

I want to save the sexual tension swirling in me for when Mikhail comes crawling through my door, begging me for forgiveness and to put him out of his horny misery.

I'm perched on the end of the bed in my lingerie and my loosely-buttoned shirt when the lock finally clicks open and Mikhail steps inside.

I curl my legs underneath me, sit tall, and wait for the groveling to start.

But Mikhail doesn't drop to his knees. His tongue doesn't loll out of his mouth. Cartoon hearts don't explode out of his eyes.

He stops in the doorway, looking like an exhausted, less put-together version of the man who locked me in this room eight hours ago, and crosses his arms. "Is this all a game for you, Viviana?"

None of the Mikhails in my imagination ever said that, so I'm not sure how to respond.

His jaw shifts. "I didn't lock you in here as a joke."

"That's good, because it wasn't funny," I snipe back.

He drags a hand through his hair. His tie is loose around his neck. "I needed you to understand where I'm coming from. I thought you'd sit in here and think about—"

"You sent me to my room to 'think about what I've done?'" I snort. "I'm not a child, Mikhail. You can't lock me away every time we disagree."

"I don't have a choice when we disagree on what your safety is worth!"

I roll my eyes. "You spent all day in the office. If you're safe there, then I don't see why I wouldn't be."

"You don't see because you've never *seen it*," he growls. He paces away from me before he spins back, eyes pleading with me to listen. "You've never walked into your own house to find your family butchered."

The oxygen in the room is sucked out in an instant. Suddenly, I want one hundred more layers to hide in. I want to look like Joey in that one episode of *Friends*. "*Could I have any more clothes on?!*" Because the next-to-nothing I'm wearing is a slap in the face to the trauma Mikhail has been through.

Trauma I should have thought about before I spent all day sexting him when he was trying to protect me.

"I've lost my family before, Viviana. I know what my enemies are capable of. They don't want to kill me; they want to *destroy me*." His voice breaks at the same time my heart does. "Killing you would be a surefire way to make that happen."

I lunge across the room just like I did eight hours ago. But this time, I throw my arms around Mikhail's neck. "I'm sorry."

His hand slips under my shirt and spreads across the bare skin of my back. It's warm and firm and comfortable. "I need to know that you understand what's at stake."

I nod against his chest and take deep breaths of the woodsy citrus scent of him. "I understand."

"I'm not going to lose you," he mutters into my hair. His voice is so soft I'm not even sure he's talking to me.

But I hear him loud and clear.

I hold him tighter.

Mikhail and Dante and the family we're building are enough for me. They're more than enough.

They're all I need.

42

VIVIANA

"You should invite someone over."

I roll over in bed, my head pillowed on my arm while I watch Mikhail do the entire world a disservice by buttoning a shirt to hide his bare chest. I'm distracted by the valleys and ridges of him and only manage a weak, "Huh?"

"You can't leave, but that doesn't mean someone can't come here to see you." He shrugs. "A friend or… whoever."

"Anatoly is my only friend."

Mikhail looks mildly horrified. "That can't be true."

If I wasn't so tired, I probably would have kept that confession to myself. But it's early and I'm not thinking clearly. "It's hard to make friends when you're on the run for six years. And it's not like there are a lot of options around here. Anatoly makes friends everywhere he goes, but Raoul keeps things strictly professional."

He bobs his head back and forth, reluctantly agreeing. "Fair enough."

"Mrs. Steinman is a hit with the under-seven crowd, but she thinks lingering before and after Dante's tutoring sessions makes for a 'confusing power structure' for Dante. As soon as his session is over, she bolts."

I can't even blame her for that. She's being paid to teach Dante, not socialize with his grown adult mother. And I'm not desperate enough to pay her to be my friend...

Yet.

"There *was* Stella, but..." My voice trails off. Mikhail doesn't react, but I know he hasn't forgiven himself for not suspecting Pyotr was a spy. Anatoly still flinches any time there's even a passing reference to Stella. It's a tender subject and it's easiest not to talk about her.

Mikhail glances up at me while fixing his shirt cuffs. "I would stay, but there's still a lot of organizing to do at the new offices."

"And you called in sick yesterday."

"I didn't call in sick. I don't need to call in sick at my own company. I told them I was busy."

It wasn't a lie. Mikhail *was* busy.... ordering in lunch from my favorite cafe, playing with Dante in the pool, and thoroughly distracting me from whichever movie it was I convinced him to watch with me. We didn't even make it through the opening credits, so I'm really not sure.

It was a nice day and a *very* nice night, but it felt loaded. As the day went on, I found myself waiting for the other shoe to drop.

I still am.

"What was all that about, anyway?" I ask as casually as I can. "You never take off work."

"We spent a week in Costa Rica."

"Because I was in danger."

He frowns. "There was also the cabin."

"I was in danger. Again." I peek up at him. "Do you see why I'm worried? You don't stop working unless my life is at risk."

Mikhail kneels on the edge of the bed, his large hands cupping my face. "You have nothing to worry about, Viviana. Everything is fine."

"So I can leave the mansion again?"

"*Almost* everything is fine." He drops my face and pulls on his jacket. "As long as you stay here, everything is fine."

Tears prick the backs of my eyes and I turn away, blinking fast. Maybe I can fan them back into my tear ducts or dry them before they hit my cheeks. Mikhail explained why I need to stay on the property and I trust him. He's been through a lot. If I can make his life easier by following his rules until this war is over, I will.

That doesn't mean any of it is easy.

The bed dips under his weight. "Don't cry."

I swipe at my stupid tears. "You weren't supposed to see that."

"I want to see everything when it comes to you, Viviana." He grips my chin, tilting my face up to his. "You don't need to hide from me."

"I'm not hiding; I just don't want you to worry about me all day. I think I'm just tired and stressed. It's making me emotional."

"I want to make this bearable for you."

"'Bearable' is such a low bar and you are leaping over it, Mikhail. I swear, I'm okay." I shove on his rock-solid chest. "Now, go. You're going to be late."

He leans his chest against my hand until I can't hold him back. My arm buckles and he falls gently against me, brushing his thumb over my damp cheek. "I'm the boss; I'm never late."

I snort. "Don't say that in front of your employees. It wouldn't be good for morale."

"The only person's morale I care about is yours." He presses his lips to mine for a soft kiss. And another. My stomach swoops as the gentle kisses turn more heated. They deepen and expand until his hand is cupped around the back of my head and I'm clinging to him, putting wrinkles in his clean shirt.

He starts to press me down into the bed, but I break away, panting. "Okay. Morale is officially very high."

"It could be higher," he growls, sinking his teeth into my bottom lip.

My stomach does another nervous flip. I chuckle and shove on his chest. "Mrs. Steinman is going to be here in a little bit. I need to get Dante out of bed and feed him breakfast. We don't have time for this."

He groans in frustration, but I manage to walk him to the door.

Just before he slips into the hall, he hooks me against his body. "Later."

I have to press my thighs together at the dark promise in his voice.

"Later," I agree. "Later."

Mikhail looks me over from head to toe, his eyes snagging on the way the t-shirt of his that I'm wearing barely reaches the tops of my legs. He bites a knuckle and forces himself down the hallway.

I close the door, still feeling off-kilter from the kissing and his attention. My head is foggy and my limbs tingle. I blink hard a few times to center myself.

Then I sprint to the bathroom and drop to my knees in front of the toilet.

"You and Dante can't leave the mansion." Anatoly glances over his shoulder to make sure Dante is still focused on the stacks of blocks singing and dancing on the television. He lowers his voice. "We're in a war."

I roll my eyes. "Do you think I don't know that?"

"If you did, you wouldn't be asking me to take you on a field trip."

"It's not a field trip," I hiss. "I have an appointment."

He leans against the island and crosses his arms. "An appointment for what?"

"Nothing."

He snorts. "Okay. I'll be sure to tell Mikhail all about how I risked your life to take you to your secret appointment for nothing *before* he disembowels me."

I arch a brow. "Please don't tell me you're scared of Mikhail."

"Yes. Yes, I absolutely am," he says with no hint of shame whatsoever. "You've met your husband. He's scary. Especially when it comes to you."

I sigh. This was a bad idea. To be fair, I didn't brainstorm very many options before I decided Anatoly was my best one.

Making a rope out of my sheets and rappelling down the side of the mansion was a top contender, but I don't think I'd have the upper body strength for that on a good day. And today has *not* been a good day. I've thrown up everything I've eaten all morning. If I didn't get nauseous and throw up halfway down the do-it-myself rope, I'd probably pass out from low blood sugar alone.

I feel a little woozy right now, actually.

I grip the edge of the counter and Anatoly tracks my movements. He watches me with a careful intensity I recognize. These Novikov men miss nothing.

"What's wrong with you, Viv?"

"Nothing is *wrong* with me. I'm sick. Sometimes, humans get sick. Then those humans need to go see a doctor. It's fine."

Anatoly is out of his chair with his phone in his hand in a second. "If you're sick, I'll call Mikhail. We'll get a doctor here and—"

"No!" I slap his phone away. He fumbles with it in mid-air for a second before he manages to get a grip on it.

"What the hell is wrong with you? You're acting insane." Then he leans back, assessing. "And now that you mention it, you look like shit."

"Gee, thanks." I cross my arms and mutter, "Hugging a toilet all morning will do that to you."

"You're throwing up? Is it a stomach bug?" He waves his arms between us like he's an air traffic controller.

"Something like that." I chew on my lower lip. "I'm pregnant."

Anatoly's eyes widen. "Again?"

I shrug. "I think. I d-don't know. I'm having all of the same symptoms I had with Dante."

Overly emotional? Check.

Nauseous? Check.

Nipples so sensitive I want to scream when a light breeze blows? Double check.

"Then you should still tell Mikhail." He waves his phone in front of me. "Not telling him shit is how things get complicated."

"Telling him the news before I'm sure could also complicate things. I don't want to get his hopes up, Nat. He really wants this."

Anatoly sags. "I know he does, but that doesn't mean I can lie to him. He'll know I've taken you through the gates the second we leave. There's no way to hide it."

He's still talking when my phone buzzes. I grab it from the island and almost can't believe what I'm seeing.

"What is it?"

I turn my phone around, biting back a smirk. "The perfect excuse."

MIKHAIL*: I'm telling Anatoly to bring you to the new Cerberus offices today. I want to have lunch together and give you a proper tour.*

Anatoly groans and looks up at the ceiling. "Why can my life never be easy?"

"Is that a yes?"

He jabs a finger in my direction. "It's a 'fuck you' for getting me into messes like this."

"Was *that* a yes?"

He points to the stairs. "Go get dressed for your booty call with your husband. We'll stop at the clinic on the way."

I blow Anatoly a kiss, which he swats out of the air. But I don't care if he's annoyed. I might be pregnant.

And in a few hours, I'll know for sure.

43

VIVIANA

I only have time to read half of the chart on gynecological disorders before the doctor comes in.

She's wearing burgundy-colored scrubs and has an alarmingly large travel mug of coffee in one hand. "The test was positive," she says as soon as she's in the room. She doesn't even look at me. She has all the inflection of someone reading out their WiFi password. It's the way a robot would deliver news, no emotion whatsoever.

Surely if she was delivering good news, she'd say it with a little more gusto.

I frown. "Positive for what?"

Finally, she looks up at me. "You came here for a pregnancy test, correct?"

"I peed in a cup. I guess I'm not sure who did which test, but I left my sample in the bathroom next to—"

"You're pregnant," she interrupts. "The strip turned pink."

My stomach churns and I'm not sure if it's nausea or anxiety. I check to make sure there is a trash can within arm's reach just in case. "Are the tests in your office more accurate than the ones I can buy at the drugstore?"

"Nope. They're the exact same thing, just without the pretty plastic wrapping."

Okay, now, I'm sure: it's anxiety.

"Then what's the point of coming here to confirm it?"

"You need a positive test on record to be referred to an obstetrician as a patient." She tucks her clipboard under her arm and shrugs. "It's bureaucratic."

"Is there anything more... conclusive? I took a pregnancy test a few months ago that said it was positive, but it turned out to be a false positive."

"False positives are very rare," she says flatly. "Only one percent of positive results are false."

"Then I guess I'm one in a hundred."

The joke falls flat. Probably because the doctor lacks the human capacity for humor. She also lacks anything even resembling bedside manner.

"So?" I press when she says nothing. "Is there a test that's more conclusive?"

She sighs like I'm the worst part of her day. "Stop in at the lab on your way out. I'll order a blood test."

"When will I have the results from that?"

"It depends on how busy the lab is. Could be this afternoon, could be four days. I'm not sure."

I'm not sure is some half-assed code for *I don't care.*

"Thanks for narrowing it down for me," I mumble.

Finally, she chuckles, but I'm not laughing.

Anatoly shifts the car into park. "I think you should tell him."

I fake a gasp. "You do? I can't believe that. You definitely haven't been saying that every thirty seconds since we left the clinic."

To be clear: he has in fact been saying it every thirty seconds since we left the clinic. From the moment I told Anatoly the test came back positive, it's all he's been able to say.

"Sorry." He shrugs. "I just think you should tell him."

I reach over the console and punch his shoulder. "I know! Stop saying it."

"I'll stop saying it when you tell my brother you're having his baby."

I level a glare at him. "Are you going to be able to keep it together when we see him? Given what you do for a living, I would've guessed you'd have a better poker face."

"What is it you think I do for a living?"

"Whatever Mikhail tells you to," I guess.

"Exactly," he snaps. "I am man enough to admit that when my brother tells me to jump, I don't even ask, 'How high?' I just start jumping. So, no, keeping secrets from him isn't one of my many, many skills."

I spit the ginger lozenge I stole from the clinic's lobby into a napkin and wedge it in the pocket of the passenger door. "Then you have an elevator ride's amount of time to practice. Because I'm not telling him today. I'm not telling until I get the results back from the blood test."

If the doctor was right and false positives are rare, then I'm probably pregnant. That doesn't mean I'm ready to start shouting the news from the rooftops. Especially because, as much as I wanted this, the news still makes me feel like I'm going to hurl. Or maybe that's the morning sickness.

All I know is, the next time I tell Mikhail I'm pregnant, it's going to be for real.

We can't afford any doubts.

The old Cerberus Industries was located on the third floor of a crumbling building downtown. There had been some surface-level updates here and there over the years, but the building was dark brown brick and the terrazzo tile floors were yellowed and chipping.

The new Cerberus Industries belongs in a sci-fi movie. It's all sleek, chrome lines and wall-to-wall glass. There's almost zero chance that a bathroom on the fourth floor could leak through the ceiling unchecked for years and make a conference room on the floor below into an unusable sewer. So, a definite upgrade.

"This place almost makes me want a desk job," Anatoly sighs, adjusting the lapels of his well-worn leather jacket and cracking his tattooed knuckles.

"Oh, yeah," I muse. "You'd fit right in."

As soon as the doors open, a petite woman with tortoise shell glasses and a crisp pantsuit grins at us. "Welcome to Cerberus Industries. How can I—" Her mouth snaps shut at the sight of Anatoly walking out of the elevator. It takes her a couple seconds to regain her composure. "How can I h-help you?"

Anatoly grins and tosses her a wink. "Thanks, but I know my way around."

He moves to walk past her, and I'm positive she's going to let him. Anatoly has a way of getting exactly what he wants from women. But just as he's edging past her desk, she darts out and plants every bit of her five-foot-nothing frame in front of him. "I'm sorry, but I need to know who you're here to see. It's protocol."

His smile sharpens. "I'm here to see Mikhail Novikov."

"Mr. Novikov is busy. If you leave your name, I can give him a message."

"I'm not leaving my name with his—" He eyes her up and down. "Are you his new assistant?"

She straightens her jacket. "I am. And Mr. Novikov told me to let no one in to see him except for his wife."

I step forward and raise my hand in a friendly wave. "That's me. I'm his wife." The words still feel bizarre coming out of my mouth. "I'm Viviana and this is Anatoly, Mikhail's brother."

"Oh, God." The woman's cheeks turn a deep shade of pink. "I'm so sorry. I should have guessed. I'm Adriana."

"Security is usually my job, but that's okay. You can make it up to me next time," Anatoly tells her as he tries, once again, to waltz past her down the hall.

Once again, Adriana stops him. "I'm sorry, Mr. Novikov, but Mr.—er, the other Mr. Novikov only gave clearance for his wife to come to his office."

"Of course he did." Anatoly's shoulders droop. "And where am I supposed to go?"

Adriana bites the corner of her mouth, clearly holding back a smile. "He told me to tell you to find yourself some lunch and come back in an hour."

Anatoly narrows his eyes. He may jump whenever Mikhail tells him to, but he doesn't take orders from anyone else. I can sense an argument brewing, so I dart around them before I'm stuck in the middle of it.

I can hear Adriana and Anatoly talking behind me, but I hurry down the hall. I'd rather do this without Anatoly, anyway. I don't trust him not to crumble and tell Mikhail about the pregnancy the moment we're through the door.

I'm halfway down the hall before I realize I have no idea where Mikhail's office is. It's a maze of solid wood doors with empty name plates screwed into the walls. Everyone is still getting settled. I'm contemplating turning around and asking for Adriana's help.

Then, a deep voice beckons me from the door to my right.

"Come in, Viviana."

There is a tall, thin window set into the wall next to his door, but the blinds are drawn. I have no idea how Mikhail knows it's me outside the door, but I'm also not surprised.

I push the door open. "Could you be any more obvious about the fact that this is a booty call?"

The words are still hanging in the air when I look around his office and realize, yes, he could be a *lot* more obvious.

And that's exactly what he's being.

"Mikhail!" I hiss his name and slam his office door shut. I flick the lock closed, but the metal bolt doesn't seem sturdy enough. I want bars and chains. I want a moat dug into the floor outside of his office to make sure no one comes in here.

Not until the projector is turned off. And burned. And the ashes have been scattered to the winds.

"Do you like it?" Mikhail kicks his feet up on his desk and gestures to the wall, where a slideshow of the naked photos I sent him the other day are on a nonstop carousel. Around and around and around I go, wearing less and less clothing until the pictures start all over again.

"What if I was someone else? What if you called the wrong person in here and they saw this?"

"Then I would have told them to leave." He dips his chin, smirking up at me. "Because I'm waiting for my wife."

44

VIVIANA

Mikhail turns away from me to stare at the slideshow he made. We're both watching it. The pictures flicking through one by one. Each frame that passes makes me blush that much harder.

"We already talked about my little photoshoot," I mumble. "I said I was sorry."

He tips his head to the side, appreciating a landscape photo of me lying on my stomach across the bed. My knees are bent, ankles crossed. I am my own harshest critic, but even I have to admit it's hot. The lace thong does absolutely nothing to cover the curve of my ass and my arms are squeezing my chest together.

"Sorry for what?" Mikhail asks thoughtfully.

I tear my eyes away from the slideshow and focus on him. The way he swallows. The finger drawing slow circles along his knee. *Is he imagining he's touching me?*

"You were pissed about these pictures," I remind him. "You hated them."

He turns to me, his icy blue eyes laser-focused. "I was pissed that you missed the point. I was pissed that you used your entire day to punish me."

"Punish *you*? I was the one locked in my bedroom. If anyone was being punished, it was me."

Mikhail stands up and paces slowly around his desk. His sleeves are rolled around his forearms. I can see the way his muscles work as he flexes his hands at his side. His pants pull taut across his muscular thighs… and the large bulge centered between them. "You wouldn't say that if you knew how fucking hard I was all day. It was a special kind of torture."

"Because of me?" I whisper.

He tips his head towards the wall where the pictures are still flashing. Another one is of me from the neck down, kneeling on the bed. One hand is curled over the red lace of my panties. The other is cupping my breast.

My instinct is to be embarrassed. To ask him to turn them off. My eyes want to focus on the stretch mark over my thighs and the mushy cellulite of my hips.

But Mikhail doesn't let me.

He moves behind me, his heat burning through the thin layers of my clothes. His breath on the back of my neck brings my entire body to attention.

"I had to come to my office between meetings and fuck my hand because I couldn't focus on anything but the way you looked with your legs spread on the bed." His hand slips over my shoulder and lower, circling my breasts. My nipples ache, but for the first time in days, it's a good kind of ache. "I was supposed to be talking numbers and projections, but the only thing I wanted to know is how wet you were."

"Very," I breathe, leaning back against his hard chest. His cock presses into my lower back. "I was so worked up. I never…"

His mouth is hot on my neck. He slides his hands up my waist, spreading his fingers across my ribs like he wants to hold as much of me as possible.

"Never what?" he growls in my ear. He asks the question like he already knows. He just wants to hear me say it.

I squeeze my thighs together and grind my ass against the bulge in his pants. "I never finished. I couldn't. I knew my hand would never satisfy me the way you could."

"No one can satisfy you the way I can." He works his hands around my waist and slips one inside my pants. The second his finger strokes over my soaked center, I'm putty. I sink into him, my head on his shoulder. "Can they?"

"No," I gasp.

He shoves my panties aside and dips into my wetness. He teases me up and down until he's teasing agonizingly slow circles over my clit. "Say it, Viviana. Tell me."

I squeeze my eyes closed, already fighting off my climax. "No one can satisfy me the way you can, Mikhail. No one has ever fucked me like you do."

He takes his hand away and I think I said something wrong. Then he grips my chin and forces my eyes to the wall. "Look at yourself. Look at how dirty you are for me."

A blush creeps up my chest and my neck. I've never sent dirty pictures before. I had never even considered it before the other day. But Mikhail makes me crazy. He drives me to do things I would never do: like, oh, I dunno… fuck him in my bridal suite the night before my wedding to his brother.

Or watch a slideshow of myself projected on his office wall while he undresses me.

Once my pants are gone, Mikhail kicks my ankles apart, spreading my legs. Then he slowly bends me over his desk.

"Keep looking at yourself," he orders as he slides his own zipper down.

"I want to look at *you*," I whine.

"Then maybe this will be a fitting punishment for the hell you put me through the other day, after all." He slides the string of my thong to the side and strokes his head up and down my opening. I stretch my arms long in front of me, gripping the far side of the desk so I don't melt into a puddle of goo on the floor.

The slideshow starts over. It's me sitting in front of the camera, my skirt hiked high on my thighs and my shirt gaping open. Add a couple inches to the skirt and do up one more button and it could be a professional headshot. I'm not even sure why I sent it.

But Mikhail growls. "That one is my favorite."

I huff out a laugh. "That one? Why?"

"Look at your eyes." He strokes himself through my wetness, teasing us both. "That's the look you give me when you want me. When you look at me like that, I know I'm about to be inside of you."

I'm about to tell him that I always look at him like that when he pushes into me. I moan, arching back to take him deeper. But Mikhail teases in and out of me. He moves in toe-curling increments, taking me a little deeper with every thrust.

I reach back and drag my nails over his thighs. He's still wearing his pants and it's doing something for me. The thought of him zipping up his pants and wearing these clothes into a meeting minutes after being inside of me... I like it.

"You're going to smell like sex the rest of the day," I gasp, bucking my hips back to meet him. "You're going to smell like me."

He groans and drives into me, finally buried as deep as he can go. He grabs a handful of my hair and bends my neck back so I'm looking at the screen again.

"Once I fuck a baby into you, I want you to take these pictures again."

The words are on the tip of my tongue. *I'm pregnant now. You've already fucked a baby into me.*

But I don't want him to stop. I don't want this moment to be sweet or tender.

I want to feel depraved.

"I hope it happens now," he snarls, our bodies slapping together. "Any time I see you and the way you're growing my child, I'll remember you like this: bent over my desk, dripping wet for me."

My pussy quivers around him. Pleasure pulses through me and I know he feels it based on the way he grunts, his fingers digging deeper into my hips.

All at once, he pulls out and flips me over.

"Mikhail!" I whine, instantly sliding my hand between my legs. "I'm so close."

"Me, too. But not yet." His eyes are black as he reaches for my shirt and shoves it over my chest. He palms my breasts, making my sensitive nipples scream. I hiss and he likes it.

So do I.

"You lured me here with lunch and now, you're edging me on your desk?" I whimper, sounding every bit as pathetic as I feel. "It's cruel."

"I'm not edging you, Viviana." He drags a finger between my breasts and over my belly button. He slips between my legs and parts me, examining the most intimate part of me like it belongs to him. Because it does. "I want to test out a theory."

I sink my teeth into my lower lip. "What theory is that?"

He leans over me, kissing my stomach and my hips. Then he grins over the length of my body. "I want to know if you taste as good as you look."

He drags his tongue over me and I cry out. My fingers find their way to his hair and I tug on him, not fully sure if I'm pulling him closer or pushing him away. The sensation building is too big. I don't know what to do with it.

His tongue delves into me as he hooks my legs over his shoulders. I clench my thighs around his ears, terrified he'll leave me like this.

"Is this better than your hand?" he murmurs between kisses to my clit.

My back arches off the table. I can't answer him, but the cry I let out has to be enough. He has to know that he's absolutely destroying me.

He thrusts his tongue into me again and then grabs my wrist. He brings my hand between my thighs and he doesn't need to tell me what to do.

I circle my fingers over myself the way I wanted to the other day. It wouldn't have been enough then, but with Mikhail tongue-fucking me, it only takes a few strokes before I'm airborne.

"Mikhail!" I moan, rolling my hips against his mouth to take him deeper. He has to band his arm across my hips to keep me from bucking off the desk.

"We're so much better together," he growls and I feel the vibration of it inside of me. Then he stands up and slams himself inside of me.

I'm still pulsing when he fills me.

"Oh, fuck." My leg is hooked over his shoulder and he turns and kisses my knee, my calf. He thrusts into me, prolonging what was already an earth-shattering orgasm. "You feel so good, Viviana."

I'm coming down and my vision clears. I get to watch as Mikhail pumps into me. His brows are pinched together. His square jaw is like granite, clenched tighter than I've ever seen it.

Knowing the pictures I sent could bring a man like Mikhail to this is intoxicating.

Then he looks down at me and explodes.

He spills into me in long, steady strokes. I feel the heat of him seeping through every part of my core. When he's done, he lets my legs fall to the side and collapses against my chest.

"Fucking hell." He presses a lazy kiss to the underside of my breast. "You look so good when I make you come."

"What a coincidence. I *feel* so good when you make me come." I laugh and run my fingers through his sweaty hair.

After a few minutes, he stands up and finds my clothes. He slides them over my legs.

"I need to clean up."

He shakes his head, a dark look in his eyes. "Don't. The only way I'm going to be able to let you leave this room is if I know I'm still inside of you."

Some small part of me wants to be embarrassed and argue. *What if people can smell him on me? What if they know what we did in here?*

But Mikhail was right before: I'm dirty for him.

So I do exactly as he says.

45

MIKHAIL

Viviana sucks on the tip of each of her fingers and I'm a second away from sweeping our lunch off the table.

"Keep that up and I'll cut this meal short."

"Who, me?" She gives me wide, innocent eyes, but her mouth twists into a smirk.

I click my tongue. "My wife is a tease."

She sucks her middle finger all the way into her mouth. "*'Tease'* implies I'm not willing to follow through."

I'm halfway out of my chair when there's a loud, exaggerated knock from the other side.

"Hello?" Anatoly calls, dragging the single word out for several seconds. "It is I, Anatoly Novikov, a person who does not want to see either of you naked. Can I—"

"Come in, Anatoly," I snap.

"You've welcomed me in, but I repeat: I do not want to see either of you naked."

Viviana blushes, but she can't help but laugh. There's a reason my brother is one of her only friends in the mansion —he's annoying, but he manages to make it charming.

Finally, he cracks the door open and peeks his head inside, one eye squinted open. When he sees we're clothed and eating, he sighs in relief. "Thank God."

"I don't know what you thought you were going to see."

He arches a brow. "You know exactly what I thought I was going to see. I'd say it out loud, but I'd hate to embarrass Viviana."

"Too late," she chimes in, kicking the toe of her shoe against his leg.

He laughs and ruffles her hair like they're siblings. In a way, I guess they are.

It's laughable imagining a world where Viviana would be my in-law. I was never going to be her fun, goofy brother. If she'd married Trofim, I would have become the man who killed his own brother to get with his wife.

There's no world where this woman isn't mine.

Anatoly leans back against the wall. "Your new assistant is a hardass, Mikhail. She wouldn't let me past her desk until it had been exactly one hour. I swear she was counting the seconds."

"She's good, but she hasn't figured out the phones. She keeps dropping all my calls."

Viviana stands up, brushing crumbs off her lap. "The phones are a bitch. I can help her."

"You don't need to. Either she'll figure it out or I'll fire her." I shrug. "Doesn't matter to me."

"I don't mind showing her the ropes." She smiles, one eyebrow arching. "You can express your gratitude later."

My cock twitches, but Anatoly groans and waves his hands in front of him. "I'm glad you two made up, but I didn't miss this. You all are uncomfortable."

"Then leave."

"I would, but I have news." He smirks, knowing there's no way I'll kick him out now.

"*I'll* leave." Viviana blows me a kiss and then turns to Anatoly. "I'll wait for you in the lobby."

I watch my wife sway out of the room. When I look back at my brother, he's shaking his head. "I repeat: *un-com-for-ta-ble.*"

"Say what you need to say. I have work to do."

"Yes, you must be swamped, now that you took a ninety-minute lunch to fuck your wife in the office." He narrowly dodges the pen I throw at him. "Relax, I'm done now. I'm happy for you. Really, I am. It's nice to see you like this."

I don't ask what he means. Because I already know. It's been a long time since I've felt like this. Maybe never.

"What news do you have?"

"The shipment will be here next week. It's confirmed with the Chinese manufacturer."

My pulse quickens with excitement. "Who knows?"

"The manufacturer, you, and me. And Raoul, obviously."

"No one else?"

He nods. "No one else. And as far as Christos Drakos knows, the shipment is arriving in three weeks. I planted that false information with half a dozen different sources. If he hasn't heard about it yet, he will soon."

"Good. I don't want him fucking up the deal." I drum my fingers on the desk, thinking.

"We've covered our bases," Anatoly tells me. "It's going to be fine."

I shrug. "Maybe. *Or*, while I'm distracted with this shipment, Christos is going to find a way to get revenge for the way I murdered his brother."

"He hasn't yet."

"Exactly. That is why I'm worried. Why hasn't he retaliated?"

"Because Damon's weeping widow passed along your threat and Christos is doing the smart thing for the first time in his life and backing off?" Anatoly guesses.

I want that to be true, but I'm not alive today because I assume the best in people.

"Stay close to Viviana," I tell him. "And Dante. I don't want either of them out of your sight until I know what Christos is up to. Even when they're in the mansion."

Anatoly scratches the back of his head. "She's already chafing at the leash you have her on, Mikhail. She'll go crazy if I'm following her from room-to-room around the mansion all day."

"But she'll be alive." I lean forward, lowering my voice.

"You're the only person I trust to watch them, Nat. It has to be you."

Something I can't read flickers across his face. Just for a second. Then he nods. "Of course. I'll take care of them."

Viviana wasn't wrong: I smell like her.

It's been an hour since she and Anatoly left, but I swear Raoul sniffs the air when he walks through my office door. He looks around like he expects someone else to be in the room.

"Viviana and Anatoly left?"

"You're the one who followed them here," I remind him. "You should know."

Anatoly would have thrown a fit if I told him that I was asking Raoul to follow him and Viviana to and from my office. He would have taken it as an insult no matter how much practical sense it makes.

If Anatoly and Viviana were followed and attacked by Christos or Agostino, I wanted to have the element of surprise on our side. That was Raoul. He was like the backup parachute: you don't jump out of a plane expecting the first parachute to fail, but you're an idiot if you don't plan for it just in case. It has nothing to do with not trusting Anatoly and everything to do with the fact that I'd never be able to forgive myself if something happened to Viviana.

Raoul looks around the room again like he still isn't sure.

"I assume they made it back to the mansion okay?" I prod.

Raoul runs a hand through his hair and it strikes me that I've never seen him fidget. I've never seen his eyes dart around the room the way they are right now.

He won't look at me.

"Raoul," I bark. Instantly, his eyes are on me and his shoulders are back. "What the fuck is going on?"

"Have you spoken to Anatoly?"

I ease back. "Yeah. He told me about the confirmed shipment. He planted false information for Christos to find, so everything is covered there. We're looking good."

Raoul's shoulders drop. "That's all he said?"

Shit.

My bullshit detector is world-class after everything I've been through. I trust it. But I still rewind through my interactions with Anatoly today, searching for something I missed the first time.

Nothing.

"Stop asking questions and tell me what is going on," I demand.

Raoul sits down in the chair across from me and I immediately know this isn't going to be good. "I followed Anatoly's car from the moment they left the mansion. He never saw me," he says. "I know he didn't see me because... he made a stop."

"What kind of stop?"

"At a nearby clinic."

I stand up before I know why. My body is ready to move even while my mind is wrapping itself around the information.

She went to a doctor's office *before* she came to see me. The first time I let her leave the house in days and she lied to me. Anatoly, too.

"What kind of clinic was it? *Where* was it? If she's sick, she should have told me."

"I didn't want to come to you without answers, so after I followed Viviana and Anatoly home, I went back to the clinic. I met with Viviana's doctor."

"And?" I press.

"She's pregnant."

He says it quickly like he's ripping off a bandage, but the news spreads through me slowly. It's a toxic swirl of dread and rage that turns my blood cold and pools at the base of my spine. "She would have told me."

She would have told me, right?

After everything we've been through, all the false starts and stops, Viviana wouldn't keep this from me.

Raoul looks down at the floor. "The doctor didn't want to tell me, but I threatened her. It wasn't a nice clinic and it didn't take much for her to show me Viviana's charts just to get me out of her face. Her first test was positive and they confirmed it with a blood test."

I was inside of her, telling her how much I wanted her to carry my child.

Once I fuck a baby into you, I want you to take these pictures again, I told her. *I hope it happens now. Any time I see you and the way you're growing my child, I'll remember you like this.*

It was already too late. She knew she was pregnant.

But she still didn't tell me.

"You're sure Anatoly was with her?"

Raoul nods. "He walked Viviana inside. He put his phone number as an emergency contact."

He sat in my office, alone, and said nothing. I told him how much I trusted him. He promised me he would take care of Viviana and Dante.

But he didn't tell me.

"I don't know what is going on, but if Anatoly didn't tell you, I'm sure he has a good reason," Raoul offers.

It's not like Raoul to try to persuade me—usually, that's Anatoly's job—but Raoul wants this to be a misunderstanding as much as I do.

"What reason can you come up with?" I ask.

Raoul looks away and I have my answer. There *is* no reason. Not a good one, anyway.

Viviana and Anatoly are hiding something from me. And I'm going to find out why.

46

MIKHAIL

I have the entire drive across the city to think about what I'm going to say to Viviana and Anatoly, but the moment I see her waiting for me in the kitchen, my mind goes blank except for one word.

Mine.

"Hey there." She smiles, a question in the pinch of her brows. A question she doesn't have time to ask before I've sliced my way across the kitchen and thrown her on the countertop.

Her smile falters. "What are you—"

I crush my mouth to hers. She yelps in surprise, but the sound is lost in our kiss. I swirl my tongue into her mouth like I'm searching for an explanation there. Like I'll find the answers I want at the back of her throat.

She whimpers and strokes her fingers gently through my hair the way someone might try to soothe a wild stallion. Not her worst choice, but there's no soothing me right now.

I hook my fingers under the band of her jeans. She barely has time to raise her hips before I'm shucking them off her legs and onto the floor.

Her eyes go wide. "Mikhail, the house isn't empty."

I pull her shirt over her head and toss it over my shoulder.

I know exactly who's here. I texted Anatoly on my drive home to keep Dante busy and then stand by. I'm not sure what it means that he followed my orders. Is he watching us now?

I rip her panties with one sharp tug and work my middle finger into her. She's wet and my cock twitches when she tightens around my finger. I stroke into her and her lips part on an exhale. Her eyes flutter closed.

Not everything is a lie, then. This *is real.*

She hugs herself to me, her breath heavy and warm against my neck. "S-someone could see us."

I pull back and look into her eyes. The green is nearly eaten away by black desire. "I want to fuck a baby into you."

This is her chance. Her opportunity to confess everything. I'm offering Viviana a second chance I wouldn't give to anyone else. *Tell me the truth.*

But Viviana scrapes her nails through my hair and nods. "Please, Mikhail."

Fine. So the truth wasn't in her mouth; maybe it's in her pussy.

I free my aching cock and drive every inch of myself into her.

She is mine. It's a bone-deep echo that vibrates under my skin. Every inch of this woman belongs to me. The way her back bows as I fill her. The way her mouth falls open in a silent scream. Everything from her head to her curled toes to the way she squeezes my cock from the inside belongs to me.

So I slide out of her completely and then claim her again.

She bucks her hips against me, taking and taking and taking. I grit my teeth and barrel into her. Our bodies slap together until my skin stings from the contact.

It still isn't hard enough.

Rage still simmers under my skin, an itch I can't scratch.

"Oh God, Mikhail." Viviana loops her hands around my neck and relaxes back, surrendering her body to me. Her breasts shake with every thrust.

They're bigger, I realize. The change is subtle, but it's there. She's pregnant and her breasts are swollen and *she didn't fucking tell me.*

Mine.

The word must slip out between my clenched teeth because Viviana writhes against my body. "Yours," she pants. "I'm all yours, Mikhail."

The lie falls from her lips so easily. How many more have there been? How long has she been lying to me?

I wrap my fingers around her throat to quiet her. The next time she utters a word, I want it to be the truth.

Her eyes flare wide for a second. Then she smiles. She arches a brow in a dark challenge.

I don't need encouragement. I tighten my hold, digging my fingers in harder with every thrust.

Red creeps up her face and the sick beast inside of me takes notice. She's under my control. On *my* cock.

She's mine.

I want to clamp my hand around her neck as much as I want to kiss away the welts my fingers are leaving. I want to fuck Viviana and take care of her and destroy her until she's in tiny pieces that only I can put back together.

She tries to press her chest to mine, but I push her away from me until her back is flat on the counter and every inch of her is bared to me. I look down and watch the way she takes me. The easy way I disappear inside of her. We fit together perfectly.

I squeeze her throat harder and her back arches, straining for air. Her fingers wrap around my wrist, and I think she's going to pull me away so she can breathe. Instead, she pulls me tighter. Viviana looks into my eyes and presses her neck more firmly against my palm.

And I erupt.

The orgasm hits me sideways and I have to release her throat so I don't fall over. She gasps for air and I brace myself on either side of her body.

"I'm coming," she moans. But it's a waste of breath—I already know.

I feel her, pulling and clenching. Black creeps into the edges of my vision as she drags the tail end of my orgasm out of me.

She melts against the counter, arms spread, legs limp. Her body shakes with a soft laugh. "Holy shit, Mikhail. What was that—"

"Are you fucking Anatoly?" I snarl.

I'm still inside of her. She's still pulsing softly around me. But I can't hold it in for another second.

She goes perfectly still except for the expression on her face, which morphs from shock to confusion to anger in a second. "What are you talking about?"

I slide out of her and zip my pants. She scrambles to cover herself, but her clothes are on the floor and she's still perched on the edge of the countertop. I like that she's naked.

It means there's nowhere to hide.

"Don't fucking lie to me," I growl. "Raoul saw the two of you walk into a clinic together this morning."

Her mouth falls open in shock, but nothing comes out. She just blinks at me.

"I hear congratulations are in order."

"Mikhail…" she says softly.

"I've been trying to figure out why you wouldn't tell me and the only thing I can come up with is that it isn't mine. Because if this was my baby," I say, laying my hand over her stomach, "you would have told me when I had you bent over my desk."

She reaches for my hand, but I jerk away. I pace across the kitchen floor, putting some distance between us before I turn into an animal and fuck her again.

"You would have told me when I was fucking you from behind, waxing poetic like a goddamn fool about how much I wanted to see you carrying my baby."

"Mikhail." She slides off the counter, her bare feet slapping against the tile. I wonder if she's cold before I remember I shouldn't care.

"If that was my baby," I continue, "you would have told me when I stood here *five fucking minutes ago* and told you I wanted to fuck a baby into you."

She seems to wilt when she realizes she missed her chance to come clean. "This isn't how I wanted to tell you. I wanted to—"

"You wanted to keep it a secret until you could come up with a cover story?" I finish for her. "Or was this some kink of yours? You've been with two of the three brothers, so it was well past time to bag the last?"

The words are barely out of my mouth when Viviana swings at me. I snatch her wrist out of the air and she quickly comes at me with the other one.

"You asshole!" She tries to kick me and I pin her ankle between my thighs. She hobbles on one leg, naked and furious. "Let me go!"

"You're going to hurt yourself if you don't calm down."

"You can't say something like that and then tell me to calm down!" she cries out. "If you really think so little of me that you think I'd sleep with your brother, then you shouldn't care if I get hurt. So, let me go!"

I let her ankle drop, but just as she gets both feet under her, I spin her around and crush her to my chest. She wriggles her naked body against me, grumbling and fighting. "Let me go!"

"Why?" I spit, holding her tighter.

"So I can kick your smug, stubborn ass!"

"No." My voice is low, the words whispered against the back of her ear. "Why didn't you tell me?"

All at once, Viviana softens. She sinks against me, the fight suddenly gone. "I was going to, Mikhail. I was… waiting."

Her body is warm and liquid in my arms. I was just inside of her, but I want it again. My cock twitches and I let her go. "Waiting for what? You had two positive tests! Were you going to wait until you had the baby just to be extra sure?"

"I didn't want to get your hopes up again." She snatches her jeans off the floor and pulls them on. The insides of her thighs are a mess and it satisfies some twisted part of me.

"I'm a grown man, Viviana. My hopes are fine."

"I didn't want to get *my* hopes up, either."

"Who the fuck cares about Anatoly's hopes, right? Makes perfect sense that you'd tell him before you'd tell your husband."

She marches over to where her shirt is draped across the coffee pot and pulls it on. When she turns to face me, some of that fire is back. "You've made it impossible for me to leave this house on my own. I had to take someone with me to the clinic and since Anatoly is my *friend*—" She places special emphasis on the word. "—I asked him to go with me. He was pestering me to tell you from the moment we left the clinic."

"He was right. You should have told me."

He should have told me. And he's going to have hell to pay for keeping it from me.

"Don't be mad at him. I begged him not to tell you. I was just waiting for the blood test to confirm things. It's more reliable. And since I had the false positive before, I didn't want to—" She stops, her mouth turning down in a frown. "Wait… You said—*Two* positive tests? I only took one. I was waiting for the results for the other test."

"Raoul threatened the doctor and saw your chart. Both tests were positive."

She stares at me with wide eyes. I can practically see the news sinking in.

She's pregnant.

She's pregnant.

This isn't an accident or a surprise. We decided to start a family. Viviana and I made the choice to grow our family and now… it's here.

We're having a baby.

And suddenly, nothing else matters.

Viviana's full lips twist into a dazed smile. She blinks back tears. "Mikhail—"

A knock at the front door interrupts her.

I was going to wait until later to ream Anatoly for lying to me, but now is as good a time as ever. Luckily for him, I'm in a surprisingly good mood.

I walk past Viviana to the door and yank it open.

But it isn't Anatoly standing on the porch.

"Mikhail Novikov, I am a federal agent," A bald man holding an FBI badge advances on me as his colleagues stand behind him, guns pointed at my chest. "And you are under arrest."

"Mikhail?" Viviana tears around the corner. Her hair is a mess from my hands and her neck is red. *At least she's wearing clothes.* "What's going on? What's happening?"

I don't have the luxury of time to explain everything. So I say the only things that matter.

"I love you. Get Nat."

47

VIVIANA

I love you. Get Nat.

What does that mean?

I mean, I know what it *means*, but it doesn't do anything to quiet the torrential downpour of questions flooding my brain.

I'm frozen on the doorstep as scrawny, dour men that Mikhail could knock out in a second drag him down the front steps of the mansion. He's a head taller than all of them. There's no way they could keep him down if he wanted to resist.

Hell, maybe *I'll* charge down there and take a few swings. With the adrenaline pumping through me, it might be a fair fight.

A bald agent puts his hand on the back of Mikhail's head and I want to break his wrist. How dare they? *He's mine.*

They shove him into the backseat.

"I love you, too!" I yell back just as the door closes.

I don't know if Mikhail heard me. The dark car slips down the driveway as quietly as it arrived. I'd still be frozen in the doorway if a large hand didn't land on my shoulder.

I scream and spin around into a solid wall of muscle.

"It's me," Anatoly says evenly, grabbing my shoulders to steady me.

I lean back to look up at him. There's a tight frown on his face. *He knows.*

I pound my fist into his chest. "Where in the hell were you? They just arrested Mikhail! Why weren't you here?"

He gently grabs my wrists, keeping distance between us. "I thought you might like to have at least one person here to guard you and your son while Mikhail is away. If I had come out to rubberneck, they would have taken me in for questioning, too."

He's making a good point, but I struggle against his hold anyway. I twist and fight and yank on my wrists because I have no idea what else to do.

Mikhail is gone.

The FBI took him.

And I don't know when he's coming back.

Slowly, my fight drains away. I don't realize I'm crying until Anatoly drops my wrists and pulls me in for a hug.

"Don't cry, Viv. He'll be back."

"When?" I sob into his shoulder. "And what'll happen when he does?"

Anatoly doesn't answer either question.

The mansion becomes *Free Mikhail HQ* within the hour.

Anatoly calls Raoul and he races here. He got the heads up that Mikhail was being arrested thirty seconds before the FBI knocked on the door. There wouldn't have been enough time to warn Mikhail even if he tried.

They pace around the kitchen, circling each other and tossing out ideas, and the two of them have never looked more like brothers. They are opposites in every conceivable way except for the most important one: they love Mikhail.

"This is about Cerberus," Raoul says when he hangs up with one of a dozen phone calls he has made to contacts all around the city. "He's being brought in for financial fraud. They think he started the fire to get the insurance and hide evidence."

"He wasn't even there!" I argue. My skin flushes when I remember where Mikhail was instead.

He was on the private balcony with me. It was the night he told me he loved me. The night he bought me a star and apologized. The night we had makeup sex so good that I had no choice but to bare my soul and tell him I was pregnant.

Fuck… maybe I should stop telling him I'm pregnant. Bad things happen when I make pregnancy announcements.

"Mikhail wasn't at Cerberus Industries, but you were," Anatoly jabs a finger at Raoul. "If anyone in our family is responsible, it would be you."

Raoul narrows his eyes. "Unless you want me to go turn myself in, that isn't helpful."

Anatoly holds up both hands. "I'm just saying. These feds don't even have their facts straight."

"They also don't have any evidence. If they did, there would be formal charges."

I sit up. "Does that mean he's coming home?"

Anatoly grimaces. "They can hold him for three days without charges."

Three days. It doesn't sound like a long time. Then again, the last hour has felt like a century.

I bolt out of my chair and run across the kitchen. I barely make it to the trash can before every measly thing I managed to eat in the last hour comes back up.

Anatoly is there, rubbing my back, when I stand up. "It's going to be okay, Viv."

I spit and rinse my mouth out with water from the sink. "I'm fine."

"You're not fine. The stress can't be good for the baby." Raoul is watching me carefully.

I want to ask him how he knows about the baby, but there's no point. Raoul knows everything. And as soon as he found out, he told Mikhail.

I'm not even mad at him. He did what I should have done.

Anatoly leads me back to a chair and pushes a plate of crackers towards me. "You need to eat something, Viv. Mikhail will kill me if he gets home and you're a wreck."

Deep down, I know Mikhail didn't really think Anatoly was the father. From the moment Anatoly and I met, he has been a friend. More than that, he's loyal to Mikhail. The only reason Mikhail accused me of sleeping with Anatoly is because he was surprised and angry. I don't even blame him.

"You were right, Nat. I should have told Mikhail about the baby as soon as I found out. I should have told him when we got to his office. I should have—"

"None of that would have changed *this*," Raoul interrupts. "The feds were going to arrest him either way."

"At least I'd know how he feels about it all," I mutter. Then I shake my head. "I'm sorry. Mikhail is being tortured for all we know and I'm thinking about myself."

"He's at the police station, not Guantanamo." Anatoly slides my plate closer, giving me a firm look until I grab a cracker and nibble on the edge. "Mikhail can handle himself."

"What does Daddy need to handle?"

I didn't hear the small footsteps padding down the stairs, but I turn around and find Dante standing in the doorway. His sweats are rolled twice at the ankle because they're a size too big and he's holding a stuffed pterodactyl under his arm.

He's so small and his dad is being detained by the FBI and all of that plus pregnancy hormones makes me want to curl into a ball and weep.

Thankfully, Anatoly jumps up before I can fall apart.

"Nothing, kiddo!" Anatoly snatches the pterodactyl out of his hand and pretends to fly it around Dante's head, booping the end of his nose with it. "Did your movie get over?"

Dante shakes his head. "No. I'm hungry."

"Amazing. A problem I can solve!" Anatoly scoops Dante onto his shoulders and marches him towards the kitchen. Then he stops and turns around. "It's okay if he has a bowl of cereal for dinner, right?"

I swipe the tears out of my eyes and stand up. "How about *I* solve this problem?" It'll be nice to have something useful to do.

Dante is much less excited at the prospect of seared chicken and roasted carrots, which means I'm doing my job as his mother.

Right now, getting Dante a well-rounded meal and not falling apart is the only thing I know how to do.

The rest of it is a complete and total disaster.

48

MIKHAIL

It's late, but the mansion is lit up like a lighthouse at the end of the drive. "They're waiting up for you," Raoul warns.

We haven't said a word to each other the entire drive. Anatoly never would have let me sit and brood like this, but Raoul knows when to stay quiet.

"You shouldn't have told them I was being released tonight."

"If you think that was an option, then you have no idea what you're about to walk into." He shifts the car into park and kills the engine. "Viviana has barely slept. Every call Anatoly or I have taken, she's been pressed to the other side of the phone, listening in. She's worried about you."

"You should have told her I can take care of myself," I growl.

Raoul sighs, so I know he told her precisely that. Multiple times, I'm sure. None of it would have made a difference for Viviana.

I love you, too. She screamed it just as the FBI agent slammed the car door closed. She couldn't see me through the dark window tint, but I could see her. She crumbled against the doorframe like she'd never see me again. She was terrified… *for me*.

It's a new feeling.

"I've endured worse interrogations than that," I add.

The agents interrogating me knew I wasn't going to crack the moment they walked into the room. It was like a game of chicken, seeing who could wait the other out. Since I'm free, I guess that means I won.

Won the battle, at least. The devil only knows if the war will continue.

"I know that, but I didn't think mentioning all the times you've been tortured would make her feel any better."

"No, probably not." I drag a hand down my face. "We should have had a warning this was coming. What the fuck happened, Raoul?"

"I've been trying to figure that out. No one in my usual network knew a thing. Whoever cooked this up, it was kept way under wraps."

"Or your informants are lying to you."

Raoul hesitates before relenting. "Or they're lying to me. Yeah. It could be someone on the inside feeding information to the feds."

Bright light slices across the driveway and we both look over as the front door opens. Viviana is in the doorway, Anatoly standing just over her shoulder. They're both squinting into the darkness towards the car.

"Anatoly lied about taking Viviana to the clinic, but he's loyal," Raoul says quietly. "He had nothing to do with this."

"I know." I knew it when I charged into the kitchen two days ago and accused Viviana of having an affair. I didn't really believe either of them would do that to me. "I'm just fucking tired. I want to be able to trust the people around me."

Raoul doesn't go near that confession and I don't blame him. We aren't in the habit of sharing our feelings. But it's late and I have half a mind to scoop Viviana and Dante up and drive straight back to that cabin in the woods. I wouldn't mind burying my head in the dirt for a while. Maybe forever.

Fuck the Bratva.

Fuck this war.

Fuck everything that isn't the three—soon to be four—of us.

Suddenly, Dante shoves between Viviana and Anatoly. He has one hand on the doorframe, swinging out into the dark looking for me.

I can't hide from what's coming. I don't want to.

Viviana and Dante spent years on the run and I won't do that to them again.

Dante bounds down the porch the second my car door opens. "Where were you for so long?" He jumps, trusting me to catch him. I do, balancing him in the crook of my arm. My wrist is still sore from the cuffs, but my sleeves are long and Dante can't see the bruising. "Mama said you'd come back, but it took forever and ever and ever and—"

"I just had to take care of some things, but I'm back now."

He narrows his eyes. "Forever?"

I can't promise him forever.

I want to tell him that I'll always be here for him, but I'm not sure that's a promise I can keep. Not when the Greeks and Italians are teaming up to take me down. Not when they might have help from someone I consider an ally.

There are a million things I don't know, but one thing I know for sure: Dante doesn't need me to be honest with him right now.

"Forever," I tell him solemnly, tickling his side. "I'll always be around."

He hugs my neck and, all at once, I understand why Viviana didn't tell me about the baby. It was easier to keep the secret until she was sure. It was easier to lie than to live with disappointing me again.

The problem is, *I'm* the one who should be protecting *her*.

Dante runs off to talk to Raoul, peppering him with questions about where we were and if there were bad guys.

"The only bad guy there was me," Raoul chimes in.

Dante laughs and Raoul looks more than a little annoyed that Dante thought it was a joke.

Suddenly, the scent of vanilla and honey wraps around me. After two days of burnt coffee and dust, Viviana smells like heaven.

"I didn't tell him where you were," Viviana whispers. She starts to reach for me, but tucks her arms around herself instead like she isn't sure whether she's allowed to touch me or not. "I didn't want to scare him."

I grab her wrist, unpeel her arm from her waist, and tuck it around me. She sinks against my chest with a dreamy sigh. "Are you okay?"

"I'm fine." I grab her chin and tilt her face up to mine. There are purple shadows pressed under her eyes, which are red-rimmed like she's been crying. "And I'm happy about the baby."

"You are?" Her eyes are glassy again.

"We were trying for a baby," I remind her. "We both wanted this. Of course I'm happy."

No matter how fucked the timing is.

She just hugs me tighter, her cheek pressed over my heart.

Anatoly is watching nervously from the door. I catch his eye. "We need to talk—you, me, and Raoul. My office in ten."

He nods and disappears into the house.

Viviana pulls back. "You just got home. Can't this wait until—"

"It can't wait." We've already lost so much time. We're lucky there wasn't an attack while I was in custody.

Dante runs over and wraps his arms around my legs again. "Can you put me to bed, Daddy?"

I ruffle his hair and gently nudge him towards his mother. "Not tonight."

Something I can't read flickers across Viviana's face, but she tucks it away and slaps on a smile. "Just you and me tonight, bud. What should we read?"

I walk into the house before they can decide and it feels like I'm stepping through a portal. Like my life is divided cleanly into two halves.

I wish that was the case. As it is, the two halves are on a collision course. And there's no telling what kind of carnage will be left behind.

"If there was anything to know about who tipped off the feds, we'd have it by now." Anatoly has given up his usual spot on the sofa in exchange for anxiously pacing across the room. "No one knows a fucking thing."

"Or they're lying to us." It's the same theory I offered to Raoul outside, but it hits Anatoly a bit differently.

He stiffens, stopping his pacing long enough to face my desk. "I know I fucked up by not telling you about taking Viviana to the clinic. If you want to hash it out now, we can. But I think we both know we have more important shit to handle."

I shrug. "What we're trying to figure out now is who we can trust. Can I trust you?"

"With your life," Anatoly vows without hesitation.

"Then there's nothing else to hash out."

I circle a hand in the air and it's like hitting "resume" on a movie. Anatoly starts his pacing again and Raoul leans against the edge of my desk. "Maybe Christos or Agostino infiltrated the FBI."

"Even if they did, their word wouldn't be enough to get me arrested. The FBI knows better than to take the word of one crime boss against another. They don't have enough evidence for a conviction, but my lawyer said they had credible testimony from an informant."

Anatoly frowns. "What kind of informant?"

"Someone the FBI would trust to know what I was up to," I explain. "Someone on the inside."

Anatoly curses under his breath, but Raoul doesn't move. His brow is furrowed. "We already don't have the manpower to match a Greek-Italian alliance. If they also have someone feeding them information from the inside, we're fucked."

"I know," I growl. "Why the fuck do you think we were trying to take out Christos or Agostino before all of this shit went down?"

"It'll be impossible now," Anatoly grumbles. "They've made a move and they'll have their guard up, ready for a response from you."

"As they should be. This can't go unanswered. We have to be on the offensive."

"We don't have the manpower," Raoul repeats through gritted teeth.

"Then fucking get it!" I snarl.

The room goes quiet, but I don't give a damn. This has gone on for too long. There have been excuses and reasons why we couldn't end this war, but none of that matters now.

"Get the manpower," I repeat. "I'm not going to sit on my ass and wait for another attack to roll in. We need to make a move before they land a fatal blow."

It's been a long time since the day we all found Anzhelina

and Alyona dead, but I know Anatoly and Raoul are right back there with me.

Only this time, it's Viviana and Dante they're seeing on the floor.

"We'll fight back," Anatoly agrees softly.

Raoul nods. "Whatever it takes."

49

VIVIANA

I'm still awake when Mikhail slips through our bedroom door.

It's been two days of not knowing where he was. Two days of wishing he was here. Now that he is, I wonder if he wasn't safer in custody.

He's padding softly across the floor, but he stops when I roll over to face him. "You should be asleep."

"Probably," I agree. "But I'm not tired."

It's not true; I'm exhausted. That doesn't mean it's easy to lie down and turn my brain off.

"Stress isn't good for the baby."

"Tell that to the men trying to kill my husband."

He kicks off his shoes next to the bed and climbs in next to me. "If they were trying to kill *me*, I'd have a lot less to worry about."

"Everything is such a mess," I whisper. "If you'd just married Helen, then—"

"Then I still would have come to my senses, divorced her, and gone looking for you." His hand strokes warm circles into my lower back. "Nothing would have changed, Viviana. It was always going to end up like this."

It's sweet, in a way. The idea that Mikhail and I are destined to be. It would be a pretty picture if all this pesky war and bloodshed would stop getting in the way.

"Just call off the war."

"I can't just—"

"Surrender," I continue, talking over him. "Wave the white flag. Whatever it is you have to do to make it stop. Why can't you do that?"

"You grew up the daughter of a don. You know why."

"Tell me anyway."

He rolls onto his back, staring up at the ceiling. "Because they won't stop coming for me even if I stop fighting back. Surrendering will just make it easier for them to get to you and Dante."

"So, what? That's it? They decide they want to come after you and you're forced into this fight? It's not fair. You should get to back down if you want to."

"I don't *want* to back down. War is in the job description. I knew what I was signing up for when I overthrew Trofim. It's the world I was born into."

"And I was born into a family who wanted to trade me to the highest bidder!" I retort. "I didn't like it, so I left it behind."

"Your father isn't letting us forget it, either," he mumbles.

He's not wrong. I left, but that life is still breathing down my neck. Down all of our necks.

I frown. "I'm the reason you didn't marry Helen. And the only reason my father is after you is because I ran away. This is all—"

"It's not your fault," Mikhail interjects.

I shake my head. "Maybe I should have stayed away. Dante was probably safer with you when I was gone."

"You wouldn't say that if you'd seen him," Mikhail says darkly. "He's better with you around."

"Except I'm the picture in the center of several dartboards right now. The closer Dante is to me, the more likely he gets hit." My stomach churns. I've been nauseous for days, but this is a new kind of sickness. "I'm his mother, Mikhail. He's supposed to be safe with me."

"Maybe it's time we consider…" Mikhail pauses, considers his words carefully. I know whatever he's about to say, I'm not going to like. "The mansion might not be the safest place for Dante right now."

I sit bolt upright. "No."

I knew the boarding school conversation would come back around sooner or later, but I'm not ready for it now. I thought we'd circle back when Dante was seventeen… and a half.

Maybe in his last semester of senior year he could transfer to a boarding school in the city.

And visit me every weekend.

"You said it yourself: the closer he is to you, the less safe he is."

"That doesn't mean I want to send him away!" I fire back.

Mikhail sits up and drags a hand over his face and I can see the exhaustion etched into every line of his face.

"We should go to sleep," I announce. "I haven't had enough sleep—ever—to have this conversation. Let's sleep on it and talk about it later when we're more rested."

Considering we're in the middle of a war and I'm pregnant, I don't think sleep is in the cards for us for the next eight years. At least.

"We aren't sending him away forever, Viviana."

"He won't be here with us."

"He'll be close by. The boarding school I found is close by. It's in the city."

I shake my head. "You told me it was in Moscow. You wanted to send him to Russia."

"I'm trying this new thing. It's called compromise." He nudges my arm with his shoulder. "You ever heard of it?"

He's trying to be cute, but I'm not in the mood. He's my husband, but he's also the man who wants to send my baby boy away. "I'm familiar, but I didn't think you were."

"That's why I said it was new." He sighs. "I don't want this, either, Viviana… if that makes you feel any better. But that doesn't mean it's not the best choice for Dante."

He's right. I know he's right, but I can't bring myself to say it. I can't bring myself to say anything. If I open my mouth, I'll fall apart.

Mikhail must be able to sense my resignation because he grabs my hand and kisses my knuckles. "He'll be safer there, Viv. I wouldn't send him if I didn't believe that."

"But Mrs. Steinman is my school!" Dante looks at me with wide, blue eyes. "I already have a teacher."

"Mrs. Steinman is a tutor. She isn't the same as school," Mikhail explains. "You're going to go to a place with more teachers and other students. It's a big building with lots of classrooms."

It looks like a prison.

Mikhail showed me pictures online this morning and told me to "keep an open mind." Well, my mind was wide open and now, it's stuffed full with pictures of that brick building outfitted with quadruple-layered glass that could probably withstand everything up to and including a nuclear bomb.

According to the website, there are metal detectors, a three-point sign-in system, and fencing and guards around the perimeter of the school.

He'll be safe there, I tell myself for the umpteenth time this morning. I keep repeating it, but the words don't seem to stick.

So what if it's safe? Dante is a kid. He needs fresh air and sunlight *and his mother.*

"Is there recess?" Dante asks.

"You'll get breaks," Mikhail tells him. "It won't be school all the time. Sometimes, you'll get to hang out with your friends and spend time in your room. There's a gym and a movie theater. There's a restaurant in the lobby and you can—"

"We're moving there?" Dante turns his Bambi eyes on me, waiting for an answer.

But my mouth goes dry.

How am I supposed to tell my son I'm abandoning him in a bombproof building full of strangers?

He'll be safe there.

This is the right choice.

Mikhail reaches over and pats Dante's knee. His large hand swallows most of Dante's leg. "*You'll* be moving there. You're going to have your own room."

"Where are you moving?" he asks, his eyes still locked on mine.

"*We* aren't moving," Mikhail explains. "Your mama and I are staying here."

He'll be safe there.

He'll be alone.

This is the right choice.

He needs me.

I clench my fists tightly in my lap, trying to keep it together. I promised Mikhail I could do this, but that was before I had to stare into my six-year-old's teary-eyed face. That was before a mother's worst nightmare was sitting in front of me with a wobbly chin and questions I can't answer.

"I'm going alone?" Dante's voice breaks and this might actually be torture.

"You'll have a blast." Mikhail tries to sound upbeat, but there's nothing upbeat about what we're doing here. "The school isn't for adults. It's for kids. You'll make friends and learn so much."

Dante stands up and the sight of his too-long pants hanging over his socked feet does me in. A sob wrenches out of me.

He grabs my hand. "I'll be good, Mama. I won't be naughty."

"This isn't—" I swallow down another sob. Tears fill my eyes and I have to blink them back furiously just to be able to see Dante. "You're a good boy."

"Then why don't you want me anymore?" His voice is watery and my heart cracks in half.

"Dante, that's not—" Mikhail sighs and I can't listen to him explain this. I can't sit here and pretend I'm not dying inside.

I fumble towards the door, crying so hard I can't see.

This is the right choice.

Even if nothing about it feels right at all.

50

MIKHAIL

The plan, as far as Viviana knew, was to wake up early, have breakfast, and drive to Dante's new school together.

Which is why Dante and I left before sunrise.

I never planned to lie to her about this. She wanted to be there to help Dante settle in and I told her we could make that happen. Then she burst into tears while ordering him curtains.

Leaving him in a dorm room, no matter how nice it is, is going to break her. So I took a page out of her book and lied to spare her feelings.

It's early enough in the morning that Dante dozes on the drive there. The guard at the gate checks my ID and notes my license plate number before letting us onto the property. Another guard stationed by the front doors takes our names and prints a visitor's badge for me after we park and get out. Then we walk through a metal detector.

The director gave me a full tour of the building when I enrolled Dante. It's the only place in the city that might be even more secure than the mansion. The bonus is that this building isn't under attack from two different crime families. Dante will blend in here.

Still, I'm not taking any risks.

Raoul and I met in a parking garage halfway between the school and the mansion to switch cars just in case anyone was tailing us. And no one outside of Viviana and my brothers knows Dante is enrolled here.

I've done everything I can to keep him safe.

It's what I tell myself when I see his naked twin-sized bed and bare walls.

He has to jump to pull himself up onto the tall bed. Seeing his little legs dangle in the air almost swings me to Viviana's side of the issue. *He's too young for this. He needs to be with his parents. He can't be alone.*

But I'm not doing this because I want to get rid of him. I'm not doing this because I think he's ready.

I'm doing this because it's the right thing to do.

No matter how much it hurts, I have to do what is best for my family.

"Your mama will call you tomorrow," I tell Dante, hugging him tight to my chest. "We'll visit you often and you'll come back to the house for long weekends."

He sniffles, trying hard not to cry. "When it's safe, can I come back?"

I want to ask how he knows it isn't safe, but it's mine and Viviana's kid we're talking about here. It would be shocking if he minded his own business.

"As soon as it's safe, I'll come pack you up myself." I kiss the top of his head. "You're safe here and this is just for a little while."

I mean it. Still, on my way out, I shove a wad of cash into the hands of the administrator in charge of Dante's block of rooms. It's more than she makes in a year, and I promise her double if she takes extra good care of Dante.

Then I get in my car and leave my son behind.

But fucking hell, it hurts like the devil to do.

Anatoly is standing in the entryway with a pained look on his face when I walk through the door. I don't even have time to ask him what's going on before I hear a loud crash from upstairs.

"Welcome home," he greets with forced cheer. "How did the drop-off go? Was Dante okay?"

Another loud bang echoes through the house, followed by what sounds like splashing water. I point at the ceiling. "What the hell is that?"

"Oh, your wife is rampaging through the upstairs and destroying everything in her wake." He says it casually, breezily, like he's telling me she's in the shower.

"Why aren't you stopping her?"

He pulls a steak knife out of his back pocket and holds it in front of me. "Because she threw this at my eyeball and I've decided I don't care what she does as long as she's not trying to murder me."

Another thud rattles the entire second floor. It sounds like it's going to come down on top of us. I can't even begin to imagine what Viviana is doing to make that much noise.

"She's a third of your size, Nat."

"No, she's a mama bear without her cub," he retorts. "That woman is the most dangerous thing on the planet right now. I will go through hell and high water for you, brother, but I'm not setting foot near *that*."

I want to tell Anatoly he's exaggerating.

Then I make it up the stairs.

The pictures that were on the hallway walls are now in tatters on the floor. A vase is smashed into the carpet like someone not only shattered it, but stomped on it for good measure. And just like Anatoly said, there's a steak knife sticking out of the wall, still quivering with the impact force.

Viviana's old room is more of the same chaos. Shit everywhere, pillow feathers floating lazily through the air.

The only room I peek into that is untouched—aside from the clothes and stuffed animals we packed—is Dante's.

Something bounces off the inside of my bedroom door and I'm sure I won't be as lucky.

I ease down the hall, waiting for a break in the shredding and smashing that I realize isn't going to come. So I push the door open and step inside.

Or at least, I step as far as I can before there's a boiling sea of clothes, jewelry, and shoes blocking my path. I'm about to pick my way through the mess when another bundle of clothes comes flying out of the closet, followed by the drawer they must have been in.

The drawer is solid wood, but Viviana manages to hurl it across the room and hit the bed frame. A chunk of wood splinters away and the front of the drawer breaks off with a pained, groaning crack.

I don't give a shit about the furniture or the house. But if she doesn't stop this, she's going to hurt herself.

I hop over a tangled mass of hangers and make my way to the closet. Viviana is standing in the middle of it, our tipped-over dresser on the floor next to her with the bar she ripped out of the wall balanced on top. She's still in her cotton pajamas, her skin shimmering with sweat.

"Viviana."

Every muscle in her body goes rigid. She turns to me slowly and I almost expect not to recognize her. As if she's been possessed by some vengeful spirit.

But she looks at me and… it's still Viviana.

Her eyes are swollen from crying, but they're as green as they've ever been. Her mouth is twisted into a scowl, but her lower lip is ever-so-slightly fuller than the top.

She's the woman I love—and she's a wreck.

I stand in the doorway, my arms opened wide. "Take it out on me." Her brows pinch together and I wave her forward. "Whatever you're feeling, *malysh*, let it out on me."

Viviana is frozen in the middle of the room for only a second. Then she launches herself at me.

51

VIVIANA

I hate him.

From the moment I woke up alone in bed, walked across the hall, and found Dante's room empty, I've hated Mikhail.

Finally, I get to do something about it.

I throw every single ounce of my weight at him, but he barely sways on his feet. I claw at whatever parts of him I can grab—his sleeves, his hair, his clothes.

"You're a liar!" I snarl. "You're a filthy fucking liar and *I hate you, I hate you, I hate you!*"

I don't recognize my own voice. The thoughts in my head belong to someone else, too.

As soon as I tore through the mansion and realized my baby boy was gone, I became another person. Someone broken and desperate and wild.

I wanted to kill Mikhail.

Now, here he is, standing in the mess with his arms spread like some kind of savior, and I have never wanted to hurt anyone as much as I want to hurt him.

No one has ever taught me to fight. There was no reason to. My father didn't care if his daughter knew how to throw a punch. As long as I could smile and nod, I knew everything he wanted me to know.

I wish I'd taken a kickboxing class in the years on the run. Something, anything, that could make this an even fight.

Seams rip and my fists ache from pounding against his chest, but Mikhail doesn't move. Doesn't defend himself. He stands there and takes it without flinching.

"That's it," he encourages softly. "Whatever you need to do, Viviana."

"Shut up!" I punctuate the point with two poorly-placed jabs to his ribs. "Fight back!"

"I'm not going to fight you."

I fall back, already panting and out of breath. There are a lot of rooms in this mansion. Destroying them all one by one took a lot out of me. "Why not?"

"Because that's not what you need."

"Don't fucking tell me what I need!" I hiss, top lip curled back like a hyena. "Don't steal my son from me in the middle of the night and then dare to tell me what I *need*."

"I didn't steal him. We agreed to send him to the school," he explains with infuriating calm. "You know it's the right choice."

I fling myself at him again. This time, I take aim at his annoyingly pretty mouth. That's what got us into this mess in the first place. Everything sounds better when it comes from a face like that.

My fist cracks against his jaw. It's the first half-solid punch I've landed. As soon as I do, pain radiates up my arm.

"Ow! Shit!" I pull back and Mikhail follows me.

His face is creased with worry. *For me.* I just punched him in the jaw and he's concerned about me.

"I hate you," I spit one more time, shoving him away from me.

I try, at least. Mikhail doesn't budge. He reaches for my hand, trying to inspect it. "Did you break something?"

I draw my foot back and kick him in the shin. Finally, he grunts, but he doesn't stop trying to triage my hand. Meanwhile, my toes feel like I just kicked a steel beam.

"What are you, the fucking Bionic Man?" I grimace, hopping on my good foot and flexing my toes. "Goddammit!"

Mikhail growls in frustration. Then he grabs me by the arms, picks me up, and toes shattered wood and clothes out of the way to drop me on the edge of the bed.

"Don't touch me!" I try to twist away from him, but he pins me in place.

"Then stop trying to punch me!" he snaps, his calm finally withering away. "You're hurting yourself."

I narrow my eyes. "Don't act like you care about me now. You're a liar. You told me we would take Dante together. *'We made this decision together, Viviana.'*"

"We did."

"You *lied*! You did what you thought was best without asking me."

"Because you can't be rational when it comes to Dante."

"Don't do that!" I shriek, jabbing a finger at him. "Don't treat me like some insane, emotional woman!"

He throws his hands in the air, flailing around to highlight the carnage I left in my wake. "Look around, Viviana. This looks pretty insane!"

He's not wrong. The room is destroyed. It's going to take the entire staff all day to clean this up. We'll need a new bed. New art on the walls. A new dresser.

The destruction is sobering in ways I wish it wasn't, so I focus on Mikhail. On the pain that cuts through me like the knife I hurled at Anatoly when he tried to defend Mikhail's actions. Every time I look at Mikhail's face and remember what he did—that Dante is gone—my chest aches.

"And you look pretty heartless." I jab at the rip I left in his shirt, directly over his heart. Like I was trying to claw my way through his skin and rip it, still beating, out of his chest. "I should have known better."

He arches a brow. "Known better about what?"

"I should have known better than to trust you. I mean, look at your father! Your brother!" I can feel my mouth running away with me, but I don't hit the brakes. I slam on the gas, actually, leaning forward to fling every word at him. "You pretend to be better than them, but you're a Novikov through and through. You don't care about anyone but yourself."

For the first time, Mikhail flinches.

Finally, I've landed a blow… and it doesn't feel at all like I thought it would.

"Do you feel better?" Mikhail asks evenly after a painful moment has dragged past us.

My teeth grind together. I clench my jaw to keep myself from blurting out the truth.

"Because if you're done," he rasps, "it's my turn to tell you what I know about you."

I brace myself for everything I deserve. Mikhail was right: when it comes to fighting him, I'm always the one who will end up hurt. It's coming in *three, two, one…*

"You, Viviana Novikov," he says, firing my new last name at me like a bullet, "care so fucking much about everyone in your life. About me. And, most of all, about Dante."

I frown. This isn't where I thought this was going. I'm perfectly still on the edge of the bed, waiting for the shoe to drop. For him to throw the knockout punch.

"You've spent your entire life sacrificing yourself—your happiness, your freedom, your desires—to make sure Dante was safe and cared for. You worked your ass off for six years to take care of him on your own."

"What are you—" I start.

But Mikhail presses the pad of his thumb to my lips, silencing me. "You don't know how to let someone else take care of the two of you."

I swat his hand away. "You lied to me."

"Because you couldn't handle it," he fires back. "You were going to fall apart and it would have scared Dante. He was finally okay with leaving, and I didn't want you to make things worse for him."

"I'm his mother! I wouldn't make things worse. I would have—"

"Sobbed," he finishes. "You would have fallen apart the same way you did here, except you would have done it in front of Dante and all of his classmates and his teachers."

I want to tell him he's wrong, but I can't. This explosion has been brewing inside of me for days. Weeks. The moment Mikhail brought up boarding school again, it was only a matter of time.

"When you're thinking clearly, you know sending him away is the right call," he says gently. "I didn't want one moment of weakness to undo everything."

"You *left* me," I blurt. My voice breaks and I slap a hand over my mouth. Angry tears burn in my eyes.

Mikhail's face softens. He curls warm fingers around my jaw. "The only way for me to take care of you was to leave you behind. Just for a little while."

I'm still angry. Livid, actually. Rage is still simmering low in my belly.

But I don't hate him. Of course I don't. How could I? Mikhail did what he does best, what he's always done: he made the tough call and stuck around to face the consequences.

There's still so much energy sizzling under my skin, but I don't want to hit him. I don't want to destroy anything. I want to… I don't know what I want.

As always, Mikhail does.

He spreads his arms again, his voice a low rumble. "Take it out on me, Viviana."

I throw myself at him again, but this time, I wrap my arms around his neck. I curl my body against his strong chest and let him hold me as I kiss the scratches on his throat and the red welts on his cheeks.

His hands grip my butt, pinning me against the erection I feel growing between us. "I'm so mad at you," I pant between kisses.

"I know." He walks me to the bed, laying me back as he falls over me.

His weight presses me down and I scrape my nails over his shoulder blades and the thick bands of muscle on either side of his spine, trying to draw him closer.

His beard scratches along my jaw and my collarbones. My flimsy pajamas are like gauze in his hands. He rips my top in two with one tug. Then his palms are over my breasts. He rolls my nipples between his calloused fingers and the nervous energy under my skin finds purpose.

It demands *more*.

I slide my hand between our bodies and find the hard length of him. He groans, a deep, strangled sound low in his throat, when I wrap my hand around his cock and stroke.

"Like this," I croak, opening my thighs to make more space for him. "Take me like this, Mikhail."

I don't want to wait. I don't need him to take me to the edge. I'm already there. I've been here for hours. Now, I want to fall with him.

He presses hot kisses to my collarbone and my pulse point. His teeth nip at my earlobe before he breathes, "Whatever you need, Viviana."

Mikhail shoves my panties to the side and wastes no time. He presses me open, parting me gently at first. Then he slides deep.

The only reason I can survive a morning like the one I just had is because, deep down, I know Mikhail will take care of me. Everything he's ever done has been to take care of me. Even now, when he's ripped my quivering heart out of my chest and packed it up for boarding school, I know he's only doing what he thinks is best.

I hate it, but I trust him.

I'm livid with him, but I love him.

He slides away and then fills me again. Each time he pulls back, he comes back even harder. Faster.

"You've got me." His arms bracket either side of me, the muscles flexing and straining with every thrust. Mikhail rises over me, driving into me harder and harder. "Fuck, you've got me, Viviana."

I kiss the flushed skin of his chest. I hold onto him with my arms and my legs, memorizing the way he feels. The way his weight pins me to the mattress and how he can stretch me to my breaking point, but make it feel so deliriously good.

I come hard, digging my nails into his back and burying my scream in his chest. Mikhail curses and falls, too. He grips my hips and spills into me, holding our bodies together until he slides out and grabs my face instead.

"I'm going to do everything in my power to protect our family." His eyes are bright blue and almost pleading. He brushes tears from my cheeks with his thumbs, and I didn't even know I was crying. "I've failed before—but I'm not going to fail with you and Dante and our new baby."

"I know," I sob, circling my hand around his thick wrist.

He kisses my forehead and whispers. "I'm going to take care of you."

I believe him.

52

VIVIANA

I stop at the base of the stairs to adjust the sleeves of my dress.

Maybe it's stupid to dress up for a doctor's appointment, but I'm about to see my baby for the first time and it feels kinda like a job interview I can't afford to mess up. Plus, almost as momentous, it's the first time I've been out of the house in two weeks.

The last time I was out was to visit Dante at his new school. It took most of my energy not to weep every second we were there, and the rest of it was spent not wadding Dante up like a contraband movie theater snack and smuggling him out of the building in my purse.

I got to see Dante again last weekend when he came to the mansion to stay. For two days, life felt normal. We swam and colored and watched movies. I slept in his twin-sized bed with him and we made smiley face pancakes for breakfast.

Now, it's been a week since I've seen him and two weeks

since I've seen a human not under Mikhail's employ—so, yes, I'm wearing a dress. And makeup. And I curled my hair.

Sue me for needing to feel normal.

It's just a doctor's appointment, but if Mikhail wants to take me out for lunch afterward, I don't want to show up underdressed. He wants to get me an iced coffee and a pastry after a long, lonely two weeks in the mansion? More power to him.

I swirl my lips together, smacking my gloss into place, and walk casually into the kitchen…

To find Raoul waiting for me at the counter.

He has a set of keys in his hand. "Are you ready to go?"

I look around like Mikhail might be hiding in the pantry or dangling from the chandelier. "I'm ready, but where is Mikhail?"

The look on Raoul's usually-stoic face says more than enough.

"He's not coming," I grit out. "Is he?"

"Something came up."

I can't tell whether Raoul is lying or not, but it doesn't matter. Mikhail booked this appointment for me. He pulled strings to get me in with, in his words, "the best doctor in the city." He swore up and down that I was going to get the absolute best care imaginable and he would take care of everything.

Apparently, that doesn't extend to showing up for me.

"Does he know it's a scan?" I ask. "Does he realize we're going to see the baby?"

If everything goes well, I think.

I was up late last night Googling the stats on miscarriage before eight weeks, just because I love throwing gas on the raging flames of my anxiety, I guess. A not-insignificant part of me is positive the doctor is going to impale me on that ice-cold internal probe for nothing.

This will be another false positive. Another disappointment.

The only thing that kept me from calling off the appointment and locking myself in the bathroom was the thought that, if the worst happens, I'd be able to reach over and squeeze Mikhail's hand. When the negative thoughts rose to the surface, he'd be there to keep me grounded.

Apparently not.

"He knows." Raoul tips his head towards the garage door. "Are you ready?"

I grimace and nod. Something tells me Raoul won't be holding my hand.

The ride to the doctor's office is silent and tense. Raoul and I have never been the chattiest. I don't think spending forty minutes badmouthing his boss would change that, so silence is the safest choice.

I'm actually determined to be miserable and have the worst possible time, only because I know Raoul is logging every single emotion on my face and will report it all back to Mikhail. Then I walk into the office of Dr. Rossi.

"You must be Viviana!" He grins at me under an impressively thick mustache. "My newest VIP."

I can't help but return his smile. "VIP?"

"Very Important Patient," he explains with a cartoonishly salacious wink. "Your husband is a delightful, terrifying man. He made me swear to take good care of you. Several times."

"That sounds like Mikhail."

"Of course, I would have taken care of you even without the threats because I am very good at my job." He says it in a way that doesn't sound like bragging. I just… trust him.

It's a nice feeling to have towards your doctor, especially when he lifts my thin exam gown ten minutes later and starts brandishing the internal ultrasound wand for my exam.

I'm staring at the ceiling, trying to ignore the pressure between my legs and the black square of the screen to my right. Not to mention the swirling black hole of dread yawning open in my stomach. Dr. Rossi can probably pick up my anxiety in the ultrasound.

Maybe that's why he lays a hand on my knee. "Easy there, Viviana. Everything will be alright."

I love him.

Sure, he's in his early seventies and his office is littered with photos of his wife and five kids, but I'm not deterred so long as he isn't. I need someone right now and this man is all I've got.

"I know these exams can be nerve-wracking, but you have nothing to worry about."

"How do you know that?"

He smiles and turns the screen to face me. "Because I'm looking at your baby right now. Why don't you join me?"

I turn and my heart stops. The world stops. Every dark, angry, anxious thought in my head disappears.

"That's my baby," I breathe. It looks like a little gummy bear on the screen. Nubby legs and arms, no neck in sight. "It's beautiful."

"I agree," Dr. Rossi says proudly. "Absolutely gorgeous. Especially that heartbeat. Strong as an ox, eh?"

He isolates the flickering white speck on the screen and a crackly *whoosh-whoosh* fills the room.

"So, the baby is…" *There? Real?* I'm not sure how to finish the sentence. I'm afraid if I do, this will all disappear.

"Perfectly healthy," Dr. Rossi finishes for me. He clicks around on the screen, taking pictures. A small printer to the side spits out the black-and-white images. "Cute as a button, too. I can tell. I have a knack for this kind of thing."

I laugh and it feels like a sigh of relief.

I just wish Mikhail was here to feel it with me.

Dr. Rossi hands over my pictures and leaves while I re-dress. A few minutes later, he comes back in with a stack of pamphlets. "We did the fun stuff first. Now, it's time for the business side of things. I have some information for you about prenatal testing."

"Is there something you're looking for?" I ask with a spike of panic.

"It's something I recommend to all my patients. When it comes to babies, knowledge is power. The more you know, the better you can prepare."

I flip through the pamphlet, my eyes skimming over the pages. In the photos, a woman grins as she reads her results. Her husband is right behind her, squeezing her shoulder and smiling alongside her. Every page is filled with happy families and beaming couples.

"The test also reveals the gender of the baby," Dr. Rossi explains. "I'm not sure if that is something you're interested in, but the test allows you to know the gender well before the usual twenty-week anatomy scan."

I never found out the gender with Dante. Somehow, I just knew he'd be a boy.

Mikhail and I haven't talked about whether we want to find out this time. We haven't had time to talk about much of anything. Even the announcement was interrupted by the FBI, though I decide not to tell Dr. Rossi about that particular wrinkle in the story.

"You can discuss with your husband before you make a choice. Just let me know and we'll see you back within two weeks to draw blood and—"

"I want to do it," I decide all at once.

He frowns for the first time since I walked into his office. "There's no rush. You can take your time."

"Not necessary." I sit tall, shoulders back. "I want the test."

If Mikhail wanted to be part of this pregnancy, he'd be here. As far as I'm concerned, he doesn't get a say. Not when he can't even bother to show up for appointments.

With a shrug, Dr. Rossi sends me to the lab for a blood draw and then I'm spat back into the lobby where Raoul is waiting for me. If he wants to see the sonogram pictures or know anything about the baby, he hides it well. His job is to escort me to and from the appointment, not ask questions. So he doesn't.

It's another silent, stuffy drive back to the mansion. As the residential roads become more and more familiar, the little bit of joy I managed to scrape together in Dr. Rossi's exam room fades like the skyline behind us.

I have a healthy baby. I should be celebrating. I pinch the stupid hemline of my stupid dress and feel ridiculous for ever thinking there might be a date afterward.

Mikhail comes and goes whenever he wants, and I'm always just *there*… waiting for him. Demanding nothing.

How could I make demands when he's in the middle of a war? It seems unfair. But it's also unfair that, for the second time in my life, I'm experiencing my pregnancy alone.

Mikhail missed everything with Dante. That was my fault, I know. But I thought this time would be different.

He promised he'd always take care of our family. I just didn't realize the price would be doing this life without him.

53

MIKHAIL

Stakeouts usually involve sitting in cramped cars for hours on end. A meal break for greasy fast food if I can spare the time.

But tonight is no normal stakeout.

For weeks, I've been working towards and waiting for this shipment of weapons to arrive. When Cerberus went up in flames, I wasn't sure we'd pull everything together in time to be able to handle the influx of product and cash.

Now, the ship is in the harbor and all the years of work are coming to fruition. I think that's deserving of a drink. Though I'd prefer to have it with my woman on my arm.

The rooftop bar is encircled with glowing heaters, fighting against the chilly air off the water. The harbor is lit up below. City lights glint off the surface of the Hudson.

"Your drink, Mr. Novikov." The waitress slides a glass in front of me and leaves a second one on the table. "And for your wife."

When the server first sidled up to my table, she flipped her hair and batted her lashes at me. She asked how a man like me could be drinking alone.

"Because my wife is running late," I told her succinctly.

The way she deflated gave me no small amount of joy.

But when the door to the stairwell opens at exactly seven o'clock, it's not Viviana walking towards me.

Raoul is nearly unreadable—he probably is to everyone else on the roof—but I know him. His shoulders are tense and his eyes dart nervously from right to left. He'd rather be anywhere else.

He sits down in front of Viviana's drink. "Is this for me?"

"Only if you want a mocktail. Where is Viviana?"

He examines the drink for a second before tossing it back. He grimaces. "Too sweet."

"Because it wasn't for you," I growl. "Where is Viviana?"

The plan was for Raoul to escort Viviana to the rooftop and then find a spot closer to the ship to make sure the delivery went off without a hitch. If he's here, it means something went wrong.

"At home. She told me to tell you... Fuck me... '*Something came up.*'"

I close my hand around my drink tight enough that the glass is in danger of shattering. Viviana hasn't left the house in a week. The only thing on her schedule was an appointment with Dr. Rossi, which I know went well because Dr. Rossi texted me, per my orders, as soon as Viviana left his office.

She's pregnant and the baby is healthy. She should be thrilled. We should be celebrating.

"What came up?"

Raoul sighs. "If I had to guess, she's pissed you didn't make it to the appointment."

I fling my arms wide. "I've been a little fucking busy."

He nods in agreement and... there it is. I've been busy keeping the Bratva running and making sure six years' worth of work didn't go down the drain, and Viviana is mad I missed one appointment.

I'm barely sleeping to make sure she and Dante are safe, but she's going to stand me up because I couldn't escort her to the doctor's office *one goddamn time.*

"Fucking pregnancy hormones," I grumble. I tip back the rest of my drink and start towards the exit. "If you want to take over the watch, I can go drag my wife out of bed and—"

"I think it'll turn out for the best. Viviana wouldn't want to be here for this next part."

Raoul meets my eyes for only a second before he looks away. He wasn't nervous to tell me about Viviana.

There's something else.

I lower my voice. "What's wrong?"

He looks past the rooftop to the harbor below. "I got a call from our contact with the Port Authority on my way into the city. Our shipment is... Fuck me, this one is worse... It's gone."

I whip around and squint towards the water as if I'll be able to see cartoon burglars making their way down the gangplank with burlap sacks of my money slung over their shoulders. "Gone. As in… Fuck. You're positive?"

"I confirmed it on my way up. The ship was intercepted. Someone cleaned it out."

Fuck.

I turn to face him. "You know who took it."

He sighs. "I do, yes. So do you."

"Fucking Christos," I snarl. "How?"

Almost no one knew about this plan. I didn't even tell Viviana more than the broad strokes of it. We kept it tight so this wouldn't happen.

"I have a lead," he admits. "I can follow up on my own if you'd rather deal with Viviana."

I shake my head. "Viviana isn't going anywhere. I want to meet the dead man who double-crossed me."

A little bloodshed usually clears my head, but each time my fist connects with the man's shattered jaw, I see Viviana. I see Dante. I see the last weeks of my life flutter away like a tearaway calendar in a movie montage.

"Weeks—months—*years* of my life spent on this business strategy. Buildings were burned and purchased to make this deal happen. Millions of dollars invested with some of the most powerful men in the world standing behind this shipment." I shake my head and grab the man responsible for tonight's fuck-up by his bloodied collar, lifting him onto his toes. "And you sold the info to Christos for *twenty fucking grand?*"

Raoul suspected a rigger on the cargo ship was to blame immediately. We paid him fifty thousand—more than his annual salary—to falsify the shipping reports. Then James turned around and pocketed another twenty to sell everything he knew to Christos Drakos.

"He tortured it out of me," he whimpers, looking from me to Raoul. "I didn't want to tell him."

"Then you shouldn't have told him," Raoul intones simply.

I drop James on the floor. He falls on his already-broken femur and screams. It doesn't matter. No one is around to hear him. No one who will save him, anyway.

I pace around him. "You're lying to me."

He pulls in his good leg, trying to draw himself in tight. Like the fetal position will save him. "I'm not! Christos tortured me! He—"

"If he'd tortured the information out of you, you'd be dead," I growl. "You would have given him what he wanted and he would have snipped you like the loose end you are. He wouldn't have paid you off."

His eyes go wide and I know I'm right.

"What happened," I explain slowly, drawing a knife out of my back pocket, "is that you got greedy. You thought you could make even more money by working as a double agent."

He shakes his head. "No. I wouldn't—"

"You would. You *did*. The question now is, *Why?*" I slowly carve the knife through the air and the dramatics are paying off. James can't look away from the blade.

Finally, he snaps. "My son!" he blurts. "He's sick. My son is sick. He needs treatment and it's expensive. I thought—I thought I could make enough money to heal him."

"A sick kid?" I frown. "Was there a cat stuck in a tree, too? Or maybe there was a bomb under the hospital and Christos would kill all the invalids if you didn't tell him about the shipment."

"I'm telling you the truth!"

"No, you're not," Raoul drawls behind me. "You are single with no family in the city. No wife, no children. You've worked on the ship for six months and were on construction before this. Originally from Atlanta. Your parents are Harold and Janine."

He blinks at Raoul, dumbfounded. "How did you—"

"We chose you because you have no ties to the city." I kneel down, the knife wedged under his chin. "We chose you because no one would miss you. Because you are *expendable*."

"Please. Don't." He's shaking. The smell of urine fills the air and I wrinkle my nose, but don't draw away.

I sigh. "Poor James. You were hand-selected because you would be easy to kill and dispose of if it came to it. Unfortunately, that's exactly what it's come to."

Tears stream down his cheeks. "Please… you can't."

"Remember your fake son—the one who's dying? Well, I have a *real* son. And a *real* wife. A family, James. Tonight, you put all of them at risk."

"I'm sorry," he sobs. "I didn't know."

"I know." I nod, tossing the blade behind me. It clatters across the floor. "But now, you do."

He looks hopeful for a second. Then I drive the heel of my boot into his nose and give him every ounce of what he deserves.

54

VIVIANA

Sending Raoul to the bar without me was a strong choice. Especially because I actually really wanted to go.

A night celebrating with Mikhail on some glitzy rooftop somewhere? Yes, please. Sign me up. Even if the closest I can get to a drink right now is juice and soda water, I want to go out. I want to stop feeling like a mole person and spend a fun night with my husband.

But not like this.

The only time I get to be with Mikhail is on *his* terms. He's too busy to show up for me, but I'm supposed to strap my bloated, pregnant body into a dress and heels the moment he snaps his fingers? It's not exactly the give-and-take relationship I always dreamed of.

Which is why, when I finally hear the front door open at two in the morning, I'm sitting in bed with a book I don't care about in my lap and one hell of a bone to pick with my other half.

I can hear muffled voices and footsteps. I'm itching to jump out of bed and charge downstairs, but I don't want to look even half as desperate as I feel. So I wait.

And wait.

And wait.

Naively, I imagined Mikhail would see that I wasn't with Raoul, hop in his car, and be back at the mansion to drag me out of bed within an hour. We'd scream and fight at first, sure. But by the time we made it to the bar, we'd have made up. Preferably in the backseat of his car. Twice.

Now, he's *in* the mansion—and he still isn't coming to find me.

"What the hell?" I mutter, tossing my book to the end of the bed.

By the time I hear him coming down the hallway, I have our entire argument mapped out in my head. Every point he could make, I can counter it. I'm ready.

It takes all the restraint I have left to wait until the door has just barely cracked open to start talking.

"You're finally home," I note coolly. "I almost didn't bother waiting up for—"

My planned speech careens off the rails when Mikhail steps into the room... covered from head to toe in blood.

"Oh my God." I throw the comforter back and slide my legs to the edge of the bed. "Where have you been?"

Are you okay? Are you safe? Those are the questions I'm too upset to ask.

"Busy."

He peels his bloody shirt over his head and I don't see any wounds or bruises on his body. So the blood isn't his, which should be nothing but good news. But in the back of my head, I wonder who he killed and why they were more important than me.

"I had a scan this morning."

"I know." He kicks his pants off and tosses them in the ruined pile with his shirt. It's been months of living with Mikhail and seeing him every day, but I'll never get over the way he moves. The strength that ripples through him. Even with nothing on except a pair of black briefs, he's a weapon.

"If you knew about it, that means you *chose* not to show up, then. Don't you even want to know how it went?"

He's covered in a dead man's blood and we're talking about my doctor's appointment. It's weird, but this is our life, apparently.

He shakes his head. "I know how it went. Dr. Rossi texted me as soon as you left his office."

"I have a phone, too. You could have texted me."

"I wanted it straight from the source." If that's his way of saying he doesn't trust me, it's as subtle as a chainsaw.

"You promised me I wasn't going to be one of those Bratva wives whose only purpose is to birth your children."

"Not tonight, Viviana."

The strain in his voice is impossible to miss. I should let this go. I should—"It has to be tonight," I snap. "Because I never know when I'll see you again."

He turns to me, his bloody hands in tight fists at his sides. "We're at war."

"And *we're* having a baby. You and me. The two of us. If it's bad timing for you, you have no one to blame but yourself. You did this. You didn't have any trouble clearing your schedule when you wanted to 'fuck a baby into me.' The war didn't stop you then."

His eyes narrow. "Things have escalated since then and you know it. If I wait until all my enemies are dead to fuck my wife, we'd never have a family."

He's right.

There will always be more enemies. Another war. An ever-growing list of things to be scared of. The enormity of what exactly I've signed up for hits me all at once.

"Maybe that would have been a good idea," I hiss. "Maybe our original arrangement was smart all along: we're business partners. I handle the house and you handle the Bratva."

"You never wanted that." He snorts and turns towards the bathroom. "These pregnancy hormones are making you crazy."

Without thinking, I grab the book from the end of the bed and fling it at him. My throw goes wide and the book clatters against the wall.

He turns towards me slowly, his jaw clenched. "Not tonight."

But it's too late to walk away now. The space in my heart where I've tucked every fear and doubt and concern for the last few months is overflowing. There's no more room to stuff it down. It has to come out.

"This life—the one with us and Dante and our baby—isn't less important than the Bratva."

"I never said it was!" he bellows. There's blood drying on his neck. It shifts as he swallows, as tension radiates through him.

"You don't have to say it, Mikhail. You show it every single day. Every day that you aren't here. Every day that Dante isn't here."

His eyes flare, a warning written on his face. "I didn't make that decision alone."

"No, but you've done everything else alone!" I cry out. "I thought sending Dante away was for the best at the time, but now... Now, I wonder if you weren't trying to get him out of the way."

He's across the room between one blink and the next. He leans in close enough that my nose fills with the copper tang of someone else's blood.

"Look at me, Viviana," he snarls. "If I wanted to get rid of you and Dante, I could. I would have done it already. Months ago. *Years* ago."

My heart is racing and I flash back to the night all of this started. To Mikhail storming into my bridal suite, this dark, vengeful presence. I didn't know anything about him then. As grateful as I was that he'd saved me from a lifetime married to Trofim, I was terrified. I had no idea what he would do or what he was capable of.

I'm just as terrified of him now.

I swallow past the fear. "Why don't you? You clearly aren't

interested in having a family. If you were, you'd bother to show up when—"

He wraps his sticky hands around my throat and drives me back against the wall. I'm so shocked, I don't even scream. I could. His hold on my neck is loose enough. But his hand is shaking. He's working hard not to hurt me, and I have no clue when that control will snap. I don't want to push him.

We stare at each other for a few seconds or minutes. I'm not sure. Time slips and morphs and I see too many emotions to count shutter across Mikhail's face.

Then, just as fast as he crossed the room, he's gone.

I can still feel the warmth of his hand around my throat when the bathroom door clicks closed and the shower starts.

55

VIVIANA

I try to ignore the noises coming from the kitchen—shuffling feet, plates rattling together. If Mikhail doesn't want to see me, that's fine. I'm not going to force myself on him again. It didn't exactly go well the last time.

When he got out of the shower a couple nights ago, he walked straight past the bed and out of the room. I haven't seen him since.

So, no, I'm not going to bombard him in the kitchen and start another fight.

But there's no reason I can't peek in and see if it's really him, right? This is my house, too. I'm allowed to walk around freely.

I tiptoe down the hall and ease around the corner. I'll just catch a glimpse of him and then be on my way.

"It's me." Anatoly waves from behind the refrigerator door. "You aren't as sneaky as you think you are."

Hope curdles into disappointment in my chest. "I wasn't trying to be sneaky."

He huffs out a laugh. "Sure. You aren't trying to be sneaky, just like Mikhail isn't trying to avoid you."

I drop down in the closest barstool. "Did he tell you that? Did he say he was trying to avoid me?"

Anatoly pulls out an armful of chef-prepared meals and dumps them on the counter. One of the containers has mold growing up the inside wall. I'm not surprised—I haven't eaten anything but sleeves of salted crackers and obnoxiously sugary cereal in days. And if Mikhail is eating, he isn't doing it here.

"No, he didn't say he was trying to avoid you. That is my point." Anatoly dips his chin, looking at me from under his brows. "You're both liars."

"I'm not a liar."

"Said the liar," Anatoly retorts. "You were sneaking down that hall—with all the grace of a horse in tap shoes, by the way—to catch a secret glimpse of your hubby because you're too afraid to walk into his office and talk to him."

"I'm not afraid," I mumble.

I can still feel Mikhail's hand around my throat. When I close my eyes, I see the fear burning in his. I didn't understand it in the moment, but since I've had days on my own to think about it, I realized something: for a second, Mikhail was just as afraid of himself and what he was capable of as I was.

"And Mikhail," Anatoly charges on, ignoring me, "is, once again, burying himself in work and responsibilities to procrastinate dealing with his personal life."

I don't want to ask and give Anatoly the satisfaction of knowing I care, but I can't stop myself. "He's done this before?"

"After Alyona and Anzhelina," he says quietly. "It went on for years, actually... Until he met you."

My heart twinges. I fiddle with the hem of my shirt to hide the fact that my hands are shaking. "Maybe Mikhail just likes work. Maybe this has nothing to do with me and this is just how he is. He's a workaholic. Everything comes second to the Bratva."

Anatoly is quiet for long enough that I look up. He's watching me, looking unusually somber.

"What?"

He breathes softly. "I wasn't born under the same pressure Mikhail was, being a bastard and all. Even as the second-born, a lot was expected of Mikhail—from Iakov and everyone else. Boys picked fights with him growing up just to say they beat up a Novikov. Then there was Trofim... God, he was such an asshole. Still is, I'm sure, wherever the fuck he is." Anatoly blows out a harsh breath and continues. "Mikhail couldn't let his guard down unless he wanted to risk getting hurt. And that was before he had people who depended on him."

"He wanted that," I point out. "He overthrew Trofim so he could run the Bratva. He wanted to—"

"He wanted to make sure no one had to live under Trofim's thumb," Anatoly corrects. "If you think becoming *pakhan* was all about power for Mikhail, then you don't know him as well as you think you do."

I could argue with him, but he's right. I know it was about more than that. No matter how upset I am with him right now, Mikhail is a good man with a good heart.

Even if he works hard to make sure no one ever sees it.

"If Mikhail hadn't taken over, I would have left the Bratva," Anatoly admits.

"Really?"

He nods. "There was no good reason for me to stay. Not after Trofim killed my mom. The only reason I stuck around is because I wanted to support Mikhail. Even still, I would have given it all up for the right person."

"For Stella?" I guess.

Anatoly's eyes darken for a second. Then he shakes his head, waving away the question. "All I'm saying is, there are a lot of things more important to Mikhail than the Bratva."

I want to believe Anatoly, I really do. But no matter how hard I try, there's no part of me that can imagine a future where Mikhail isn't running the Bratva. Where death and war aren't constantly intruding on our doorstep.

I knew all of that when we got married—*twice*. But I thought I was agreeing to face it together. If I'd known I'd be facing it all alone, I'm not sure I would have made the same choice.

Anatoly warms something up for dinner and leaves, but I stay at the island. I sit there for a long time, thinking through everything Anatoly said, everything Mikhail and I have been through. I'm not specifically waiting for Mikhail, but I don't flee to my room when I hear him coming in the front door late.

He walks down the hall towards the kitchen and I hear his steps falter when he sees me at the island. Then: "You should be asleep."

"I can't. Not until we talk." I turn to face him. His beard is longer than I've ever seen it and his hair is sticking up like he's run his hands through it one too many times today. He looks tired and there's probably a better time to do this, but I have no idea when that would be. I'm not sure it would ever come. Now is all I've got.

His jaw clicks. "About what?"

"About where you've been."

"You know where I've been," he says wearily. "I've been scouring this city for any sign of your father or Christos Drakos. They stole from me and they've threatened the Bratva. I have to respond."

"I heard about that."

Anatoly filled me in last night on the lost weapons and the financial fallout. The war is ramping up.

"Then why even ask?" He drops his keys in a bowl in the center of the island. The noise shatters the quiet and I realize how quiet it has been for days.

"I know where you've been, but I want to talk about it," I clarify. "I want to talk about the fact that you haven't been *here*."

His hand curls into a fist. He slides it off the counter, hiding it at his side. "Staying here doesn't keep you safe."

"What if I don't want to be safe?"

He frowns, and I realize I'm not even mad at Mikhail anymore. I'm just tired.

"I don't think 'safe' is my biggest priority," I explain softly. "I'd rather have you. I want my son to be here with me. I want our children to know—*really* know—their father."

Because, wow, what a father he would be. Without all of the noise and pressure and threats of violence, Mikhail could really sweep up this whole fatherhood thing. He'd blow every male figurehead I've seen up close and personal out of the water without even trying. Our kids could be so, so lucky, and I want that for them. More than anything.

Mikhail is looking right at me, but he's never felt further away. The week we spent in the cabin feels like another life. The version of Mikhail that taught Dante to fish and cooked us all dinner feels like another person. My stomach churns. I feel the loss of what could be like a physical, ripping ache deep inside of me.

He takes a breath. "I want our children to survive. That's my priority."

I want to argue with him, but I don't know how. Mikhail cares about this family as much as I do, but we care about it in different ways. We want different things. And I have no idea how to make that work anymore.

"You should be asleep," he says again, dragging a hand over his jaw. "You take care of yourself and the baby; I'll deal with everything else."

Before I can even begin to figure out what to say to that, his phone rings.

Somewhere deeper in the house, another phone rings at the same time.

Mikhail frowns, hesitating for only a second before he answers it. "Hello?"

I hear an echo of this conversation happening in the other room. Anatoly's on the phone, too. *It's a coincidence. They both got a phone call at the same time, that's it. Everything is fine.*

I believe my own lies until Mikhail's face goes completely white. He lowers the phone slowly like he can't physically hold it up anymore.

"What's wrong?" I ask as footsteps thunder through the house behind me.

Anatoly whips into the kitchen, breathing heavily. "Mikhail."

I look from Anatoly to my husband, lost as something unspoken passes between them.

"What is it?" I demand. "What's happening?"

Anatoly opens his mouth to respond, but Mikhail beats him to it. "It's Dante," he breathes, our son's name catching in his throat. "He's missing."

56

MIKHAIL

Viviana already looked worn. As soon as I walked in the kitchen and saw her slumped at the counter, I wanted to wrap her in my jacket and carry her upstairs. I haven't been around as much as I wish I could, and I don't think she's been sleeping. She looked exhausted and sick. Her collarbones were poking out of the wide neck of her t-shirt, and I thought, *I don't have the bandwidth to worry about her health on top of everything else.*

Now, this.

"He's missing." I barely get the words out before Viviana buckles.

The only reason she doesn't crack her knees on the floor is because Anatoly catches her. He helps her into a chair, but it doesn't matter. Viviana is up and on her feet again a second later. She stumbles towards me.

"Where is he?" she rasps. "Mikhail!"

My mind is whirring. It's chaos, but I've always thrived here. When everyone else panics, the fog clears for me. For the first time in days, I feel like I'm exactly where I'm meant to be.

I pull out my phone and call Raoul. He answers on the first ring.

"Dante," he says. I have no idea which informant told him, but I'm glad. It saves us time.

"Find him, Raoul."

"I'm already on it."

He hangs up and I text the guards at the front gates. I want every available set of eyes, ears, and hands looking for my son. Nothing else matters.

"Anatoly."

My brother is in front of me before I can even look up. "I'll go look for him."

I shake my head. "No. Stay here with Viviana."

I know he hates doing nothing while the rest of us search for Dante, but there's no one else I trust to watch her. There's also no one she trusts more. I'm including myself in that category.

Viviana grabs the front of my shirt. Her fingers are cold. "I want to come with you. Wherever he is, I want to—"

"I don't know where he is," I tell her.

I hate that it's true.

I hate that I didn't see this coming.

I hate the way she's looking at me right now.

Tears well in her eyes. They spill over when she blinks, pouring down her cheeks. "Is it Christos? Is it—Is he—He has to be okay, Mikhail."

She breaks, falling against my chest.

I hold her for a second. For one second, I let myself wrap an arm around her waist and hug her to my chest.

Then I pass her to Anatoly.

"I'm going to find him, Viviana. Dante is going to be okay."

The voices in my head beg to disagree. *He might not be okay. It might already be too late. You fucked up and now, Dante is paying the price.*

I quiet the dark thoughts and focus on what I can control. "Whoever did this is going to pay with their life. I promise you that."

Viviana wraps her arms around herself. She's trembling and wide-eyed, split open in a way I've never seen before.

I tip my head to Anatoly. "Take care of her."

"With my life," he vows quietly.

I grab my keys and jog to the garage. As the door closes behind me, Viviana wails. I think she drops to the floor, but I know she'd rather me go look for Dante than return to comfort her.

So I keep moving and I don't look back.

I make it to the doors of a nightclub—the third Greek-owned business I've hit in the last hour—and Raoul is already there.

We've been working off of the same list. He started at the bottom, I started at the top. Now, we've met in the middle and there's still no sign of Christos.

Which means there's no sign of Dante.

"Christos isn't here," Raoul confirms, furiously tapping out a mess on his phone. "I'm following other leads, but Christos hasn't been seen anywhere tonight. Are you sure it was—"

"It was him," I snap. "Christos was caught on the school's security cameras an hour before Dante went missing. He paid off one of the guards at the front gate."

The school called to tell me that no one on Dante's floor could find him, but "you shouldn't panic. We are doing everything we can to locate him. I'm sure he just wandered to another building."

But I knew. An hour before the school was willing to admit that Dante was gone, I'd already put my entire Bratva on the scent. I've reached out to every ally and called in every long-forgotten favor. In a matter of hours, I've turned this city upside down.

Still, no one has seen my son.

Raoul pockets his phone and paces. "We can put a man at every known Greek hangout. We can watch and see if Christos makes any moves, but that could take days."

"Too long," I snarl. "We don't have time. That's my son, Raoul."

An old ache rises in my chest. One I know all too fucking well. I know what it's like to lose a child. I can't do it again. I won't.

Viviana is safe at the mansion with Anatoly, but if anything happens to Dante, she'll be gone, too. She blames me for this, and I agree with her. I'm the one who sent him away. I'm the one who separated them.

If I can't bring him home, I'll lose them both.

"We don't have time to waste."

I push past Raoul and through the blacked-out double doors of Christos's club. It's a weeknight, so the dance floor is sparse. But multi-colored lights strobe around the room and music thumps through the speakers.

A waitress in a mini skirt and fishnet top peels away from the bar and makes her way over to us with a smile. "Would you two gentlemen like a table or booth?"

"Take me to the office," I order.

"I can get you a private room." Her eyebrow arches. "I'm available for dances. I'd be happy to take care of you."

Usually, I'd let the woman down easy, but my patience ran out hours ago. "If you want to take care of me, then take me to your boss," I say. "I only came to kill one person tonight, but I'd be happy to add you to the list if you push me."

Her eyes go wide. She looks from me to Raoul and I watch as recognition flickers across her face. She knows us. I'm sure our faces are on a "kill on sight" sign somewhere in one of the back rooms. Christos doesn't like anyone toeing into his territory.

She swallows and nods. "Okay. Follow me."

Her hips don't sway nearly as much as they first did as she leads us across the dance floor to a door in the back right corner of the club. We step into a dim hallway that still feels painfully bright after the strobe lights from the main room.

I think about Dante being held in a place like this, scared and alone while music thumps through the walls. I focus on all the arts and crafts I can make with Christos' intestines to keep myself from tearing the building apart brick by fucking brick.

The waitress takes us to the middle of the hallway and then points to a door straight ahead. "He's in there—and, if anyone asks, I didn't bring you back here."

"Won't they already know?" Raoul asks, his eyes flicking to the two obvious cameras affixed to the ceiling.

"The system doesn't work," she replies. "The cameras haven't recorded anything for a couple weeks now. Not at any of Christos's clubs. The dancers think he's planning something."

"Like what?" I ask.

She holds up her hands in innocence. Her long, silver nails reflect the dim fluorescent lights. "I don't mess with that side of things. I'm here to make money and feed my kids."

"Keep everyone out of this hallway for the next half-hour and I'll forget we ever met," I tell her.

She nods and hurries back into the club like her life depends on it.

As soon as the door closes behind her, I kick open the door at the end of the hall.

"What the hell?" The square-shaped man behind the desk starts to stand up, his face twisted in a scowl. Then he sees me.

He doesn't need a refresher the way the waitress did. He recognizes me immediately.

His face falls and he drops back into his chair. The metal legs squeal under his weight. "This area is for employees only."

"That's perfect. Because I've got a job for you." I gesture for Raoul to close the door and it clicks shut a second later. The music from the club is even more muted. No one will hear him scream. "You tell me everything I want to know. In return, I won't kill you."

His eyelids twitch. "If you want money, I can open the safe. The bar has cash. I can clear it out for you, if you want."

I pull the gun out of my pocket and aim it at his forehead. "I'm not interested in cash. I want to know where Christos Drakos is tonight."

Sweat drips down his forehead. His collar turns a darker shade of gray as panic soaks through his shirt. The room smells stale and bitter.

I hope Dante isn't in a room like this. I hope he isn't with a man like this.

"Mr. Drakos owns the club, but I don't know anything about—"

His lie is lost to a yelp as I press the barrel of the gun to kiss his forehead. "You have no fucking clue what *I* know, apparently. Because I know for a fact that you have at least one useful piece of information for me in that block head of yours."

He's shaking from head to toe. "I swear I don't know anything! I don't know where your son is."

There it is.

I feel Raoul stiffen behind me so I know he heard it, too. A confession. As good as, anyway.

I cock the gun, ignoring the man's sob of terror. "Explain to me how a random *mudak* like you, sitting in the back of a dingy club with low-rent dancers, knows my son is missing before almost anyone in the world?"

His eyes widen as he realizes what he did. What he said.

"You've already betrayed your boss's trust," I explain, tracing the round line of his face down to his fleshy jaw with my gun. I wedge the barrel there against his neck. "So you might as well save your own worthless life in the meantime."

He licks his lips and blows out a shaky breath. "What do you want to know?"

57

VIVIANA

The second Mikhail touches the door to leave, my insides twist. It's a searing pain that drops me to my knees.

"Viviana?" Anatoly is there, grabbing my arm and trying to pick me up. But the pain is so intense I can't get my feet under me. All I can do is fold myself forward and press my head between my knees.

Dante is missing.

My son is gone.

I know it's true, but I can't make sense of it. I can't wrap my head around a world where the little boy I've devoted every minute of my life to for over six years isn't healthy and whole and well and *here.*

"It's going to be okay, Viv." Anatoly pats my back. It's the same way I used to soothe Dante when he was sick. Long, slow circles between his tiny shoulder blades. "Mikhail is going to take care of everything."

But *I'm* the one who takes care of Dante. It's always been me.

When he was a baby, I handled every middle-of-the-night nursing session because there was no one else. He had me and I had him and that was enough. I worked to buy the mountain of diapers he needed. I bought him clothes and, when he outgrew them in two months, I bought him more. I held heating pads to ear infections and I sang away the nightmares.

Anything Dante has ever needed, I've been there.

Now, when he needs his mama more than he's ever needed me, I'm not there.

"He's gone." My voice is broken. It comes out in a strangled whisper. "He's gone."

"You have to get up, Viv." Anatoly scoops me up and places me on the barstool. "Mikhail is taking care of it. Everything is going to be—"

His voice cuts off so suddenly that I look up. Somewhere behind the haze of panic and grief, I register that Anatoly looks sick.

His face is still pale from the news about Dante, but now, Anatoly is staring down at the floor.

At a smear of blood on the white tile.

I run the last few minutes back and can't understand where it came from. Was Mikhail bleeding? Did I hurt myself when I fell?

I turn back to Anatoly and he's looking down at his arm now. At a red spot on his forearm. The same arm he just curled underneath me to lift me off the floor.

"Are you hurt?" It comes out in a hoarse whisper.

Anatoly jumps. Like he was so deep in his head he forgot I was here. He shakes his head slowly. "It's not mine, Viv."

"Then whose—?"

No.

Even as I stand up, I don't believe it. I can't. Life has been a bitch to me more times than I can count, but she's not a monster. Surely, I've had enough slices of shit pie for a lifetime. I don't need a double helping on the worst day of my life.

But I grab the back of my shorts and they're wet. My fingers come away bloody. The stool I was sitting on is smeared with blood. It's bright red. Fresh.

"No," I whisper like that might make all of this disappear. "This isn't happening."

My eyes flicker back and forth over all the evidence, taking it in but not absorbing it. Meanwhile, Anatoly grabs his keys and loops his arm through mine.

We're halfway to the garage door before I dig my heels in. "We can't leave."

"You're bleeding, Viv." He explains it slowly, sounding out every syllable.

"Dante is missing," I respond just as slowly. "We have to stay here."

"You need to go to a hospital. You could be—Fuck, I don't know! But you're pregnant and I know this isn't good."

"Not good" is an understatement. This is cruel and unusual punishment. My son is missing and now, I can't even keep the child in my own womb safe? *I'm a failure.*

Guilt threatens to bring me to my knees again, but I don't have time for that. It isn't helpful now.

Anatoly pulls me towards the door. "We have to go."

"We can't leave. Mikhail told us to stay here!"

He did, didn't he? I don't remember what he said. Everything after "Dante is missing" is a blur.

"If he knew you were bleeding, he'd tell me to get you to a hospital," he argues. "There is no way I'm letting anything happen to you or your baby on my watch. We need to go."

I pull back, sliding my wrist out of his grip. "What if Dante calls?"

As soon as the words are out of my mouth, I know it's ridiculous. Dante doesn't have a phone. He wouldn't even know my number if he had one.

"What if he comes back?" I try again, but… no. I blow out a shuddering breath. "He doesn't know the address. He can't— He's too little to find his way back."

He's alone and helpless and he needs me and I'm not there.

Anatoly grabs my shoulders, dipping down so he's looking in my eyes. "Dante doesn't need to be able to find his way back, because Mikhail is looking for him. Mikhail is going to find him."

My chest hitches with a sob. "I should be out there, too. He's my baby, Nat."

Anatoly's eyes go glassy and he pulls me close, squeezing hard. I can tell he needs a hug as much as I do. But when he lets me go, his eyes are clear and his jaw is set. "Mikhail is going to find Dante and he'll make sure whoever did this pays with their life. In the meantime, I'm taking you to the hospital whether you want to go or not."

I don't want to go. At all.

But like almost everything else in my life at the moment, I don't have a choice.

"You're perfect! Nothing is wrong."

I want to slap the emergency room doctor in the face. I know it's not his fault. How would he know that nothing is perfect and absolutely everything is wrong? For some crazy reason, the world hasn't stopped because my son is missing. To everyone else, this is any normal day.

I slide my hands under my thighs to control myself. "I'm not losing the pregnancy?"

"Bleeding can be normal for the first twelve weeks," he explains with a smile. "But you did the right thing by coming to get checked over. You're a very responsible mother."

It's like the man is reading from a list of all the worst things he could possibly say to me at this moment. *If I was a responsible mother, my son would be at home in his bed instead of God only knows where.*

Sensing how close to the edge I am, Anatoly lays a hand on my shoulder. "She's free to go, then?"

The doctor probably thinks Anatoly is my husband. Or the father of my baby, at least. I don't even care. If it means I don't have to talk and try to pretend my world isn't crumbling around me, then he can think whatever the hell he wants.

"Yes, but she needs to rest," the doctor tells him. "Take it easy for the next couple days. Call her doctor if she has any more spotting."

"Call her doctor or bring her here?" Anatoly asks, a tinge of panic in his voice. "Should I have called her doctor the first time?"

The emergency room doctor is saying something about how it's good to stay in contact with my physician since Dr. Rossi will be more familiar with my case, but I stop listening when I hear a muffled vibration. Like a bloodhound on the scent, I leap at Anatoly's pocket and wrench his phone out of his pants.

"Fucking hell, Viv." He squirms and tries to pry me off of him, but I see Mikhail's name on the screen and I don't care about anything else.

I answer it. "Mikhail?"

There's a beat of hesitation. "Where's Anatoly?"

I push past the annoyance that Mikhail called Anatoly, not me. That he doesn't want to talk to me now.

"Have you found Dante?" I haven't moved in the last half hour, but I'm breathless. "Where is he?"

"Is Anatoly with you?" Mikhail bites out.

Who cares about Nat? I want to know about Dante!

Anatoly reaches for the phone, but I twist away from him. "He's here. Where is Dante?"

"There are no phones in the exam rooms," the doctor says. "If you could turn that—"

I round on him, top lip curled. "Fuck off!"

The doctor recoils and looks offended, but he should just be grateful I didn't slap him. Anatoly ushers him towards the door. "You really should fuck off. She can get scary."

As soon as the doctor is gone, I put the phone on speaker. "Where is Dante?"

At the same time, Mikhail repeats, "Is Anatoly there?"

Anatoly takes the phone, holding it between us. "I'm here."

"Why the fuck are you at a hospital right now?" Mikhail snarls.

"How do you know about—" Anatoly's voice fades into a groan. "Fucking Raoul and his trackers. Tell him to stop tailing me!"

"Then stop taking my wife out of the mansion without my consent."

I'm torn between being offended Mikhail thinks I need his permission and the way he says, "my wife." A lot has happened in the last few days, but those words still send a warm flutter through my chest.

"I was bleeding."

The confession hangs in the air for a second before Mikhail exhales. "Are you okay?"

"I'm fine." The reality of how bad this doctor's visit could have gone hits me all at once. I swipe the tears off of my cheeks, hoping Mikhail can't tell I'm crying through the phone. "Everything is fine. The baby is okay."

Mikhail sighs. "Thank God."

"But where is Dante? What do you know?"

I don't actually expect anything. It's only been a couple hours. How much could Mikhail have done in this short amount of time? Anatoly and I only managed to make it to the hospital and go to an appointment. There's no way Mikhail was able to find a kidnapped child.

"I know where he is."

I grip the edge of the exam table to keep from dropping to my knees again. A sob that has been lodged in my throat for the last two hours breaks free. "You found him?"

"I know where he is," Mikhail repeats. "I don't have him yet. But I'm on my way."

"Where?" I blurt.

I can hear Mikhail's stern frown through the phone. "Viviana needs to go home and rest, Nat. You need to stay with her."

I guess that means he's done talking to me again.

I snort. "I'm right here. You can talk to me."

They continue talking to each other, ignoring me entirely. "I'll stay with her, but tell me where you're going to be. In case shit goes sideways." The line goes quiet and Anatoly curses under his breath. "You need to fucking tell me, Mikhail. If something happens to you and Raoul, I want to know how to find you."

If something happens to you and Raoul.

It was stupid of me to think Dante was the only one in danger here. If someone was willing to risk Mikhail's wrath to kidnap Dante, they'll definitely fight to keep him. Mikhail and Raoul and everyone fighting alongside them are putting themselves at risk, too.

I could lose everyone in one night.

"Christos is holding him at an abandoned shopping mall." Mikhail's voice shakes and I know he's feeling the exact same thing I am.

There's a difference between knowing your son has been kidnapped and then finding out where he is, *who* has him. It's been a nightmare from the first second, but now, it feels devastatingly real.

I know where he is, and I need to be there.

"Get the address," I whisper to Anatoly. "Say you need it for backup."

Anatoly waves me off, but I elbow him in the side, mouthing for him to ask. Finally, he scowls at me, but says, "Send me the address."

I'm not sure if Mikhail can hear me whispering, but his response makes me think he can.

"I have backup lined up already. I don't need you there."

Anatoly rolls his eyes. "I'm useless to you, I get it. Consider me Plan Z. Backup for your backup."

"You're not useless, Nat. I need you to take Viviana home and stay with her. Tie her down if you have to."

"Hey!"

"I mean it," Mikhail interrupts. "I can't worry about anyone or anything else tonight. There's too much on my plate right now."

"Then don't worry about me! That'll free up some room on your plate," I snap.

"If I could turn it off, I would," Mikhail mutters quietly enough that I almost don't hear him. He clears his throat. "We're headed to the mall now. I'll send you the address and update you when there's something to know. For now, *take her home.*"

I realize a second too late that the call is ending. "Be careful!" But the screen is already black.

"He'll be careful," Anatoly assures me. "Mikhail and Raoul know what they're doing."

"You aren't worried about them?"

I study Anatoly and he may not be worried, per se, but he's antsy to fight alongside his brothers. He's been the designated babysitter for weeks. He has a lot of pent-up energy and nowhere to put it.

"It could be a trap." I don't want to give voice to all of my darkest thoughts, but I have to. "They could be bombarded as soon as they get there. Dante might already be—" My throat closes.

I can't say it. I can't even think it.

Dante is okay. Mikhail will save him.

Anatoly pockets his phone. "Of course I'm worried. But I trust them. You should, too."

"I trust them, but I—I can't go back to that mansion and sit and wait for them, Nat. I have to do something. Don't you want to be there to help? Aren't you tired of sitting around and doing nothing?"

His jaw works side to side and I realize too late what I said.

"I didn't mean—"

"The only thing that will happen if we show up at that mall tonight is Mikhail will be pissed and distracted. He'll go in to find Dante, but his head will be outside with you."

"He can forget about me long enough to save our son!"

But I hear Mikhail's whispered confession in my ear. *If I could turn it off, I would.*

Anatoly ignores me. "I'm going to do the best thing I can do. I'm going to take you home and make sure he doesn't have to worry about where you are tonight."

I chew on my lower lip. "I'm sorry, Anatoly. You do a lot for him—for *me*. I didn't mean it."

He sighs and then wraps a heavy arm around my shoulders, shaking me gently. "I know. You get worked up and think with your lizard brain. Lucky for you, I'm here to keep a close eye on you."

I bump his hip and shove him away. "You're an asshole."

He smiles, but in the next second, it wilts. There's nothing to smile about tonight.

We go back to the house and do the only thing we can do: wait.

58

MIKHAIL

The mall is a dark smudge against the cloudy sky. Cracked asphalt stretches out in every direction. Weeds and scraggly blades of grass have pushed their way through, but in every other way, the place is a hulking, desolate wasteland.

And my son is inside.

The manager at the club told us as much as he knew—Christos was planning something big. All the security cameras at Greek-owned clubs around town had been turned off in case Christos needed to use them as a stash point.

He didn't want evidence tying Dante to any of his business. But if the plan went off without a hitch, he wouldn't need them.

"He owns some big piece of property outside the city," the manager said.

I knew what he was talking about immediately. Christos invested in the mall in the late 1980s. When it closed for good a few years ago, he didn't bother selling it. The retail side of things never made him much money anyway. He gets much more use out of it now that it's abandoned and forgotten and doesn't draw any unwanted eyes.

"Do you think she'll stay away?" Raoul stands next to me, assessing the bland exterior of the building.

"If Anatoly knows what's good for himself, then yes." After the clinic fiasco, I don't think Anatoly would risk taking Viviana anywhere against my wishes again.

Then again, I know my wife. She has a way of getting what she wants.

"It's going to kill her not to be here."

"It might kill her *to* be here."

Sure, Viviana being an onlooker to a raid like this is dangerous, but it's more than that. If things inside don't go the way we're hoping, I don't want her anywhere near this place.

"There are some things you can't ever get out of your head," I add softly. "I don't want her to ever know what it feels like to see her own child dead."

I wouldn't wish that pain on anyone.

Suddenly, Raoul claps a hand on my back. "No one is going to experience that today. Because we're going to go in there and save your son."

Raoul isn't usually the cheerleader type before a raid, but I don't mind the energy today. We could all use a little pep in our steps.

I'm not the only one who's exhausted; the men are tired, too. It's late and we've trekked all over the city in a matter of hours. But when I make the call to storm the building, no one hesitates.

They just *go.*

We hit every entrance, clearing the rundown building room by room. Distantly, I hear gunshots echoing through the dusty air and harried footsteps across the tiles. This mission isn't about stealth. It's not about the element of surprise. There's no way Christos kidnapped my son and thought, for even a second, that I wasn't going to tear this world apart until I got him back. He knows I'm coming at him with everything I have.

So this mission is about being fast and being thorough.

I search an old retail space, kicking over a box of moth-eaten clothes in the back room to make sure it's empty.

"Clear!" I call as soon as I'm back in the main walkway.

Raoul pops out of the space just ahead of me. He shakes his head, but still yells, "Clear!"

The voices are getting louder. My men are converging from every direction. Soon, we'll meet at the heart of the building.

What if no one finds Dante?

What if he isn't here?

What if this is a trap?

We don't have any other leads and I already killed the manager from the club. He didn't know enough to be useful, anyway. But he knew a six-year-old was going to be kidnapped and he did nothing to stop it. He's lucky all I did was shoot him in the head.

Raoul is in front of me, walking past the wide-open mouth of what was once a lingerie store, when gunshots ring out.

He hits the floor and I dive sideways, crouching behind a tiled planter. The tree inside withered up and died a decade ago, if not more, so it offers zero cover.

Raoul is sprawled on the floor six feet away from me. He isn't moving.

"Raoul?" I hiss.

No answer.

My heart is pounding, but my hand is steady. I ready my gun, prepared to charge into the store alone to find whoever fired those shots.

But I don't have to.

Raoul crawls over to me, pulling himself behind the planter just as a bullet cracks the tile where he was lying a second ago.

"Shit," I breathe. "I thought you were hit."

"I kind of was." He lifts his arm, revealing a burn mark across his bicep where a bullet grazed him. He shakes it off and gets his weapon ready, too. "Do we have a plan?"

"You take the left, I take the right, and neither of us die," I suggest.

He smiles. "My thoughts exactly."

On a silent count of three, I roll out from behind the planter, get to my feet, and weave into the store. Raoul is a dark blur to my left.

The electricity in the building is off, so the back of the store is dark. I don't want to fire at random and risk hitting Dante, but the broad-shouldered shadow pointing a gun at me doesn't have the same concern. Bullets whizz past my head, but I keep my focus trained on him.

When I'm close enough, I aim for his head.

The first shot ricochets off of a metal shelving unit in the wall behind him. He ducks, dropping his gun. My second shot hits him in the neck.

He falls behind a rack of skimpy clothes, loudly choking on his own blood.

There's a muffled curse from the corner of the store, and Raoul descends there. Something flickers in the air—a small, silver flash. I don't have time to follow it. I check to make sure the man I shot is down and then position myself behind Raoul to back him up. But he doesn't need it. He's standing on the other man's neck.

"Where is the kid?" Raoul snarls.

"Nearby," I announce. I don't know how I know, but I do. I feel it. "He threw something when you got close."

"I heard it hit the floor," Raoul confirms. He drives his heel into the man's throat. "What was it?"

His tongue swells out from between his blue-tinged lips. "Nothing."

I reach for the door behind his head, but it's locked.

"Was it a key?" I guess.

The guard sinks into the floor like he wants to dissolve there.

"If you want to watch him, I can find the key," Raoul offers.

I wave him off and turn to face the door. "I don't need it."

I draw back and then, with everything I have, throw my shoulder into the door. The knob and bolt don't budge, but all it takes is one blow and the cheap, hollow door caves in. I ram it with my shoulder twice more, until there's a sizable dent. Then I grab the clothes rack behind me and spear it into the opening.

Splinters and wood dust explode into the air, but I ignore it all as I widen the hole. Once I've punched through to the other side, I reach through the door and turn the lock.

The back room smells like the employees left in such a hurry they forgot to clean out their lunches. It's rotten meat and curdled milk. As much as I want Dante to be in here, I don't want him to be stuck in this hellhole.

I throw an arm over my nose. "Dante?"

The guard outside the door says something, but Raoul quiets him with a kick to the face.

Everything goes quiet and I listen—not moving, not breathing. "Dante?" I call again.

Seconds tick past so slowly it's painful. Then, finally, I hear rustling.

It could be a mouse. Or a homeless person hiding out in the bowels of the building. But why would two of Christos' guards be assigned to guard the rat population?

"Dante?" I edge slowly around a tall shelf in the middle of the room so I can see the back corner. "It's me, kid. It's Dad."

There's another shuffling sound, and I can see a small shadow near the ground. Tiny limbs shifting against the dusty tile. Then, the sweetest sound I've ever heard.

"Dad?"

For the first time in hours, I take a full breath.

I almost black out with sheer relief as I leap around the corner and pull Dante into my arms. He's shaking and whimpering, but he's breathing. His chest is rising and falling. His arms and legs are attached. He's as perfect as he was the last time I saw him, and I've never been more grateful for anything in my life.

"I found you." I say it for my sake as much as Dante's. I need to drive the point home.

Only now, when he's in my arms, can I admit that I wasn't sure how this day was going to end. I couldn't think of a single reason why Christos would kidnap my son and keep him alive. Let alone guarded by two terrified, inexperienced guards.

It makes no sense, but I don't fucking care. Not when he's here and he's alive.

Dante buries his face in my neck. "I want Mama."

"I know, kid. God, she wants you, too." I actually have to blink back tears thinking about how happy Viviana is going to be.

He pulls back. His eyes are almost swollen shut from crying and his nose is bright red. He swipes at it with his sleeve and talks through hiccups. "P-please don't t-take me back t-to school. I w-want to go h-home."

"You're not going back, Dante. You're coming home." I cup my hand around the back of his head and hold him close. "Where you belong."

Raoul binds the living guard with a rope he fashioned out of left-behind lingerie and then drags the dead one far enough away from the door that Dante won't see him. He's experienced enough trauma for one day. No reason to pile on more of it.

I trust Raoul with my entire soul, but it's still hard to hand Dante over to him. I place my son in his arms and look in his eyes. "Take care of him, brother."

"With my life," he vows, dipping his head.

Then he hustles out of the store with Dante cradled against his chest.

The best thing for Dante is to get back home with Viviana as soon as possible. The best thing for the future of my family is for me to stay behind and find out as much as I can from the unlucky guard who survived.

He's shaking on his side on the floor, his hands and legs hog-tied with red and black lace. I've never seen Raoul without a pair of zip-ties on him, so I have to assume using the lingerie was a way to add insult to injury.

I'll allow it. This asshole deserves whatever is coming to him.

I squat down in front of him and he closes his eyes. Like I'm some boogeyman who only exists in his imagination. Like he can wish me away.

I snatch the lace muzzle off of his mouth and grab his jaw, forcing his eyes to me. "Tell me everything you know."

"Nothing!" he cries, shaking so hard his jaw rattles against the floor. "I don't know—"

He's interrupted by my gun. Two shots—one in each thigh.

Blood sprays and he howls. His back bows, his body trying to escape the inescapable pain. I like it a little too much. So I fire again—this time, into his shoulder.

Blood soaks through his pants and his shirt. It spills onto the floor and he has to strain his neck to keep his face out of it.

"Take number two." I tap the gun against his temple. "Tell me everything you know."

He's gasping for air. A bullet fragment could have hit his lung. If so, I have even less time with him than I thought.

"Talk fast," I bark.

"I'm just a guard," he moans. "Christos told me and—" He glances over to the dead lump in the corner and then quickly away. "Me and Tobias were sent here to guard this door. We weren't even supposed to open it. He didn't want us talking to the kid."

"How long did you know he was planning to kidnap my son?"

His mouth slams shut.

"Lying won't save you now," I snarl. "How long?"

"Two weeks," he admits in a whisper.

Since the day I dropped Dante off at school.

I'm a fucking idiot. I thought he would be safe there, but it just put an even bigger target on his back.

My knuckles are white around the gun. My finger itches to tighten on the trigger, but I hold back. "Why?"

"Because you didn't marry Helen."

"No," I bark. "I mean, *why?* Why keep Dante here? Why put two guards who don't know what the fuck they're doing in charge of watching over my son?"

It was all too easy. There was no one manning the exits. No defense between the doors and this room. Christos kidnaps the son of a *pakhan* and then holds him in a back room with two guards on him. It's almost like it was—

"It was a trap," the man gasps. His eyes are wide. I can tell he's coming to the same conclusion I am. "Christos told us you wouldn't come for the kid. He said we didn't need many guards because you wouldn't even know the kid was missing until it was too late. By the time you figured it out, the kid was supposed to be on a plane headed to—Fuck! There was no plane, was there?"

Christos played us both.

He knew I'd drop everything to track down Dante. The question is: while I'm standing here, what is Christos doing?

He's still lost in his own revelation, so I press the gun against his temple. His wide eyes focus on me. "What is Christos doing right now? What was his plan?"

He shakes his head. "I have no idea. I don't know anything else. Please don't kill—"

His brains splatter on the wall before he can finish his thought.

I sprint out of the store, my phone already pressed to my ear.

Anatoly answers on the first ring. "You found him, brother! Raoul just called. Thank God. How are—"

"Dante was a distraction," I interrupt. "Christos is up to something. Until I know what it is, don't let Viviana out of your sight."

I want to be there with her. I want to be the one to walk through the door with Dante in my arms. I want to see the relief on her face and hold both of them in my arms.

But there isn't time.

59

VIVIANA

My heels ache from pounding into the tile over and over again, but I can't sit down. When I stop moving, my brain turns on. And when my brain turns on, things get dark. *Fast*.

Anatoly waves at me from the dining room, what he has deemed to be a "safe distance" away from my manic pacing and prowling. "You do remember that Mikhail found Dante, right? He saved your son's life? You heard that part."

"I heard it," I grit out.

Raoul is the one who called to deliver the news. I'm not sure I'll ever get the sound of Dante weeping in the background out of my head. It will haunt my nightmares until I'm dead.

But he is alive.

He's coming home.

And Mikhail wasn't with him.

My husband didn't even bother to call me to tell me the

news. No, he sent our son home with Raoul and then called Anatoly to tell him not to let me out of his sight.

I *want* to be in Mikhail's sight! The only thing I want in the world right now is to be with my family, but Mikhail is still working.

"This is how it's always going to be," I whisper hoarsely to myself.

"Things are tense right now. They'll get better." Anatoly does his best to sound certain, but when I look over at him, all he can manage is a sympathetic grimace.

Once upon a lifetime ago, I would have believed him. I thought love could fix everything. My father wanted me to marry a filthy rich, influential man—but once he saw how much I loved our maid's son, he'd change his mind, right? He wasn't heartless; he just didn't understand how I felt about Matteo. Once he saw that, he'd let us be together. After all, he wanted me to be happy, didn't he?

I got the answer to that question when my father slaughtered Matteo in front of me. Along with a lifetime supply of trauma, that moment taught me a valuable lesson.

Love can change you, but it can't change the world.

As much as I want Mikhail to put our family first, we will always come second to the Bratva. Because that's who Mikhail is. It's who he was raised to be.

No amount of loving him will change that if he doesn't *want* to change.

"Just give him time," Anatoly urges softly.

He's watching me like he can see what I'm thinking. I give him a tight smile.

Then the door opens.

I don't think. I don't make a single conscious decision. On pure instinct, I run for the open door. I run for my son.

Dante is so small and frail, curled against Raoul's chest. But as soon as he sees me, he starts wriggling and writhing, trying to get free.

"You shouldn't pick him up," Anatoly reminds me. "You're supposed to rest."

His voice is a million miles away. It's not in this room; not in this reality. The only thing that exists is me and my son.

"Dante!" I sob, dropping to my knees just as Raoul sets him on the ground.

He leaps for me and I fold him against my body. I bury my face in his golden brown hair and I rock with him, back and forth, back and forth. It's the way I held him as a baby. I would hold him all night, rocking him in the dark, terrified that I would lose him.

I can't believe I ever let him out of my sight. What was I thinking?

He's shaking in my arms, so I stroke his back. "You're okay, baby. I'm here. I'm not letting you go."

And I don't.

I hold Dante until he stops crying. Then, I carry him upstairs —despite Anatoly protesting the entire way—and give him a bath. While I rinse the dust and sweat out of his hair and wipe off his pink cheeks, he holds my hand over the lip of the tub. He keeps hold of it while I read him books in bed. Every so often, he gives my fingers a squeeze like he wants to remind himself I'm still here. Even as his eyes drift closed, he doesn't let go.

I almost lost him.

Something about lying here with him is driving it all home. He's safe and I now know with painful clarity that that isn't a guarantee. We got so lucky, and I can't count on that again.

I won't leave his life up to chance.

He's still breathing deeply when I slip away from him and tiptoe out of his room. I have no idea what time it is, but the house is dark. There are no voices coming from downstairs.

So I move silently down the hall and into my old bedroom.

When Mikhail first brought us here, I stashed a duffel bag under my bed, filled with everything I'd need if Dante and I had to get gone fast. It was my emergency exit plan. I almost forgot about it.

There's a fine layer of dust on the top of the bag when I pull it out from under the bed. I sweep it off and unzip it.

There are a few changes of clothes, a roll of cash that could get us three or four nights in a cheap motel—but only if we're okay sharing with bedbugs—and toothbrushes. The bare necessities.

Except, Dante needs more than this. For years, I thought as long as Dante and I had each other, we had everything we needed. It's a romantic idea, but things have changed.

He needs his father. He needs stability.

"But he won't have that here, will he?" I whisper to myself.

The truth hurts, but it's still the truth.

I blink back tears and zip the bag closed. I hike it over my shoulder and stand up…

Just as the door behind me opens.

Mikhail is a dark shadow against the hallway light, but I'd recognize the shape of him anywhere. "What the fuck are you doing?" he growls.

The anger is back in a second. It was buried under relief for a few hours, but it has clawed its way back. My hands shake on the straps of the bag. "Sounds like you already know."

"No, I don't." He steps into the room. "Because there's no way you would be stupid enough to be packing a bag after the night we just had."

"You're right. Let's just pretend I'm getting ready for bed," I snap. "I can't wait to wake up alone tomorrow and wonder who is coming after my family next. Why don't you disappear to *take care of something* again so I can get back to it?"

His eyes narrow. "I saved Dante."

"After you put him at risk in the first place!"

It's the first time I've said it out loud. The first time I've admitted to myself how much I blame Mikhail for what happened today.

Pain ricochets across his face before it hardens into the mask I know so well. It has slipped a few times—when he took us to Costa Rica, to the cabin—but it took me a while to realize that I wasn't slowly softening him. I wasn't going to swoop in and change the big, bad *pakhan.*

He wasn't opening up to me gradually until, one day, there would be no secrets. The sweet, tender, vulnerable moments we had were exceptions to the rule. Once we got home, it was always right back to the status quo.

I.

Can't.

Fix.

Him.

"Do you want me to tell you I fucked up?" His shoulders rise and fall in an angry shrug. "Because I know I fucked up. It's why Dante is back here with you instead of back at that school."

"He's here because Raoul drove him home."

"I gave the order."

"There! *That.*" I snap my fingers and point. "*That* is the problem, Mikhail. Our son was kidnapped and you gave the order for him to be driven home by someone else. He was kidnapped and—"

"I know he was kidnapped!" he roars. "I realized that when bullets were whizzing past my head as I rescued him."

I almost lost them both.

Tears burn in the backs of my eyes, but I hold my chin high. "He was kidnapped and you still couldn't come home to us."

"Because Christos is coming after you." He flings his arm towards the door like our enemies are waiting their turn in the hall. "I had to make sure they couldn't get to you. I'm going to keep you all safe."

I sigh. "That's great, Mikhail. But it doesn't mean anything if you are never here."

"How can you say it doesn't mean anything?"

"Because Dante may be safe in this mansion, but he's going to grow up terrified of the outside world. He's going to feel like his father cares more about the Bratva than him. I can't let him live like that." I lay a hand over my stomach. "I can't let either of our kids live like that."

Mikhail's blue eyes are wild. He looks like a caged animal, scanning the bars of this conversation, looking for the way out. "If you have it your way, our kids won't *live* at all. You all would be killed out there."

"Only because you won't make a choice."

"What choice?" He moves closer. He looks down the end of his nose at me and it's crazy how much I want to fall against his chest. It would be so easy to push this fight aside, to push it to the backburner once again and let him hold me.

But I can't do that.

Not anymore.

"The choice you need to make between me and the Bratva. Between the family we're building and the one you were born into." I meet his eyes and I hope he can see how serious I am. This isn't my pregnancy hormones or stress. This isn't some heat-of-the-moment ultimatum.

This is *real*.

"You knew what you were signing up for when you agreed to marry me, Viviana. This isn't a surprise to you. You knew who I was."

"I thought I did," I admit. "But then our son was kidnapped because you can't give the Bratva up. You don't know when to let go."

He raises a hand like he's going to grab me, but he tugs it through his hair instead. "I don't need to give anything up. I'm going to kill Christos and your father and—"

"And then someone will take their place. There will always be another threat and it's killing our family. Don't you see that?" I take a deep breath. "You have to choose, Mikhail: the Bratva or our family. You can't have both."

He closes the distance between us. His chest brushes against mine with every ragged breath. "Or what?" he growls.

I swallow down my nerves and the bone-deep instinct to curl against his chest. "Or I'm leaving. *We're* leaving—me and Dante."

"You'll die out there," he breathes.

I nod. "We might die in here, too."

He traces my face. *Really* looks at me for the first time since he walked in the room, and he knows I'm serious. I can see it dawn on him that I'm going to leave.

He's going to choose us.

No other man in my life has chosen me, but Mikhail will. He loves me the way I love him. I'm sure of it. I've seen it.

Maybe I can fix him.

"You think you're going to die if you stay here?" he asks softly.

I nod.

He takes one step back and another. He moves with purpose, his eyes never leaving mine. "I say we test that theory."

By the time I understand what he's saying, he's pulling the door closed between us.

The duffel bag slips off my shoulder and I lunge for the narrowing gap, but the chance for escape clicks closed. The bolt slides home.

"You can't keep me here forever!" I pound on the door, but it's solid.

I'm sure Mikhail is already gone, but then his muffled voice reaches me through the wood. "I don't need to keep you here forever, Viviana. I just need to keep you long enough that you don't go out and get yourself killed."

"There's always going to be another threat. It's never going to end, Mikhail. We can't keep going like this." I press my forehead to the wood as my voice wavers and breaks. "*I* can't keep going like this. I won't. I've wasted enough years of my life running and hiding. I'm done with that. You have to choose. If you don't… you'll lose me either way."

I wait for a response, but it doesn't come.

Mikhail has made his choice.

He's gone.

60

MIKHAIL

You have to choose. If you don't... you'll lose me either way.

Viviana's voice follows me down the stairs and through the mansion. The words play on a loop in the back of my head as I start my car and drive numbly through the dark.

I don't know if it's the way I am or the way my father raised me to be, but I don't doubt myself. Ever. I make a decision based on the information in front of me and I know it's the right thing to do. Even if everything goes to shit, I know I did the best I could with what I had.

But since the moment I followed Viviana back to her apartment and saw that little boy with my eyes hiding behind her legs, I've had doubts.

Should I have stopped her from leaving the bridal suite the night I saved her from Trofim?

Was bringing her and Dante back to my mansion the safest decision for them?

Am I bringing death and loss into their lives or was it there from the beginning?

It's a nonstop mental assault of doubt and guilt and worry that doesn't go away no matter what I do, no matter what I choose.

So how can I choose *this*?

I park the car and climb out before I fully realize where I am. My feet find the grass and, even in the dark, I pick my way down the familiar path.

The air is cold. My breath fogs against the black sky. When I sink to my knees, the frozen ground pushes back. It's the first time I've stopped moving in… shit, days, maybe. *Weeks.* My restless joints want to riot, but I sink down in the crunchy grass.

"Viviana was right," I mutter. "I've been away too much."

There is no response. It used to be my favorite thing about this place. As bleak as it was to come here, I could say what I thought—what I *felt*—without any judgment.

Now, there are so many things I'd like to ask Alyona. I want to hear what she'd say.

I study the weather-rounded edges of her tombstone. "I wasn't there for you at the end. I couldn't save you. But before that… did you feel alone?"

"Yes."

I startle for half a second before I recognize the deep voice. I clench my teeth without turning around. "You shouldn't be here, Anatoly."

My brother appears in my peripheral vision. He bends down, laying two roses on the ground in front of me. "When I saw you driving away, I grabbed these from the vase on the dining room table. I figured you were coming here."

"You shouldn't be here," I repeat. "You should be—"

"Watching Viviana and Dante? Yeah, I know. That's what I always do."

I snap my eyes to him. "If you want to complain about your workload, now isn't a great time. It's been a shitty day."

He stares down at the flowers and shakes his head. "I'm not complaining. I never do. Not now. Not when it was Alyona and Anzhelina I was watching, either."

"You were the only other person I trusted to take care of them."

"Which is why I was there... all the time," he explains, glancing over at me. "Alyona joked a few times that I was her common law husband because of how much time I spent at the house with her and Anzhelina."

"We were at war," I grit out. "I don't know how many times I have to explain this. People were trying to kill us. I was the only thing standing between my family and death."

And I failed.

The twin headstones in front of me prove that well enough. Anzhelina's is so small.

"I'll be the first to admit that I don't know what that kind of pressure feels like," Anatoly says. "I mean, I've never had a real family. I had my mom, until Trofim took her from me. And I always had you, even when you were a punk little kid.

Now, there's Raoul, too. But growing up, I wanted a mom and dad. I wanted family dinners and vacations and all of that Norman Rockwell bullshit." He sighs. "I'd give all of this up in a second if I could have that."

You have to choose. If you don't... you'll lose me either way.

"You don't have to choose. Who says you have to choose?" I drive my knuckles into the cold ground, frustration buzzing through my veins. "People work and they have families. No one else needs to choose."

Anatoly turns to me, eyebrow arched. "Are you actually comparing yourself to the suit-and-tie type? Your life couldn't be more different from theirs. Unless you really think most white collar men have a body count."

"That's not the point."

"It is, though," he insists. "Our world is different. It's dangerous and bloody. As much as I like all of that most of the time, it's not what I want to live for. I want people to come home to, more than I want people to defend, if that makes sense."

I wish it didn't.

As soon as I saw Viviana and Dante together—as soon as I understood who they were to me—I felt an overwhelming urge to protect them. A few times, I've been able to forget about protecting them long enough to take in the whole experience. When we get out of the city and away from all of the chaos, the picture sharpens and I can take in the finer details.

When Dante slides his hand in mine while we're walking aimlessly through the trees.

The way Viviana curls against my chest in her sleep.

Right now, those tiny moments are all crushed under the weight of responsibility.

"I think I was getting close with Stella," Anatoly admits quietly. He swipes a hand over his face, but it's too dark to see if he's crying. Even if he is, I don't want to see it. I feel shitty enough as it is. "But I didn't move fast enough and… I lost her."

I shake my head. "*I* lost her. I should've known Pyotr was a spy. If I'd been paying attention, then—"

He holds up a hand to stop me. "I didn't come here to blame you, Mikhail. I don't blame you. I never did. I'm just here to tell you that the world we grew up in is a tiny sliver of what's possible out there. And if you want to test some of those other options out… well, no one would blame you."

He says it like it's as simple as trying on a hat. Slipping one off and popping another one on.

What he's suggesting, what Viviana is asking—it isn't some minor thing. They're asking me to give up who I am. Who I've been for thirty-five years.

"I can't. You know I can't. Too many people depend on me."

"Because you don't give us a choice!" Anatoly laughs. "You take on everything by yourself and don't give anyone else a chance to figure it out on their own. But I promise you, the men you lead are capable. They'll land on their feet even if you aren't there to catch them."

I know he's right, but… "This is our family's legacy."

He turns to me, his eyes wide and clear. "You're my *pakhan* and I respect the hell out of you. But I'm also your brother, so please hear me when I say, *Fuck our family's legacy.*"

A surprised laugh bursts out of me. "Otets is probably rolling in his shallow grave hearing that."

"Good," he spits. "It's what the fucker deserves. He definitely doesn't deserve your loyalty."

"I'm not loyal to him. I'm not doing any of this for him."

"Okay." Anatoly slides his hands in his pockets. "Then who are you doing it for?"

The question hangs in the air between us, unanswered and unanswerable.

After a beat, Anatoly pats me on the shoulder. "I'll see you at home." His crunching steps grow quieter until they're gone.

"Who the fuck *am* I doing this for?" I whisper to myself.

When I decided to overthrow Trofim and take the Bratva for myself, I was doing it for me. I'd lost Alyona and Anzhelina. I had nothing else—*no one* else. The last thing I wanted was for the only other constant in my life to be run into the ground because my brother was an incompetent psychopath.

Being *pakhan* made sense then.

Now, I have Viviana and Dante.

Does it still make sense?

"She's right," I breathe. "Viviana is right. This world is killing them. It's destroying us. The way it destroyed you."

I could have taken Alyona and Anzhelina and fled the city. I wasn't *pakhan* yet; we could have outrun the war and lived a quiet life. But I stayed. I stayed and I fought in my father's war because I thought it was my duty. That misplaced loyalty cost my family their lives.

I already lost one family to the Bratva.

I won't lose another.

61

VIVIANA

He didn't choose me.

You should never give an ultimatum you're not ready to suffer the consequences of. I know that. But I never really thought Mikhail would walk away.

Even when he locked me in this room and I slid to the floor, too weak to stand, I didn't really believe it.

In my mind, there is no future where Mikhail and I aren't together. I'm not sure what a life without him even looks like now. I can't go back to lonely apartments and fake names. But I have no idea what else there is.

I'm staring into the dark of my bedroom, contemplating what lies ahead for me and my children, when the knob above my head twists.

I don't have time to think about who it is or what they want with me. I only have time to crawl just clear of the door before it swings open so hard it bounces off the wall.

I'm on my back, staring up at the looming silhouette of…

"Mikhail?"

He came back for me, I think before I can stop myself. *He changed his mind.*

I bury the thought deep down. I survived him walking away from me once—if sitting on the floor in a dissociative state can be considered "surviving." I don't know if I can do it again.

Mikhail is squinting into the room, scanning far above my head like he's looking for me. But at the sound of my voice, his eyes snap down to where I'm huddled on the floor.

He sinks to his knees in front of me. He smells like cold air and frost. His fingers are freezing when he curls them around my face, tilting my chin. "Are you okay?"

"I'm—" My mouth hangs open uselessly. *What am I?* After everything that has happened today, I'm hollowed out. I'm exhausted and heartbroken and terrified of the future. I try to say something—*anything*—but the word lodges in my throat. A sob escapes instead.

Mikhail curses under his breath and picks me up. He cradles me in his arms, and I want to hate it. I want to hate *him*. It would make things a lot easier.

"Where are you taking me now?" I ask. "A cell?"

"I'm taking you to our room." He carries me through the door. Just like he said, he walks down the hall towards his room. *Our* room. "I shouldn't have locked you in there in the first place."

His arms tighten around me and I commit every detail of it to memory. The solid wall of his chest. The way his arms flex around my body, effortlessly strong. The way his warm breath whispers against my cheek.

I don't know how long any of this will be mine, and I don't want to forget it. Because if Mikhail can't give the Bratva up, I really will leave. I have to.

No matter how much I want to stay.

The room is dark and he doesn't bother with a light. "You need to rest. That's what Dr. Rossi said after your appointment."

"Stop being so nice," I whisper, even as I lean against his chest. "It only makes things harder. If you're just going to leave—"

"I'm not going anywhere." There's a hard edge to his voice, but I don't think it's directed at me.

He lowers me into our bed and starts to turn away. To grab the blankets, I think. Like I could possibly want to sleep right now. I grab his wrist and hold onto him like my life depends on it. Right now, it feels like it does.

"What does that mean, Mikhail?"

He turns his hand in mine until he's cradling my fingers and brings them to his lips for a kiss. "It means I'm sorry, Viviana."

My heart is pounding as I ask, "For what?"

"For walking away from you." His blue eyes pierce through the darkness. The mask I'm used to is gone now. The Mikhail in front of me is the one I know—the one I fell in love with. "I'm sorry for hesitating for even one fucking second when the choice has always been clear."

He kisses my knuckles again. Then his mouth moves to my wrist. My forearm. He tastes my skin like he's starving, making his way to my neck. His stubble scrapes against my jaw and I tilt my head to give him better access.

"What are you saying?" I breathe.

I genuinely need him to explain himself because, with the way he's touching me, my thoughts are fuzzy. This is the way it's been since that very first night. My body comes alive when Mikhail is close to me, but my brain shuts down.

I gather my wits enough to grab his shoulders and push him back.

Mikhail backs away, but his eyes are glazed over and black. I can tell he doesn't want to move away from me.

"What are you saying?" I repeat, shaking my head to rearrange my muddled thoughts. "I gave you a choice, Mikhail. I told you to choose, and you—"

"I choose *you*." He kneels between my legs and grabs my hands. His thumbs stroke over my skin like he has to remind himself I'm still here. Like today reminded him, the same way it did me, how fragile everything is. "I choose you every single time."

My heart pulses at the base of my throat, but I swallow it down and hold myself still. "I know you love me."

"Entirely," he agrees, licking his lips.

Heat stirs low in my belly, but I ignore it. We've always had this part figured out. It's everything that happens outside of the bedroom that we've had trouble with.

"I know you love me. *You* know *I* love you," I add. "But that isn't enough. Unless you're willing to walk away from the

Bratva and everything your family has built, we can't be together, Mikhail. I can't keep doing this if—"

"I'm willing." He falls forward, catching himself on his hands, which are on either side of my body. He crawls over me until I'm forced back against my pillow. His voice pitches low. "Eager, too."

His erection brushes high on my thigh. I chew on my lower lip. "I'm serious, Mikhail."

"So am I." He crawls another few inches closer until all I see when I look up is his face. The strong, square edge of his jaw and the bright blue of his eyes. "The only reason I'm doing any of this is for you and Dante. But if you want me to give it up, then I will."

"I don't want you to do this because *I* want you to. I want *you* to want it."

I feel ridiculous arguing with him. *He's giving you what you want, you dummy. Shut up and take it!* But if he's doing this for the wrong reasons, it will all backfire later. I don't want a few months of bliss to go up in spectacularly devastating flames when Mikhail realizes he isn't happy.

"Do you want to know what I want?" he whispers. He drops his mouth to my neck. Goosebumps flare everywhere his lips touch.

I swallow. "Tell me."

"I want to wake up next to my wife every morning." He kisses the skin beneath my ear. "Every night, I want to fall asleep next to you, wrapped around you… buried inside of you."

My body throbs as if in agreement with that plan.

He scrapes his teeth over my jawline and then soothes away the ache with his tongue. "I want to raise babies with you, Viviana. I want to go to the park on a sunny day and watch our kids play. I want to hold your hand while I drive instead of keeping both hands on the wheel in case we're attacked. And—" He groans, deep in his chest. "I want to be there to climb into the tub with you and ruin every single bath you ever try to take."

I laugh in surprise. "Hey!"

"Don't worry," he shushes me, biting back a smile. "I'll make sure you enjoy it."

My heart is so light it feels like a balloon in my chest. Like we could both float out of this bed, flying over the mess our lives have become in the last few weeks.

"That's a pretty picture," I say, a tinge of sadness creeping into my voice. "But there are a lot of people who would work hard to make sure that doesn't happen."

"Which is why I need you to give me some time." He strokes a finger under my chin. "I have a plan, but I need time to set it in motion. I need you to be patient with me. Can you do that?"

The last few weeks felt impossible because there was no end. I kept straining for some light at the end of the tunnel, but it was all darkness.

Now, Mikhail is giving me a timeline. He's promising me that this will end and our lives will start.

I couldn't muddy through the dark forever, but how long would I wait if I could be sure Mikhail would be on the other side?

"I've been nothing but patient for six years, Mikhail." I press my palm to his chest. I can feel his heart thudding against his ribcage like he isn't entirely sure what my answer is going to be. *As if I ever had another choice.* My mouth tips into a smirk. "I'll wait forever, as long as I know you'll be there at the end."

Mikhail's eyes flare. Then he falls over me.

The distance between us dissolves. His hands slide under my shirt, cupping my breasts and kneading my nipples until they're in hard, desperate points. His erection nestles between my legs. I press my legs together and roll my body, stroking him with my thighs.

"Fuck," he moans, dropping his forehead against mine. "If you want me to be patient, you better slow down."

I squeeze my thighs together again. His eyes flutter closed. "I don't want to slow down."

He circles his mouth over my breasts, sucking on my nipple through the thin material of my shirt. "But I want to take my time with you."

"We have a whole lifetime for going slow." I slide my hand between us and slip under his waistband. He's warm and hard against my palm. When I give him a rough stroke, he jerks, pumping into my fingers like he can't help himself. "Right now, I want you inside of me."

Mikhail growls deep in his chest. He shoves his pants down and slips my loose pajama shorts to the side. He hesitates for a brief second when he first parts me, when he dips into my wetness and groans at how ready I am for him.

Then he pushes into me with one smooth, continual thrust.

My back bows. I gasp and arch off the bed until I'm barely lying down at all. Mikhail bands an arm around my lower back and holds me in the air. He balances me against him, letting me adjust to the way he fills me.

With a kiss to the underside of my breast, he slides away and drives back in.

We writhe and move with each other. Mikhail leads, gripping my hips and driving into me. Then he rolls over, spinning me so I'm sitting on top of him, straddling his hips.

He keeps his hands spread across my thighs so he can control my pace even when I'm riding him.

I press him back into the mattress and kiss the hard ridges of his abs, the broad sweep of his chest. I circle my hips and work myself onto his length again and again. When we hit a new angle, I gasp. Mikhail pumps into me until I'm putty in his hands. Until I collapse against his chest and scream against his feverish skin.

I clench and spasm and Mikhail holds himself deep inside of me, groaning as I fall apart on his cock. As soon as I go limp, he wraps an arm around my waist and rolls us over.

"I want this," he growls, slamming into me. "I've wanted this from the first time I ever saw you, Viviana."

I'm still coming down from the first orgasm, but Mikhail is taking me there again. His words and his body and the perfect way we have always fit together are destroying me from the inside out.

"Mikhail..." I curl my fingers through his hair, tugging on the roots.

He silences me with a kiss, swirling his tongue against mine. I realize with a startled laugh that it's the first time we've kissed. Only Mikhail could drive me out of my mind without any physical foreplay whatsoever.

Just the nearness of him—the way he talks to me and how much I want him—are enough. I'm always ready for him.

I will always choose him.

"Come inside of me," I pant. "Fill me up, Mikhail. Fuck me like you love me, please."

His movements stutter for only a second. Then he roars. He empties himself into me until he collapses.

I wrap my arms around him, more than happy to be crushed under his weight.

We fall asleep like that, with him still inside of me. Just the way he wanted.

62

MIKHAIL

I wake up achingly hard.

Viviana must feel me shift next to her. Her eyes are closed, but her hands find me. She rolls onto her side and backs into me. "Mikhail…"

My cock twitches. "Viviana, I want—"

"Me, too."

I slide into her and we fuck slowly, lazily. I bury my nose in her hair and flatten my hand across her stomach.

I never had a choice. Not when it comes to her.

I'll always want this.

I slide my hand lower to circle her clit and find her wet. *Really* wet.

Viviana moans and clenches around me. I want to ignore the little voice in the back of my head telling me something is wrong. I want to silence it and keep fucking my wife.

But I can't.

I pull my hand away. Viviana groans in protest and reaches for my wrist. "Don't be a tease, Mik—"

I barely hear her. I'm too busy staring at my bloody fingers.

My silence must catch her attention because she looks at me over her shoulder, her smile slipping. "What is it?"

"You're bleeding."

"What?"

I slide out of her and there's blood on me. On her. On the mattress. *Everywhere.*

I'm out of bed in a second. I grab a towel from the bathroom and wet it under warm water. I come back and Viviana is staring down at the stain. Her cheeks are red.

"I'm sorry. I didn't know—"

"Don't apologize for bleeding." I swipe the towel over her. She moves like she wants to do it herself, but I level her with a glare. "Sit still. Let me take care of you."

"I'm fine," she protests, but she lets me work.

I clean her up and then grab her hand, pulling her to standing. "Can you walk?"

"*I'm fine*," she repeats. "The doctor told me this could be normal."

"*Could be* normal. Which means it could also not be normal at all." I lead her towards the closet. "We're going to the hospital."

She pulls on my arm. When I don't stop, she spins around so she's in front of me. "Mikhail, I'm okay. I'm sorry I got blood everywhere, but it's probably just because we had sex. *Really* great sex. It can happen during pregnancy."

"I'll believe it when I hear that from the doctor."

I fire off a text to Dr. Rossi and then Viviana lets me dress her. Her lips are twisted into a frown, but she doesn't argue. She knows damn well it won't change anything.

The sun is nothing but pale yellow light behind the horizon when we get on the road. We only slept for a few hours at most, but I'm not tired at all. My stomach is twisted in knots.

"Everything is fine," Viviana says as if she can read my mind. "The baby is okay." She reaches over and plucks my hand from the steering wheel. I let her twine her fingers through mine. "Everything is going to be just fine."

Dr. Rossi arrives at the hospital five minutes after us. I've already demanded Viviana be given a private room and a nurse is rolling in a portable ultrasound machine when he walks through the door.

"You were at the emergency room yesterday," he notes, reading from her chart. "The doctor who examined you didn't call me." He looks over the paper, eyebrow arched. "Nor did either of you."

Viviana wilts. "I'm sorry. I wasn't thinking. We panicked."

Calling it "we" is generous. *I wasn't even with her.* Saving Dante ranked high on the list of priorities. He's safe in bed right now because of what I did, and I don't regret it. But it's another reason I need to let this world go. I want to be able to be there for Viviana whenever she needs me.

Dr. Rossi smiles and sets her chart aside. "All is forgiven, of course. Let's take a look at what's going on."

"She's bleeding," I tell him. I'm sure it's on his chart, but I say it anyway. "It started while we were sleeping."

"After we'd…" Viviana's cheeks flush. "Well, we had intercourse."

Dr. Rossi is a professional and doesn't react at all as he sets up the machine. "Some bleeding can be normal after sex."

He presses the wand to her stomach. He pokes and prods for only a second before an image fills the screen.

Our baby.

"This little one has gotten bigger since I last saw it," Dr. Rossi coos warmly. He zooms in, isolating a small flutter on the screen. A rhythmic whooshing sound fills the air. "Listen to that heartbeat! It's beautiful. Very strong."

Viviana reaches out and grabs my hand. "The baby is okay?"

"It's perfect," I answer under my breath.

I can't take my eyes away from the screen. We *made* that.

I felt the same way the first time I saw Anzhelina. I've been responsible for taking a lot of people out of this world. It's a new experience bringing them into it.

Dr. Rossi chuckles. "That's right. You weren't at the first scan. This is Dad's first time seeing the baby."

I turn to him. "Is Viviana okay?"

"As far as I can see, everything is fine."

"Why would she be bleeding if she's fine?"

"It won't do a lot to make you feel better, but as much as science has figured out about the human body, it's still a mystery."

"You're right. That doesn't make me feel better at all," I drawl.

Dr. Rossi thinks for a second. Then he snaps his fingers and reaches for Viviana's chart. "I have something that might make you feel better: the results of the NIPT test."

"Does that mean it's good news?" Viviana asks.

"It's great news. Your baby didn't test positive for any of the chromosomal disorders we tested for. It also means I know the sex." Dr. Rossi wags a brow. "If you want to know."

Viviana tugs on my hand. Her green eyes are hopeful. "Do we want to know?"

"Do you?"

She chews on her lip. "It would make it easier to buy clothes and paint the nursery."

I almost forgot about a nursery. Alyona planned Anzhelina's down to the most asinine detail. I told her it was certifiable to commission art for a newborn's walls, but she insisted. And I let her. I was busy with work, anyway. Preparing the nursery gave Alyona something to do.

Now, Viviana and I will do that together.

Fucking hell, *we are having a baby.* Not a six-year-old who comes barreling into my life already walking and talking, but a baby. A helpless, tiny baby.

My track record with those isn't great.

Viviana shakes my fingers, bringing me back to the moment. "Well?"

I swallow down the bitter thoughts and turn to Dr. Rossi. "Might as well find out."

He checks the chart one last time to confirm the result. "Congratulations, you two, on your healthy baby girl."

"A girl!" Viviana squeals, clapping her hands over her mouth. "Dante is going to have a little sister."

"We're going to have a daughter."

Another baby girl. I smile and hug Viviana, but the news drops like a stone in my stomach.

I'm happy. Really, I am. I want this.

I wanted it ten years ago, too.

When I lost Anzhelina, I swore I'd never have another family. There wasn't a choice with Dante. But this… This is a choice.

Dr. Rossi leaves and Viviana pulls me closer to the side of her bed. "What are you thinking?"

I blink and paste on a smile. "I'm happy."

"But…?" she prods.

I shake my head. "It's nothing."

Viviana brings my hand to her lips. She kisses my knuckle and presses her cheek to my curled fingers. "It's okay if you have mixed feelings, Mikhail."

I clench my teeth. "We're having a baby. This is what we wanted. We're supposed to be overjoyed."

"You and I have never done what we're *supposed* to do. Why start now?" She shrugs. "I mean, I'm happy, but I'm scared, too. I'm worried I don't know how to have a family in the traditional sense. Not after the way I grew up."

"Are you scared I'll be a bad parent? That I'll turn into a man like our fathers?"

She palms both sides of my face and forces me to meet her eyes. "Listen to me: that is the one thing I have never, ever been scared of, Mikhail. You've suffered so much in your life, but instead of letting it make you cold and cruel, you've used it to become a better man. That's how I know you have enough love in your heart for this baby *and* Anzhelina."

I stiffen, but Viviana strokes her fingers over my cheeks. "How did you know?" I mumble.

"Because I'm a parent, too," she says softly. "I can't imagine what you're going through and I won't tell you how to feel, but I have no doubt that you'll love this baby girl the same way you loved Anzhelina. The same way you love Dante. Love isn't a finite resource. When you have a child, you don't have to make room for them in your heart. It grows to fit them. There's always enough to go around."

I want to believe her. Maybe someday, I will.

But not tonight.

Still, I kneel next to her bed and cradle her face in my hands. "I love you. And I'm happy."

She kisses me softly. "Me, too."

63

VIVIANA

The hospital room is beige and bland. Anatoly snuck in some French fries and a strawberry milkshake when he brought Dante to visit for lunch, so the food situation isn't as miserable as it was a few hours ago, but as soon as they left, it was back to the beige, bland silence.

Back to Mikhail pacing the room, back and forth and back and forth across the scuffed terrazzo tiles. The only time he stops is to stare through the blinds at the city around, his dark brow furrowed.

Even full of worry and anxiety, Mikhail is the only bright spot in the room for me.

That selfishness is the only reason I've let him pace in stormy silence for so long. I don't want him to leave.

"I'm getting dizzy," I complain when he turns away from the window once again to continue pacing. "You don't have to stay. You asked me to give you time and I said I would. If you have things to do, you can go."

Mikhail turns to me. His blue eyes clear like he's coming out of a dream. He's been deep in his head ever since Dr. Rossi told us that I'm having a baby girl.

He'd never admit it, but he's terrified. Having a little girl probably feels like he's trying to replace the daughter he lost. There's a part of me that hoped we would have another boy for that very reason. I always knew this was a possibility.

Just a couple months ago, Mikhail vowed to never have a real family ever again. A lot has changed since then, but old habits die hard.

"I want to make sure you're okay."

I laugh. "Dr. Rossi said I was okay yesterday. The only reason I'm still here is because *you* insisted. I could probably track down a nurse and get myself released in five minutes."

Mikhail draws closer to the bed, a devilish smirk tugging the corner of his mouth. "You'll have to get through me first."

Heat settles low in my belly. It's been there since Mikhail pulled me out of bed yesterday and dragged me to the hospital. Nothing kills the mood faster than unexplained vaginal bleeding, I guess.

"Gladly," I purr.

Mikhail's eyes darken, but I see the moment he realizes what I'm doing. When he does, he turns away from me and starts pacing again. "You need time to heal."

"There's nothing to heal," I whimper, slumping deeper under the scratchy blanket. "If I didn't know any better, I'd say you're just pacing around this room as a way to procrastinate."

Mikhail hesitates long enough that I know I struck a nerve.

"I'm sorry," I blurt. "I didn't—"

"No." He drops down into the armchair next to my bed. "You're right. I'm not exactly thrilled about what I have to do."

"Giving up the Bratva?" I guess, steeling myself for the answer.

I worried Mikhail might regret choosing me, but I didn't think it would happen quite this fast.

"What comes with it," he corrects, his elbows resting on his knees. "The danger it puts you and Dante and—our baby girl in."

The knot of anxiety in my chest loosens, but doesn't disappear. With the life I've lived, I'm not sure it will ever fully go away. "You have a plan, then?"

"I do. It's…" He chuckles humorlessly and drags a hand over his neck. "It's fucking crazy. People are going to think I've lost my mind."

"Have you?"

Mikhail's blue eyes find mine and hold. He bridges the space between us without moving a muscle. I feel him inside of my head, my heart. The connection between us is a tangible thing. I hope it never goes away.

"No," he says firmly. "This is the most certain I've felt about a decision in a long time. I know I'm doing the right thing. But I'm not used to putting my trust in other people."

I sit up tall. "Who are you putting trust in? What kind of trust?"

Will they hurt you? Will you be safe?

Now, Mikhail really does bridge the space between us. He leans forward and takes my hand. I don't realize how cold my fingers are until they're curled against his. "I don't want to keep secrets from you, but the less you know now, the safer you'll be."

"Mikhail, if this is dangerous, then it isn't worth it. Nothing is worth your safety."

"You are," he fires back. "Dante is. The future we're working towards is worth my safety."

"But it's not the future I want if you're not in it!" I cry. Tears spill over my cheeks and I swipe them away. "God, I'm tired of crying. It feels like it's all I do anymore."

Mikhail brushes my tears away. "Hormones."

"Yeah," I mutter. "Hormones and… I've been here before. Kind of. With Matteo."

Mikhail doesn't say anything. He just holds my hand tighter, waiting.

"I was just a kid, but, at the time, I really loved him. I thought we could overcome anything—*anyone*. I took a risk and tried to escape the world I was born into. I tried to run away and live out my fantasy with Matteo. Then my father murdered him in front of me."

"I'm not scared of your father, Viviana," he says gently.

"Maybe you should be. You're going to have to face him at some point, right? He's mixed up in all of this. And he knows how much you mean to me, Mikhail. If there was ever a way for my dad to use up all of his anger and get back at me, hurting you would be it. He'll take a shot if you give him one."

"Then I won't give him one." He kisses my knuckles. "I'll be careful."

I bite my lower lip and nod, trying hard to blink back tears. "You mean everything to me, Mikhail. Absolutely every—"

The words choke off in a sob.

Suddenly, my scratchy blanket is gone and Mikhail is sliding into bed next to me. He curls his warm body around mine, enveloping me until I can't move in the best imaginable way. "I'll do absolutely everything I can to be safe," he whispers against my temple. "Getting home to you and Dante is the only thing that matters to me."

I press my forehead to his chest and breathe deeply. I sync my breaths with his. I count seconds to the rhythmic thump of his heart.

Being with him like this will never get old. I spent years alone in my bed, wishing someone else in the world could hold me like this. Wishing someone could *know* me. Not my fake name or the fake life I'd propped up like a facade, but *me*.

And here he is.

Slowly, my hand slides from his ribs to the taper of his waist. And lower still. Mikhail catches my wrist when I move for his waistband. "You need to rest."

"This is how I rest." I tip my chin up, pressing a kiss to the pulse in his throat. "Being with you is rest. It's the only time I can just… *be*."

His fingers splay across my lower back, laying claim to the skin exposed by my flimsy hospital gown. "I don't want to hurt you."

"Then take me slowly, Mikhail." I thread my fingers through his and guide his hand to my hip. "Take your time."

He tucks a strand of hair behind my ear, watching his fingers move over my cheek. Finally, his eyes find mine. He leans forward until we're a breath apart. I inhale the mint and citrus scent of his skin—the smell of home.

His lips are shockingly gentle against mine. It's a slow, easy kiss that makes me desperate for more. But I'm desperate for this, too. For the press of his tongue against mine. For the way we explore each other slowly with teeth and lips and tongues like we have a lifetime.

Eventually, his hands slide down my body. He traces the dips and swells of me until I'm a pile of melted contentment in the bed. He hooks a hand behind my knee and curls my leg over his hip. When he finally presses into me, I sigh with relief.

"Tell me if I hurt you." His whisper is breathy and uneven. He's holding himself back.

I cradle his stubbled cheek and press our foreheads together. "The only way this will hurt is if you leave."

He angles my hips and slides deeper. "I won't leave, Viviana. There's nowhere else I'd rather be."

We move together slowly, our panting breaths mingling together between us. If the nurses notice my vitals spiking, they mind their own business. No one comes into my room to interrupt. It's just me and Mikhail in a slow, relentless build to my climax.

When I whimper that I'm close, Mikhail claims my mouth. He seals our lips together and swallows every cry as I pulse around him.

When it's his turn, I curl my fingers through his hair and he buries his groans in my neck.

He lifts his face to reveal that his cheeks are flushed and he's smiling. But it fades when he sees the tears slipping down my face. "Did I hurt you?"

A watery laugh bubbles out of me. "No. I just… I even cry when I'm happy now."

Amusement burns in his eyes when he presses a kiss to my forehead. "Then I see a lot of crying in your future, Viviana."

I hope like hell he's right.

64

MIKHAIL

"We don't need to do this now," Raoul says. His voice echoes in the empty parking garage below the hospital. It's the crack of dawn and visiting hours are closed to everyone who hasn't paid off the guards and the nurses. "We can wait until Viviana is home and—"

I shake my head. "I'm tired of waiting."

"It hasn't even been a day since you told me about this plan." There's a tinge of annoyance in my second's voice.

"You're just mad that you haven't had weeks to prepare."

He shrugs. "I like my routines. And what we're doing right now? It's not part of my normal routine."

There's nothing "normal" about what we're doing. Not for us nor any other *pakhan* in existence. It's not every day that men in power cede all control of their life's work to their long-time enemies.

I suppose that makes me a trailblazer.

"I want you here with me, Raoul, but I understand if you'd rather not be on the call. I know all about family drama, and I won't make you face yours if you aren't ready to—"

"I'm ready," he assures me. "It's been a long time since I've spoken to my father. I'm ready to put this all behind me."

The call comes in at the exact minute Raoul said it would. He hands the phone to me. I trust that he's ready to speak to his father, but I'm still *pakhan*. We're breaking a lot of traditions today, but I should still be the head of this negotiation.

"Ruben," I say in greeting. "It's been a long time."

"It has, Mikhail. Which is why I'm curious to know what this call is all about."

Aside from the slight Colombian accent, he sounds so much like Raoul. If Raoul himself wasn't standing next to me, I could be convinced I was talking to him on the phone.

"It's always straight to business with you," I remark. "Like father, like son in that respect."

"Is my son there?" Ruben asks.

I hold the phone out to Raoul. It's not a video call, but he still dips his head slightly in a show of respect. "Hello, *Padre*."

"If the two of you are calling me together, I can't assume it's good news," Ruben rumbles. "Whatever you think I've done, I promise you I haven't. We're at peace, Mikhail. Things got ugly last time. I have no desire to go back there again."

"Ugly" is one word for the murder of my wife and child. Even the knowledge that Ruben wasn't fully to blame for that particular war crime doesn't take away the sting.

I clench my jaw. "This isn't about a war, Ruben. I'm calling about peace. A deal, actually. Between the two of us."

"Go on…"

"The deal is simple," I explain. "I want to cede control of the entire Novikov Bratva to the Falcao Cartel."

The silence is loaded. I imagine Ruben pulling his phone away from his ear to check who he called. After a few seconds, his voice crackles through the line. "You're kidding."

"I'm not one for jokes, Ruben. I'm completely serious."

"Then you're insane."

I shrug. "If I am, then you should take advantage of it. My insanity is going to make you the most powerful man in the Americas."

I considered dissolving the Bratva. Tearing it apart piece by piece and scrapping it for parts. All of it felt messy. The power vacuum it created would be filled by *someone*, and I didn't like the idea of not knowing who that would be. Or whether they would come for me to ensure I didn't change my mind and want my Bratva back.

In the end, handing the Bratva over to Ruben felt right.

It's what I should have done during the war ten years ago. But I didn't know when to let go back then.

Now, I do.

There's another long pause before Ruben breaks into a cackling laugh. "I always knew you were a crazy son of a bitch, Mikhail. I just never thought I'd be happy about it."

After half an hour of back and forth and repeatedly assuring him I'm serious, Ruben and I have reached simple terms.

He'll own everything even tangentially connected to the Novikov Bratva—old grudges and enemies included—and I'll make a clean break. I have no say over how he chooses to wield his new power and he doesn't speak to me about his business ever again.

"What about my son?" Ruben asks. "What is Raoul going to do?"

I turn to Raoul. "What *are* you going to do, brother?"

As always, Raoul takes his time with the question. When he finally looks up, he's smiling. "Whatever the fuck I want."

The fluorescents lining the hospital hallways are still dimmed when Raoul and I make it back to Viviana's floor, but her room might as well be a beacon.

Every light is on, including the lamp next to the bed, and Dante is directing a remote-controlled dinosaur across the tiles. He cackles every time the dinosaur disappears under the hospital bed only to reappear on the other side. Every time it falls over, it lets out a loud *roar*.

"Who gave him *that*?"

"Mistakes were made and regrets have been had," Anatoly mutters from the corner beside the door. Based on the way he's holding his arms, I think his fingers were shoved in his ears. "The kid was sad you two were in the hospital. What was I supposed to do, *not* buy him an extremely loud, obnoxious toy to make him feel better?"

Dante sees me and his eyes go wide. "Dad! You have to watch this."

He sends the dinosaur in a circle around my feet before it trips on Raoul's shoe and lets out a roar. Dante giggles and races over to set the toy on its feet again.

Viviana is sitting on the edge of the bed, watching all of it with a wide smile. I cross the room and press a kiss to her cheek. "Are you ready to go home?"

"Since the moment we arrived," she teases. "Then again, the dinosaur might convince me to spend another day here. Dante isn't going to turn that thing off until it breaks."

"Sorry," Anatoly sighs again. But as he watches Dante chase the dinosaur into the connected bathroom and back out again, giggling the entire time, I don't think Anatoly is really sorry at all.

Viviana presses a hand to my shoulder. "Since Raoul is smiling for the first time in... *ever*, I'm going to assume everything went okay this morning."

I told her the broad strokes of my plan late last night. When she teared up and told me passing the Bratva to Raoul's family was a fitting eulogy to Alyona and Anzhelina, I knew I was doing the right thing.

"It went perfectly."

"And how do you feel?" she asks.

I take a deep breath. For the first time in years, the heavy weight in my chest is gone. I turn to Viviana and kiss her, stroking my thumb down her neck. "This part of my life is almost over. And the next part is about to start. I feel great."

We convince Dante to carry his dinosaur friend through the still-quiet hospital hallways. The second we're in the parking garage, the dinosaur is back on the ground and Dante is running and grinning behind it.

"Watch where you're going," Viviana calls after him. Her voice echoes off the concrete pillars. "Stay away from cars."

There are no cars to speak of. The garage is almost as empty as it was when Raoul and I were here an hour ago and the gates letting cars inside don't open to the public for another hour. A few doctors and nurses have started showing up for their shifts, but otherwise, we have the place to ourselves.

The dinosaur is chugging along at least twenty feet in front of Dante when it hits a rock and topples over with a roar.

Dante breaks into a run to pick it up…

Just as an engine roars from around the corner.

The headlights flash as the car lurches forward, heading straight for my son.

65

MIKHAIL

"Dante!" Viviana shrieks.

I don't pause to think. There isn't time for it. I lunge forward and slam my hand into Dante's back to knock him out of the path of the car.

He's small and he goes flying, skidding across the concrete ten feet away. I whip around and wrap my arm around Viviana, yanking her back in the opposite direction just before the car careens into the central wall of the parking garage.

Viviana and I hit the ground with a pained grunt. The ruined car is hissing behind me and the air smells like gasoline. Somewhere, the remote-controlled dinosaur is still roaring.

Viviana shoves off of me and crawls towards the car on her hands and knees. I realize she's looking under the wheels. "Dante!"

"He was out of the way. He's okay."

He's okay right now. But the next few seconds will determine if it stays that way.

The windows of the car are deeply tinted. I can't even make out a human shape in the driver's seat. Was this a freak accident? Was it intentional? Until I know, I'm not taking any chances.

I rise to my feet, gun aimed at the windows. "Get out of the fucking car!"

The doors don't open. Nothing happens.

From the other side of the car, just out of sight, Dante starts to cry.

Viviana gasps and runs forward, but I grab her around the waist. "Let go of me!" she cries out, scratching at my hands. "We have to get him!"

I shake my head and point towards a concrete pillar behind us. "I will. You need to get behind cover before—"

The order is lost in a barrage of gunfire.

Viviana screams, and I duck her down and run towards the pillar. My heart is pulled in two directions—towards Viviana and Dante—but I'm only in a position to help one of them.

Bullets embed themselves in the concrete in front of us, whizzing past our heads. The air is thick with dust and Viviana starts coughing as we duck behind the wall.

I stop for half a second to breathe before I press Viviana flat against the pillar. "*Stay. Here.*"

I don't have time to make sure she heeds the warning. I spin around and dart towards the car to my right.

A bullet deflates the rear tire, so I squeeze myself between the concrete wall and the hood of the car. I need to get to Dante, but drawing attention from him is effective, too. I'd rather have the guns aimed at me so he can get away.

"You let your guard down, little brother," a familiar voice sneers. I peek over the hood and, through a haze of cement dust and gunsmoke, see Trofim standing next to the open driver door. His gun is pointed at me. "You let yourself get distracted by *my* fiancée."

Trofim is so fixed on me that he doesn't notice Anatoly and Raoul tucked into the elevator alcove behind him. They're hidden beneath the crunched hood of his car, but I can see them from my angle.

The two of them whisper something to each other. Raoul crouches down, moving in the direction of Dante. But Anatoly's sights are set on the back of Trofim's head. It's not hard to imagine what his plan is.

Trofim fires again. The shot glances off the side view mirror and I duck behind the front bumper. "This is what I'm saying —distracted. It won't even be fun killing you."

A volley of shots punch through the windows of the car I'm hiding behind. Glass rains down on me and I shake it out of my hair.

"Hurry up, Anatoly," I mutter.

I could have dealt with Trofim by now, but I don't want to risk hitting Anatoly as he creeps up behind him. Or face Anatoly's wrath for killing Trofim before he got the chance.

Dante is still crying. I pray it's just over a scraped knee and nothing worse.

I crawl to the passenger side of the car and peek over the hood. Trofim pivots to shoot just as Anatoly rises up like the Grim Reaper over his shoulder. Anatoly raises his fist like a hammer and brings the full force of it down on the top of Trofim's head.

Trofim's eyes roll back in his head and his legs buckle. He crumples to the ground.

"Ah, shit," Anatoly moans. "He wasn't supposed to pass out."

I come out from behind my cover just as Viviana screams. "There's someone else in the car!"

I follow her finger back to the smoking car. I can see Dante huddling against the wall next to the crash, his entire body shaking and the dinosaur toy still clutched in his hands.

Then the passenger door flies open. I can't see Dante anymore. All I can see is a man darting out of the car, headed straight for him.

"Dante!" I break into a run, but I won't get there in time. It's too far. The man is too close.

I'm not going to make it.

But I don't have to.

Raoul leaps over the hood of the car, landing like a fucking superhero between Dante and the man, who I can now see is Agostino.

Then a gunshot echoes through the garage.

For one second, I think it was Raoul's gun. He's holding it in his hand, after all. But his barrel is pointed at the ground. And blood is spreading across the front of Raoul's gray shirt.

And the gun in Agostino's grasp is smoking.

Raoul's eyes go wide a second before he collapses to the ground.

66

VIVIANA

Everything happened so fast.

As soon as Anatoly knocked Trofim unconscious, I got my first clear look into the car. I didn't know the shadowy man in the passenger seat was my father, but I knew he wasn't a friend. I yelled out to warn Mikhail, but Raoul jumped into action first. The door opened, Raoul leapt in front of Dante, and then…

I can't bring myself to look, but based on the way Mikhail is shouting, I know enough.

Mikhail was taking cover behind a white hatchback, but he isn't worried about cover now. He tears across the parking garage like he thinks he's invincible. Right now, he might be.

"Agostino!" he roars, rage practically rippling behind him as he charges at my father.

My father whips around. His face pales when he sees Mikhail coming towards him. He's frozen for a second before he ducks behind the car…

And comes back up with Dante in his arms.

No!

I don't realize I've spoken—or moved—but everyone turns to me. I'm stumbling across the garage, my arms outstretched. "Don't hurt him!"

"Then tell your husband to give me space," my father bellows back.

Mikhail slows down, but even from this distance, I can see the murder in his eyes.

"I told Trofim this was a stupid plan," my father mutters almost to himself. "We should have struck when it was just Mikhail and the Colombian, but Trofim wanted Viviana to watch. Now, he's dead and I'm left cleaning up his mess."

He wanted me to watch. Watch my husband die. My son, too, probably.

My stomach churns.

"This is your mess," I tell him. "You got involved with Trofim because you hate me. After all these years, you're still mad *at me*. So let Dante go and take me instead."

Dante is wide-eyed and shaking in my father's hold, and I can't look at him. If I do, I'll collapse. The only way I can save him is to stay strong.

"Why would I want you now?" he spits. "You're useless to me. You're pregnant with another man's baby. Trofim is dead."

"As good as," Anatoly agrees. He's standing over Trofim's unconscious body, gun at the ready. "As soon as he wakes up and knows it was me."

"Even Christos is losing interest in Mikhail," my father adds. "Now that Helen is re-engaged, he doesn't want revenge. I have no alliances, nothing to gain… You are *nothing* to me."

"Careful," Mikhail growls.

My father cackles. "*I* should be careful? I'm the one with the leverage." He pats Dante on the shoulder hard enough that Dante winces. "What a way to meet my grandson, huh?"

There's so much to unpack there, but only one thing matters. "Let Dante go."

"Not until I know I will walk out of this parking garage alive," he retorts. "I'm not letting him go until I know you aren't coming after me."

Mikhail sneers and starts to say something, but I charge ahead. "We'll let you go. I never wanted to kill you, Daddy."

His eyebrow arches suspiciously. It's been a long time since I've called my father "Daddy." It feels foreign rolling off my tongue, but who needs dignity? Not me. I just need my son.

My father hesitates for a second before a sick smile twists across his face. "That's the problem with you, Viviana. You're always lying to me. It makes it impossible to trust you."

"You can trust me on this! If you let Dante go, I won't hurt you."

"What about your husband?" He eyes Mikhail nervously. "Can you guarantee that?"

Mikhail doesn't turn to look at me. He's laser-focused on my father's hands around our son's neck.

My father just shot one of Mikhail's best friends in the chest and is now holding his son hostage. There's no saying what kind of hell Mikhail has planned for him.

I dodge the question. "We just want Dante safe."

"In that case—" He takes a step backward, dragging Dante's much-shorter legs across the cement. "You won't mind if I take Dante with me and dump him a block or two from here. Just to make sure I can clear the area before you come looking for him."

"No!" I lunge forward, but my father flexes his fingers around his gun. It's a silent threat.

He'll kill him if he needs to.

"He'll be fine," he says coolly. "Besides, it will be good bonding time for us."

My father takes another step towards the exit when, suddenly, a loud roar echoes behind him.

He jolts, loosening his grip on Dante just enough that Dante squirms away from him and runs, full-tilt, towards me. The distraction gives Mikhail time to close the gap.

Before my father can react, Mikhail swipes his gun out of his hand and has his arm around his neck.

"Mama!" Dante leaps into my arms, the remote control for his dinosaur still in his hands.

I cradle him against my chest. "You're okay, baby. No one is going to hurt you."

"Please. No." My father's pleas echo through the empty parking garage. All of the arrogance has drained out of his voice, replaced with raw fear.

"You just tried to use my son like a bartering chip," Mikhail growls, squeezing my father's neck until his face is red. "Was using Viviana as one her entire life not enough for you?"

"This was Trofim's idea!" he cries. "I never wanted to come here and take you on. He blackmailed me into—"

Mikhail drops him to the ground and kicks him in the stomach. I twist Dante away so he can't see.

"You did so good, bud." I kiss his cheek. "You were so smart."

He sniffles. "My dinosaur scared him away with his roars."

"That was genius. You scared him and escaped. I'm so proud of you."

My father's groans fill the space, but I hold Dante against me, shushing him as he whimpers. "Please," my father whines. "Viviana, please! Don't let him kill me."

The hair on the back of my neck stands tall. My father doesn't deserve another second of my time, but... he's still my father.

Anatoly appears in front of me. His eyes are still trained on Trofim's limp body, but he's talking to me. "I'll take Dante if you want to go deal with that."

I'm not sure what Anatoly means, but sitting here huddled in a corner while Mikhail cleans up my mess seems selfish. So I kiss Dante and promise him I'll be right back. Then I stand tall, press my shoulders back, and cross the parking garage.

Gunsmoke is still wreathed in the air. Cement dust has settled like a fine powder on the ground. My shoes crunch over shattered glass.

Mikhail must hear me coming because he drags my father to his feet, the gun pointed at his temple, and faces me. "What do you want me to do, Viviana?"

I lose some of my confidence. I don't know anything about torture. Even seeing my father like this, bloody and limp in Mikhail's grasp, makes me nauseous. "You're leaving it up to me?"

"As Agostino said, he's *your* father. The decision should be yours."

My father whimpers and blood spills over his lower lip. "Vivi," he coos, using the nickname he gave me when I was a child. I only heard it when he wanted something from me. This time is no different. "I went about things the wrong way, but I only ever wanted what was best for you. You know that, don't you?"

His lip is busted and there's a mottled bruise around his eye. He's pawing weakly at Mikhail's hand around his neck, but he doesn't have a chance of breaking free.

He's weak.

He has always been weak.

"You controlled every element of my life," I say softly. "You sold me to ruthless men for alliances that benefited you. You killed the boy I loved because he was born without money."

"I wanted you to be protected," he gasps.

"You wanted to protect yourself. It was never about me. I was just a way to get what you wanted: security." I frown, taking in the pathetic scene in front of me. "You are terrified of the people around you and you were willing to sacrifice me to save yourself. Why should I do anything different?"

"Because I'm your *father*," he says again, as if it means anything. "We are blood, Viviana."

I try to feel something. Part of me wants this moment to hurt just so I know I'm not half the monster my father was.

But I feel nothing as I turn to Mikhail. "He stopped being my father a long time ago. Kill him."

Horror flickers across Agostino Giordano's face for an instant before the bullet tears through his skull.

67

MIKHAIL

Agostino hasn't even hit the ground when I grab Viviana.

"Are you okay?"

She pulls her eyes away from her father's body and nods. "I'm okay."

I run my hands across her shoulders and down her arms. I trace the shadows under her eyes and the quiver in her chin. She's pale and shaking, but she's okay. Not a scratch on her.

I turn to lay eyes on Dante.

They were both out of my sight for too long. I should have gotten them away from the fight, but there wasn't time. I wouldn't have even had time to save Dante, if it hadn't been for—

I cut the thought off at the root. I need to compartmentalize. One thing at a time.

Anatoly is standing on the other side of the smoking car with

Dante latched onto his side. They're looming over Trofim, who is still unconscious on the ground.

"Is Dante hurt?" I ask.

Dante shakes his head at the same time Anatoly answers, "No. He's a little hero. Saved himself over there."

Anatoly sounds chipper for Dante's sake, but I know he's compartmentalizing, too. It's the way we were trained.

I scan the garage, but it's empty. There's no one else standing. No one else to check in on.

They're okay.

Everyone else is okay.

So I drop to my knees next to the only person who isn't.

Raoul hasn't moved since he dropped. He's soaked in an angry red puddle of his own blood. When I roll him onto his back, there's no resistance. No groaning.

Nothing.

I know it's not good, but I roll him over anyway. I lift his shirt and examine the wound the way I have a hundred times before in a hundred different shootouts. But this time, my hands are shaking as I apply pressure to the gaping hole over his heart.

Fluid spurts out of the wound when I first press on it, but it quickly slows.

He has no blood pressure. His veins are stagnant and his heart has stopped and my brother-in-arms is dead on the ground in front of me. I know that, but I check for a pulse anyway.

Nothing.

Viviana kneels on Raoul's other side. Gently, she takes his blood-crusted hands and folds them over his chest. Her voice wobbles as she whispers, "Thank you."

The reality that he's gone crashes down on me all at once. I hang my head. "He saved our son."

This day will play in my head on a loop for the rest of my life. I'll always wonder what I should have done differently.

Viviana reaches over Raoul's body and squeezes my arm. "Tell me what you need, Mikhail. Let me help."

My head is a fucking mess, but I blow out a breath. I've always worked best under pressure. This shouldn't be any different. "Dante shouldn't see any of this. He's been through enough. And I don't want him to remember Raoul like this."

"I'll take him back inside," she offers. "We can wait for you and Anatoly in the hospital."

I don't like the idea of her being out of my sight, but with Agostino and Trofim dead or incapacitated here, she's as safe as she's been in months.

I nod. "Stay close to the guard stationed at the back exit. Call me if anything changes. I'll come find you when we're done."

Viviana moves to stand, but hesitates. She sinks back to her knees and takes my face in her hands. "You are not responsible for this, Mikhail. You did everything you could."

The words are nice, even if they don't do anything to make me feel better right now. I kiss her palm and watch her leave, Dante tucked in her arms.

"Does Raoul still have zip-ties in his jacket pocket?" Anatoly calls over the still-smoking car between us.

I hate snooping through his pockets, but I slide my hand inside his jacket and pull out thick black zip-ties. Now that I've burned through my adrenaline, it takes every ounce of energy left in my body to propel me to my feet and around the car.

Anatoly spots the ties in my hand and his face splits into a sad smile. "I always told him it was pointless to bother with zip-ties when we could take no prisoners instead. If he was here, he'd give me shit for using them now."

If he was here.

He *is* here. He's less than ten feet away.

But we both know that isn't true. Raoul isn't here in any way that counts, but there's still work to be done and bodies to dispose of. The world doesn't stop spinning, even if it feels like ours has.

Trofim is still prone on the cement, a thin stream of watery blood pouring out of his open mouth. "Do the zip-ties mean you're taking Trofim prisoner?"

Anatoly bends down and zip ties our brother's wrists tightly enough that his fingers look like red, swollen sausages.

"I would love to drag out his punishment, but we have a funeral to plan thanks to this fucking—" He blows out a sharp breath. "Believe it or not, I'm ready to be done with Trofim. Aren't you?"

I study the emotion in my chest. I sort through the tangled web and search for anything having to do with Trofim, but…

there's nothing. Somewhere along the way, all the rage I carried for him disappeared.

I just want him gone.

The car is leaking a steady stream of gas and oil and the smell is becoming distracting. Something under the hood is sputtering like it could catch any second.

I tip my head towards the crash. "What do you say we make sure Trofim can't come back from the dead a second time?"

"Music to my ears." Anatoly grins viciously. "Do you have a lighter?"

I toss him the one from my pocket and Anatoly's eyes dance as if he's staring into the flames already.

Silently, we get to work. We'll have witnesses soon enough; we need to move fast. He heaves Trofim's unconscious body over his shoulder and drops him back in the driver's seat. While I'm dragging Agostino's corpse into the passenger seat, I notice Anatoly securing Trofim's hands to the steering wheel.

Together, we carefully move Raoul's body into the backseat of Anatoly's car, far out of reach of the flames.

"What are we going to do with him now?" he asks quietly.

I drape a blanket over him and close the door. "We're going to give him a proper funeral."

"A big blowout," Anatoly agrees. "The kind Raoul would have hated."

I laugh, but it's bitter. I imagine it will be for a long, long time.

"What is the plan if Christos pops up to finish the job these two couldn't?"

"Christos is Ruben Falcao's problem now." I thought that would taste bitter, too, but it doesn't. Handing off this lifestyle to someone else feels like a gift. "In honor of Raoul, I'm ready to put this shit behind me and do whatever the fuck I want."

Anatoly clasps his hand with mine and pulls me in for a quick hug. "Let's start with arson, shall we?"

I usher Anatoly towards the wreck with a wave of my hand. "You do the honors."

He gives me a ridiculously deep bow. Then he turns towards the crash. Faintly, I hear him whisper, "This is for my mom."

Anatoly tosses the lighter into the driver's seat.

The car catches instantly. The heat from the initial explosion sizzles like a sunburn across my skin. Anatoly jogs back to me and watches the fire spread. Flames lick across the interior until the windows shatter from the heat. The paint peels and rolls back like sizzling flesh as the car is entirely engulfed.

"He's not making it out of there," Anatoly mutters.

"I thought you wanted him to know it was you."

He shrugs. "I'll tell him when I see him next."

"In hell?" I roll my eyes. "I hate to break it to you, brother, but you aren't half as bad as you think you are. I don't think hell will take you."

"I guess time will tell. With the deal you just made this

morning, it looks like I'm about to start living a reformed life. Maybe we'll both change our ways and earn our wings."

The Bratva signet ring on my pointer finger burns in the residual heat. The hot metal bites into my skin. Frowning, I twist it off for the first time in years. For the first time since I claimed it from Trofim in that hotel bridal suite six years ago.

Sirens wail far off in the distance.

There are still security tapes to be scrubbed and officers to be bribed. The usual clean-up will take even longer without Raoul—just the first of many, many times I'll feel his loss over what's left of my lifetime, I'm sure.

The flames grow and soot spreads across the concrete ceiling. The sirens are getting closer every second.

It all feels like goodbye. A funeral pyre to the life I used to lead.

I turn the ring over in my palm once and then again. Then I hurl it into the flames.

"Time will tell," I repeat.

I clap Anatoly on the back and we walk out of the parking garage together.

EPILOGUE: VIVIANA
SIX MONTHS LATER

I'm convinced this can't be happening until Dante screams.

"You peed on the floor!" He flings across the narrow kitchen and attaches himself to the wall like it's Velcro. His arms are spread flat like if he moves even an inch closer to me, he'll touch the puddle at my feet.

"I didn't pee!" I stare down at the floor and my own cloudy reflection in the water pooled between my legs. "I just…."

My water broke.

It's not shocking. It *shouldn't* be shocking. I'm four days away from my due date. The weekly doctor's appointments and countless strangers in public who smile at me and say, "You look like you're about to pop" are proof of that. I *am* about to pop.

But I still didn't expect to pop here. Now.

"I have to take you to school," I say, trying to organize the suddenly wild thoughts in my head. "It's my turn to take you to school."

I could still make it. The private school Mikhail and I chose is only five minutes from the house. It's why we moved into this quiet neighborhood in the first place. We wanted to be close enough to walk him to school on nice days. Though my swollen ankles haven't felt up to walking in four months, at least.

The car drop-off line is fast. I could swing through the line, drop him off at the front doors, and then—

"But you peed!" Dante shrieks again, wrinkling his nose. "Do you need a diaper now?"

"I didn't pee!" I grit out. "And no more potty talk."

Usually, that rule is for all of the poop jokes that Dante and his band of six-year-old school friends think are the absolute height of comedy. If I wasn't frantically trying to reorganize the day's plans—driving Dante to school, one last waxing appointment before the baby comes *in four days*, a trip to the grocery store to stock up on freezer meals—I'd probably let it slide. I mean, it does look like I peed my pants.

"But you pottied!" He sticks out his tongue and closes his eyes. "It's so yucky. This is the yuckiest thing I've ever seen."

I snatch a roll of paper towels from the counter and throw the whole roll into the puddle. "Go get your dad. Now!"

"To tell him you peed?"

I pinch the bridge of my nose. "Yes. Tell him I peed."

Dante slides down the wall and then darts down the hallway. I hear his frantic footsteps pounding up the stairs.

Maybe I did pee. Lord knows this little girl likes to headbutt my bladder. It's her favorite place to hang out. If she isn't curling her feet under my ribs until I'm crying in pain, she's bashing her head against my bladder like it's downright hilarious.

"What's the verdict?" he asks as he sweeps into the room.

I stand up to see he has my hospital bag slung over his shoulder. I've been calling it my "go bag" and storing it under our bed for old time's sake, but Mikhail never found the joke especially funny.

I nod my head, ignoring the sudden shakiness in other parts of my body. "It's real."

Mikhail walks towards me and Dante yelps behind him. "Watch out for the pee!"

But Mikhail doesn't worry about it. He grabs my face and forces me to look at him. "You're ready for this, Viviana."

Instantly, the knot of panic in my chest eases. I take my first deep breath since I heard the splash. "We need to get Dante to school."

Before Mikhail can say anything, the garage door flies open and Anatoly is standing there in head-to-toe leather, a child-sized motorcycle helmet tucked under his arm. "One just-barely-over-the-speed-limit motorcycle ride for a Dante Novikov. Is Dante Novikov here?"

"Uncle Nat!" Dante careens around the island and snatches the helmet out of Anatoly's hands. He has it on his head and is tearing into the garage before he can even say goodbye.

Anatoly grins. "Good luck having a baby, Viv. While you're gone, I'll take care of this one."

The garage door closes and I spin towards Mikhail. "How did Anatoly get here so fast? I thought he was on a motorcycle trip to Alaska."

Anatoly has used his time away from the Bratva to take up every dangerous hobby he can imagine. Skydiving and backcountry skiing came and went quickly, but he has a motorcycle now and he spends most weekends racing on dirt tracks in the middle of nowhere. It's a good thing he still keeps in touch with the Bratva doctor, because his medical bills would be astronomical by this point.

"He got back two nights ago. I asked him to sleep in the pool house just in case the baby came early."

"Why didn't you tell me?" I snap.

Mikhail arches a brow. "Because every time I tried to make plans for the delivery, you waved me off. You always said we had plenty of time to prepare."

"We do!" I frown. "Well, we *did*. She wasn't supposed to get here for four more days. She was supposed to arrive on her due date when I was fully prepared."

I chew on my lower lip. I'm not sure what "fully prepared" feels like, but I kept expecting it to just snap into place. At some point, I'd be ready for this.

"We Novikovs aren't big fans of doing what we're supposed to do. You pointed that out to me once. I took some precautions. You're welcome." He curls a hand over my cheek. "Now, I'm going to drive you to the hospital so we can have our baby."

"I can't do this," I whimper.

"Don't be ridiculous, Viviana." Mikhail loops an arm around my lower back and leads me towards the garage. "You can do anything."

∼

"You're a liar!" I narrow my eyes at my husband as I simultaneously squeeze his calloused hand with every ounce of strength in my body. "You're a dirty, no-good, filthy liar."

He winces as my contraction peaks and my grip on his hand gets crushing. My hold loosens as the pain wanes. "I've been called worse. What did I lie about this time?"

My top lip curls back in a snarl. "You told me I could do this, but I can't. I can't do this." I tip my head back and scream it to the ceiling in case the nursing staff can't hear me. "*I can't do this!*"

Mikhail brushes my sweaty hair away from my face. "You absolutely can do this, Viviana. I still believe that."

"Says the man not having contractions every sixty seconds. Says the man who isn't going to push a whole human out of his body in—Fuck! Probably never," I grit as another contraction tears across my stomach. "This is going to last forever. I'm probably dead and this is my punishment."

Mikhail offers me his hand. His fingers are bright red from using them as a stress ball, but my capacity to feel bad for him is nonexistent. I latch on again and squeeze like this is all his fault.

Which it is!

How many times did he say he wanted to "fuck a baby into me"? Well, we never discussed the other side of that. When the baby has to come out!

"All your fault," I groan before my ability to speak is lost in a scream.

Mikhail wipes my forehead with a cool cloth and slips his other hand behind my back to knead the knotted muscles with his thumb. "What exactly do you think you need to be punished for?"

"For stabbing your brother. For lying to you about Dante. For selling my heart and soul to the devil for love." I throw my hands up. "Or for all the times I broke the pay-it-forward chain in the drive-thru. I've gotten a lot of free coffees over the years and I never paid them back."

Mikhail laughs and it's a beautiful sound, but I also want to squeeze his lungs until he's in as much pain as me—yet another reason I deserve to be punished.

"Free coffee isn't a reason to be punished. Plus, I'm not sure if you've heard, but I'm an honorable man now." His lips press against the shell of my ear. "I met a woman and she dragged me into the light."

For half a second, my moon-sized bump isn't demanding all of my attention.

For one fractured moment, I'm focused on Mikhail's lips on my ear. On his warm breath against my skin.

Then another contraction rips through me and my back bows as I scream. "Fine! Then I deserve to be punished for rambling on and on to everyone who would listen about how much I wanted a natural childbirth."

"Studies show the recovery is easier with a natural birth," Mikhail says flatly. "You taught me that."

Mikhail didn't read any of my pregnancy books, but he might as well have. I read massive sections of them out loud to him every night in bed for months.

"That may be true, but the birth is torture. I want drugs!" I slap my hand over the nurse's call button repeatedly. The middle-aged nurse, who I forgot has been standing between my legs for the last ten minutes, gives me a wave. "You asked for drugs twenty minutes ago and it was too late then. It's definitely too late now. The doctor is on his way."

"Dr. Rossi," I growl. "This is his fault, too! He recommended that book on natural childbirth."

"After you *asked* him for a book on natural childbirth," Mikhail chuckles. He kisses my sweaty forehead. "How about we wait until the baby is out? If you still feel like wreaking vengeance once our baby girl is here, I'll help."

I fist the front of his shirt and drag him closer. "No takebacks. You have to keep your word."

"With you? Always."

Again, I'm almost free of the pain. Looking into Mikhail's eyes, I can almost forget where we are. What's about to happen.

Then a strangled curse tears out of my throat as Dr. Rossi rushes in the door.

"Let's have a baby!" He grins, pulling on a pair of gloves.

And thirty minutes later, we do.

The second Dr. Rossi holds my wrinkled, slimy, perfect baby girl in the air, the pain disappears. I'm still exhausted. Still coated in sweat and blood and plenty of other fluids I don't ever need to know about.

But none of that matters.

"She's here." I grab Mikhail's hand, but I don't squeeze. I bring his knuckles to my cheek and nuzzle my face against his warmth. "Our baby is here."

"You did so good." He kisses my temple, whispering in my ear again and again. "You did so, so good."

The nurses clean her off and lay her on my chest. I remember this moment with Dante. I was shaking and terrified, realizing all at once how much the tiny, helpless baby in my arms needed me. I was all he had in the world. *He* was all *I* had.

That isn't true anymore.

"You're so perfect," I whisper, sliding my finger into her chubby palm. "Your brother is going to love you."

"What about me?" Mikhail teases. "She hasn't met me yet."

The baby turns toward Mikhail instantly, searching. Tears well in my eyes. "She recognizes your voice."

"Good. I didn't spend all those months talking to your bump for nothing." Mikhail lays his large hand over her small body. His eyes are wide with genuine wonder. It's the first time I've ever seen Mikhail look terrified.

"Do you want to hold her?"

He starts to shake his head, but I hold her out before he can. He has no choice but to take her in his arms. He's clumsy at first. His shoulders are raised practically to his ears and he stares down at her like she might suddenly backflip out of his arms. After a few seconds, he relaxes into it. And it's the most natural thing in the world.

A father holding his baby.

My husband holding our child.

I wasn't sure I'd ever see it.

Suddenly, Mikhail catches my eye. "Thank you."

"For giving birth? Believe me, if I could have passed the buck, I would have."

He shakes his head. "Thanks for not giving up on me. Thanks for... Thanks for not letting me give up on *this*."

You'd think I'd be all out of spare fluids, but you'd be wrong. Tears pour down my face as I grab Mikhail by the belt loop and pull him into my bed. He holds our daughter and I rest my head on his shoulder, breathing in this new life we created.

Our daughter, yes. But everything else, too.

"This is how it's always going to be, isn't it?" I whisper.

He turns and kisses my forehead. "I think that's how it usually works with happily-ever-afters."

EXTENDED EPILOGUE: VIVIANA
TWELVE YEARS LATER

Click here to check out the Extended Epilogue to the Novikov Bratva duet!
https://dl.bookfunnel.com/j001hgcfo6